AFTER TWILIGHT

Dee Davis

IVY BOOKS • NEW YORK

Sale of this book without a front cover may be unauthorized. If this book is coverless, it may have been reported to the publisher as "unsold or destroyed" and neither the author nor the publisher may have received payment for it.

This book contains an excerpt from the forthcoming paperback edition of *Just Breathe* by Dee Davis. This excerpt has been set for this edition only and may not reflect the final content of the forthcoming edition.

An Ivy Book
Published by The Ballantine Publishing Group
Copyright © 2001 by Dee Davis Oberwetter

Excerpt from *Just Breathe* by Dee Davis copyright © 2001 by Dee Davis Oberwetter.

All rights reserved under International and Pan-American Copyright Conventions. Published in the United States by The Ballantine Publishing Group, a division of Random House, Inc., New York, and simultaneously in Canada by Random House of Canada Limited, Toronto.

Ivy Books and colophon are trademarks of Random House, Inc.

www.randomhouse.com/BB/

Library of Congress Catalog Card Number: 00-107761

ISBN 0-8041-1966-X

Manufactured in the United States of America

First Edition: January 2001

10 9 8 7 6 5 4 3 2 1

To Robert,
the love of my life.

There is a moment after twilight when the world hangs in balance, neither here nor there, and anything is possible. . . .

Prologue

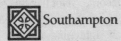 Southampton

"I DON'T WANT a divorce, Alex. I want a husband."

Lightning flashed as the glass pane shook with the force of the wind. Kacy felt it vibrate under her fingertips. Rain pounded against the French door, running in rivulets down its face, partially obscuring the wildly gyrating trees outside. The path to the beach, beyond the trees, was totally invisible, the downpour acting like a moving curtain, obliterating almost everything.

"I *am* your husband, Kirstin." Alex's voice was tense, a low counterpoint to the fury of the storm.

She turned to face him, alarmed at how his use of her first name could sound so wrong, so foreign. "Maybe in name, but . . ."

He cut her off with the wave of a hand. "In all ways." His eyes narrowed, telegraphing his meaning.

She shivered. "It isn't like it used to be."

His smile was slow, almost lazy, and it didn't reach his eyes. "Well, perhaps it's time you learned to be a little more adventurous."

She clenched her fists, wondering how she'd managed to get herself in this position. By marrying a stranger, the little voice in her head calmly announced. Thunder rattled through the living room. The lights flickered, went out, and then came

1

on again. She squinted as her eyes adjusted. "I need someone who loves me, Alex—"

"Loves you?" His look changed to derision. "And that's why you eloped with someone you hardly knew? Come, Kirstin, be honest, you married me for the same reason I married you." His hand snaked out and he jerked her to him, his tongue tracing the line of her lips. "You want me, Kirstin." He pressed against her. "You want this."

"Alex, I . . ." She tried to push him away, to find the right words, to face the reality of what he'd become. "Not like this, please."

"Fine." He stared down at her, his jaw tightening, then he released her, his handsome face mottled with anger. "Have it your way." The words exploded from his lips and he pushed past her, throwing open the door. Rain lashed into the room, instantly soaking them both.

"Where are you going?" She placed a timid hand on his arm. She'd never seen him this angry.

He shook off her hand and turned, his hair already plastered to his head. "Out."

"But the storm . . ." She gestured toward the torrent of rain pounding the paving of the patio.

"It beats the hell out of being here, with *you*." Each word was clipped, designed to wound. She flinched as if she'd been struck, watching helplessly as he headed out into the storm.

"Alex, wait." She followed him, the wind snatching away her words. He was only a dim shadow now, moving down the path toward the beach, illuminated at off moments by a flash of lightning. She took a step toward his retreating figure, surprised at the strength of the wind. For every step forward, it seemed to beat her back two. She sniffed, her nose filling with rain and tears.

Coughing, she fought her way forward, urged on by the dark silhouette of her husband heading for the beach, feeling the wet sand suck at her feet. Alex was almost to the dock, his frame bent at the waist as he tried to maneuver. Their little sailboat bobbed violently in the roiling ocean. Surely he wasn't going to try to go out in that?

"Alex," she screamed. Again the wind tore away her words, throwing them back at her with an almost angry savagery.

She neared the ocean's edge, still a hundred feet or so from Alex and the boat. He'd managed to climb out on the dock. In the recurring lightning, she could almost make out his features. It was like watching him in strobe lighting. There and gone, there and gone, there and . . .

A violent clap of thunder split the night. For an instant, Alex was illuminated clearly. Behind him, green in the eerie flash of light, a huge wall of water served as a backdrop. There was a roaring sound and she opened her mouth to scream.

One minute he was there, and the next, with a flash of the strobe, he was gone, leaving nothing but darkness and rain. Again the lightning lit the beach, but this time it was empty.

Horrifyingly empty.

The dock, the boat . . . Alex.

They were gone.

Kacy fought against the wind, its strength almost a physical blockade. Driven by fear, she pushed forward, finally reaching the edge of the water. She screamed his name over and over, certain that he was there, that the storm and the lightning were playing tricks on her. Her eyes searched the horizon, looking for something, anything.

For Alex.

Alex.

Oh, God. *Alex.*

She realized she was still screaming his name, and with a force of will honed from years of practice, she shut down her terror, forcing herself to find calm. Panicking wouldn't help him.

Nothing was going to help Alex, the little voice sang in her head.

She walked into the surf, feeling the powerful pull of the water, jumping to avoid the crashing waves. She stared into the pouring rain until her eyes ached, hoping for a sign— hoping for a miracle. Only when the waves threatened to swamp her did she retreat to the beach.

She shivered as much from horror as cold and wrapped her arms around her waist.

"Alex," she called again, this time knowing it was hopeless. He was gone. Forever.

She sank on the sand, sobs ripping through her, the sound of them adding to the cacophony of beating surf, rain, thunder, and wind. She pounded the ground with her fists until her fingers and palms were bloody, her hair whipping around her, tangling in the wild wind.

Everything she loved went away.

Everything.

And this time, as always, it was her fault.

All her fault.

The wind blew and the waves crashed, the water sucking at her, its greedy fingers carving a channel around her, until she was left totally alone on an island in the sand.

Chapter 1

 Lindoon, County Clare, Ireland—two years later

KACY MACGRATH SAT on the stony promontory and stared out at the ocean. Sky, mist, and sea melded together, obliterating the horizon, the somber coloring reflecting her mood.

Gulls darted back and forth between land and water, their cries echoing off of the rocky cliffs. Mac chased each and every one, joyfully barking and leaping into the air, blissfully unaware that he was physically incapable of catching one of the darting birds.

Kacy sighed. Maybe Mac had the right idea. Perhaps ignorance was bliss. She stood up, brushed off her skirt, and whistled for the dog. Mac bounded over to her, pushing a cold nose against her leg. The wind whistled across the meadow, the sound melancholy in the half-light. She shivered, suddenly grateful for the enveloping warmth of her fisherman's sweater.

She turned to face the tumbled ruins of Dunbeg. The shape of the old ring fort was obscured by the mist, tendrils drifting in and out of the fallen stones. Centuries ago the fort had served its owners well, defending them from invaders and protecting them from the harsh Irish weather. There was something romantic about it. A sense of timelessness. She shook her head at her own fancy and turned her attention to

5

Mac, scratching the dog behind his ears. Mac's liquid brown eyes smiled up at her.

Kacy smiled back. "I think it's time you and I were heading for home."

The dog wagged his tail in agreement and took off in the direction of Sidhean, a blur of black and white against the flat green and gray of the rocky meadow. The cottage wasn't visible over the rise, but Mac knew it was there. He stopped about fifty yards away and turned back, barking as if to say, "Where are you?"

"I'm coming. Just let me get the basket." She turned back to the edge of the cliff and bent to retrieve the remnants of their picnic. Mac barked again, but something in the tone sent a shiver of anxiety up her spine. She jerked upright and spun around, heart pounding, looking for something out of the ordinary in the shadows of the misty twilight. Nothing moved.

Mac arrived at her side, his teeth bared, a low growl issuing from deep in his throat. She laid a hand on his head, comforted by the silky feel of his fur. "What is it, Mac? What do you see?"

Her eyes darted around the clearing. In the far corner of the fort, against the stark contrast of the stone wall, something shifted, moved. She closed her eyes, stepping back involuntarily. Mac growled again.

She sucked in a breath and blew it out forcefully.

This was silly. There was no sense in jumping at shadows.

"Shadows," she repeated the word out loud, and opened her eyes, ready to face whoever was out there.

The fort was empty.

Nothing was there.

She stroked Mac's ears. "It was just our imagination, a trick of the mist." She spoke more for herself than the dog. Still, she could feel him relax. "Probably just a gull." She forced herself to sound positive. Mac wagged his tail.

"Come on, let's go home."

* * *

Braedon Roche took a slow sip of his beer and eyed the other patrons of the pub. It was early still and there were only a few people nursing the requisite pint. An old man in one corner sat with eyes closed, an open newspaper in front of him. A couple in the back halfheartedly threw darts at the tattered wheel on the wall, stopping often to exchange kisses, another type of bull's-eye on their minds.

The bartender—Fin, he called himself—polished the spigots with a flourish while having an animated conversation with someone on the other side of a small pass-through. It had been a long time since Braedon had been in a pub like this. The ones he frequented these days were the trendy places the elite liked to meet. It felt good to be here. Almost like he was home again.

Almost.

He finished the beer and walked over to the bar, setting the empty glass on the counter.

"Will you be wantin' another, then?" Fin nodded at the glass.

"Yes, please." He paused, feeling like a duck out of water, or more accurately a man without a country. "I don't suppose you have an egg sandwich?"

"Not on me." The man looked down at himself with a grin. "But I suspect my sister, Caitlin, can make you one faster than you can finish this pint." He set the glass back on the bar, foam running down its sides. "And would you be wantin' chips with that?"

Braedon felt his mouth water. It was good to be back in Ireland. "No, but if you've a packet of crisps, I'll take those."

"Name your flavor."

"Salt and vinegar."

Fin placed the crisps beside the beer and rang up the sale on an antique cash register. Its chinging pulled Braedon farther back into his past. He could almost see his mother, smell the lilac she always wore. Going to the pub had been a special treat. "For me very best boy," she'd always say.

The register drawer opened with a ding and he jerked from his reverie. There was nothing nostalgic in his past. Only pain and misery. And he'd put that all behind him. Or at least he thought he had. Hell, if all it took was a packet of crisps to bring the memories back, they couldn't be buried as deeply as he'd thought. Maybe this had been a mistake.

"Your change." Fin held out a handful of coins.

"Keep it. Buy yourself a pint."

The big man smiled. "Don't mind if I do. But I can't be drinking it alone, now can I?" He motioned to a barstool nearby.

Braedon sat and opened his crisps. It wouldn't be a bad idea to get friendly with the locals. They might even be able to help him.

The bartender looked toward the door, a smile of genuine delight breaking across his face. "Well, look what the dog's brought in. Come to escape the fairies, have you?"

Braedon followed the bartender's gaze. The man hadn't been exaggerating. The woman in the doorway was indeed accompanied by a dog. A large Border collie.

But Fin had only been half right. The woman wasn't escaping the fairies, she was one. Tiny and perfectly formed, she had silvery hair that hung like silk around her shoulders. Her face was as delicate as her body, with a tiny upturned nose and rose petals for lips.

Rose petals? Had he actually thought that?

She smiled at the bartender and pulled off her jacket. "I haven't come to escape anything." She was enveloped from head to knees in a cable knit sweater, the kind that *looked* perfect on a woman, but clearly *belonged* to her lover. Braedon was surprised at the twinge of jealousy he felt at the thought.

Her skirt only added to the ethereal image she presented.

The same color as her hair, it was gauzy, reminding him of cotton candy. In fact, she reminded him of a confection. A confection he desperately wanted to taste.

He took a sip of his beer, trying to pull his libido into control. It had obviously been too long since he'd had a woman. And his poetic mind had run amok. Cotton candy. Hell. Maybe she really was a fairy.

The dog sniffed at Braedon's shoes, and then, seeming satisfied, walked over to the fireplace and plopped down on the hearth as if he'd been doing it all of his life. Probably had, Braedon's mind whispered. He watched as the dog idly scratched, thinking that the New York Board of Health would have a field day with that. But, he sighed, this wasn't America. It was Ireland.

Home.

"I just thought a bit of company might do me some good." She crossed the room to the bar, her stride at once appealing and hesitant—almost shy.

"And you chose me. Well, now, there's a thought to make a man's day." The big Irishman handed her a half-pint of pale ale. She smiled and took a small sip, her lips caressing the edge of the glass.

Braedon shook his head, trying to clear his traitorous thoughts. He had more important things to dwell on, like saving his business, not to mention his reputation. He forced himself to focus on the conversation, wrenching his mind from the elfin woman in front of him.

"So you're sure the fairies haven't been bothering you? I mean, you do live at Sidhean," Fin was saying.

She laughed, a deep, throaty sound that made Braedon's groin tighten. "Just because I live on a fairy knoll doesn't mean I'm *intimate* with the fairies."

Braedon choked on his beer and struggled not to spit it out. She had one of those indiscernible accents. The kind that

privilege produced. Private schools and money. Her voice itself was deep and raspy, a complete contrast to the way she
looked. It stroked down him, filling him with—

"Here's your egg sandwich." Fin slapped the plate on the
bar, his interest in Braedon apparently evaporating in favor of
his newest patron. Not that Braedon could blame him. She
was more than a looker. There was something vulnerable
about her. The kind of woman a man wanted to take care of.
The kind of woman that he'd best avoid if he was going to ac-
complish anything.

He picked up his food and glass and settled into a chair at a
table across from the bar. It was close to the fire, he reasoned,
but knew it was also the perfect place to watch her. Fin bent
forward, whispering something in her ear. She laughed and
answered, but he couldn't hear her words, only the smoky
resonance of her voice.

Kacy listened to Fin, smiling at the appropriate moments,
following the gist of his conversation, but her attention was
still riveted on the man by the fire. He looked all at once right
and wrong.

He wore jeans and a sweater, but even in casual clothes the
man reeked of wealth. His loafers were shined to perfection
and she'd bet a pint those were ironed creases in his jeans. His
hair was deep brown, almost black, and it curled slightly at
the neck, as though it were trying to rebel. The rest of it was
combed firmly in place, not a hair out of line.

A reflection of the man, no doubt.

But there was more to him, something deeper, primordial,
and it called out to her. She let her eyes follow the strong line
of his jaw down to his neck and across his broad shoulders.
He was a tall man. Well over six feet, if she had to guess. She
sipped absently from her glass, trying not to stare.

Mac, the traitor, had already made friends with him. He'd
left the hearth and curled up at the man's feet. A man and his

dog. Her fingers itched to paint it. Heavens, what was she thinking? A man and her dog. *Her* dog.

"He's from New York, you know." Fin was leaning in conspiratorially. "Cosmopolitan, like you."

"Really?" She fought to keep her voice cool, determined to sound uninterested. She'd had a heck of a lot of practice hiding her emotions. She certainly wasn't going to let one over-pressed pretty boy ruin her average. "What's he doing here?"

"Why, darlin', you cut me to the quick." Fin managed to look hurt and wistful all at the same time. "He's obviously here because word has gotten out that this is the best pub in all of Ireland."

She rolled her eyes. "I wasn't talking about Finnegan's Folly and you know it."

"Aye, that I do."

"Well?" She waited, her eyes straying to the dark head bent over his sandwich.

"I don't know. He said something about a holiday. He's here to see the forts. Although I cannot understand what it is people see in those old piles of stone."

"They see history, Fin. History."

"Aye, well, perhaps they do. And mind you, I'm not complaining. 'Tis a fair amount o' business they're bringing with them."

"He doesn't look much like an historian."

"You were expecting a tweed jacket and a pipe?"

Kacy smiled at her friend and shrugged. "Well, maybe I am being a little cliché."

"Still, there's definitely more to the man than he's letting on." Fin smiled smugly.

Kacy frowned. "Why would you say that?"

"Well, for one thing he's no Yank."

"But I thought you said he was from New York."

"I did." Fin rubbed an empty glass with a cloth.

"Well, then . . ."

"He might live there, but he isn't *from* there, if you take my meaning." He lifted his eyebrows. Fin could drive her crazy when he was of a mind to.

"Fin."

He smiled, clearly recognizing he'd milked it for all he could. "He's originally from Ireland. It's in the way he talks. Mind you, he's worked hard to erase it, but the sound of an Irishman is in his soul, not his voice. I'd wager the pub the man was born on this side o' the pond."

Kacy studied the stranger. He certainly looked more like a New Yorker than an Irishman. She turned back to Fin and shrugged, trying to convey indifference. "Well, whoever he is, I doubt he'll be here long."

Fin laughed. "True enough. We're not exactly a tourist center, now are we?"

That was exactly why she'd chosen Lindoon. The perfect place to disappear. And she was good at disappearing. Of course, it didn't hurt that her grandmother had left her a cottage here. No, Sidhean had been a blessing.

"I'd best go rescue my dog."

Fin laughed. "I'm not sure it's rescuing he's wantin'."

True enough. Mac was rolled over onto his back, white belly exposed to the stranger. He wriggled in ecstasy as the man stroked his furry underside. She stared at his strong hands, trying to imagine what it would feel like to have a man like that care for her—love her.

Foolish dreams, the voice in her head whispered.

She sighed, pushing her thoughts aside. It was ridiculous to indulge in childish fantasy. There were no happy endings. She was living proof of that. And there was absolutely no sense in imagining otherwise.

She stopped at the table and opened her mouth to speak, but was suddenly struck dumb as she stared into the deepest blue eyes she'd ever seen.

* * *

Her eyes were huge. Green. Luminous. Like . . . hell, he had no idea, but they were beautiful. She was beautiful. He swallowed a huge lump of egg sandwich, wondering if he looked as juvenile as he felt.

"I was just coming to retrieve Mac."

He struggled to make sense of her words. The dog. She was talking about the dog. "He's really friendly." He patted Mac's head to emphasize his words. The dog looked at him and then at his mistress. It was almost as if he were following the conversation.

"He can be a nuisance sometimes." The dog came to her side and she rubbed him behind the ears.

Braedon found himself wishing it was him she was touching. Great, he was acting like a teenager. Next thing his voice would be cracking. "He's fine, honestly." She shifted her weight, obviously as uncomfortable as he was. They shared an awkward silence. At least he wasn't doing the adolescent thing on his own.

"Fin says you're interested in the forts." She smiled shyly.

"Yes." Great. Now he was answering in monosyllables.

"Well, you've come to the right place. The countryside around here is dotted with them." She blew out a breath, her eyes locked on his.

"So I've been told. I don't suppose you could recommend any?"

She hesitated a fraction of a second, her tiny teeth worrying her bottom lip. "There's one near my cottage. Dunbeg. It's small, but in excellent condition. There's even a souterrain."

"Souterrain?"

"An underground tunnel. The ring forts are famous for them." She frowned. "I'd have thought you'd have known about them."

"I'm sure I must have read about them. Could I see this

Dunbeg?" He held his breath, wondering what it was exactly he was doing.

"Of course. Anyone can show you the way." Her hand fidgeted with the salt shaker on the table. On impulse, he reached out and covered it with his own, surprised at the jolt of electricity that ripped up his arm.

He met her gaze and held it, his eyes trying to read hers. "I meant to say, would you be willing to show it to me?"

Her hand fluttered in his. A captive butterfly. "I . . . I mean . . . well . . . of course, I'd be happy to." She pulled her hand free.

"When?" He knew he sounded eager, too eager, but he had to see her again.

Her eyes widened and he was reminded of a deer trapped in headlights. "Tomorrow?" She licked her lips nervously.

"That would be great. How do I find you?"

"I'll be at Sidhean."

"Shee-an?"

"Sidhean," she repeated.

He nodded. "I know the word. I just wondered why your house is called the fairy knoll."

She smiled, a dimple creasing the corner of her mouth. "Because the cottage is built on one."

"I see." And somehow he did.

She looked down at her dog. "Shall we head home?" Mac wagged his tail in response, and with a wave to Fin, she turned to go.

He rose, his feet acting of their own accord. "Wait."

She turned, cocking her head to one side.

"I don't know your name."

She dimpled again. "Well, I'm sure I don't know yours either."

"Braedon. Braedon Roche."

"I'm Kacy. Kacy Macgrath." She gave him a last smile and then disappeared through the doorway, Mac following at her heels.

His heart dropped to his stomach. Kacy Macgrath. He felt physically sick. *Kirstin Macgrath Madison.* He sank onto the chair, his head spinning.

Fin appeared at his side. "You look like you could use a refill. Our Kacy has a way of doing that to a man. What can I get you?"

"Whiskey." He ran a hand through his hair, his mind in turmoil. "Make it a double."

Kacy Macgrath.

The memory of her soft curves and sensuous green eyes teased him. Oh, God, Kacy Macgrath.

The woman he'd come back to Ireland to destroy.

Chapter 2

ENRICO GIENELLI CLUTCHED his carry-on impatiently and inched forward. Passengers were lined up hodge-podge behind the yellow line, passports in hand, waiting for an available Irish customs agent. He hated this part.

Hated it with a passion.

Not that there was any chance they'd stop him. And even if they did, he wasn't carrying anything suspicious. Still, he always worried. Some last little bit of conscience. Not that there was much left. He hadn't been one of the good guys for a very long time.

He shrugged mentally and looked at the dowager standing in front of him. Too much blue in the rinse, she resembled a Muppet. Wasn't there a blue one? He smiled. He should spend more time with his nephew, but the Bronx might as well be a galaxy away from his home in Milan.

He fidgeted with the handle of his briefcase. What was the holdup? A dark haired man was arguing with a beefy looking woman in uniform. Obviously, he'd done something wrong.

Rico sighed. *Better him than me.*

"Next."

The blue hair moved forward. Two to go. He felt a trickle of sweat slide down his back. Nervous, he ran a hand beneath his collar. This was ridiculous. He'd been out of Rikers a long time now. Not that he'd been clean exactly. But he'd been careful. Really careful. Well, maybe not as careful as he should have been, but he was going to take care of that.

Someone behind him was speaking Gaelic. It sounded like gibberish. Damned Irish and their independent ways. Why didn't they just speak English?

He grinned. He sounded like an American. Which made sense. He *was* an American.

Sometimes.

He clutched the passport in his left hand. Today he was Italian. His grandmother would be proud. She'd never forgiven his grandfather for making them leave Sicily, and she'd spent the better part of Rico's childhood making certain he was well versed on the virtues of the old country. A fact that had served him well over the years.

He glanced at his watch. It was late. He'd be lucky to make it to Lindoon before dark. Not that he was in any hurry to get there. The little village wasn't exactly a hot spot.

In fact, as far as he was concerned, Lindoon had only one thing to recommend itself.

Kirstin Madison.

At least he hoped it was her. If his informant was right, she was going by Kacy Macgrath. And his instincts told him that if she needed an alias, she had something to hide. He chuckled to himself. He ought to know.

Of course, there was always the chance that his informant was wrong. He frowned, stroking his moustache. That had better not be the case. He'd paid the man a fortune. If he was wrong, there'd be hell to pay.

The octogenarian stepped up to the counter. Almost there. He blew out a breath, glancing at the dark haired man still arguing. A terrorist? If so, he was in good company.

"Next."

A bored looking blonde with a wad of gum in her mouth held out a hand. "Passport." Rico gave her the leather case, his heart beating staccato against his ribs. He really wasn't good at subterfuge.

"Eduardo Baucomo?"

He nodded. She'd butchered the name, but he wasn't bothered. It wasn't like it was his.

"Business or pleasure?"

He wanted to say both, but held his tongue. In his experience, he'd found that passport control people often lacked a sense of humor. "Pleasure," he said, thickening his Italian accent for effect.

"How long?"

"A week, maybe two."

The woman thumbed through the passport, looking for an empty spot. Eduardo had traveled a lot. Finally finding room, she stamped the page and handed the passport back, stifling a yawn. "Next."

He was through. He heaved a sigh of relief, feeling slightly foolish for all his worrying. No one knew who he was. He'd made sure of it. He headed for the car rental cubicle. He had an appointment to keep—with the elusive Mrs. Madison.

Kacy threw her jacket on the bench in the hall and headed for the kitchen. "What we need is a cup of tea." She smiled at Mac. "Okay, you can skip the tea, but I could use the company."

Mac lifted an ear and Kacy laughed, reaching for the electric kettle. After plugging it in, she threw herself into a chair with a sigh. "Well, you have to admit he was cute."

More than cute, actually, Braedon Roche bordered on magnificent. Of course, he'd look better with his shirt unbuttoned, his jeans rumpled, and his hair a mess. She rubbed her fingers against her palm, imagining what it would feel like to run her hands through his hair.

She groaned, trying to control her feelings. This wasn't such a good idea. Really dangerous. In all her life she'd let her emotions have full rein only two times. The first, she'd had them handed back to her on a silver platter. A solid silver platter. And the second . . . She felt her stomach tighten and drew in a slow breath, forcing herself to relax.

The second time had ended in disaster.

And death.

She had to face reality. She wasn't meant to have a relationship—with anyone. Her dog nestled at her feet, his head resting protectively across her ankles. Except Mac. She could love Mac.

The teakettle whistled and she welcomed the interruption. She steeped the tea, though not enough according to the locals, but the stuff they made could rot a person's gut. Adding milk, she stirred it, inhaling the scent of bergamot. Earl Grey was her favorite. She took the cup and headed for the front room, Mac trotting at her heels.

Putting her cup down on the coffee table, she crossed to the fireplace, stirring the carefully banked peat fire with a poker. Small yellow flames licked upward, sending thin tendrils of smoke up the chimney.

She put the poker back against the wall and leaned down to straighten a stack of magazines that had fallen across the hearth and onto the floor. She shot a look at Mac. "Did you do this?"

He ignored her, intent on scratching behind one ear.

"I've told you to be careful with that tail," she scolded with mock severity, restoring the stack to its proper position. She straightened, her eyes falling on the Monet hanging over the sofa. Her Monet. She smiled, for once letting herself feel pride in ownership. It was crooked.

She leaned across the sofa and righted the painting. There. Perfect. Mac looked up reproachfully. She sat on the sofa, reaching for the dog, giving him a hug. "I didn't think you did that. Honestly." She smiled and picked up her mug and a book that lay open on the table.

The Moon-Spinners. An old friend. She curled up on the sofa, took a sip of tea, and tried to remember what was happening with Nicola and Mark. Nicola thought he was dead. She read a few paragraphs, but found it difficult to concentrate.

She knew the story, knew it by heart, but somehow, tonight, Mark kept turning into Braedon, his indigo eyes warm and lazy. She sighed. In truth, Braedon Roche didn't seem like a man who smiled all that often. Maybe she could—she shook her head—*the book*, she was reading the book.

Where was she, again? Oh, yes, the body . . .

Something crashed, glass splintering against wood. Kacy sat up with a start, knocking the book to the floor. She blinked, trying to get her bearings. The fire was burning merrily, Mac was . . . where was Mac? She sat up, all traces of sleep vanishing in an instant.

She heard Mac growl. Frowning, she tried to force her brain to function cognitively. The bedroom. She'd heard a noise in the bedroom. That must be where the dog was. She grabbed the poker and moved hesitantly into the hall. She could still hear Mac and was relieved that his growl hadn't intensified to a bark. A good sign surely.

Taking a deep breath, she strode into the bedroom, brandishing the poker, hoping she looked tougher than she felt. She flipped on the light, blinking at the brightness. Except for Mac, the little room was empty. She released the air in her lungs, surprised to realize she'd been holding her breath.

The lace curtains blew inward and Kacy followed the material with her eyes, her gaze dropping to the floor by the bed. It was covered with roses.

Roses.

She sighed, her hand loosening its death grip on the poker.

A vase. It was just a vase. She bent and started picking up the broken crystal and crushed flowers. "I must have heard the vase crashing." She spoke out loud, as much to herself as to Mac. He came and sat beside her, watching as she cleaned.

"It was just the wind." As if to underline the thought, the wind whistled through the window and the curtains billowed. She stood up, dropping the pieces into the trash can.

"Maybe I need to read something a little less suspenseful." She smiled at the dog and reached across the table to pull the window closed, firmly pushing the latch into place. "My imagination is working overtime. What do you say we call it a night?" Mac wagged his tail and jumped up onto the bed.

Her eyes dropped to the picture on the table. Alex. Sun-bronzed and laughing. She picked up the photo, wondering for the millionth time why she kept it.

A reminder of what a fool she'd been.

She traced the line of his face with a finger. She'd been so blind. Rushing almost overnight into a marriage based on nothing but empty promises. Believing that he had loved her. That, finally, someone loved her. She fought her tears. Tears of humiliation. All she'd wanted was to share a life with him.

But all he'd wanted was a possession. A pretty toy. He'd used her body, but ignored her soul. For three months he'd treated her more like a harlot than a wife. And still she'd refused to accept the truth. Instead, she'd tried to win him back, but in the end, she'd driven him away.

Driven him to his death.

She clutched the photograph to her chest, the pain of his rejection threatening to engulf her. Even after all this time, she wanted him to love her.

With a sigh of resignation, she pushed her bitter thoughts aside. She'd come here to put it all behind her. To start again. To build a new life. And staring at her dead husband's picture was not helping the process.

She opened the nightstand drawer and shoved the picture

to the bottom, a pack of Kleenex covering his face. Maybe another day she'd actually be able to throw it out.

Maybe.

She closed her eyes, but she could still see Alex's face mocking her. He still waited for her in her dreams, taunting her, touching her—hurting her. And always, always, sleep prevented her escape.

She shook her head, opening her eyes, trying to banish her thoughts. But he was still there, teasing at the corners of her mind. She wondered if she'd ever truly be free of him.

Sighing, she closed the drawer, then reached over to pat the dog. At least Mac loved her. "I'll be back in a minute."

She checked the locks and windows in the rest of the house and shut off all the lights, banking the fire before heading for the bathroom.

Fifteen minutes later, she was tucked under the covers, Mac's warm body curled against the small of her back. She reached for the light and paused, realizing her hand was shaking.

Well, maybe just for tonight.

She rolled over, leaving the lamp burning, angry with herself for being afraid of the dark.

Braedon pounded his pillow, wondering how long exactly it was going to take him to fall asleep. Maybe it was jet lag. He rearranged the sheets and closed his eyes. A face floated through his mind, complete with dimpled cheek and emerald green eyes. Kacy Macgrath. So much for jet lag.

He rolled onto his back, locking his fingers behind his head. She was nothing like he'd imagined. And he'd imagined a lot. Some wild combination of Ethel Rosenberg and Marie Antoinette mostly, with a little of the Sharon Stone character from *Basic Instinct* thrown in for good measure.

The woman in Finnegan's Folly was none of the above. At

least not based on her appearance, his brain cautioned. Right. And appearances could be deceiving. Hell, he ought to know that. He'd been pretending to be something he wasn't most of his adult life.

At least she hadn't recognized his name. Or his face. He hadn't even thought about running into her at the pub. Stupid assumption. What the hell had he been thinking coming here? Matt should have come. His friend was the expert in covert operations. That's why Braedon had him on the payroll.

But this was Braedon's problem, his reputation at stake, and he intended to get to the bottom of it. He thought about his encounter with Kacy. Despite his blunder, he'd come out of it okay. She had no idea who he was. Or she was a hell of an actress.

He thought back over what he knew about her. Nothing, really. The woman seemed to appear for brief moments of time only to disappear so completely it was almost as if she'd never existed. What had Matt said? A blip on the radar screen. There one moment, gone the next.

He'd had Matt run a background check on her, and he'd come up with almost nothing. A grainy photograph that could have been anyone, and some vague memories from staff at an art school in France. She was a chameleon, blending into the background so well, no one seemed to even notice she was there.

She was evidently as reclusive as she was talented. During one of her brief appearances on the radar, she'd begun to obtain some acclaim for her art restoration. But even then, she'd worked alone and rarely if ever actually appeared in public. And, just as suddenly, she'd disappeared again altogether.

Even her marriage to Alex seemed odd. The man had been a confirmed playboy. His marriage should have been big news. But Alex hadn't mentioned it. Granted, Braedon hadn't talked to him all that often. The galleries pretty much ran themselves. But it seemed reasonable to have expected Alex to have at least mentioned his new wife.

Hell, it was only after his death that Braedon realized she even existed. And by then she'd managed to disappear again. At the time he hadn't cared. It was only now, in light of recent developments, that it mattered—her odd behavior taking on a more sinister cast.

He frowned, trying to put what he knew together with what he'd seen. The pictures didn't mesh. The reclusive chameleon didn't jibe with the vibrant woman he'd met in the pub. His instincts rarely failed him, and he had a strong notion he'd either misjudged Kacy Macgrath or seriously underestimated her.

And worse, he had the feeling he wasn't going to get any sleep until he figured out which one it was.

The bus's doors slid shut behind him with a satisfying thunk, the Q101's engine revving as it moved away from the stop. Max Madison bit back a grin. He was free. *Free.* He breathed deeply. Even with bus fumes, the air smelled better off the island. Traffic moved at a snail's pace all around him. Pedestrians jostled past him. New Yorkers, dressed to the nines, always in a hurry.

He looked down at his shabby suit, out of fashion and a little snug. He'd managed to gain weight in prison. Sort of amazing, really, when one considered that the fare was hardly nouvelle cuisine. He straightened his tie and shrugged. Well, at least it was better than a monochromatic jumpsuit adorned with only a number.

Running a hand through his hair, he scanned the street for the limo. A woman pulled her child closer as they passed him, her eyes wary, watchful. Geez, she thought he was a street person. He looked down at his suit with disgust. Where was Anson? He needed a tailor. Needed a manicure and a haircut, too. Who was he kidding, he needed a whole new life, and he was determined to get it. But first, there were some things he had to attend to.

A black limo slid silently up to the curb, one tinted window halfway down.

"Maxie, welcome back."

Nadine. He hadn't expected her to be here.

The door to the limo opened, and she stepped out, her long legs accentuated by the tight red miniskirt she wore. He felt a rumble of life below his belt. On the other hand, who was he to argue with fate? It had been a hell of a long time since he buried his johnson in anything but his own hand. He licked his lips, already anticipating the ride.

Nadine reached him just as Anson emerged from behind the wheel. He shrugged and grinned. Max swept the redhead into his arms, winking at his chauffeur over her shoulder. He kissed her thoroughly and then pulled back, his breath coming in short gasps. Damn, he needed it bad. But he needed to talk to Anson more.

"Nadine, honey, could you go over there and buy me a pint of whiskey?" He pointed to a storefront across the street.

"I thought you'd be happy to see me." She pursed her lips in a calculated pout.

"Sweetie, I am happy to see you." He placed her hand on the hard bulge of his crotch. "Believe me." She smiled and tightened her hand. "But first—" He traced the curve of her breast with a finger. "—I want some whiskey."

"Sure, Maxie, whatever." She ambled off, tottering on her high heels, looking like the bimbo she was. Anson joined him.

"What the hell is she doing here?"

"I couldn't stop her. She showed up at the brownstone and I figured you wouldn't want a scene in front of the staff."

Max shrugged and smiled. "Well, at least certain parts of her are welcome."

Anson grinned. "I take it you're not talking about her mouth."

"Not if it's empty." The two men laughed and walked toward the car. Anson was more than a chauffeur, he was Max's right-hand man. He'd trust Anson with his life. Fact was, he had on more than one occasion.

The only person he trusted more than Anson was his twin. But Alex was dead. He sobered, his desire metamorphosing into anger. "Did you find her?"

"Yup. Wasn't easy, the broad is real good at covering her tracks, but I found her."

"Where?" He felt a rush, similar to what he'd felt at the first sight of Nadine. But this was a different kind of lust. *Blood lust.* For the bitch who killed his brother.

"Ireland. She's in some podunk town in Ireland."

"Are you sure?"

"As sure as I can be. The chick keeps a low profile." Anson paused, studying his shoes.

Max raised an eyebrow. "There's more?"

"Yeah. My sources tell me Gienelli is in Ireland, too."

"Son of a bitch. If the little greaseball is there, then you can bet we've got the right girl."

"What girl?" Nadine sauntered up, her red lips almost the same color as her henna dyed hair.

He wondered what had ever possessed him to get involved with her. She thrust out her chest and pouted provocatively. D cups. They got to him every time. "No one you need to know about."

"But I heard Anson telling you about her. You're going to Ireland to see her, and some guy named Gio something." Nadine frowned, narrowing her overmascaraed eyes, obviously trying to remember his name.

Max bit back a surge of irritation and pulled her close, whispering in her ear, "Right now, baby, there's no one I want but you." Over her shoulder, he exchanged a knowing look with Anson and took the knife the other man offered him.

They slid into the car, and Anson shut the door behind them. There was a bottle of champagne on ice. Dom Pérignon, bless him. Max reached for the bottle.

"I thought you wanted whiskey." Nadine held up the bag, pouting again. God, he hated women.

"I did." He opened the bottle she offered and took a long pull. "How about you?" He held out the pint and she looked wistfully at the champagne. "Don't worry, you can have that, too." He smiled, loosening his zipper. "But you'll have to earn it."

A slow smile spread across her face and she slid to the floor of the limo. Max leaned back, trying not to explode as her mouth closed around his throbbing shaft. Now he remembered why he'd spent time with Nadine.

He took another drink of the whiskey, closing his eyes, letting the sensations rock through him. It was all a matter of timing.

Timing.

He closed his hand around the handle of the knife. It was too bad she'd overheard them. He sighed. Too bad. He arched back, shoving himself deeper into her mouth, the heat and suction threatening to undo him.

Timing.

He moaned, lifting his arm. With one quick thrust, he rammed himself down her throat, then pulled out, stabbing her at the base of her throat with the knife. One twist and it was over. He leaned against the seat cushions, gasping for breath, feeling more fulfilled than he'd been in years.

He hit the button for the window separating him from Anson. Silently it slid open. "I think we'd best make a couple of stops."

"Where would you like to go, sir?"

"The East River might not be a bad idea." He looked down at the crumpled body on the floor and then back at his chauffeur. "Oh, and I think I'd like to call on my tailor."

He slid the window shut and reached for the champagne, popping the cork. Filling a glass, he toasted himself. "One down, one to go."

Chapter 3

KACY STOOD ON the rise, looking out at the wet, green field stretching down toward the fort. The rain had stopped for the moment, but the clouds hung ominously close to the ground, and she knew it was only a matter of time before the deluge resumed.

She loved this country. Loved everything about it. The rain, the stone studded green hills. There was an ancientness here. A feeling of being part of something larger than life. She wrapped her arms around herself and surveyed her kingdom, as it were. She felt at peace here. As if at long last, she had found her way home.

She shook her head, laughing at the turn of her thoughts. Too much time alone could make a person dotty. Reaching into her pocket, she pulled out a tattered tennis ball and threw it in the direction of the fort. With a joyous bark, Mac set out after the ball, his ears streaming behind him.

The rain began again, but she only pulled the hood of her slicker over her head. Ignoring the misty drizzle, she watched Mac leap into the air to catch the ball, then return triumphantly to lay it at her feet, his body poised in anticipation of the next throw.

"Again? You're insatiable." She reached down to pick up the soggy ball, grimacing at the slimy feel of it. "Is it absolutely necessary to slobber all over it?"

She shot a narrowed-eyed look at the dog, then threw the

29

ball toward the white stone of the fort. Mac was off like a shot, disappearing behind a wall, nose buried in the grass.

Simple pleasures.

In the dark shadow of the souterrain, something shifted, black on black. She froze, the little hairs on the back of her neck standing at attention, eyes searching for something out of place, beyond the normal. The rain slackened and the sound of the surf echoed from the cliff below. A lonely gull's cry drifted across the meadow.

She wondered if she'd always be this wary.

A lifetime of living in the shadows had obviously made an indelible impression. One that could not easily be discarded. Still, her demons were long buried. There was nothing left to hide from. No one left to hurt her.

She was alone.

"Kacy?"

She whirled around at the sound of her name, heart pounding, the wind whipping her hair across her eyes. She grabbed at it, trying to see who was calling her.

The figure of a man emerged from a tumbled down gap in the fort's outer wall. She stared at him, taking an involuntary step backward, the wild ramblings of her imagination taking on solid proportions.

The man raised a hand and called again. Mac appeared in the gap, circling the stranger with excited little yips. Her stomach dropped and her heart rate abruptly changed tempo as recognition dawned.

Braedon. It was Braedon.

She rubbed suddenly sweaty palms against her sweater. He'd said he was coming, but a part of her had hoped he wouldn't. Although if she were honest, she'd have to admit it was only a tiny little part of her. The sensible part, a little voice whispered.

Smiling, she waved in return. She could see his features now and caught her breath at the sheer imposing strength of him. He was dressed for the weather in an anorak and jeans, Wellingtons, or some expensive American version, encasing his feet. God, he looked good.

She ran a hand through her hair, suddenly wishing her worn Aran sweater and faded jeans would morph into something more chic. She'd never had fashion sense. Her mother had lamented it. Her father had always tried to make light of it. But the fact remained, she couldn't tell a Chanel from a Clio, and frankly, she looked deplorable in both.

She shrugged mentally and tried to tuck her unruly hair behind her ears. Fat chance in this wind.

"I'm glad you're here." His voice was low, pitched so that it would glide under the sound of the wind. It caressed her and a sensuous shiver twisted down her spine.

Her gaze locked on his, her breath coming in little gasps. She opened her mouth, but couldn't find words. He smiled, his hands settling on her shoulders, gently pulling her nearer. She sighed, closing her eyes, waiting for his touch, his kiss.

A rumble followed by an ominous crash splintered through the meadow, shattering the moment. Braedon grabbed her hand and pulled her low to the ground, his eyes searching the area, trying to locate the source of the noise.

Except for the whistle of the wind against the cliffs, the meadow was silent. Mac raced off toward the far wall, his bark echoing off the stone circles. Braedon stood, pulling her with him, his arm locked around her.

She leaned into his strength, her fear evaporating. "It was the fort." She pointed to a heap of rubble lying against a remnant of stone wall.

Braedon's gaze followed hers and she felt him relax. "It caved in."

She nodded and then stepped from the shelter of his arms, suddenly embarrassed at the intimacy. "It happens a lot. Especially when it rains."

"But these things have been here for centuries. Why would they fall now?" He raised a skeptical eyebrow.

"Because farmers take the stones. They use them to make new walls. And they don't really care which stones they take. So bit by bit the wall becomes more unstable until—"

"Until the whole damn thing comes tumbling down." He stared at the rubble.

"Exactly."

Mac barked, leading the way as they set off to examine the remains firsthand. The rubble was in a corner between three sets of walls, two forming a right angle and a third stretching off behind them like the tail on a *Y*. The hill dropped off toward the third wall and Kacy knelt by the edge of it. "There's a souterrain here."

Braedon joined her. "That's the underground passageway you were talking about."

"Right. This place is riddled with them. It's a wonder the fort doesn't fall into the passages below." She shifted a couple of rocks. "There was an entrance here. The stones have covered most of it. See?" She stood back, pointing to what was left of an archway at the bottom of the wall. A black hole gaped beneath it, partially blocked by the rubble.

Mac was sniffing at the entrance, whining.

Kacy grabbed his collar. "No, Mac. It isn't safe."

Braedon eyed the hole, his eyes narrowing. "For anyone."

Kacy met his gaze, confused. "What is it?"

He gestured to the ground at her feet.

She looked down, her eyes settling on the clear imprint of a man's foot. "Oh, my God, someone could be trapped in there." She started forward, reaching for the fallen stones. He pulled her back.

"Look again."

She did, her eyes staring at the footprint, trying to see what he saw.

"It's facing out, Kacy."

"Out?"

"Away from the tunnel."

She sighed with relief. "So there's no one trapped inside?"

"No. Whoever left this print was leaving, not coming."

"That's good, right?"

"For him." Braedon still looked pensive. He placed his hands on her shoulders. She could feel the warmth of his hands all the way through her sweater. "Look, Kacy, I don't want to jump to any conclusions here, but wouldn't you say it's a little coincidental that there's a footprint right where a wall suddenly falls down?"

She stared at the footprint, then looked up at him, frowning. "Maybe it's an old footprint."

"In this weather?" He gestured to the moisture laden sky.

"So what are you implying? That somebody made the wall fall? That doesn't make any sense at all." She searched his face, trying to understand where this was coming from.

"I'm not saying anyone did anything on purpose. I'm just saying that this footprint is fresh, and that I'd bet anything there's a connection."

"Braedon, there wasn't anyone here. If there had been, Mac or I would have seen him."

"Not necessarily. Not if he didn't want to be seen."

She stepped back. "Braedon, you *are* scaring me."

"I'm sorry. I guess I just have a suspicious mind. It was probably just a kid. A prank."

"Maybe so." She thought about the movement she'd sensed earlier. Had there been someone here? Someone watching her? She shivered and pushed the thought aside.

He wrapped an arm around her. "You look cold. What do you say we head for Finnegan's and a hot toddy? You can show me the fort on a drier day."

As if to underscore his words, the rain began to fall in earnest. She bit her lip, considering her options. Her heart and body were of one mind and her brain quite another. She looked up into the blue of his eyes.

Her brain lost.

"Why don't you come to Sidhean? It's closer."

Braedon sat on a bench in Kacy's hallway, watching her pull her sweater over her head. The heavy cotton cable slid up her torso, exposing first the soft curves of her jean-clad hips and then the swell of her breasts beneath the jersey of her T-shirt. He sucked in a breath and tried to concentrate on removing his boots, but his mind was stuck on instant replay and he found himself wishing for slow motion. A wet nose nuzzled against his hand, bringing him back to reality with a thud.

"I think you've made a friend for life." Kacy laughed, the sound filling him with warm sensations he wasn't sure he could identify. Wasn't sure he *wanted* to identify. "I'll just go and put the kettle on. The front room's in there. Make yourself comfortable." She headed for a door at the back of the hall.

He told himself this was the perfect opportunity to have a look around, to try to find something to implicate her, but his feet seemed to have other ideas and he found himself following her.

The kitchen was bright and cheerful, a pleasant change from the wet, gray afternoon. In contrast to the ancient walls of the cottage, the furnishings seemed wrong somehow. Not exactly out of place, just not what one would expect to find in a tiny cottage on the edge of the Burren.

People here barely scratched a living out of the land. They didn't have antique French refectory tables and priceless Welsh dressers. He ran a finger along the edge of the dresser, enjoying the feel of the smooth, worn wood. And they certainly didn't fill those dressers with Waterford and Pickard.

He frowned, looking over at Kacy. She was humming softly, her back turned as she puttered with the tea things, carefully arranging the pot, sugar bowl, and cream pitcher on a tray. He was reminded suddenly of his mother. She had loved tea time, always insisting they use their best china.

He glanced at the cups Kacy was reaching for. His mother's best had certainly not been Limoges. His practiced eye recognized it even from here. He surveyed the rest of the kitchen. The ancient Aga in the corner looked right at home, and beside the cooker was the requisite ice box. An ancient one at that. The only appliance that seemed out of place was the microwave—but even it had the battered look of second-hand. He frowned at the incongruity. Another puzzle. Kacy Macgrath seemed full of them.

He stopped himself, confused at his own indecision. In New York, he'd been so certain of her guilt. But here, in her kitchen . . .

He blew out a breath, trying to bolster his resolution. She had to be guilty. Everything pointed to her. And he wanted her to be guilty.

Didn't he?

He watched her arranging the tea things, impatiently pushing back the strands of hair that fell in her eyes. Right at the moment, guilty or not, all he wanted was to run his hands through the soft silky mass of her hair.

He shook his head, clearing his thoughts. He needed to stay focused. If she was guilty, he'd find out soon enough.

"Almost ready." She turned to him, a biscuit tin in her hands. "Could you open this? I can't seem to manage it."

He reached for the can, surprised at the spark that leapt between them when their hands touched. Kacy jerked back, her eyes wide. She'd felt it, too. He couldn't decide if that pleased him or scared the hell out of him. Neither, he decided, yanking the tin open with more force than necessary.

Biscuits flew everywhere, landing on the floor and the cabinet, even in the sink. "I'm sorry, I guess I was a little overexuberant." He shrugged, reaching to retrieve several from the counter.

She smiled, adding a couple that had landed on a shelf to the plate on the tray. "It's okay. Mac certainly thanks you."

Sure enough, the dog was happily gobbling up the fallen plunder. Braedon sighed. "Well, at least he helps with the cleanup."

Mac barked in agreement and the teakettle whistled in dissonant harmony.

"If you think you can manage, why don't you take the tea things into the front room. I'll pour the tea and follow you in a sec." She reached for the tea tin and began spooning leaves into the pot.

"Right." He picked up the tray. "I'll just be in here, then." He sounded like a damn schoolboy. A lower-class Irish one at that. He'd worked half a lifetime to eradicate the accent. These days, it only surfaced when he was rattled.

And Kirstin Kacy Macgrath Madison definitely rattled him.

She had no business getting involved with anybody. None at all. She was not capable of making a good decision when it came to relationships. Her marriage had been a sham. One of the more painful things she'd ever had to endure. Almost as painful as . . .

She shook her head. This was not the time to think about her father. Kacy poured the hot water into the pot and tried to make herself see reason. Unfortunately, the irrational part of her brain was firmly in control.

There was just something about Braedon Roche that spoke to her. Something she saw in him that reflected her own need. She suspected he kept his protective walls every bit as high as hers. There was a connection. She'd felt it at Fin's and she felt it now. Like a current running between them, linking them intrinsically.

She was out of her mind.

She slammed the lid on the teapot, checking the tin to make sure it did in fact contain tea and not some crazy aphrodisiac. She wasn't usually like this. Good Lord, she was standing in her kitchen thinking about cosmic connections with a total stranger. Next thing she knew she'd be blethering on about true love.

God, she needed her head examined.

"Can I be of any further help to you?" he called from the parlor.

She heard the hint of Irish lilt in his voice. Fin was right. "No. No. I'm fine. On my way." She grabbed the teapot and pushed through the swinging door into the front room.

He was standing in front of the sofa, tray still in his hands, staring at the Monet. Her Monet.

"It's wonderful." He motioned to the painting with the tray, the teacups rattling in their saucers. "*The Custom Officer's Cottage.* A favorite of mine."

She set the pot on the table, and then took the tray from him and put it down, too. "You like Monet?"

"I do. I just never expected to find him here." His eyes never left the painting.

"I suppose I could take that as an insult."

"None intended. It's just that the last time I saw this painting, it was in a museum in Rotterdam."

She laid a hand on his arm and whispered, "It's still there."

"What?" He turned to face her, his expression priceless. "I know art. Well, at least a little. I know a Monet when I see one."

She flushed, suddenly feeling insecure. She wasn't in the habit of sharing her secret. She never knew how people would react. Her father had said it was a poor rendition, and Alex had accused her of lying. She wasn't certain she wanted to risk someone else belittling her.

The Monet was special. It was something that belonged

only to her. Braedon was watching her. Waiting for an explanation. She breathed in and out—oxygen for fortification. "It's a copy."

He'd moved closer now and was looking at the painting, really looking. "A damn good one." He turned to face her, his eyes narrowed to tiny blue slits, the intensity drilling into her.

"Who painted this, Kacy?"

She swallowed. In for the penny and all that. "I did."

Chapter 4

◈ "You?"

All traces of any connection between them vanished in an instant. The walls were back in place, higher than ever. Braedon's look sent a shiver down Kacy's spine.

"Yes, me." Her voice came out a whisper. She sat down on the sofa and stared at her hands, not sure exactly what she had done, feeling like a schoolgirl caught red-handed by the nuns, nevertheless. So much for telling the truth. She swallowed and attempted a weak smile.

His frown only deepened. "When?" The question shot out and hung between them in the air.

"In college. I studied art restoration. The idea is to try to match the original as closely as possible. I thought it would be interesting to see if I could copy the entire thing. Right down to the paint used." She gestured at the Monet. "This was my attempt."

"I see." The line of his face softened, although the edge was still in his voice. "And have you painted others?"

She chewed on her bottom lip, wondering where these questions were coming from. Still, there didn't seem any harm in answering. At least the angry look was gone. "One or two. But they didn't turn out as well."

"Where are they?"

Suddenly her own anger flared. "Excuse me, did I miss

something? I don't believe I realized this was an inquisition."
She met his gaze full on.

His face changed as the impact of her words hit him and he
fidgeted uncomfortably. In a flash, the interrogator disappeared
and the charming man from the pub was back. "I'm sorry, I
didn't mean for it to sound that way. I'm just interested. Unfortunately, sometimes I come across as too intense."

Warning bells went off in her head, but he smiled at her,
and they stopped as suddenly as they'd started, as if someone
had stuffed pillows under the clappers. "It's okay," she said,
accepting his apology. "I'm probably overreacting."

He sat down, reaching for a cookie, looking incredibly
at home on her sofa. Right somehow. She shook her head,
struggling to pick up the train of the conversation.

"Your artwork," he prompted.

"The copies." Her brain clicked back on, for the moment
stifling her libido. "A friend of mine has one of them. It was a
Gainsborough. Really bad rendition, but Kathy needed cheap
art." She felt herself relax.

"And the other?"

"A Martin."

"Fauvism, an interesting choice." Both eyebrows lifted,
almost disappearing behind the dark hair falling onto his
forehead.

She shrugged. "I think it's in my studio, somewhere."

"You have a studio?" He'd relaxed completely now. Maybe
she *had* overreacted. Somehow the thought relieved her. She
didn't want to be cautious around this man.

"Well, it's a big name for a little room. It's just off the
kitchen. Used to be a storage room, but the light is good and
so I decided to paint there."

"You use it for work?" He was being polite now, going
through the social motions. He sat back against the sofa cushions, one leg crossed casually over the other.

She sipped her tea, surprised to find that her hands were shaking. "No. Not really."

He frowned. "But I thought you restored art?"

She shook her head. "I studied it. Even worked for a little while, but then I quit."

"Didn't you like it?" He tipped his head to one side and raised an eyebrow inquisitively.

"I loved it. There is so much that goes into restoring a painting to its original state. I specialized in Dutch miniatures."

He reached for his teacup, taking a sip, regarding her with curious eyes. "But if you loved it so much, why did you stop?" He leaned forward, interested again, the intensity back in his eyes. His moods were mercurial.

"Family commitments." Despite her attempt to keep the words light, they came out in staccato succession. She swallowed, trying to control her emotions. Accentuate the positive. After all, her life was in the here and now. "I am thinking about going back to it. I've had some recent inquiries. A professor from Italy called about a consultation. So I've decided maybe it's an omen. Time to dip my fingers into professional waters again."

"And you can do that from here?"

"I think so."

Mac dropped down onto the rug at Braedon's feet, cookie crumbs clinging to his whiskers. He reached down and scratched the dog between the ears. "So what made you choose to live here?"

Because she'd been running away, and it was the perfect place to lose herself—again. Old habits died hard. And Alex's death had only intensified them. But that was hardly an answer for polite conversation. She forced herself to smile. "Lindoon or Ireland?"

"Both, I guess. Seems an isolated spot for someone with your occupation."

"I like Ireland." She shrugged.

He swallowed the last of his tea and put the cup and saucer back on the tray. "But why Lindoon?"

She paused, trying to order her thoughts before she answered. "In a way, this is my home."

"You're from here?" He raised a skeptical eyebrow, reminding her of Mr. Spock.

"No. Obviously not. But my granny was. This is her cottage, and her father's before her, and so on." She shrugged. "It's the closest thing to a family I've ever had."

He studied her for a moment and she felt bare under his probing eyes. "She certainly did well for herself, your granny."

Again, she had the distinct feeling that this was more than a casual question, but this time she was ready with an answer. Everyone was surprised at the contents of the cottage. "No. The things are mostly mine."

"I see," he said, although his voice clearly indicated he didn't. "For an unemployed artist, you're doing pretty well for yourself."

She felt her hackles rise again. "Not that it's any of your business, but most of these things were inherited. They're family pieces. Except for a small trust fund, they're all I have. So I guess you'll just have to adjust your image of me as a poor starving artist living in a hovel in Ireland." She glared at him, wondering if she had the nerve to throw him out.

"I'm sorry. I was out of line. I was just surprised to see all this here." He gestured at the priceless antiques scattered about the room.

How could she adequately explain her need to have her father's things around her? A futile effort to fill the void he'd left in her heart. She shook her head, banishing the past, and smiled at Braedon, accepting his apology. "It's all right. You're not the first one to mistake me for something I'm not."

His steady gaze met hers and she tried to read the message written there. Whatever it was, it made her heart beat faster. The man was an enigma. One moment making her want to throttle him and the next making her want to lose herself in his arms. One thing was certain, though, Braedon Roche had gotten under her skin.

The doorbell chimed.

"Saved by the bell." She flashed him what she hoped was a carefree smile and went to answer the door.

The man on the threshold could only be described as dapper. He was small and round, with a neatly trimmed beard and moustache. All he needed to look perfect was a bowler and an umbrella. Sort of a cross between Santa Claus and Mr. French.

"Good day, signora." *Okay, Mr. Italian.* The little man smiled, his eyes crinkling at the corners. "I am Professor Eduardo Baucomo." He bowed politely. "You are expecting me, no?"

She felt rather than heard Braedon come up behind her. Goose bumps rose on her arms as his warm breath caressed the back of her neck. She blinked at Professor Baucomo, trying in vain to remember why they were still standing there.

"Kacy?" Braedon's voice was impatient and Baucomo looked at her expectantly.

She jumped, pulling her riotous thoughts in order. "Of course I was expecting you, Professor, please come in." She backed up to gesture him into the house, colliding with Braedon in the process. His body was hard against hers and she resisted the urge to rub against him. She jerked forward, breaking the contact.

The professor looked confused and slightly amused as he watched the two of them. "I have come at an inopportune moment?"

"No." They both answered at once, sounding more like guilty children than adults.

"I see." The little man shifted uncomfortably from one foot to the other.

"No, really. I was just leaving." Braedon sat on the bench and began pulling on his boots.

"Please, Professor, have a seat in there." She pointed to the parlor door, trying to calm her surging hormones. "I'll be with you in a moment."

The little man smoothed his moustache and disappeared through the sliding doors.

Braedon shrugged into his jacket.

"I'm sorry. I really do need to meet with him. He's come all this way just to see me."

He put his hands on her shoulders, his blue eyes suddenly intense. "Have dinner with me tonight."

Say no, her brain instructed firmly. She stared up at him, her heart in her throat. "All right." So much for logic. She was a wimp, a great big wimp.

He grinned, his teeth white against his tan. "Fin's?"

"As long as we're not going for the food." She smiled, suddenly feeling absurdly happy.

"Personally, I think I'm more interested in the view." His eyes traced a slow path from her head to her toes and back again.

She flushed under his heated gaze. "I'll . . . I'll meet you there."

He squeezed her shoulders and leaned close, his lips brushing hers.

Lightning.

White, hot lightning.

One instant he was kissing her good-bye, and the next, he was out the door without a backward glance. She stood on the top step, watching him walk away until he disappeared into the mist, a finger pressed to her lips.

Rico stood in front of the sofa, staring at the painting. It was good.

Damn good.

Of course, with his unique expertise, it was obvious to him it was a copy. But he doubted there'd be many others who would realize they weren't looking at an original Monet. He ran a finger along the bottom of the canvas. The paint was even old.

He blew out his breath in a soft whistle. Damn good.

"I'm sorry, Professor Baucomo. I didn't mean to keep you waiting." Kacy Macgrath breezed into the room, holding out her hand.

He raised it to his lips, using the moment to examine her more closely. She was a beautiful woman. Nothing like he'd imagined. Fragile, almost wispy. A good breeze would blow the girl away. Yet there was something tangible about her, too. A woman a man could depend on. He smiled, lingering over her soft skin. For an old man, he had a foolish young heart. "It is no problem. It is me who should be apologizing. I have interrupted a—what do you call it—afternoon delight?"

"It wasn't anything like that, really."

He watched as a slow pink flush crept across her cheeks. So rare to see innocence in young people these days. Despite his preconceived notions, he found that he liked Kacy Macgrath. "I see." He let the words trail off provocatively, unable to resist the urge to tease her.

"Professor Baucomo, I've only just met Mr. Roche."

His jovial mood evaporated instantly. He knew he'd recognized the man. Braedon Roche. If he was here, that spelled trouble. *La Madre di Dio.* Things were always so complicated. He pushed the thought aside. "Well, perhaps something will develop?"

Again she blushed. So, Roche was romancing her. If he were twenty years younger he'd probably romance her, too, but right now his objective was far more simple. He just needed to know what she knew. And to do that, he needed her trust. "I was admiring your painting. It's marvelous, an exceptional copy."

A tiny dimple flickered at the corner of her mouth. "Thank you."

It couldn't be. Wasn't possible. He forced himself to speak. "May I ask who did it?" He held his breath, almost afraid to hear the answer.

She was grinning, and suddenly he felt like he'd heard a joke but missed the punch line. She sobered and laid a hand on his shoulder. "The painting is mine, Professor Baucomo."

His admiration for her grew a notch. "Please, it's just Professor," he mumbled, climbing onto the sofa for a closer look. "This is fabulous. I cannot believe you have let a talent like this languish here in this backwater." He pulled his attention away from the painting to look at her.

"I like my home." She shrugged.

"But with talent like this, you should be working." He eyed her closely, looking for something beyond the guileless enthusiasm he saw reflected in the green of her eyes.

"Well, now, I thought maybe you could help me with that." Her lips curved into a shy smile, and his old heart actually turned a flip-flop.

He turned back to the Monet, examining it more closely, amazed at her expertise. "How did you manage the paint?"

"A technique I developed for restoring." She joined him on the sofa, her enthusiasm matching his.

"On your own?"

She nodded. "My professors said it couldn't be done." The smile changed to an impish grin. "I wanted to prove them wrong."

He touched the paint carefully with an index finger; even the texture felt right. His admiration ratcheted right off the charts. She was good. *Really good.* Whatever her sins, they'd work around them. He rarely found anyone who understood his passion for copying another man's work, and the idea that perhaps he'd found a kindred spirit was beyond excitement.

It was bliss.

* * *

Braedon knelt beside the muddy entrance to the souterrain. The footprint was gone, obscured by the rain. He'd expected as much, but he was disappointed nevertheless. His
rational mind told him he was making mountains out of
molehills, but his intuition told him otherwise. Something
here wasn't as it seemed.

Hell, who was he kidding, nothing in Lindoon was as it
seemed. And Kacy Macgrath was at the top of the list. He'd
come here to prove she was more than she claimed to be. That
she, along with her dearly departed husband, was responsible
for the problems that were plaguing his gallery. But now that
he was here, he found himself doubting the instincts that had
brought him back to Ireland.

He blew out a breath and stood up, still studying the rubble
at his feet. Kacy was probably right. It was just a cave-in
caused by the rain.

And she was exactly what he'd thought she was. She'd all
but admitted she was a forger. A really good forger, at that.
But then that was part of the problem. Most criminals didn't
display their handiwork in their living rooms and then brag
about their accomplishments to a stranger.

So maybe she wasn't most criminals.

He ran a hand through his hair in frustration. She certainly
wasn't hurting for money. Maybe she wasn't even Kirstin
Madison. Maybe his sources were wrong. He knew he was
grasping at straws. The truth was he wanted her to be innocent.

He watched as the gulls darted in and around the stone
walls of the fort. He glanced back at the souterrain, frowning.
Something was definitely off here. He just couldn't put a
finger on it. But he would. Oh, yes, he would. He hadn't made
a fortune by letting details slide. Sooner or later, he'd find
answers.

And in the meantime, he intended to get to know Kirstin

Kacy Macgrath, or whoever she really was, a little bit better. He grinned, remembering the way her lips had quivered under his kiss. Hell, if he had his way, he planned to get to know her a whole lot better.

Enrico Gienelli whistled to himself as he walked down the hall of Mrs. Macnamara's bed and breakfast. The elderly lady was as deaf as a doorpost, but otherwise unremarkable. Which is exactly what he wanted.

He'd been a little concerned that Braedon Roche might be staying here as well. Lindoon wasn't a very big place, but Mrs. Macnamara had informed him that the nice American fellow was staying in the room above Finnegan's Folly.

Nice American fellow, his Aunt Rosa. Braedon Roche was a shark. A cold-blooded, bottom-feeding shark. And Kacy Macgrath had best be careful of him.

Rico was surprised at the strength of his feelings. He wasn't one to risk his carefully constructed life blithely. In fact, he'd come here to protect it. He smiled, thinking of the two hours he'd spent happily discussing—no, arguing about—art with Kacy Macgrath. Then they'd examined the miniatures he'd brought with him. His sources hadn't exaggerated. She had true talent.

And then there was the Monet. The Macgrath, he should say.

Whatever Kacy Macgrath was hiding, his gut told him it didn't have anything to do with Alex. He'd bet his reputation on it. And he damn sure wasn't going to let a predator like Braedon Roche get his teeth into her.

He twisted the key in the lock on his door and went inside, already removing his jacket and loosening his tie. He'd brought a bottle of Chianti with him from Milan. He couldn't wait to open it, to celebrate his marvelous new find. Why, with proper training, she'd be better than he was.

"Good evening, old friend. Fancy meeting you here."

Rico froze, hand in the air, tie dangling uselessly from limp fingers. The lamplight from beside the bed cast long shadows across the room, its pale gold light illuminating the harsh, handsome features of Max Madison.

Chapter 5

"I THOUGHT YOU were—"

"Incarcerated?" Max smiled, the lamplight making his features appear almost demonic. "I was, but the parole board seemed to think I had paid my debt to society, as it were."

"Alex's debt."

Max shrugged. "Whatever."

"So, what are you doing here?" Rico played for time, knowing full well why Max was in Lindoon. The same reason he was. To find out how much Kacy Macgrath knew. With Alex dead, the only way the forgeries could be linked to them was through Kacy. She was the weak link.

"I could ask you the same thing." Max sipped wine from one of Rico's crystal glasses.

Evidently he'd found the Chianti. Pity. Rico dropped the tie on the bed and reached for a second glass, pouring himself some of the wine. "I came to tie up loose ends. With my paintings popping up all over Europe, it seemed best to check all the angles."

Max raised his eyebrows. "I thought you had people to handle these things for you."

Rico shrugged. "I do. But sometimes it pays to check on things yourself." He'd severed most of his connections to organized crime years ago. There were no "people" unless he called in favors, but he saw no point in enlightening Max.

One thing prison life had taught him was that a person had to keep his cards close to the vest. And he didn't trust Max Madison any more than he trusted the other men he'd met in Rikers. In fact, in many ways he trusted him less.

"So . . ." Max paused, eyebrows raised.

Projecting a calm he didn't feel, Rico savored the wine in his glass, turning it in the light, examining the color. Then with false bravado, he sniffed it, letting the Chianti linger in his nostrils, tantalizing his palate. "So, nothing. She doesn't know a thing."

"The hell she doesn't," Max exploded, literally coming out of his chair, rage marring his handsome face. "The bitch killed my brother."

Rico felt a chill run down his spine. He forced his voice to stay calm. "What in the world would make you think that?"

"She came out of nowhere. Married him overnight. And then suddenly he quits coming to see me. Three months of nothing. No calls. No letters. *Nothing*."

"And that makes her a murderer, how?"

Max tightened his grip on the wineglass. "In all the years I was in the joint, my brother never missed a visit—until he met *her*. She lured him away from me, and then she killed him."

"That's ridiculous, Max. Just because the girl married your brother doesn't mean she murdered him. There's no connection at all."

Max's jaw started working, a red flush staining his face. "There's the money."

"What money?" Rico stared at his old cellmate.

"Mine. And Alex's. There was a bank account. Offshore. Alex deposited my share of our little endeavor there."

"I know. I have an account there, too, remember?" Rico took a sip from his glass.

"*Have* being the operative word." Max slammed the crystal

down on the table, and Rico winced. Baccarat was not meant to be manhandled. "My account has been liquidated."

"And you think Ms. Macgrath is responsible?"

"Who the hell else could it have been?" His face had gone from cerise to crimson.

"Alex."

"No." The single word echoed through the room. Max took a menacing step forward, and despite himself, Rico flinched. "Alex would never have betrayed me. He's my brother. He would have been nothing without me. We were a team."

A fairly lopsided team when one considered the fact that Max had just spent a number of years locked in Rikers Island for something his sainted brother had done. But Rico knew better than to mention the fact to Max.

"It had to have been Kirstin. I think she knew about the forgeries. That's why she married Alex."

"And then killed him?" Rico narrowed his eyes, considering the proposition, then rejecting it. He'd bet all his ill-gotten gains on the fact that Kacy Macgrath wasn't capable of killing anyone.

"Yes. She poisoned Alex against me, and then murdered him for the money. My money."

"You have any proof?"

"No, but I'll get it. And then I'll make her pay." He tightened his fingers, the stem of his glass snapping under the pressure, wine splashing against the brocade of the chair, the spreading stain bloodred.

Rico shivered. If he wanted to keep his new friend alive, he needed to think of something fast. Something to stall Max. "Even if you find the proof, you don't want Ms. Macgrath coming to any harm. At least not yet."

Max sat back down, normal color returning to his face. "All right, I'll play. Why don't I want her to come to immediate and irreparable harm?"

Rico bit back a smile, knowing he had the upper hand, for

the moment at least. "Because she might know where your money is."

Max pursed his lips thoughtfully. "I wouldn't mind finding the money. It is mine after all."

"Right. So all we have to do is find out where it is, and then—"

"Then I can have my fun with that murdering whore."

"Well, that's one way to put it." Rico sipped the rich wine, wondering why in the world he'd ever allowed himself to get involved with the brothers Madison. They were poison. He should have known better.

He sighed, already knowing the answer. Vanity. It was his major shortcoming and no doubt would be his ultimate downfall, but he'd be damned if he'd let a man like Max Madison be the one to bring him down. "There's more you should know." He watched the younger man's eyes narrow. "Braedon Roche is here."

"In Lindoon?" Max slammed a fist on the table and Rico winced.

"Yes. And it gets worse."

Max leaned forward menacingly. "How much worse?"

Rico shrugged. "He's romancing your dear brother's widow."

"Son of a bitch." Max jumped to his feet and strode to the window, fists clenched. "That means he knows about the forgeries."

"Oh, he knows. I told you, they've been popping out of the woodwork everywhere. I'm surprised you haven't heard."

"You forget, I've been out of circulation." A muscle in Max's jaw was twitching, one fist clenching and unclenching.

Rico smirked. "Could it be the infallible Anson is slipping? I thought he could ferret out anything."

"Leave Anson out of this. Just tell me what's been happening."

"Fine. It's simple, really. A month or so ago, there was an

appraisal. For insurance purposes. And surprise, surprise, the painting was a forgery."

"Why now?"

"You mean as opposed to two years ago?" He shrugged. "It was a fluke. But once the first was discovered, every painting sold at a Solais gallery was suspect. I seem to remember telling you we were taking a chance, reproducing so many."

Max waved a hand in the air. "Quantity is not the issue anymore. What matters is that Roche has linked it to Alex. Or at least he suspects something. Otherwise he wouldn't have gone to the trouble to track down my brother's widow."

"True." Rico stroked the thin line of his moustache, watching the wheels turn in Max's head. "Why don't you let me see what I can find out? I've already got an in with Ms. Macgrath. All I have to do is gain her trust."

Max frowned.

"If it doesn't work, then we can try it your way."

"And what if Roche figures things out?"

"He can't. The trail stops with Kacy. If she's innocent, she'll have nothing to tell him. And if she did kill your brother, it's doubtful she knows we're involved or she'd have already done something about it—about us. So either way, we win."

"And she loses." Max looked eager. Too eager.

"And—" Rico pointed a finger at him. "—if you wait, maybe you can retire a rich man."

"I am a rich man."

"All right then, a richer man. One can never be too rich, my friend."

"Fine." There was a grudging note of agreement and Rico accepted that it was the most he'd get.

"Good. I'm glad we're in accord, because I think the best thing you could do now is go home. It surely won't help matters if they see you, especially Kacy."

Max straightened, his lips thinning with decision. "No. I'm not going anywhere. I'll stay in the next village, and I'll try to keep out of sight. But there's no way I'm taking a chance on her slipping away from me. I'll wait a little while longer, but you listen to me, Rico, sooner or later the bitch *will* die. And if I have my way, I'll be standing over her when it happens."

Rico's wine suddenly tasted bitter. He wanted to save Kacy, but he wasn't sure he had the power to do so. There really wasn't room for attachments in his line of work anyway. He sighed, feeling it all the way down to his toes. At the end of the day, the only thing that really mattered was that he was clear and free of this whole nightmare.

He held up his glass. "To success."

Whatever that might be.

"So, was your visit successful?" Anson started the car.

The strips of asphalt that passed for roads in Ireland were too narrow for a limousine, but Max had no intention of doing without a driver. He touched the leather of the little Mercedes's seat with a loving hand. No sense in doing without the finer things either, even in this backwoods hellhole.

"More or less." He met his chauffeur's gaze in the rearview mirror. "The old fool believes the girl is innocent."

"And you?"

"I haven't changed my mind, but I'm afraid the stakes have changed."

Anson frowned. "How?"

"Roche is here."

"Braedon Roche is in Lindoon?"

"That's what I said." Max fingered the door handle with irritation. "He's made the link to Kirstin, Anson."

"You're sure."

"I'm sure. The paintings have been discovered and he suspects Alex."

"Has he connected it to you?"

"I don't think so, but he will. I know his type. Like a dog with a bone. He'll chew on it until he finds all the answers."

"So what are you going to do?"

"I don't know yet, but maybe there's a way to lay the whole thing at the old man's feet."

"And the girl?"

Max smiled, images of her begging for mercy filling his mind. "Well, I predict the little professor will help us with that, too."

"I don't get it."

"You don't have to. Just know that when the dust settles, we'll be in the clear and Kacy Macgrath and her *friends* will be dead." He leaned back and closed his eyes. Revenge was tiring. "And, Anson, do hurry. I find that I'm famished."

The night was moonless and overcast. Dark enough that the lights at Mrs. Macnamara's bed and breakfast looked like a beacon, promising warmth and protection from the evils of the night. She had to get a car. This was getting ridiculous.

The road was slick and she had to fight the bicycle to maintain traction. She stared at the yellow glow from the windows and suddenly wished she was visiting Irene instead of heading for Fin's—and Braedon.

Which said a lot. Irene Macnamara was a talker. And since she couldn't hear the answers, it made for long and often confusing conversations.

Kacy steered to the left, passing the drive, heading down the lane to the village. Stone walls lined the road on either side. Like countless other Irish stone hedges, these were layered with dense vegetation, hazel and brambles tangling with gentians and cranesbill.

The lane felt like a green tunnel on sunny days. In the dark, it took on a more sinister cast. Usually it didn't bother Kacy, but tonight it seemed bleaker than ever. She stopped for a moment, bracing herself with her foot, pulling her raincoat closer around her.

It was just a road. She went down it almost every day.

The wind moaned and the leaves lifted, fluttering into a skittering dance. She swallowed and tried to think of the pub, full of light and laughter. She failed miserably, her brain insisting instead on replaying the bridge scene from *The Legend of Sleepy Hollow*.

She should have brought Mac.

A trailing branch rubbed against the back of her head. She jumped, stifling a scream.

This was ridiculous. There was no headless horseman, and she had a date waiting for her. She pictured Braedon. Blue eyes, brown hair, broad shoulders, and . . .

She sucked in a breath and started to peddle. It was just a road. A thread of light lit the pavement in front of her, the arc expanding rapidly. Her first thought was relief. Light was definitely good. Even light accompanied by humming.

Humming?

The noise increased as it neared and Kacy recognized the mechanical whine. A car. It was a car.

Company.

A second thought snuck into her brain, insisting on being heard.

The car was coming too fast.

She peddled to the side of the road, the wall preventing her from pulling completely out of the way. Still, she should be safe. She turned to look back and was blinded by the light. The noise of the engine swelled, threatening to overpower her.

She dove off the bicycle just as the bumper of the car hit it, the momentum sending her sprawling into the wall, her head cracking against the stones. It was over in a second, and the car and its light disappeared around a bend, leaving her in the dark rain. Kacy's last thought was that the son of a bitch hadn't even stopped.

*   *   *

"Why are you slowing?" Max leaned forward, peering out the window.

"We just ran someone off the road. Do you want me to stop?" Anson tossed a glance over his shoulder.

"Could you see who it was?" Max picked at the leather ridge on the trim of the seat with his index finger.

"No. Looked like a woman. But it's really dark out there."

"Did she see us?"

"No way. The lights were in her eyes." Anson smiled into the rearview mirror.

"Drive on then." He waved a hand in dismissal, his mind already turning back to his plans for his brother's soon to be departed wife.

"Whatever you say, boss."

Max frowned, the mental picture evaporating. Anson only called him boss when he disapproved of something. "You think we should go back?"

The chauffeur was quiet a moment. "Yeah."

"So we can rush the woman to a hospital?" Max sneered.

"No. So we can make sure she's dead."

Max tipped his head back and laughed. God, he loved Anson. "I applaud your tenacity, but I think we'll leave her to fate. We have more important things to think about."

Chapter 6

HE'D BEEN STOOD up. Braedon paced in front of the door to the pub, stopping every pass to look out the window at the rain spattered street. He'd have thought he was beyond getting upset about this sort of thing, but he obviously hadn't figured Kacy into the equation.

"Whoa, man, if you don't quit your pacing, you're sure to wear a hole in me floor."

He stopped and walked slowly back to the bar. "Sorry, I guess I wasn't thinking."

Fin's lips twisted into a wry smile. "I'd say 'twas just the opposite. I'm not a betting man, mind you, but if I were, I'd say your problem involves too much thinking."

Braedon sighed and sat on a stool, swinging around to face the man. "That obvious, is it?"

"Afraid it is." Fin tilted a glass under a spigot. "She'll be here, you know."

Braedon fought the urge to say "who." He'd already made fool enough of himself. "Why do you say that?"

The barman opened a packet of peanuts and poured them into a bowl on the bar. "Two reasons. One. Kacy doesn't lie."

Fin obviously wasn't talking about the same Kacy. If his hunch was right, the woman *was* a lie. Braedon reached for a handful of peanuts. "And two?"

Fin smiled. "I saw the way she looked at you. Believe me when I say it. She'll be here."

Braedon swallowed the nuts, the bulk of them sticking in his throat. "You think a lot of Kacy."

Fin sobered. "That I do. She's one hell of a woman. And if I thought I had a prayer, I'd give you a run for your money."

"I see." Braedon wasn't really surprised that Kacy inspired such fierce loyalty. It was just that the whole thing was so at odds with his original thoughts about her. "How long have you known her, Fin?"

"Well, off and on all her life, I guess. Her granny lived here, and from time to time she'd show up and stay, starting when she was a just a little sprite."

Braedon found himself imagining Kacy as a child, her long hair pulled back in ribbons. "So you were friends?"

"No. She always kept to herself. And she was rarely here more than a day or two at a time. She had an odd sort of childhood. At least that's what me mam said. Her mother never was very clear on who exactly Kacy's father was, if you know what I mean, but there was always money to burn. And then, when her mother died, we all expected she'd come here to live. But she didn't."

"Where'd she go?"

Fin shrugged. "I don't know the whole of it. I do know she was in the States just before coming back here." He smiled, his eyes crinkling at the corners. "But I think being here again has done her a world o' good."

Braedon recognized the sparkle in his eyes. Hell, he probably had one of his own. Kacy seemed to do that to a man. "I'd wager it hasn't hurt you either."

The smile turned into a grin. "Can't say that it has. I've certainly come to know her better."

"And you've become close?" He picked up a peanut, rubbing it between his fingers.

Fin frowned for a second, considering the question. "I suppose so, in a manner o' speaking."

"That's certainly a cryptic statement." Braedon popped the peanut in his mouth.

The other man smiled. "Well, now, I don't think I meant for it to be. It's just that our Kacy's sort of a contradiction."

"In what way?"

"It's hard to put into words. On the one hand, she's almost like a child discovering the world for the first time. Open, kind of inviting." He paused, scratching his head. "I think being back here has done that."

"She was closed before?" Braedon struggled to assimilate this new information.

"Well, *closed* isn't really the right word. *Shut down* might be better. She was devastated over the death of her husband. I've never seen a person in that kind of pain before."

"What happened to him?" Braedon tried to keep his voice conversational.

"He drowned during a storm. Swamped by a wave." Fin placed a glass under the spigot, drawing a beer. "I think she saw the whole thing. Can you imagine anything more horrible? Watching someone you love die and not being able to do a thing about it."

Actually he didn't have to imagine it, he'd lived it. "You said, you think she saw it. Don't you know?"

"No, not the whole of it. I've been able to put bits and pieces together. The basics. But she won't talk about the rest. Keeps it all bottled up inside. In fact, she won't talk about her past at all. That's the contradiction I was talking about. As long as you stay in the here and now, Kacy's an open book, all smiles and dimples."

Braedon lips quirked into a grin. He remembered that dimple. "But?"

"But if you try to dig any deeper, she shuts you out. Closes the castle gates, so to speak."

"Circles the wagons."

"What?"

"Nothing, it's an American term. Means the same thing." Braedon had spent years circling his wagons. He was an expert.

Fin nodded, his brow furrowed. "I guess the real answer to your question is that Kacy isn't close to anyone, Braedon. There's a part of her I'd bet she's never shared with a living soul, certainly not with me." Fin put a glass down in front of him.

"You're saying she has secrets?" Braedon downed half the beer with a single gulp.

"Everyone has things they'd rather be keeping to themselves."

"True enough." He sat back, waiting.

Fin blew out a breath. "The truth is, you might have a real shot at getting her to open up."

"Me?"

"Aye. In all the time I've known her, I've never seen her react to anyone the way she did with you. It was there in her eyes." Fin studied him for a moment, his eyes narrowing. "You'd best not be hurting her. I may not hold the key to her heart, but I care about her just the same, and I'll not tolerate any man toying with her."

Braedon held up a hand. "I've no intention of hurting her." *Unless she was guilty.*

"See that you don't."

"See that you don't what?"

They both turned at the sound of her voice. Anger warred with relief, relief winning by a nose.

She was leaning against the doorframe, looking literally like something the cat had dragged in. Her hair was a mess, with leaves and brush helter-skelter in the tangle. Her raincoat gaped open, her dress smeared with mud. One arm of her coat was ripped at the shoulder. She stepped into the light.

His heart skipped a beat. "You're hurt."

She smiled crookedly, wiping at a streak of blood on her cheek. "Good deduction, Sherlock."

He reached her side just after Fin, who wrapped a strong arm around her waist. She smiled at him gratefully and Braedon ground his teeth, jealousy rearing its ugly head. "What happened?"

"I had a fight with a car and the car won." Fin settled her into a chair, and she leaned back, closing her eyes.

Jealousy evaporated as he knelt beside her, taking her hand. She looked so fragile. He felt so helpless. "Fin, call a doctor."

"No." Her eyes flickered open. "I'm fine. I just need to clean up."

"Kacy, you've been hurt. You need a doctor." He stroked her hand with his thumb.

"I said, I'm fine."

Braedon met Fin's gaze and the other man shrugged. He blew out a breath, admitting defeat. "Well, at least let Fin call the police."

"For what? A car that's probably miles from here by now?"

"Did you see who it was?" Fin's voice sounded anxious, mirroring Braedon's concern.

"It was too dark. And the headlights were in my eyes."

"Did the driver stop?"

She shook her head. "No. And he had to have seen me. Or at least heard my bike hit the bumper."

"Bloody bastard," Fin exploded, then shot a sheepish look in Kacy's direction. "Sorry."

She smiled up at him. "It's all right. I've actually spent the last half hour calling him a heck of a lot worse."

"You walked here?" Braedon raised his eyebrows in surprise.

"Well, the bike has seen better days. Me, too, for that matter." She shot a grin in his direction, and he basked in its warmth, marveling at her spunk.

"I still think we should call the police." He reached out and pushed the hair back from her head, revealing a gash above her eyebrow. It was small, but still bleeding slightly. He ran a finger lightly across the skin above it. She shivered at the contact, her pupils darkening with something he couldn't quite identify. He leaned forward, his eyes dropping to her lips.

"Why don't you go in back and let Caitlin have a look at you?" Fin's words broke into the moment and Braedon pulled away.

She shifted on the chair, wincing with the motion. "I think that's a good idea. A quick wash and a cup of tea and I'll be right as rain." She looked up at Braedon. "Will you wait?"

"I'll be right here."

"There now, that ought to hold you." Caitlin O'Brien sat back to admire her handiwork. "You're sure to have a wallop of a bruise by the mornin', though."

Kacy touched her bandaged temple gingerly, feeling the movement in her shoulder. "I suspect more than just one."

"Well, 'tis lucky you are that it wasn't worse." The redhead nodded in accompaniment of her thoughts, her riotous curls bobbing in time with the motion.

Kacy frowned. "I just wish I'd gotten a look at the car. It would give me great satisfaction to haul the jerk who was driving in front of the constable."

"Aye, 'twould do us all good. And if I was a bettin' woman, I'd say for certain it was a tourist. They're always dashing about the roads as if they owned them. You'd think the lane was a bloody autobahn."

"Well, hopefully, whoever it was won't be back. I'm not sure I could take a second round. And I know my bike can't." In fact a decent burial was about all it was good for at this point.

"I've got a spare you can use, if you like. At least until you can get yourself another."

Kacy stood up, stretching slowly, testing her stiffened muscles. "Just at the moment, I'm thinking of getting a Land Rover. Or better yet, a tank."

Caitlin laughed. "Well, then, in that case, I'd say whoever was driving that car is best off in another county."

"I suppose I'd better be getting back in there." Kacy looked down at herself doubtfully. She was wearing a pair of Caitlin's sweats, the sweatshirt proclaiming that she was from the University of Dublin. Ironic, when she thought about how long it had taken to decide what to wear in the first place.

Caitlin eyed the getup appraisingly. "Not exactly the date look. 'Tis sorry I am that I've not got anything better. But most of my clothes are in Dublin. And you're so much smaller than me." She looked down at Kacy, smiling at the disparity in their heights. Fin's sister was almost six feet tall. And despite the fact that she was willowy, her sweats threatened to swallow Kacy.

"Maybe that's just as well. I've been having second thoughts about having a date anyway." And third thoughts and fourth thoughts . . .

"With *him*?" Caitlin tipped her head toward the doorway leading to the common room of the pub. "Lord in heaven, if I had a chance with a man like that one, believe me, I'd not be letting the opportunity slip through my hands."

"It's just been such a long time since I even thought about the word *date*. Let alone the actions that go along with it."

"Well, now, if you ask me, that's the problem." Caitlin reached out to take one of Kacy's hands. Blue eyes meeting green. "You've been too long without a man."

"But Alex—"

"Is dead and gone." Her friend smiled, her eyes speaking volumes. "And from what little I've been able to pull out of you, 'tis more than a blessing. He certainly was not the right one for you."

"Maybe, but he charmed me into believing in fairy-tale endings. I guess I should have known better."

"Well, there's no sense beating yourself up about it. Everyone makes mistakes now and then. Especially when it comes to men." She smiled knowingly.

Kacy pulled away and stood up with a smile, the sentiment not quite reaching her heart. Alex's betrayal still hurt. "That's exactly why I don't need to be dating anyone. My powers of judgment obviously leave something to be desired." And that was an understatement. She thought back on her last night with Alex, shivering.

"Go on with you." Caitlin gave her a playful tap. "Out of the frying pan, into the fire."

Kacy stood her ground, eyeing the door with trepidation. "That's exactly what I'm afraid of."

Where Braedon Roche was concerned, incineration was not out of the question.

"Well, there you are." Fin's voice filled the pub. "We were just wondering if maybe you'd slipped out the back way."

Braedon was by her side almost before she could step into the room, his hand warm under her elbow. "Are you all right?"

His eyes burned down into hers and she bit back the desire to answer no. Absolutely not. "I'm fine." At least as fine as she could be under the circumstances.

"Come over here, by the fire. Your hands are like ice." He led her to a table near the hearth and helped her settle into a chair.

"I've got a cuppa for you." Fin set a steaming mug on the table. "Laced it with a wee drop o' whiskey. I thought it might put the color back in your cheeks."

The two men were hovering over her like overprotective mamas. It was charming and claustrophobic at the same time. "Thanks, Fin. I'm sure this will do a world of good." She reached for the mug and sipped slowly, the heat and alcohol combining to warm her from the inside out.

She met Braedon's worried eyes. "Why don't you sit down?" She tipped her head toward the chair beside her. With almost simultaneous movements, the two men tried to sit in the chair, Fin winning by a nose. Kacy bit back a giggle and watched as Braedon shot Fin a telling look.

"Oh. Right." Fin flushed and jumped up. "I'd best be seeing to the bar."

Braedon sat down in the vacated seat and reached for her hands. "You really are all right?"

"I'm a bit sore. And probably will be more so tomorrow. But aside from the insane desire to sit on the road with a shotgun and blow away unsuspecting speeders, I'm fine."

Braedon smiled and released her hands, reaching for his beer. "Sort of a dramatic entrance for a dinner date, wouldn't you say?"

"Well, I wanted to make certain I had your attention." She smiled at him over the rim of her teacup.

His answering grin was slow and provocative. "Oh, I think you can safely say you have that."

"So, how long are you planning to stay in Ireland?" Kacy stirred the beans on her plate aimlessly, her head tilted to one side as she waited for an answer.

Until I find out the truth about you. Hardly a suitable response. "I don't know, really. This is the first holiday I've had in a long time."

"You look like a man who never vacations." Kacy eyed him as though he were an interesting painting she was restoring.

He bit back a smile. Usually he was the one doing the scrutinizing. "And what exactly is that supposed to mean?"

She smiled. "I don't know. Lack of laugh lines. Perfect creases. Not signs of a restful life."

"Well, I always seem to be putting out one fire or another."

"Doing what?"

"This and that. I dabble in a lot of businesses. Investing where I see a sign of profit."

She nodded sagely, sipping her tea. "A mogul."

"Well, I don't know if I'd go that far, but I definitely keep my finger in more than one pie."

"That would explain why your name seems familiar."

He almost choked on his sandwich. "My name?"

"Yes. I know I've heard it somewhere before. I just can't put a finger on where." She shrugged, obviously dismissing the thought.

He released a breath. Relieved. Time to turn the tables. "So, Fin tells me you came here from America."

She frowned and shot a look at the barman, mumbling something under her breath, then, with a sigh, she met his gaze. "I was living in Southampton."

Now seemed the perfect time to steer the conversation to Alex. "So what made you leave?"

Her face hardened. All emotion—all life—draining away instantly. It was as if he'd pressed a button and a mask had dropped firmly into place, obscuring the real Kacy from view.

Fin's paradox.

He reached over to cover her hand with his, wanting nothing more than to bring back the sparkle in her eye. "I didn't mean to pry."

Just as quickly as it had descended, the mask was gone. "You didn't. There's just nothing to tell. I thought I'd be happier here. Besides, I wanted to look after the cottage. It's my heritage, after all."

"Don't you miss the social whirl of the Hamptons?"

"I'm not much of a party girl, I'm afraid. I'd rather be alone with a canvas and a brush. Boring, I know, but there you have it." She smiled at him almost apologetically, but there was a spark of something else, too. If he hadn't known better, he'd have thought it was defiance.

"I dislike the social crush myself. Avoid it like the plague if I can." The tension between them eased, the conversation back on safer ground.

"Well, then that's something we have in common. I'm afraid my idea of a good time is a good book and a cup of tea." She shrugged. "So Lindoon suits me perfectly."

"I can see why. It's an enchanting place." He picked up his beer glass, staring into the amber depths. "Still, I'd think you'd get homesick now and then. Want a hot dog or a soap opera or something."

She laughed. "I miss silly things. Like strawberry Jell-O and Pillsbury crescent rolls."

"Ah, yes, spoken like a true gourmet." Although he had to admit there were days when he'd kill for a good lamb stew or hot soda bread or a tall glass of Smithwick's. Something no one in the States seemed to be able to reproduce authentically.

"Well, I told you, I like things simple."

The color had come back to her cheeks, the slight flush accentuating the white of the bandage over her eye, reminding him of her recent ordeal. "I suspect you're tired."

She nodded slowly, a soft smile playing about her lips. "It has been rather a long day. Would you mind if I called it an early night?"

He stood up, offering her his hand. "Not at all."

She took his hand. "The thing is . . ." She stopped, her teeth worrying her bottom lip as she considered something. "I don't have a way home." Her eyes met his, her look apologetic.

"Oh, God, how thoughtless of me. And here I've been keeping you captive."

Her mouth curved upward, her dimple peeking out. "I've enjoyed every minute of it. Well, maybe not the almost getting run over part. But dinner was lovely." She stifled a yawn.

And he felt like an out and out rotter. "Just hang on a minute. I'll go get my keys."

Kacy leaned back into the soft upholstery of the blue sedan. It smelled of rental car and Braedon. She closed her eyes, letting the smell of him surround her, soothe her. She'd never met anyone like him. His intensity frightened her and fascinated her all at the same time. He was a contradiction. One she desperately wanted to explore. Beyond the intensity, there was gentleness—an intrinsic goodness.

She smiled at the romantic turn of her thoughts. It wasn't like her to wax poetic. It must be the whack on the head.

"You all right?" His voice was soft and warm, intimate, almost tender.

"I'm fine. Just a little tired."

He pulled up in front of Sidhean, the wheels of the car crunching on the gravel drive. The house was dark. A shiver of apprehension ran down her spine, and she leaned forward, staring at the cottage.

He braked, bringing the car to a halt. Killing the engine, he turned to face her. "Something wrong?"

"Probably not. I just thought I left the lights on. Mac's in there."

"I tell you what. I'll go and check things out. You stay here."

She glanced at the dark house and then out into the dark night. She hated to admit to being afraid, but just at the moment the dark house with Braedon looked a lot less scary than the dark night all alone. "I'm coming with you." She tried to keep her voice steady, but the telltale tremor was there.

He hopped out of the car and came around to the passenger side to help her out. With his hand under her elbow, she felt braver.

Braedon held out his hand when they reached the steps. "I need the keys."

She felt herself flush and was grateful for the dark. "It's not locked."

He swung around to look at her and even in the dim light she could see his frown. "You left your house open?" His voice was sharp, accusing.

"No one locks their doors around here. For God's sake, this is rural Ireland. I don't even know if there is a key." She sounded apologetic and hated herself for it. It was her house, after all.

He opened his mouth to respond and then snapped it shut, seeming to think better of it. His hand closed around her arm, his anger communicating itself through his touch. He turned the knob and opened the door, releasing her to reach inside and flip on the lights.

Light had never looked so good. She pushed past him into the hall. "Mac? Sweetie, where are you?" Nothing moved. Fingers of dread danced along her skin. "Mac?"

"Stay here." Braedon's voice had lowered to a whisper. He grabbed a cane from the urn by the door and moved slowly toward the kitchen.

An unearthly keening filled the room.

Mac.

Kacy ran forward, fear spurring her on. Braedon reached the kitchen first, holding the door for her. The sound of the cry still echoed in her ears. He flipped the light on and Kacy searched the room for her dog. "He's not here." There was a note of desperation in her voice. The wailing started again. This time louder, almost echoing through the walls.

She grabbed his arm. "Braedon, it's coming from the pantry."

He went to the connecting door, yanking it open, the walking stick held point out. Kacy skidded to a stop behind him, then stepped back involuntarily when the keening began again.

"Is there a light?"

She nodded, unable to make her voice work, and pointed to a cord dangling above the door.

Braedon stepped into the storeroom, still brandishing the cane. With a click, light flooded the little room and there was a whimper and another whine.

Mac.

She pushed past Braedon, her only thought the welfare of her dog. He was lying on the floor, his left leg twitching, his tongue lolling. He tried to sit up, but his limbs seemed to have a mind of their own. He finally managed to struggle to a sitting position, but he listed to one side, head hanging, resembling a furry, black-and-white drunk.

Kacy locked her arms around him, keeping him stable, alarmed at the feel of his pounding heart. "What's wrong with him?" She looked up to meet Braedon's eyes, comforted by his steady gaze.

"I don't know, but we'll find out. You stay with him, I'm going to go call the vet."

"The number is by the phone." It was all she could manage. Her head throbbed and her dog was sick or poisoned or worse. She buried her head in Mac's soft fur. He was shivering uncontrollably.

Oh, please, God, she prayed, don't let him die.

Chapter 7

 "KACY, HE'S GOING to be fine." Paddy Fitzgerald stood up, brushing off his worn, corduroy work pants.

She sagged with relief, grateful for Braedon's arm around her. "So what happens now?"

"Nothing. He'll sleep it off. Should be right as rain in eight hours or so. I'll come out first thing in the morning to check on him, but I doubt he'll be needing me."

"Thank God." Relief flooded through her. "I don't know what I'd do if I lost Mac." Braedon's arm tightened as he pulled her closer.

"Do you have any idea what caused this?" She felt the vibration of Braedon's voice through his chest.

Paddy rubbed his chin thoughtfully. "Well, now, there's no way to say for sure, but if I had to state a reason, I'd say the pup was drugged."

"Deliberately?" Kacy stared at the vet. "I'd just assumed he'd gotten into something he shouldn't have."

He nodded, his face grim. "The symptoms are right. It could have been acepromazine."

"I beg your pardon?" She took a step toward Mac, breaking contact with Braedon, shivering at the loss of his warming touch.

"Acepromazine. It's a drug I use sometimes to relax an animal."

She knelt by her dog, stroking his head, grateful to see that he had fallen asleep. "How?"

" 'Twould be easy enough." He shrugged. "Pop a capsule into a bit o' meat and the animal never knows what hit him."

Braedon crossed his arms, his eyes narrowed thoughtfully. "There's no way something like that could happen accidentally."

It was a statement, not a question, but Paddy answered anyway. "I suppose it could, but it'd take a mighty long string o' coincidences. There's honestly no way to tell for certain without examining the contents of his stomach." Paddy dropped his stethoscope into his bag and snapped it shut.

Kacy shivered, looping a protective arm around Mac. "You're not going to do that?"

Paddy laughed. "No, child. I'm not." He sobered, his gaze meeting Braedon's. "I'd see to it you keep the cottage locked for a while. 'Twas probably no more than a prank, but it's best to be careful."

"I'll make certain they're safe and sound." Braedon's voice was firm.

"Good." Paddy picked up his bag and held out his hand. "I'd best be on my way. No sense in worrying Mary."

Braedon shook the vet's hand. "I'll walk you to your car."

"No need for that. You stay with Kacy and Mac." He headed for the door, stopping on the threshold to call over his shoulder. "Keep him warm, and I'll see you in the morning."

Braedon nodded and then turned back to Kacy, running a hand through his hair, leaving it in wild disarray. She'd bet that didn't happen very often. "I'm glad he was home when I called."

"Me, too." She rolled her shoulders, trying to ease her aching muscles. Stroking Mac's head, she tried to process all that had happened. She met Braedon's gaze, frustration and fear battling inside her. "Why would someone do this?"

He shook his head, his mouth tightening into a thin line. "I'm not sure we'll ever know."

"I just keep thinking about the car. And Mac. All of it."

"Kacy—" He frowned at her, his look intense. "—is there a reason someone might be trying to hurt you?"

No, her mind insisted. Maybe, a little voice revised. She sighed. Either way it wasn't something she was ready to discuss. It was too soon for that kind of trust. "No, there's nothing. It's probably just coincidence. The important thing now is to make certain Mac is all right."

"Paddy says he'll be fine, and I'd bet the farm he's not the type of man to make rash promises." He held out a hand. "Come on. Mac's not the only one who's had a rough night."

She nodded, and after tucking a blanket around her sleeping dog, let him pull her up into the kitchen.

"You wait here." He gestured to the kitchen table. "And I'll check the rest of the house."

She nodded absently, sinking onto a chair, resting her head in her hands. How could this have happened? Who would want to hurt Mac? Or had they been trying to hurt her? She cringed, sick to think that somehow Mac might have suffered because of her. It seemed that whatever she did, wherever she went, someone always got hurt.

All she wanted was a normal life. A chance for the happiness that most people took for granted. But it seemed no matter what she did, no matter how far she ran, disaster followed. She'd married Alex in an effort to shed the old and make a new start, but she'd only traded one prison for another.

Then instead of finding release after the horror of his death, she'd been thrust into another nightmare. One filled with goons carrying handguns. And, as always, Millicent was there in the background. Waiting for her to make a mistake. She threaded her fingers through her hair, fighting a wave of hopelessness. She'd battled so long to step out of the shadows. Yet every time she took a small step forward, it seemed that something—or someone—pushed her back.

"I can't tell if anyone has been here." Braedon walked into the room, the sound of his voice breaking into her thoughts. "The front room and your studio look fine, but your bedroom is a shambles."

She blushed, ducking her head in embarrassment. "That'd be me. I couldn't decide what to wear." She shot him a rueful look and then looked down at the overly large sweats. Suddenly she started to laugh.

It began as a bubble of amusement, but soon burgeoned into something bordering on hysterics. Tears mixed with laughter and she slipped into sobs, her shoulders shaking with the release of emotion. She felt his arms circle around her, pulling her close, and she buried her face in the soft warmth of his sweater.

Suddenly she pushed back, aware that she was allowing herself to rely on someone else. And that was against her number one rule. Relying meant trusting and she wasn't allowed to trust anyone. Her father had drilled it into her head. Over and over. No one could be trusted. Ever.

"I'm . . . I'm all right now. I just need a shower. And bed." The minute the word was out she wanted to yank it back. Bed wasn't something she wanted to think about while she was in the same room as Braedon Roche. And she was more than just in the room with him, she was in his arms.

Oh, Lord, she was in his arms.

She pulled away, mumbling something about tea and almost fell, her legs buckling under her. His strong arms locked around her again, righting her, his voice warm against her ear. "Here now, let me help you."

She leaned back against him, allowing herself just a minute. One minute. Then she'd go back to looking after herself. But it felt so nice, just for once, to let someone take care of her. No. She had to be honest. She was nothing if not honest.

Well, most of the time. And the truth was she wanted *Braedon Roche* to take care of her. Wanted it more than she'd ever wanted anything in her life.

Braedon carried the tea tray into the bedroom. He could hear the soft whoosh of water coming from the shower behind the closed door of the bathroom. His brain instantly formed a vivid, graphic picture of Kacy. Setting the tray down on a table, he tried to clear his mind. The picture intensified.

He needed a distraction. Tea. He'd drink tea. He took a cup and filled it with the potent brew, adding sugar and milk. Somehow it was impossible to entertain lascivious thoughts while sipping tea.

He smiled, surveying the small bedroom. Without all the clutter, it looked much like the rest of the cottage, exquisitely furnished. The mahogany four poster dominated the room, a brightly patterned quilt adorning the bed—the kind only someone's granny could make. He ran a hand across it, feeling the tiny handmade stitches, for a moment transported back to his childhood. Memory shifted and he saw his mother, frail and dying.

He pushed back the pain, banishing the vision, and returned his attention to the room. Lace curtains covered each window, a pristine white. One floated out, billowing in the breeze from an open window. On one side of the bed, a large occasional table was covered with books and decorative pieces—a vase, a pewter candlestick, a crystal bowl. The entire scene looked like something from a magazine photo layout.

Everything was perfect. *Too perfect*. At odds with a woman who'd earlier left every garment she owned scattered about the room without a second thought. He was back to Fin's paradox.

He frowned, his gaze sweeping across the room again. There was nothing of Kacy here. The room was beautiful in a

House & Garden kind of way, but there was no soul. No heart. Nothing personal.

There wasn't even a photograph in the room, and now that he thought about it, none in any of the other rooms either. Odd. Almost compulsively, he reached for the little drawer in her nightstand. Surely there would be something there, a small clue to the woman in the shower.

He stopped, hand on the drawer pull, suddenly aware that he was trespassing. The water in the shower was still running. Curiosity battled with decency. Curiosity won.

He opened the drawer, staring at the usual assortment of night things. Vaseline, tissues, a flashlight. Nothing personal, certainly nothing worth snooping for. He started to push the drawer back into place. It stuck a little and the motion shifted the packet of tissues, revealing a small silver frame.

Alex Madison stared up at him.

It was a casual picture, taken on a beach somewhere, surf and sky providing an azure backdrop to the laughing man. His hair was wet, slicked back, and his crooked smile hinted of promises. Hedonistic promises. Braedon was suddenly certain that the photographer had been Kacy.

Not Kacy—Kirstin Madison.

He looked back at the picture, feeling like a voyeur. It was an oddly intimate portrait. A private moment shared between two people in love. Or at least in lust. He felt a surge of jealousy and marveled at the inappropriateness of the feeling.

If he was right, the man in the photograph had out-maneuvered him, taken Braedon's trust and used it to sabotage his business empire. Without the sterling reputation he'd worked so hard to build, he was nothing. And Braedon had been *there* before, and he had no intention of going back again. One hand tightened into a fist, and he fought the urge to throw the little picture across the room. Damn Alex Madison. And damn his wife.

"What are you doing with that?"

He spun around, guiltily clutching the little frame. She was standing barefooted, wrapped like a cocoon in a terry cloth robe. Her eyes were narrowed, the angry red line of her gash vivid against the white of her face.

"I'm sorry, I—" He stopped, cutting himself off. Take the offensive, not the defensive, his brain cautioned. Lessons learned long ago. Out of the corner of his eye, he saw the cellophane wrapped tissues. "I was looking for a tissue. Figured this was the best place." He gestured toward the drawer. "I didn't mean to pry. It was just lying there." He shrugged in what he hoped was an innocent fashion.

She crossed the room and snatched the photograph from him, tossing it back into the drawer and slamming it closed. "It's private." She turned back to face him, sparks shooting from bottle green eyes.

He held up a hand. "I said, I'm sorry."

She relaxed a little, her eyes returning to their normal size. "So you did." Her hand fluttered around her neck, as though it was uncertain where to land. He watched with interest as it finally curled around the lapel of her robe, holding the material from both sides together.

"Who is he?" The question hung in the air between them, her hand starting to flutter again. He captured it in his own and held it, feeling her leaping pulse against his skin.

She chewed at her bottom lip and tried to tug her hand away, but he pulled her closer instead, until they were only a few inches apart. She was so tiny, barely coming up to his chest. She had to tip her head to see him.

There was pain in her eyes—and resentment. He was torn between the need to take her in his arms and comfort her and the need to grill her until she told him everything he needed to know.

"Kacy?"

Her eyes continued to reflect her inner turmoil, and he

waited quietly for the outcome, wondering if she'd trust him, wanting her to trust him.

She sighed and met his gaze, hers filled with an equal mixture of resolve and trepidation. "He was my husband."

"I thought so." He answered quietly, waiting for the fireworks. He didn't have to wait long.

"You know about Alex?" She sucked in a breath, sparks flying again.

"Fin told me."

"Fin talks too much." The anger drained from her face, dissipating as quickly as it had come. She ran a trembling hand through her hair.

"I'm sorry, Kacy."

"There's nothing to be sorry about. It was a long time ago." She closed her eyes, effectively ending the conversation. "I'm so tired."

He knew he should be asking her more, hitting her while she was vulnerable, but the pain reflected on her face was more than he could bear. Maybe he was getting soft, or maybe she really was innocent. Either way, there would be another day, but right now, she needed to rest. Really rest. And he had a lot to think about.

"Come on. I'll help you into bed." He smiled at his choice of words. It wasn't often that he said something like that to a beautiful woman and meant nothing more than the words themselves. Hell, he *was* going soft.

He tucked the quilt around her shoulders, not surprised to see that she was already half asleep. "Good night, princess," he said, pressing a quick kiss on her forehead.

"Good night, Braedon." Her response was mumbled, her mind already well on its way to oblivion.

He moved away from the bed.

"Braedon?" It was a plea.

"I'm here."

"You won't leave, will you?" It was the cry of a small child.

"No, Kacy, I'll be right here."

She nodded, snuggling down into the covers.

He moved to the doorway and reached for the light switch.

"Braedon?"

"I'm here, Kacy."

She opened her eyes, her emerald gaze meeting his. "Please don't turn out the light. I'm ... I'm afraid of the dark."

He watched her until her eyes drifted shut again and her breathing became soft and even.

"No, Kacy," he whispered, "I won't leave you in the dark."

Kacy woke with a start, her eyes opening to the soft glow of lamplight. The room was lost in shadows, and for a moment she was disoriented. She frowned at the face of her alarm clock. Two o'clock. She reached automatically for Mac and was momentarily surprised to find the bed empty. Then memory came flooding back. Her accident—Mac. She sat up, worry lacing through her.

"It's all right." A gentle hand smoothed the hair back from her forehead. *Braedon.* She winced at the pain in her temple, but allowed him to help her settle back into the pillows.

"Mac—"

"Is fine. Sleeping like a baby. I checked on him just a few minutes ago."

She let herself sink back into the bed, sleep overcoming her. With a concerted effort, she raised a hand, stroking the back of it along his cheekbone. "Thank you." He smiled, and for just a moment, she felt safe and secure. She sighed, knowing that it was just an illusion, but loving the way it felt anyway.

Closing her eyes, she drifted into the arms of Morpheus, amazed at how much he resembled Braedon Roche.

* * *

She looked so innocent lying there. Her head nestled in the crook of her arm, her hair splayed out across the pillow. Braedon clenched a hand, wanting nothing more than to tangle his fingers in the silky softness.

Cleaned up, the cut across her forehead was clearly superficial, but the welt above it was already turning an angry purple. He worried about concussion. She'd obviously hit her head pretty hard.

She tossed and turned, even calling his name once or twice. But she slept, and he figured that probably meant she was okay. Hell, who was he kidding? He hadn't a clue. He could frighten a boardroom full of executives into selling their company, but he had no idea how to take care of this woman.

He glanced at his watch, the luminous hands lining up on twelve and five. He yawned and flexed his shoulders. Almost morning. He'd wake her in a few more minutes. He'd been waking her every hour or so, just to assure himself she was all right. Something he'd seen in a movie. He had no idea if it had been of any value, but it gave him something to do and he was a man of action.

Mac padded into the room. He'd come to about an hour earlier and polished off a bowl of dog food, evidently none the worse for his ordeal. The dog jumped up on the bed before Braedon could stop him, laying his head in his mistress's lap. Without waking, she turned, her hand unhesitatingly finding Mac's head, fingers stroking the soft fur. The dog sighed and closed his eyes, everything right with his world again.

Braedon ran his hand over the stubble on his face, wishing suddenly that his world could be put to right so easily. Everything was so damn complicated. And somehow, Kacy Macgrath was at the center of it. He smoothed a stray tendril of hair back from her forehead.

Her eyes fluttered open and she smiled sleepily. "Has it been an hour already?"

He felt his face break into a grin. Simple pleasures. He'd had too few in his life. "It has. And I can see by the gleam in your eye that you're doing fine."

Her dimple deepened. "Mac, too."

"Mac, too," he echoed, still feeling absurdly contented. "Now go back to sleep."

She reached for his hand. "You should sleep, too," she murmured, drifting off before he could answer.

There had been trust in her eyes. Braedon felt a flash of guilt. He should have told her who he was from the beginning. But if he had, would she have trusted him?

Braedon rubbed his eyes and settled back into the chair. Hell, he couldn't remember the last time he'd taken care of someone. The last time he'd been needed for something other than his business acumen.

A picture of his mother flashed through his brain. She'd needed him, but he'd let her down. Old sorrow coursed through him, pain that he'd thought long dead and buried. He looked at the sleeping woman and wondered what it was about her that made him feel so vulnerable.

He snorted at the train of his thoughts. Braedon Roche was vulnerable to no one. He'd seen to that. Practiced it every day for years. It was the cornerstone of his success.

So why, suddenly, did he wonder what he'd lost with the transformation?

Chapter 8

 "YOU'RE STILL HERE." Kacy narrowed sleepy eyes at Braedon.

He turned, spatula in hand, grinning. "Well, top o' the morning to you, too. Is that all the thanks I get for convincing this beast of a cooker—" He gestured at the Aga. "—to cooperate in my attempt to fix you breakfast?"

The brogue was back. "My head hurts." It sounded ungracious, but she felt like hell. Despite her pounding head, she smiled. He looked so, well, domesticated.

"Have a seat. It's almost ready." He stirred something in the frying pan that smelled like heaven and then poured tea from the teapot into a cup. "With milk, right?"

She nodded, yawning. It was odd to have a man in the kitchen, but she could get used to it. At least *this* man.

He set the cup on the table with a flourish. "Your tea, madam." She bit back a giggle and sipped the brew, letting its warmth and fragrance soothe her. She watched as Braedon prodded the contents of the skillet again with the spatula, a tea towel tucked into his waistband serving as an apron.

He looked a far cry from the slick city boy she'd met in the pub. Had it only been two days ago? His face was shadowed with the beginnings of a beard and his hair was a tangle of riotous brown curls. His shirt was untucked and his shoes had gone AWOL, leaving a broad expanse of argyle exposed under the hem of his jeans.

He looked younger, more carefree. He rubbed a hand across his face. And tired. He looked tired. Of course, he'd most likely had little or no sleep. At least she'd been allowed fifty-five minute naps. He, on the other hand, had kept vigil all night. "You must be exhausted."

He shot her a grin. "I've certainly slept more, but between you and Mac, I had my hands full."

"Mac." She looked around frantically for her pet.

"Relax, he's fine. He's sleeping in the front room."

She ran a hand through her hair. "Oh, Lord, Paddy's coming."

"He's already been here." He scooped two sausages onto a plate. "He was here at first light."

"Why didn't you wake me?" Her mouth watered as he slid a poached egg onto a slice of toast.

"Didn't seem much point." He added a broiled tomato to the plate. "I figured you needed your sleep. I'd have woken you if there was anything you needed to know."

She waited for him to say more, but he was too involved with the bacon. There was probably black pudding as well. She couldn't remember when she'd last had a real breakfast, let alone someone to cook it for her. "And?"

He looked at her, plate in hand, eyebrow lifted. "And what?"

She blew out a breath in exasperation. "And what did he say about Mac?"

"Oh, right. Mac's fine. It wasn't a pleasant evening for him, but there won't be any lasting effect."

"Thank God."

He put a plate with enough food for the entire village in front of her. "So how come Mac is Mac?"

"You mean his name?" she answered over a fork full of sausage and egg.

"Um hmm." He laid a second plate on the table and sat down across from her.

"It's short for Mackintosh."

"The computer?" He cut into his tomato, carefully layering it with egg and sausage, concocting what looked to be the perfect bite.

She watched him chew, fascinated with the way his jaw rippled with each motion, his lips moving together almost sensuously.

"Kacy?"

She pulled her gaze from his mouth and met his smiling eyes. The rat. He'd been watching her watching him. She blushed. "No. There's been a dog named Mackintosh around here for as long as I remember. Mac is number twelve, I think. My granny's mother was Scottish. A Mackintosh from a clan near Inverness. There's an old tower house there that I've always wanted to visit."

He spooned sugar into his tea. "Do you still have family there?"

She nodded, swallowing a bite of black pudding. "A cousin. But the connection is distant and I've never met him." She forked another mouthful. "This is really good. I take it you have some in-country experience."

His face went from jovial to guarded in two seconds flat. She was startled at the transformation. "I used to live in Dublin."

"I . . . I wasn't trying to pry." She put down her fork and reached across the table to lay a hand on his arm.

He met her gaze, his softening. "It was a lifetime ago." He pulled away, the gesture somehow symbolic of a greater separation. Their playful intimacy vanished and her heart sank, her hand lying lifeless on the table, alone. The mogul was back. She almost expected to see neatly pressed jeans and a cleanly shaved face staring back at her.

"I thought I smelled breakfast." Fin O'Brien strode into the room, cap in hand.

They both jumped. Kacy pulled the edges of her robe together, feeling the heat of a blush staining her cheeks. She stood awkwardly. "We were just eating." Well, there was a blinding glimpse of the obvious.

"So I see." Fin's eyes twinkled as he looked at the two of them. "I wasn't intending to interrupt anything. I knocked, but you didn't answer."

She stared at him uncomprehendingly, her mouth open, waiting for some form of vocal control to return.

Fin's mouth split into a grin. "I've come for the painting. You invited me?"

Kacy closed her mouth with a click of teeth. "So I did."

Braedon grinned at her lazily, offering no help at all. Nothing. The man was infuriating. "Fin, have a seat. There's plenty."

Fin dropped into a chair. "Don't mind if I do."

Braedon crossed to the Aga and started filling a plate for him. "Pudding?"

"That'd be grand." Fin actually rubbed his hands together in anticipation.

Kacy sat down again, massaging her pounding temples with her index fingers.

Fin frowned at her, his look one of concern. "Are you all right?"

"I'm fine. Just a bit of a headache."

"Well, that was quite a tumble you took. I worried about you being all alone, but it seems I hadn't the need. You were obviously in good hands."

Kacy had no idea if the choice of words was intentional, but if possible her face burned even brighter. And Braedon, damn him, was just standing there enjoying the show, looking like he'd been cooking in her kitchen for years instead of hours.

"Here you go, old man."

Fin dug into the food like he hadn't eaten in a week, which was ridiculous considering his sister had probably fed him only a few hours ago. Despite her discomfort, Kacy bit back a smile.

Braedon settled back into his chair after refreshing their tea. "I stayed here last night."

Fin nodded. "I assumed as much."

Kacy wondered dryly if they were going to high five or something. She stared into her cup, feeling like a kewpie doll at a fair.

"There was more trouble." The amusement had vanished from Braedon's voice.

"Beyond the hit and run?"

"I think that's a little strong," Kacy began.

"Yeah. Someone drugged Mac." Braedon continued as though she hadn't spoken.

Fin looked first at Kacy and then at Braedon. "As in, doped him up?"

"Exactly." Braedon explained how they had found Mac in the storage room.

Fin frowned. "It could have been some lads from over Ennis way. I heard tell o' high jinks with some sheep."

"Perhaps." Braedon stroked his chin thoughtfully. Kacy had the feeling he wasn't buying into a teenage prank. "At any rate, I thought it best to stay here for the night."

"By all means, I'd have done the same. Have you called the Garda?"

"No. Last night it seemed more important to get Kacy to bed and see to Mac."

The two of them were talking about her as if she wasn't there. *Men.* "I don't want to call the Garda."

They both looked at her. Fin surprised. Braedon—well, she couldn't read his expression, but she had the feeling he'd expected her reaction.

"Why ever not?" Fin asked.

"I just don't want to make a big deal out of nothing. Mac's fine." As if to emphasize the point, her dog ran into the room in hot pursuit of something only he could see. Catching the scent of sausages, he skidded to a stop and crossed to Braedon, laying his head on Braedon's knee, peering up at him soulfully. Braedon took a link from his plate and fed it to Mac. It was gone in a gulp.

Fin laughed. "I guess he recognizes a pushover when he sees one."

Kacy wondered just when exactly it was that Braedon had become a fixture in her house. She closed her eyes, not certain if she wanted him to belong or not. Suddenly her solitary life seemed particularly empty.

"Kacy, are you all right?" His deep voice washed over her, warm like brandy, a mellow fire.

"Is there something wrong with the signora?" Professor Baucomo stood in the doorway, looking dapper in a pinstripe suit.

Kacy sighed. Evidently Braedon had issued invitations. She looked down at her frumpy robe. It was heading for the parish rummage sale as soon as she got it off. And for the foreseeable future, she was dressing for breakfast.

Braedon was already back at the Aga, filling yet another plate, this one for the professor. Evidently, when he cooked, he cooked for the masses. She bit back a smile. Maybe she should hang out a sign. *Breakfast by Braedon.*

"Tell me what has happened." The little Italian sat in an empty chair, his hand indicating the gash on her head.

"Somebody ran Kacy off the road last night," Fin said between mouthfuls.

"*Santa Maria.* Do you know who it was?"

"No." Braedon handed the professor a plate, his voice grim. "Whoever the bastard was, he didn't bother to stop."

"Maybe he didn't see me." Kacy was getting the distinct feeling she was invisible to more than just the driver of the black sedan. Which was good and bad. It solved the robe problem, but made it difficult to participate in a conversation that was primarily about her.

"Didn't see her?" the professor mimicked. "How could someone run a woman off the road and not see her?" His face was red and his eyes shot fire.

Fin frowned. "I don't know, but I do know what I'd like to do to him."

The professor focused on Fin. "And you are?"

"Finnegan O'Brien, at your service." Fin inclined his head in something approaching a bow.

"Ah, Finnegan's Folly." The little man smiled, and Fin broke into a grin.

"I see that my reputation precedes me."

"Let's just say that I've heard only the best." The professor turned his attention back to Kacy. "But you are all right?"

"A little banged up, but basically no worse for wear."

" 'Twas a rough night. Someone drugged Mac, too." Fin leaned forward, his heavy red brows drawn into a frown.

"The two things are related?" The little man sipped his tea, his expression concerned.

"I hope not," Kacy said, hating the tremble in her voice.

"There doesn't seem to be a connection, but the thought has crossed my mind." Braedon reached down and scratched Mac between the ears. "There wasn't any sign that someone had been in the house."

"Ah, but that, in and of itself, doesn't mean anything." The professor stroked his moustache thoughtfully.

"Fin said that there had been some pranks in the area. Something to do with sheep, right?" She looked at her friend hopefully. The discussion was turning serious and it scared her. She'd had the same thoughts herself, but hadn't wanted to face the fact that there might be a connection.

"Right. Old man Riley lost about fourteen ewes. Some-one . . ." He paused. "Well, let's just say parts were removed that were not meant to be taken from a live animal."

Kacy shivered. "I'm sure whoever did this won't be back again." She looked to Braedon for support, surprised to see him frowning.

"Well, the main thing is that you're all right." The professor patted her hand. "I hear there's a fiddle festival at the pub in the summer." He turned to Fin, obviously trying to change the subject.

"Aye, that there is. In fact, most any night there's someone picking out a tune. County Clare is known for its music and Lindoon is no exception." Fin laid his fork on his plate with a satisfied smile. "Speaking of the pub, I'd best be getting back. Caitlin can handle the opening, but once Tolly Macnamara arrives, it's best that I be there." He pushed back his chair. "I'll just be getting the painting, then, and be on my way."

Kacy gestured to the studio door. "It's in there, leaning against the far wall."

"You're sure you won't be missing it?"

"No. I'm glad for you to have it." She'd be relieved, actually. She'd never really liked the Martin. Alex had been obsessed with the original. That's why she'd painted the copy. She'd wanted to please him. Not that it had done any good. There had been no pleasing her husband.

Fin disappeared into the studio. Kacy looked at the two remaining men sitting at the table. The professor was lost in thought, absently eating his breakfast. Braedon was watching her, his face expressionless.

"Kacy, I still think you should call the Garda."

"We've been down this road before, Braedon. There's nothing to report. All's well that ends well and all that." The last thing she needed was to bring the officials down here. One thing would invariably lead to another, and Millicent would no doubt be over on the next plane, threatening her very existence.

She shivered, hearing her father's voice, a recording she

couldn't short-circuit: "Keep to the shadows, Kirstin, or you'll lose me forever. Millicent will see to it."

He was gone now, but the recording kept right on, echoing through her mind, brainwashing her, his voice changing to his wife's rasping tones. She choked on a sip of tea, managing to pour some down her face, pulling her back to the present.

Oh, she was a picture of grace today.

"It's your decision." Braedon watched as she dried her chin, his gaze colliding with hers.

"It is." She smiled to take the edge off her words.

The professor coughed discreetly. "I don't think we've been formally introduced."

Kacy pulled herself together. "I'm sorry. I wasn't thinking. You saw each other yesterday, but I guess I forgot to introduce you. Professor Baucomo, this is Braedon Roche."

"Professor." Braedon held out a hand.

"Signore Roche, it is a pleasure." The two men eyed each other and Kacy had the fleeting feeling that she was missing something.

"I'll just be on my way, then." Fin came back into the kitchen, the paper-wrapped painting under one arm. "Ta." He waved and ambled out the back door.

The intrusion broke the moment. Kacy smiled at the professor. "Braedon is interested in Irish history."

"It's a hobby." Braedon poured some milk into his tea.

The professor smiled and nodded. "A man must have many interests, no?"

Braedon inclined his head in agreement.

"The professor is the art historian I told you about. He's brought some miniatures for me to look at."

"Kacy's expertise has preceded her. A colleague of mine remembered working with her a few years ago and suggested that she might be able to help me." The professor smiled fondly at Kacy, and then turned his gaze back to Braedon.

"Where do you teach, Professor?" Braedon's question was casual, but Kacy thought she detected a hint of something more.

"In Milan."

"Did you study there, as well?"

"No. In fact what little I know is mostly self taught. My title is honorary, I'm afraid. The misguided enthusiasm of my students." He lifted his shoulders in a Teutonic shrug.

"Well, hopefully Kacy will be able to help you."

The professor nodded, smiling at her again. "I am certain of it. With her talent we will be quite the team, no?"

Kacy nodded, already catching the little man's enthusiasm.

"Well, then I guess I'll leave you in her capable hands." Braedon turned to Kacy, his blue eyes meeting hers, the expression hinting of intimacy. "And now, if you're sure you're all right, I really ought to be going, too. You and Baucomo have work to do."

Kacy nodded, unable to speak. His eyes were telling her far more than his words and she felt light-headed, almost dizzy.

"Professor." He nodded at the little man and crossed to Kacy's side, bending to brush a kiss against her lips. "Take care of yourself," he whispered, and she shivered with something she couldn't quite identify. Something warm and wonderful.

He squeezed her hand and strode into the hall. In a few minutes, the door slammed shut. Mac whined and Kacy understood. Suddenly the house seemed quite empty.

"He's quite a man, your Braedon Roche."

"He's not mine," she answered automatically, but she wished he was.

Oh, God, she wished he was.

Chapter 9

"THIS IS *MAGNIFICO*."

Kacy looked up from the little miniature she was examining. Professor Baucomo was studying one of her canvases. A watercolor of Dunbeg. "It's just a landscape of the fort on my land."

"But you've captured the light beautifully. I can almost feel the dampness, smell the threat of rain."

She dimpled, flattered by his compliment. She'd never thought much of her own work. Technically inept, her father had said. "Do you really like it?" She pushed aside the magnifying lamp and stood up, stretching. Her muscles were sore, protesting at the movement.

"But of course. I would not say it if I didn't." He actually looked a little hurt.

"It's not that I don't trust your judgment, Professor. It's just that I've always thought I was better working on other people's work."

He nodded, his eyes radiating sympathy. "I know just what you mean. I never felt that my work was of true artistic caliber. That's why I am an art historian." He shrugged. "But this," he said, gesturing to her painting, "this has imagination. There is a spark here." He moved the canvas, exposing another watercolor—this one of Finnegan's Folly. "It is here in this one, too. In the way you capture the light and shadows. It

94

draws the viewer into the work. Stimulates his other senses. It is very good, Kacy. Very good."

"You're very kind."

A shadow passed over his face. "No, not kind. Honest. I was impressed when I saw your Monet, but I am even more impressed with these." Again he gestured to the canvases. "I have friends in the art world. If you let me, I would like to arrange a showing."

"Gosh, I don't know what to say. I've always painted for myself. I never even thought of showing them publicly."

He thumbed through several other paintings, stopping when he came to an oil. He lifted it up, leaning it against an easel. "When did you paint this?" His voice was low, almost a reverent whisper.

Kacy moved to look at the painting, her stomach knotting when she recognized which one he had chosen. Angry green seas bashed at a line of cool gray sand. The skies were black, illuminated by a single flash of lightning. "I . . . I painted it two years ago."

"It is a tragic painting."

"Yes, it is." Memory flashed through her head, resurrecting deeply buried emotion. She'd forgotten the painting was in here.

The professor watched her silently for a moment, and then quietly placed the painting back against the wall. "Sometimes we paint from our pain, no? It is often our best work."

Kacy nodded, grateful that he was letting the subject drop.

"So, can you repair the damage done to Madame de Fornio?"

Kacy slid back into her chair and switched on the magnifier, positioning it so that the professor could see. "I think so. We'll start with her hat."

Braedon paced the common room of the pub, waiting for the switchboard operator to put his call through. It was one o'clock here, seven o'clock in New York. Early, but Matt should be in. It had taken all his self control not to call the man at home in the wee hours of the morning.

"I'm connecting you now, sir." The receptionist sounded solicitous. He smiled. He had to admit there were certain perks to being the boss.

"This is Matt." His friend's voice was crisp. Cautious. Matt was always cautious. Not too many people knew exactly what it was Matthew did for Roche Industries.

"Matt, how the hell are you?"

"Braedon? I should be asking you the same question. Or more accurately, *where* the hell are you?"

"Taking a holiday—in Ireland."

"Vacationing. Right, and I've got a hot date with Sandra Bullock tonight." His friend laughed into the receiver.

"All right then, call it business and pleasure."

"More business, I suspect. Something to do with the Madison woman?"

"Something like that." It had everything to do with her, but in ways he'd never imagined. And now wasn't the time to explore his conflicting feelings about Kacy Macgrath.

"Hey, whatever you say," Matt sighed. "You sign the paychecks."

"And don't you forget it, my friend." It was a long-standing joke between them. Matt was a trust fund baby. He'd left home to escape his family and had never looked back. What Matt did, he did for the pure pleasure of it. First for the CIA, and now for Braedon.

"I take it you're not calling to shoot the breeze."

"No. I need you to dig up information on a Professor Eduardo Baucomo. I think he's from Milan. Something to do with art or maybe art restoration."

"That all you know?"

"Yeah. There's really nothing out of the ordinary. Just a feeling I have. And I'm pretty sure the guy recognized me."

"You think there's something to it?"

"Maybe not. But I keep a pretty low profile, and my only real connection to the art world is through Solais."

"And you're thinking he might have a connection to the forgeries?"

"It's a possibility. A long shot probably, but I don't want to take any chances. There's too much at stake. And according to Kacy, he just approached her out of the blue."

"Kacy, is it?" Matt let out a whistle. "I see the old Roche charm hasn't lost its power."

"Just see what you can find on Baucomo," he said, ignoring Matt's curiosity.

"All right. I'm on it."

"Thanks, Matt."

"No problem. I live for stuff like this."

Braedon could hear the smile in his voice. "Well, for once, I think I'm actually hoping it comes to nothing."

"I'll call you as soon as I have something. I'll use your cell phone."

"Can't. The damn thing is on the fritz again. I have no idea what's wrong with it."

Matt laughed. "Face it, Braedon, when it comes to mechanical devices, you're inept."

"I prefer technically challenged. Anyway, until I can get to Ennis and get it fixed, you'll have to call here."

"Fine. And, Braedon, don't worry."

He gave Matt the pub's number and hung up the phone. He wasn't certain there was anything to worry about, but he had a hunch there was more to the little professor than appearances presented.

Lost in thought, Rico walked along the road leading from Kacy's cottage to the village. Kacy was far more than a good forger. She was an artist in the truest sense. And he'd discovered her.

His thoughts of convincing her to join him in his more

legally challenged pursuits faded as he considered the end-
less possibilities of promoting her work. No sense in in-
volving her in his forgery business if he could introduce her
to the world on the up and up. Maybe he'd even get out of forgery altogether. He'd be her mentor. Her Svengali. The idea
excited him. He felt more alive than he had in years.

But the first thing he had to do was protect her from
Braedon Roche.

Roche was obviously being less than honest with Kacy.
And Rico had no doubt that his motives were less than honor-
able. The man was definitely romancing her. And from what
little Rico had observed, it was working.

And that's what worried him.

Kacy was a woman of deep emotion, and Braedon Roche
was certainly not the right man for her—even if he were truly
interested. And Rico was fairly certain it was all an act. An act
designed to lead Roche to answers.

He frowned, trying to think of an easy way to handle the
problem, and then smiled. All he had to do was be certain
Kacy discovered the connection Roche had with Alex and
Solais. The rest would take care of itself. He didn't know his
protégé well, but he knew enough to know that she would not
tolerate a liar.

And, at the very least, Braedon Roche was a liar.

There was still another problem, though.

Max Madison.

Even if he took care of Roche, he'd still need to convince
Max to leave Kacy alone—permanently. There was no question in his mind now that Max was wrong. She'd had nothing
to do with Alex's death.

He'd known it from the moment he'd met her, but if he'd
had any doubts at all, the painting would have erased them.
No one could paint with that kind of agony, that kind of passion, if it weren't real. There was pain in that seascape.

Real pain.

She'd seen her husband die, and based on the painting, the memory still haunted her.

A black Mercedes pulled up beside him, the back window rolling down as it slowed. "Good afternoon, *Professor*. Won't you join me?"

Rico shuddered. Max Madison was not a man to be trifled with. He fought the instinctive reaction to run. He had nothing to hide. And Max had no reason to threaten him.

Except that he knew everything. And he wanted to protect the woman Max believed was responsible for his twin's death.

Rico sighed and slid into the automobile.

"So you've spent the day with my brother's charming widow?" Max spit out the last word as if it tasted of arsenic.

"If you mean Kacy, yes. I've been working with her. My cover, remember?"

"Ah, yes, your cover. Quite the subversive, aren't you, Rico?"

"I get by. To what do I owe the pleasure of this meeting? It wouldn't have to do with a certain hit and run, would it?"

"How did you know about that?" Max glared at him, eyes narrowed.

Rico lifted an eyebrow. "So it was you. I take it you had no idea the woman was Kacy."

Max smiled, an oily sort of grimace that made Rico cringe inside. "How delightful. If only we'd known. She came out of nowhere. Anson couldn't avoid her. Could you, Anson?"

"No, sir." Rico could see the man's smiling reflection in the rearview mirror.

"I take it she's none the worse for wear?" Max flicked at a nonexistent speck of lint on the shoulder of his suit.

"No thanks to you." Rico tried to hold on to his temper. Angering Max wouldn't further his cause.

"Pity."

"And did you also have something to do with her dog being poisoned?" Rico waited, fearing the worst.

"I told you, Rico, I intend to find out what the little slut knows. And I'm not adverse to using whatever methods might be necessary."

"You agreed you'd wait before you did anything." Rico carefully worked to modulate his voice. He was pleased to hear that he sounded calm, almost bored.

Max flexed his fingers. "So I did. But sometimes opportunity presents itself when you least expect it."

Rico sighed. "You're not seeing the big picture here."

"Big picture. Big picture?" Max's voice crescendoed, filling the car. "What could be bigger than murdering my brother?"

"She didn't murder your brother." Rico felt his own anger rising.

"And how do you know this?" Max's voice dropped, deceptively soft now.

"I saw a painting. A beautiful, heartrending painting. She was in great pain when she painted it, Max—true, gut-wrenching agony."

Max's hand flashed across the space between them, his fingers circling Rico's wrist like a vise. "A painting. You hear that, Anson? A painting." Max laughed, but there was no humor in it. With a jerk, he twisted the wrist and Rico bit his lip to keep from crying out in pain. "Make no mistake, my friend, Kristin *Macgrath* killed my brother. And anyone foolish enough to get in my way will suffer for it. Do I make myself clear?"

"Crystal." Rico barked out the word, certain the bones in his wrist were breaking.

"Good." Max released the hand as suddenly as he had grabbed it, straightening his tie with a casualness that belied the tension of the preceding moments. "Anson."

The car slid to a halt.

"Never forget who's in charge here, Rico."

The door opened and Rico slid gratefully out into the lane. He stood, rubbing his wrist, watching the car disappear into the twilight.

A long time ago, he'd paid for someone else's mistake. And now, despite his instincts to the contrary, he intended to see that Kacy Macgrath didn't suffer the same fate.

For once in his life, Enrico Gienelli was going to do the right thing.

"Where to?"

Max met Anson's gaze in the rearview mirror. "Take me back to the hotel. Then I want you to head back to Kirstin Macgrath's."

"To see what she's hiding?"

"There has to be something. Records. Bank accounts. I don't know, something that will tell us what she did with the money."

"What do you want me to do if she's there?"

"She won't be. Unless I miss my guess, Mr. Roche will take care of that for us."

A crooked smile lit Anson's face. "You do your homework."

Max steepled his hands, bringing his index fingers to his lips. "Always."

The chauffeur nodded. "What are you going to do about Gienelli?"

"Nothing, yet. The man's a coward. Self-preservation at all costs. I don't think he'll present a problem."

"And if he does?" Anson's eyebrows lifted.

"Then we'll have to take care of him."

Max cracked his knuckles, wishing he'd broken the little man's wrist. It would have emphasized his point and helped to relieve his boredom.

* * *

Kacy checked the locks on the windows in the room for the third time in less than an hour. Everything was locked up tighter than a drum. A fire burned cheerily in the hearth, but the dancing flames did little to dispel her sense of dread.

Mac slept peacefully in front of the fire. He was some comfort at least. He'd bark bloody murder if anyone were nearby. He'd also eat little pills that paralyzed him, the little voice in her head whispered. And someone had gotten close enough to give him one.

She shivered, walking into the hall, lifting the receiver for the phone. The dial tone hummed in her ear, a vital connection with the rest of the world. She sighed and replaced the handset, embarrassed at her own insecurity.

She thought of heading for the pub. Company would be more than welcome. Braedon's company, specifically. She smiled at the thought. In a very short time, he seemed to be filling a major role in her life.

But the pub was up a very long and dark road. And her bicycle was trashed.

She wandered into the kitchen, eyeing the back door.

Locked. Had she locked the front door? She was fairly certain. She frowned, trying to assure herself. Of course she had.

Blowing out a breath, she wondered how in the world she was going to make it through the night. She plugged in the teapot and then unplugged it again. Tough times call for tough measures. She needed a glass of wine.

Opening a bottle of merlot, she poured it into a Waterford goblet and headed into her studio.

Work.

What was the saying? Work will set you free? Well, she had no idea if that were true, but certainly work would keep an overactive imagination occupied. And right now, that's exactly what she needed.

She turned on the light over her drafting table and settled in to work on one of the miniatures Professor Baucomo had brought her. Madame de Fornio. The painting was old, probably from sometime in the sixteenth century. It was a family heirloom and the work was being done to preserve the heritage, not the actual painting, which made it easier for her.

When the work had to be restored rather than preserved, there were strict rules she had to follow, but simple preservation allowed more creativity. She could use her judgment. The equivalent of airbrushing an oil painting.

A very tiny oil painting.

The wind rattled against the window. She glanced up, startled to see that it was already quite dark. She looked at her watch. Only six.

Sighing, she reached for her wine. It was going to be a long night. She forced herself to concentrate on her work. The woman in the portrait was not a classical beauty, but she had a certain style. Using a small knife, Kacy dislodged a few loose pieces of paint.

The worst damage was to the top. A hat. The trick would be guessing at the missing colors. She spent the next hour removing bits of color and making notes so that she could create a color map of the original.

Reaching for her glass again, she was surprised to find it empty. The wind moaned and a branch tapped against the window. She jumped. Definitely time for a break. Rubbing her neck wearily, she decided to head for the kitchen.

After the cool silence of the studio, the kitchen was comfortingly cheerful. She felt instantly better. More secure. She corked the bottle of wine. Never drink alone, her mother had always said—usually while pouring a stout bourbon.

Tea was a much better alternative. She plugged in the kettle and was reaching for the tea tin when a low growl issued from the entry hall.

Instantly alert, Kacy grabbed a cleaver from the butcher block, not sure exactly what she was going to do with it, but feeling better holding it. "Mac?" She inched into the hallway. "What is it, boy?"

Her rational mind was informing her calmly that there was nothing to be concerned about. Her emotional mind was strongly urging her to run for the hills, literally. She swallowed and tightened her grip on the knife.

Mac was whining now, circling in front of the door. There was a single rapid knock, and then the door handle slowly turned. Kacy sucked in a breath, gripping the knife with everything she was worth. Watching, mesmerized, she followed the turn of the handle and breathed a sigh of relief when it stopped.

A part of her mind urged her to head for the phone, but her feet evidently hadn't got the memo, and she stayed firmly rooted to the spot. Suddenly the lock clicked ominously, and the door began to swing inward.

Kacy opened her mouth to scream.

Chapter 10

"I'M SORRY, KACY. God, I'm sorry." Braedon held his hands up, his face a chaotic cross between apologetic and relieved.

"You son of a bitch." She hissed the words, surprised at her own vehemence. "You scared the hell out of me."

"Well, then, we're even. When you didn't answer, I thought . . . I thought . . ."

"So it's a draw." She laid the cleaver on a table, exhaling a breath she had no idea she'd been holding.

In one motion, he was across the hallway, his arms wrapping around her. She tipped her head back, telling herself she only wanted to see him better, but when his lips descended, she opened hers willingly—savoring the taste of him, the feel of him.

He devoured her, drinking her in, until she was certain there was nothing left to give. And still he demanded more. Her body arched against him, his hard muscles burning against hers. She wanted to pull him deep inside and never let him go.

Never had she felt anything so powerful. His hands traced their way down her body, stopping to caress her breasts. Breathing became difficult, and all she wanted was to lose herself in this man.

He pulled away, his eyes burning into hers. "I came to ask you to dinner."

She fought her desire, trying to ignore the question in his eyes. God, she wanted him. Summoning superhuman strength, she stepped back. "That would be great," she said, amazed at how normal her voice sounded.

They stood a few feet apart, eyes raking over each other, his gaze tracing the curves of her body. She felt herself blush. "You should change," he said.

She fingered the hem of her sweatshirt. "I'll just be a minute." She walked into the bedroom, her breathing still coming in gasps. She heard Mac growl playfully and poked her head out the door. "Mac has to come, too. Okay?"

"No problem. I called to make sure all three of us would be welcome."

She smiled, feeling suddenly optimistic. How could a girl not like a man who loved her dog?

She walked into her closet, trying to decide what to wear. What she needed was the proverbial little black dress, but she didn't have anything that even came close. She finally settled for a silky sheath in navy. At least it was sleek and had some semblance of what she considered high fashion.

She knelt on the floor of her closet, trying to find matching shoes, and finally with relief slammed her feet into what she hoped was a pair of navy pumps.

With a quick brush of her hair, she walked back into the hallway, hoping she looked presentable. She honestly couldn't remember the last time she'd cared if it mattered. "I'm ready."

His gaze raked her from head to toe. "I'll say." His eyes abolished any doubt she could have harbored.

"Let's go." She tried to sound calm, but she kept remembering *the kiss*. Frankly, dinner was the last thing on her mind.

The three of them settled into the car, Mac with his nose on the gear shift.

"I take it we're not going to the pub?" Kacy asked.

"No. I thought considering everything that's happened, you could use a change of venue."

No one had ever thought about what she'd want. Not ever. She tried not to read more into it than there was. "Sounds great."

Braedon tried to concentrate on the road. It had been a long time since he'd driven on the left and he usually kept a mantra going in his head. *Right is left. Left is right.* But tonight he was finding it hard to focus on anything but Kacy.

Her dress skimmed her body like a glove, hugging her thighs, accentuating her bare legs. He felt like a teenager with a boner. She was enticing, to say the least. And he could still feel her soft lips opening under his, responding with joyous abandonment.

Mac sighed.

"I'm with you, boy." Braedon grinned, reaching over to scratch the dog.

"What?" Kacy turned to look at him, a smile playing at the corners of her mouth.

He hadn't realized he'd spoken out loud. "Nothing. Just a sidebar with the dog."

She smiled in earnest, her dimple popping into view. "Well, I'm glad the two of you can hold a conversation."

Mac wagged his tail and Braedon felt a little foolish. What he needed was something to get his mind off of how much he wanted to pull the car over and make love to her right here and now. Dog be damned.

He tightened his grip on the steering wheel, forcing his libido into low gear. "So, tell me, how did you get the name Kacy? It's kind of unusual, isn't it?"

"Actually, in Irish Gaelic it means brave. But that's Casey with a *C*, not a *K*."

"So someone thought you were brave, but couldn't spell?"

She shook her head, her silky hair swirling around her shoulders. "No. In my case it's a nickname. My initials are K.C. One of the nuns—"

"Nuns?"

She dimpled again, nodding. "Nuns. I was sent to Switzerland to boarding school after my mother died. Anyway, Sister Margaretta could never remember my name, so she used my initials. And before long, everyone was calling me Kacy."

"Even your family?"

A shadow passed across her face. "There was only my father. And I didn't see him that often."

He considered the information she'd just given him, mentally marking a check in the Kacy's innocent column. Boarding school in Switzerland cost money. And if she had family money, she certainly had no need to kill Alex for his. "What does the *C* stand for?"

She was quiet, worrying her bottom lip with her teeth. "It's a family name," she said finally.

"Obviously one you'd rather not share."

She studied her fingernails. "Right."

He felt like he'd stumbled onto something important. A key to understanding whatever it was she kept so closely guarded, but now wasn't the time to press. She'd already shared a lot. "Okay, then I'll guess. Let's see. Cleopatra?"

She laughed, automatically relaxing. "No."

He pretended to ponder the issue. "Cornelia."

"Yuck."

"I'll take that as a no. Hmm." He turned into the parking lot of the restaurant. "Calandra."

"Calandra? What kind of name is that?"

"Greek. It means lark."

"You speak Greek?"

"A little." He killed the engine, turning to face her. "What can I say, I'm a man of many talents."

Their gazes met and held. Breathing normally suddenly seemed difficult. He reached out, taking a strand of hair, stroking it softly between his thumb and forefinger. With a gentle tug, he pulled her to him.

Her eyes widened, her pupils dilating in anticipation, and when she licked her lips, he was lost. Leaning forward, he brushed his lips across hers, running a hand through her hair. With a groan he pulled her to him, bringing them together more forcefully. She moaned and he felt her hand at the back of his neck, stroking, kneading.

With a playful yip, Mac pushed his way between them. Braedon sat back, the separation almost physically painful.

He met her gaze, satisfied to see desire reflected in her eyes. "I guess someone is ready to eat."

Mac barked again and Kacy laughed.

Braedon stepped out of the car into the cool night air, relieved to see that there was no physical remnant of the moment. Mac jumped out behind him. "Next time, big boy, there won't be any interruptions." He shook a finger at the dog, speaking with mock severity, then walked around the car to open the door for Kacy, smiling to himself.

If he had his way, there would definitely be a next time.

The restaurant was lovely. Part of a hotel. A restored tower house, actually. No doubt a fortification left behind by the O'Briens or Macnamaras. The two families had fought for control over Clare for centuries, and their strongholds dotted the countryside, most of them in ruins.

Their table was in a quiet corner of the dining room, candlelight and soft music adding an air of romance. Not that they needed any help in that department.

Kacy shot a look at Braedon. He was studying the menu, a little frown wrinkling the skin between his eyes. Even when he looked intense, he was handsome.

Mac shifted at her feet. And she wondered if she should be thanking him or punishing him for his timely disturbance. She reached for her wineglass, grateful for something to do with her hands. She felt like a teenager on a first date. Heavens, her palms were even sweaty.

"Have you decided what you want?" Braedon closed his menu and laid it on the table.

You. I want you. She bit back a smile. That wouldn't do. "A salad, I think. I'm still on protein overload from breakfast this morning. How about you?"

"Salmon."

The waiter came and took their order, leaving a basket of warm soda bread on the table. Kacy reached for a slice the same time Braedon did, their hands colliding, sparks shooting up her arm. The man was lethal.

"So, you know a lot about me, and I still don't know that much about you." She bit into the bread, savoring the contrast of coarse bread and sweet currants. "Tell me about Braedon Roche."

"There's not much to tell, really." He lifted his glass and sipped idly.

"Well, I know you were born in Dublin."

"Actually I was born in County Cork, near Fermoy."

She frowned, trying to remember his earlier remarks. "But you said—"

"That I lived in Dublin. We moved there when I was six."

"We?" She offered him the bread basket and he took a slice. He slowly slathered it with butter. God, even the way he buttered bread was sexy.

"My mother and I." There was a finality in the way he said it, and she realized the subject was closed.

All right then, she'd try another tack. "So where do you live now?"

He smiled at her, and she was glad she hadn't pressed for more. "New York, mostly."

"Mostly?"

"I have a flat in London and a house in Colorado."

"You must be a successful mogul," she said dryly.

"Those were your words, not mine."

"So what do you do exactly?" It was an innocent question, but she held her breath, waiting for his answer.

"I'm a businessman. An entrepreneur. Mainly, I buy and sell companies."

"Forced takeovers?"

"Sometimes."

She could see him ruthlessly getting what he wanted. There was a certain steely quality about him. She doubted Braedon Roche lost very often. "Sounds exciting."

"Actually, it's pretty dull most of the time. Tell me why you chose art restoration."

Nice move; he'd avoided an answer and neatly turned the conversation back to her. She wondered how he was at chess. Probably devastating. "I wasn't talented enough to be an artist, or at least I thought so until this afternoon."

He refilled their glasses and raised an inquiring eyebrow.

"Professor Baucomo was looking at some of my paintings. He really liked them." She stopped, feeling suddenly shy.

"And?" Braedon prompted.

"And he wants to organize a showing."

"But that's wonderful. Why the concern?"

He was an observant man. "I guess I just have trouble believing him."

"But he knows what he's doing, right?"

"In his field."

"But you think it's a far cry from art historian to art critic?"

She swallowed some wine, the crisp chardonnay caressing her throat. "Yes. I guess that's it. I don't know if I can trust his judgment."

"Have you ever shown your work to anyone else?"

"A few professors in college and my . . . my father." She felt a flutter of nerves. She was edging into deep water.

"What did they think?"

"Well, the professors were encouraging."

"And your father?"

"He said I was technically deficient. That I should give up the idea of being an artist." She bit her lip, trying not to let the memory of the hurt show.

Braedon reached across the table, covering her hand with his. "Maybe he just wanted you to find an easier profession."

She frowned, comforted by his touch, but confused by his words.

"Sometimes a parent's need to protect their child is stronger than the need to praise him. Your father might have been afraid you'd be hurt if you tried to become an artist. It's a harsh profession. Maybe he wanted to protect you from that."

It was a lovely thought, but Braedon didn't know her father. "So you're saying that he discouraged me, not because I wasn't talented, but because he wanted to spare me the rejection that inevitably comes with an artist's life?"

"It's possible."

"Then why didn't he just tell me that?" She angrily brushed at the tears filling her eyes. Why did it still hurt so damn much?

"I don't know. I just know that sometimes it's hard to find the right words. Especially when you're talking to someone you love."

"My father cared about my father." She knew she sounded bitter and hated it that he still had so much power over her. She sniffed, pulling herself together. "I'm sorry, I didn't mean to get so emotional."

He squeezed her hand and released it. "Where's your father now?"

"He's dead." Kacy tried to keep her voice light, but she knew it was time to steer the conversation to a new topic. "Your mother, is she still in Dublin?"

"No." His mouth tightened. And she thought for a moment

that that was all he was going to say. He sighed, the sound reaching out to her soul. "She's been dead a long time."

Maybe she wasn't the only one with secrets to keep.

Kacy sipped her coffee, knowing that the last thing she needed right now was caffeine. She was already as jumpy as a drop of water on a hot skillet, and she could blame it on the man sitting across from her. The one looking cool as a cucumber.

Maybe he had dalliances daily, but she was sadly out of practice. Who was she kidding? Nothing in the world could have prepared her for Braedon Roche and the feelings he seemed to pull out of her.

She glanced around the restaurant, taking in the other diners. The tables were full, mostly with couples. Some enjoying their food, others enjoying each other. She blew out a sigh, watching an older couple on the dance floor, cheek to cheek. Maybe someday . . .

"Would you like to dance?" Braedon was standing beside her, his hand out.

She took it, knowing that she was probably going to regret it, but already imagining how wonderful it would feel to be dancing in his arms.

The orchestra was small, but somehow, it made it all the more intimate. They were playing a Cole Porter tune. "I've Got You Under My Skin."

How appropriate.

He danced superbly, but she'd known that he would. She leaned into him, letting his body caress hers. The muscles of his arm moved under her hand, and she felt a flutter of desire course through her.

She looked up at him, allowing herself the luxury of losing herself in the deep blue of his eyes. Their breath mingled, the smell of cognac and coffee filling her senses. His hand, splayed across her back, burned through her dress, branding her with his touch.

The other people in the room just seemed to disappear. There was nothing but the blue of his eyes, the feel of his hands, and the sound of the music. The song ended and they stopped. Kacy started to pull away, but he tightened his hold.

"One more," he whispered in her ear, and she felt a shiver run the gamut from head to toes.

The music started. Slow and melodic. "Like Someone in Love." It had been one of her mother's favorites. She buried her face in the broad expanse of his chest, inhaling the essence of him. Spicy, and thoroughly Braedon. His hand gently traced the curve of her back, his fingers leaving a trail of fire.

He pulled her closer and then closer still, until Kacy felt like they were one person, moving in unison to the soft rhythm of the music. His heart beat steadily underneath her cheek, a counterpoint to the music.

With a flourish, he twirled her away from him, and then pulled her into his arms again before she even had time to mourn the loss. Now they danced limb to limb, mirroring each other's rhythms. Thigh to thigh, belly to belly, her breasts against his chest, his heat searing her through the thin material of her dress.

She trailed her fingers up his arm, to his shoulder. He found her hair with his free hand, cupping the back of her head. Her eyes met his and she lost herself in the golden flecks dancing through his lapis eyes.

Slowly, never losing the rhythm of the dance, he bent his head until his mouth was only a few inches away from hers. His breath caressed her face, and her heart fluttered, fanning the flames of desire threatening to overwhelm her.

She focused on his strong and more than capable mouth. And with a sigh she stretched upward to meet him. Their lips touched and Kacy felt as if the room itself exploded. She was flying, wrapped in his arms, locked in a passionate kiss, the music swelling until it carried them high, higher . . .

She realized the music had stopped and, suddenly shy, pulled away. It wasn't like her to make such a public display of herself. Blushing, she held a shaking hand to her cheek. Braedon was still drinking her in with his eyes, obviously as affected by the kiss as she. He covered her hand with his, turning it so that the back of his fingers stroked her cheek.

"I think it's time to go." His voice was tight, husky, the sound making her ache deep inside.

She nodded, unable to summon words.

"You stay here. I'll go get Mac."

Again, she nodded, certain that she would trip if she tried to move. Fortunately, they had stopped at the edge of the dance floor, close to some potted palms. At least she wasn't falling apart in the middle of the room. She watched the broad expanse of his back as he walked away and clenched her fist at the surge of desire that raced through her.

Drawing in a breath, she tried to calm her ragged breathing. This just wouldn't do. She needed something to distract her.

People. She'd watch people.

Across from her, large double doors led to the hotel. She focused on the patrons in the lobby. There were two little ladies, English, she'd guess. They were trying to pile their various pieces of luggage on a trolley. And making quite a mess of it. They worked at cross purposes. One succeeding only to have the other undo what she'd just accomplished.

The British version of Lucy and Ethel. Ethel reached for her suitcase and once more got it settled on the others. But then, like clockwork, here came Lucy throwing hers on top. And the whole thing came tumbling down again. Kacy bit back a smile.

A well-dressed gentleman standing near the door was also observing the show. She stared at his suit-clad back, a tingle of recognition running down her spine. Recognition turned to dread as he slowly turned toward her, a familiar, mocking smile on his face.

Alex.

Oh, dear God, Alex.

Chapter 11

BRAEDON WHISTLED FOR Mac and turned back toward Kacy. She was standing with her hand outstretched, her mouth open, all the color drained from her face. He sprinted across the restaurant, oblivious to the people around him.

"Kacy, what is it?" He took her hand, surprised to find it ice cold. She was staring at the door connecting the dining room to the hotel lobby, totally unaware that he was there. "Kacy, honey, talk to me." He took her by the shoulders and turned her to face him. She blinked, focusing on him. "Braedon." Her voice was weak, barely a whisper. "I saw him."

"Saw who?" She was beginning to scare him. He pulled her back into the shelter of the plants.

"Alex." The word was almost a sob.

"Kacy," he spoke gently, "Alex is dead."

"I know th-that." She ran a hand across her eyes. "But I saw him." She met his gaze, hers begging him to believe her.

"Where?" He turned her around again, pulling her against him, rubbing his fingers up and down her arms. "Show me where."

She swallowed and lifted a shaking hand, pointing to the lobby. "There."

"Kacy, there's no one there."

"I saw him, Braedon. He was there. Right there. Sm-smiling at me." He could feel her trembling, shudders rippling through her body.

117

"You're tired. It's been a long day. You hardly slept at all last night. You're just reacting to everything that's been happening. We talked about him last night, so you had him on your mind. Honey, you saw someone who resembled Alex, that's all."

She jerked away, swinging around to face him, fire in her eyes. "I know what I saw."

"I'm not saying you didn't see something. I'm just suggesting that maybe it wasn't really Alex."

She met his gaze, doubt and fear battling in her eyes. "Oh, God, I was so sure." Her anger deflated as quickly as it had come. "Maybe you're right. I am tired." She placed a shaking hand on his arm. "Will you take me home?"

He wrapped an arm around her shoulder, pulling her close. "It's going to be all right, Kacy. I promise you. It's going to be all right."

He only hoped he was telling her the truth.

Max pressed the button for his floor and moved to the back of the elevator. What had she been doing here? With Roche. And she'd seen him. Recognized him. Or at least thought she had.

He smiled, savoring the stark expression of fear on her face. The idea of gaslighting her held great appeal, but first he had to deal with Roche. He'd seen them dancing, bodies writhing together. Rico had been right, the man was set on seducing her, no holds barred. The question was why?

How much did he know?

Frustrated, Max ran a hand through his hair. He'd come here to simplify things, but instead, they seemed to be getting more complicated by the second.

He frowned. Maybe Roche and the little slut had been in on it from the beginning. Maybe they'd conspired to kill Alex, and now they were enjoying the money, *his* money.

The elevator dinged and the doors slid open. Max walked

into the hallway, his jaw clenched in anger. He'd wait for Anson. Surely the man had found something. All he needed was to find out what had happened to the money, and then he would see to it that Alex's *wife* never kissed anyone again.

Kacy leaned against the upholstery of the car, eyes closed, her mind spinning. The more she thought about it, the more she thought Braedon was right. She couldn't have seen Alex.

He was dead.

It was just as he said, she was reacting to the stress of the last couple of days. The restaurant had been dark, candlelight flickering everywhere. Her imagination had obviously been working overtime. She opened her eyes. "I'm sorry."

"For what?" Braedon shot her a quick look, his eyes full of concern.

"For ruining the evening. I don't know what came over me. I mean, one minute everything is fine, and the next, I'm seeing the ghost of my dead husband. You must think I'm crazy."

"No. I don't think anything of the sort." His voice was reassuring, filling her with a peace she probably didn't deserve. "I just think you're tired."

She laid a hand on Mac's head, rubbing the little place behind his ear that sent him into ecstasy. "You're probably right. All I need is a good night's sleep, and then, poof, no more ghosts." She was babbling. He covered her hand with his, squeezing gently, and despite everything, she felt better.

"Just close your eyes. We'll be home soon."

She obeyed, hoping the motion of the car and the feel of his hand would soothe her. But her mind was still filled with the image of Alex, and try as she might, she couldn't erase the sardonic smile from his face.

"We're here." Braedon pulled into the drive and stopped the car in front of the house.

Kacy opened her eyes, surprised to see that they were already home. She blew out a breath. *Home.* Some sanctuary this had turned out to be.

"Come on, sleepyhead, let's get you inside."

He stepped out of the car, followed by an exuberant dog. Mac raced up and down the drive, releasing pent up energy. Kacy smiled, wondering if maybe it wouldn't do her good to do the same thing.

Braedon opened the door and offered her his hand. "Thanks." She looked up into his eyes, grateful for his help. Her legs felt like melted butter, and when he slid an arm around her waist, the resulting shiver made her wonder if his touch was helping or hurting the situation.

Mac ran in circles around them as they made their way to the front door. The porch lamp cast a circle of harsh white light on the top step, and they stopped there, the illumination casting long shadows across Braedon's face.

"Where's the key?"

She raised her eyebrows, trying not to smile. A bit on the arrogant side, Braedon Roche, automatically assuming she'd taken his advice regarding locking the cottage. Of course the overconfidence was well founded. She had followed his instructions. Sort of. "I hid it in the flowerpot."

"Kacy." Her name exploded from his mouth, sounding more like a curse than a moniker.

She shrugged. "I don't like carrying a purse."

He frowned, but she could see a flicker of laughter in his eyes. "At least you locked it. But next time—"

"Next time, I'll take the key with me. Okay?"

He settled his hands on her waist. "Okay."

She chewed on her bottom lip and stared up at him, waiting for . . . well, she wasn't sure exactly, but her heart was beating loudly enough to accompany *Riverdance.*

He smiled down at her, his teeth white against the shadows of his face. "You certainly are an interesting date, Ms. Macgrath."

"Is that what this was? A date?"

He nodded, his eyes suddenly intense. He bent his head and she tipped hers back, waiting for his kiss, for the touch of his lips against hers. She opened her mouth to him, reveling in the feel of his tongue against hers, exploring the heat of his mouth.

Pressing against his solid strength, she felt the steady rhythm of his breathing and the acceleration of his heart. His hands slid up from her waist. One circling her back, pulling her closer. And the other . . . the other traced a path up her arm, down her shoulder, settling at last on the curve of her breast.

She pushed against his hand, impatient, wanting more. He obliged, one finger slowly tracing the swell of her breast through the thin material of the dress. She arched against him, a low moan escaping her lips. His fingers kneaded the tender skin, rubbing her nipple between thumb and forefinger.

He trailed kisses along her neck and the line of her shoulder, sending fire sparking through her, starting a slow burn in her belly that spread to the soft place between her thighs.

"Let's go inside." His whispered words brought her back to reality, dousing the fire.

She pushed back, her breath coming in rapid gasps, her heartbeat echoing in her ears. She wanted him. Wanted him more than she had ever wanted anything in her life. But years of self-doubt slammed walls of self-protection into place, and she realized she was afraid. Afraid that if she gave herself to this man, there would be no turning back.

He put a finger under her chin, tipping it up so that he could see her. His eyes were full of hunger and need, their intensity stoking the fire inside her. "Kacy?"

The blaze threatened to rekindle. She almost lost her resolve. He looked so vulnerable. So handsome.

But no.

She had to protect herself. Be certain. This was a man she could so easily love. And loving someone gave them all the power. She wasn't sure she was ready to trust him—trust herself—that far.

"I . . . I can't do this." She looked away, staring at her feet, trying not to think about what she was turning down.

"Okay." His voice sounded strained, almost as if he were in physical pain. There was a long pause and Kacy held her breath. "If that's what you want."

It wasn't what she wanted at all. She wanted him to sweep her into his arms and make love to her until the world looked level, but that wasn't what was best for her. She had to look out for herself.

Never let anyone get too close, Kirstin. The sound of her father's voice filled her mind.

Her father was right. And this time she'd listen. "It's what I want."

Braedon leaned down and gently kissed her, his touch tender, as if he thought she might shatter. Which wasn't far from the truth.

Without another word he turned to go, and she stood on the porch, eyes brimming with tears, watching him walk away.

Braedon refused to look back. He felt like someone had gutted him with a fishing knife. The pain was more than physical. It invaded his soul. Kacy touched him in a place he'd thought was dead. And her rejection hurt. Really hurt.

He yanked opened the car door and slid behind the wheel, his traitorous eyes demanding one last look. She was fumbling with her key, the dog pushing against her knees. He slammed a hand into the steering wheel.

Damn it, he was behaving like a love struck schoolboy. This was for the best. He didn't need entanglements and certainly not with her. Even if she were innocent, and he suddenly knew with all certainty that she was, she'd still been married to the man who'd stolen his artwork and his reputation.

Guilt by association.

He ran a hand through his hair. Who was he kidding? He wanted her. Wanted to hold her, to touch her, to make love to her. And he was walking away?

With a grim smile, he opened the car door and stepped into the cool night. He wasn't going to let her slip away. He turned toward the house, his mind made up.

A sharp scream split the night.

Kacy.

With heart pounding, he began to run.

Chapter 12

KACY PRESSED A hand to her mouth, swallowing another scream, her diaphragm slamming into the back of her rib cage, making it almost impossible to breathe.

The man lay on the stairs, his head twisted back, his eyes wide. He looked like something in a movie. She almost expected a voice to yell, 'Cut,' and the man to get up and walk away.

Mac circled the body, whining and sniffing, stopping every once in a while to look back at her.

She tried to move, to call for help, but her voice seemed to have only two working levels, scream and mute. There was blood on the stairs, dripping down the riser to the hallway floor, pooling a muddy crimson against the wood of the floorboards.

Hands landed on her waist, turning her. The mute button released and a scream rose in her throat. She drew in a breath, ready to face her assailant. Braedon. The scream died, its remains trailing out of her mouth like air from a balloon.

She threw herself into his arms, burying her head against his chest, gasping for air, trying to erase the image of the dead man seared in her mind.

Braedon held her tight for a moment, his hands rubbing soothing circles into her back. Then he pushed her away, moving in front of her, blocking her view of the stairs. "Stay here."

A bubble of hysteria forced itself between her lips, sounding like a strangled giggle. She wasn't moving an inch. She hugged herself, rubbing her arms, rocking back and forth, an excellent candidate for a rubber room.

Braedon knelt by the man's body. There was no doubt in Kacy's mind that he was dead. His head looked like someone had taken it off and put it back on crooked. A broken Barbie doll. Another burst of tortured laughter pushed past her clenched teeth. A Ken doll.

"Is he . . ." Her voice barely carried across the hall and she waited, not sure that he'd even heard her.

"Yeah." Braedon stood up, careful not to disturb anything. "We need to call the Garda."

Kacy nodded, but her feet refused to move. There was safety in this spot and she didn't particularly want to leave it. Although the view left something to be desired.

"Do you have any idea who he is?" Braedon's voice was close.

She snapped out of her corybantic reverie and looked up at him. "I don't know. I can't see his fa—" She stopped, swallowing the bile that rose in her throat.

Braedon slid an arm around her. "I'll come with you, but you need to take a closer look."

She steeled herself, willing her feet to move. She could do this. Braedon was here. She could do this. Her left foot moved forward, followed by her right. And way before she was ready, she reached the nightmare-inducing face.

A stranger. It was a stranger.

"I've never seen him." She stared, mesmerized by the angle of his head and his stark, frozen features. Whoever he was, he had died a horrible death. "Was he . . . did he . . . I mean . . ."

"Looks like he fell. The Garda will be able to tell us more."

"Right." She drew in a shuddering breath and jerked her gaze away from the body.

Braedon's arm tightened around her. "Let's make that phone call."

Braedon replaced the receiver, not surprised to see that his hand was shaking. Kacy clung to his other hand like a life-line, her eyes still locked on the broken body on the stairs. "They're on their way. I think you should wait outside."

Kacy turned to meet his gaze. Her eyes were wide, her mouth set in a thin line. "No. This is my house. I won't let *him*—" She jerked her head toward the stairs. "—ruin that." She crossed her arms over her chest, eyes flashing.

He raised a hand to her face, impressed with her fortitude. She was so tiny. It looked as if a strong gust of wind would blow her away. Yet she stood here, in the face of death, deter-mined to preserve her home. A gutsy lady.

She relaxed, smiling weakly, and, for a moment, leaned into his touch. Then, with a quick breath, she squared her shoulders. "Well, best we get on with it." She turned, heading for the door leading to the parlor.

"At least let me go first." He took a step to pass her and col-lided with her back, feeling the rigid muscles of her shoulders against his chest. "Kacy?"

A little "oh" escaped her mouth, alarming him more than her scream had. She leaned back against him, all attempt at bravado vanishing. He circled her waist with his arm, his eyes scanning the room for the source of her pain.

The room had obviously been searched, methodically, from the looks of it. Books were thrown on the cabinet and papers littered the floor. Cushions from the chairs and sofa were slit, their stuffing spilling out like grotesque aberra-tions, a room gone insane.

The curtains hung lopsidedly against the window, one end of the rod wedged against the windowsill. Lamps were over-turned, magazines hung in tattered remnants off the coffee table. It was as if wild horses had thundered through the room in sheer panic.

Whoever the man on the stairs was, he had been looking for something, looking with no thought to covering his tracks.

Kacy shivered, the tremor running through her body and into his. For a moment it felt as if they were joined, as if her anguish were his.

Then she pulled away, taking a staggering step forward, her eyes locked on the far wall.

On the Monet.

Kacy's Monet.

It had been slashed diagonally from corner to corner, leaving the canvas gaping, hanging. He reached her side, gathering her into his arms.

"Why?" she whispered, her eyes meeting his. "Why?"

He shook his head wordlessly. There was nothing he could say. With a groan, he pulled her close, surrounding her with his body, trying to shield her from the destruction around them, knowing the mutilated painting was etched in her brain. He frowned, rage and anger giving way to frustration.

He didn't know how to help her. Didn't know what to do.

So he held her, stroking her hair, whispering useless words of comfort, wondering if the wetness on his face could really be tears.

Kacy sat in the kitchen, a cup of tea in front of her. Policemen roamed the house, dusting, photographing, touching everything. She remembered reading somewhere that robbery victims often felt violated. She hadn't understood. Not then. But now she knew it was an inadequate description. Her home had been desecrated. Again. Sanctuary had been broken. She felt more than violated. She felt defiled.

She lifted the cup to her lips and sipped the tepid tea. It tasted bitter. She lowered the cup, surprised that the liquid had grown cold. Everything was cold. She rubbed her arms with her hands, her nervous fingers kneading her icy flesh.

"Kacy?"

She raised her head. Frowning at the face in front of her. Fin. It was Fin.

"Angel, are you all right? I came as soon as I heard."

She dug her nails into the palm of her hand, the sudden pain helping her clear her mind. "I'm fine," she lied.

He covered her hand with his. "I'm so sorry." He waved helplessly in the direction of the hallway and parlor.

"They're just things, Fin." She ran a weary hand through her hair. "Have they . . . have they . . ." She broke off, unable to bring herself to say it.

"Yes. They . . . ah . . . just carried him out."

She nodded, chewing on the inside of her lip, turning the teacup in its saucer.

"Kacy?"

Braedon. Suddenly the room felt safer, his presence sending shivers of relief pulsing through her. "They're almost finished." He nodded at Fin and drew up a chair, one hand warmly covering her thigh. Tipping her chin up with a finger, he looked deep into her eyes.

She swallowed, tears welling at the tenderness she saw there. "I'm doing all right. As well as can be expected." Fin held out a handkerchief and cleared his throat. She pulled her gaze away from Braedon's and smiled at Fin. "Thanks. I can't seem to stop blubbering."

" 'Tis expected under the circumstances." He turned his attention to Braedon. "So they're thinking it was a robbery?"

"Yeah." Braedon blew out a breath, rubbing his temple.

"Did you tell the Garda about the other incidents?" Fin crossed his arms over his chest, leaning back in the chair.

Kacy nodded wearily. "They think the dead man may have been the one who drugged Mac."

"So he tried before?"

"Yeah. I think maybe we interrupted him when I brought Kacy home last night." Braedon leaned forward, elbow on the table, bracing his chin on his hand.

"And so he came back for a second go round. Makes sense." Fin frowned. "And the car that ran you down?"

"They agree that it was probably just coincidence." Kacy rubbed her arms, trying to dispel the icy numbness creeping through her.

"So what was the man after?" Fin asked.

"No telling, really. This place is full of priceless things." Braedon waved a hand at the Waterford lined up on the Welsh dresser.

"I hardly think there's much of a market for stolen crystal." Fin looked around the kitchen.

Kacy offered him a weak smile. "There's been a number of robberies in the area lately. Someone hopped up on drugs. The Garda seem to think the dead man is the culprit."

"Well, if he was high on something, that would certainly explain all the destruction. Do they know who he is?"

"No," Braedon answered. "And frankly, I don't think it's a priority to find out."

Kacy watched the two of them, part of her listening, another part of her trying to bury itself somewhere deep inside her, somewhere safe. The police were just going to give up. Tell her there was nothing more they could do. Like before. They'd left her alone then. And the only thing she'd been able to do was run.

She choked back a sob. Evidently she hadn't run far enough.

Fin frowned. "I don't understand."

"As far as the Garda are concerned, the matter ended here, tonight." Braedon stroked her leg absently with his palm, the heat seeping into her, easing some of the icy agony that filled her.

"Because the man is dead?" Fin sounded dubious.

"That and the fact that his death was apparently an accident."

"You mean the bugger really fell down the stairs?"

"It sure looks that way. They think he tripped. One of the risers was rotted."

"But only a little." She shook her head, surprised at her own reaction. The next thing, they'd be telling her she was liable for killing the man.

She buried her head in her hands. This was turning into something for the *Geraldo Rivera Show*. "I Killed My Burglar." She was on the edge of losing control. She knew that, even recognized that it was probably shock, but she'd be damned if she knew what to do about it. Sister Margaretta hadn't prepared her for this sort of thing.

"Kacy." Braedon lifted a hand to her hair. "No one's blaming you for this." His voice was soft, but firm.

"I know. It's just that it's all so much to take in." She smiled weakly, covering his hand with hers, and for a moment it was just the two of them in the room.

"Mr. Roche, sir?" The young officer stood in the doorway. "We're finished here."

"You'll let us know as soon as you identify the body?" Braedon squeezed her hand reassuringly.

The man nodded. "That we will. And we may have some more questions for Miss Macgrath."

Kacy lifted her head, meeting the man's kindly gaze. "Is it all right if I clean up?"

He smiled, a comforting it's-going-to-be-okay smile. "We've got all we need. 'Tis your house again." He smiled again and turned to go.

Kacy bit back a bitter laugh. Her house? She wondered if it would ever truly be her house again.

"Come now, Kacy, surely you don't want to be cleaning the place tonight? We'll get someone from the village to do it for you in the morning." Fin's heavy brows drew together in concern.

"Fin's right." Braedon moved his thumb in circles on her palm. "You need to rest."

"You know you're welcome at the pub. And if you don't want to stay there, I know Irene Macnamara would be happy to give you a room for a day or so."

"No." The word hung in the room, and Kacy was ashamed at the tone of her voice. "It's really nice of you, Fin, and I know you mean well, but I need to be here."

Braedon searched her eyes. "Are you sure?"

She squared her shoulders and tilted her chin, determined to look strong. "Positive."

"All right then, I'm staying, too."

Relief surged through her. She wanted to be brave, but the thought of doing it alone terrified her. With him beside her, she was suddenly certain she could find a way to put this behind her.

She smiled at the two men. Her friend and her . . . what? What was Braedon to her? Certainly more than a friend, but not a lover. *Yet.* The word echoed through her brain. And she sucked in a breath, wondering when exactly he had come to mean so much to her.

"Looks pretty good." Braedon stood in the restored tranquillity of Kacy's bedroom. It was magazine perfect again, everything returned to its proper place.

"That leaves the attic." She was moving on blind energy. He recognized the signs, but knew there was nothing he could do about it. Hopefully, she'd deal with it all in time. But for now, he figured she was coping in the only way she knew how. And Braedon was determined to help her.

"All right. Let me go first. I don't trust those stairs."

She nodded, shifting so that he could lead the way. The staircase was tucked into an opening the size of a small closet, the stairs themselves treacherously narrow and steep. No doubt its predecessor had been a rickety ladder.

The broken riser was covered with police tape, the exposed wood looking strangely harmless without the sprawled body to accentuate its danger. Braedon reached for Kacy's hand as they cautiously stepped over it.

"It's hard to believe that killed a man." Kacy's voice was soft but steady. She was gradually gaining control. He just hoped there wouldn't be any more surprises.

He looked down at the splintered piece of wood. "I suppose one could argue that he got his just desserts."

Kacy shuddered. "Nobody deserves to die like that."

He wished his thoughts were as kind. Personally he wished the bastard had lived, if only long enough to get his hands on him.

They stepped into the attic and Braedon reached for the cord hanging from the lone lightbulb. The room was small, angled on both sides from the pitch of the roof. It was packed with boxes and various discarded paraphernalia, some of which Kacy must have inherited with the house.

The intruder hadn't made much progress here. There were only a few boxes overturned, but their contents were strewn haphazardly around the room. Kacy sighed and bent down to pick up a file folder.

"It's like he's been inside me somehow." She straightened the papers and stuck them into an empty box. "Like he knows—" She shivered. "—or knew, things about me that no one else knows. I know it's silly, but it makes me feel dirty."

"It's normal to feel that way. The man invaded your privacy, and for most of us that's the one part of our lives we truly feel in control of. But you have to remember, no matter what he saw, no matter what he touched—" He reached to tuck a strand of hair behind her ear. "—he didn't really reach you, Kacy."

She searched his gaze, looking for answers he knew he couldn't give, but he found himself wishing that he could.

"Come on, let's get this mess cleaned up." His words broke the spell and she sat on the floor, beginning to gather papers.

He joined her and they sorted in silence broken only by his questions as to where she wanted things. Kacy kept everything. There were Playbills from shows that had long ago ended their run, papers from college, even course notes. There were photographs and letters, books and mementos. A faded corsage. A menu from some Caribbean restaurant. All the personal things missing from the rooms below, here, haphazardly stored in boxes. Memories, forcibly contained, kept well out of reach. Why?

He picked up an envelope addressed to an M. Giles. Something flickered in the back of his brain. He held it out to her. "What's this?"

She looked up from a newspaper clipping and frowned at the creamy envelope. "I don't know." Taking it from him, she held it close to her face, squinting at the address. "Wait, I remember. It was sent to our apartment in New York by mistake. After Alex—" She paused, the pain surfacing again. "—after he died, I meant to send it back, but things got a little—harried, and I guess I never did." She lowered the envelope, memories clouding her beautiful face. "It was an awful time."

Braedon took the envelope, his brain still trying to identify what it was about the thing that bothered him. "Where shall I put it?"

She pulled away from her thoughts. "I suppose it's too late to return it." She shrugged. "I guess just throw it away."

He started to toss it, but something stopped him, and he slid it into his pocket. He was probably being oversensitive, but later, when he was alone, he'd have a look at it.

"I guess I ought to throw the lot out."

His gaze found hers and he tried to read the emotions in her eyes.

"I've never been very good at letting go of the past." She

gestured to the boxes and piles of things filling the tiny space. "I keep them up here, out of sight, and I pretend that I've left it all behind. But it's always here. Always a part of me." She looked at a paper in her hand. "I can't run far enough to escape it." The hopelessness in her eyes made him ache inside.

He pulled the paper from her hand, recognizing it immediately—her marriage certificate. There was her signature and Madison's.

"It seems like a lifetime ago."

"It was."

"Maybe so, but it's still here." She touched her temple with a trembling finger.

"Marrying Alex?" He felt a rush of jealousy, angry that it had to be this man of all men who had captured her heart.

"No." She studied her hands, as if they were one of the paintings she restored.

He waited for her to continue, but when she didn't, he prodded gently. "His death?"

Her head snapped up.

"Fin told me he drowned."

"Did he tell you I was there?" Kacy laughed, a deep throaty noise with absolutely no trace of humor in it. "That I was right there?" The brightness in her eyes faded, and he knew she was far away, lost in her memories. She ran a hand through her hair, her eyes wild, seeing a storm that had blown out long ago. "And did he tell you that I killed Alex? As surely as if I'd shot him. I killed him." Her voice was little more than a whisper now, strained and anguished.

Braedon felt the hairs on his arms rise. He'd wanted this after all, wanted a confession. But now that the time seemed to be at hand, he was surprised that there was no joy in it. None at all. "Do you want to tell me about it?"

She twisted her hands together, tears glistening on her cheeks. He wanted to wipe them away, but he was afraid to touch her. Afraid she'd shatter and he'd never be able to put her together again.

"There's nothing to tell. I wanted him to come home more, spend time with me." She smiled bleakly. "Treat me like a real wife. So I confronted him. Begged him to find more time for me, quality time. But he told me he only wanted s-sex."

She choked back a sob. "And when I told him I wanted a husband, he exploded and stormed out of the house. Before I could get to him, he was gone." She lifted her gaze to meet his. "Just gone. As if he'd never existed. One minute I was Mrs. Alex Madison, and the next, I was . . ." Two great tears rolled down her cheeks and he thought his own heart might break. She buried her face in her hands, sobs shaking her slender shoulders.

Braedon shifted, moving closer, putting an arm around her shoulder. "I'm sorry. I didn't mean to make you relive it."

Lifting her head, she sniffled, her gaze meeting his. "It isn't your fault. I live with it every day of my life." She was back with him, the beach gone, and he reached to wipe away her tears.

"It's over, Kacy, let it go."

She touched his hand hesitantly with hers. "I've never told anyone before. About . . . about . . ." She stopped, unable to finish.

Covering her hand with his, he stroked her soft skin. "It's all right," he said, and he meant it. Whatever sins Kacy had committed, she hadn't been responsible for her husband's death.

It was a damn good thing Alex Madison was already dead. On top of everything else he'd done, the man had hurt Kacy. He'd treated her like a possession, something to be used and then thrown away. *The prick.* Hadn't he recognized what he had? How lucky he was?

Braedon pulled her to him, tightening his arms around her,

resting his chin on her hair. "It's going to be all right, Kacy," he whispered. And he knew that, somehow, he'd make sure that it was.

Chapter 13

OH, GOD, WHAT had she done?

Kacy ran an agitated hand through her hair, pacing back and forth across the rag rug at the foot of her bed.

She'd told Braedon about Alex.

Squeezing her eyes shut, she rubbed her temples. Considering all that had happened, she ought to be worrying about more important things than what she had or hadn't told Braedon Roche.

Easier said than done. She blew out a breath, opened her eyes, and sat on the end of the bed, staring at the closed door connecting the bedroom with the hallway and, ultimately, Braedon asleep in the parlor.

She'd admitted to Braedon that Alex hadn't loved her, and in doing so, she'd given voice to her biggest fear—that she was unlovable. No matter how hard she tried, the men she loved rejected her. First her father, and then Alex.

She wrapped her arms around herself, rocking back and forth, fighting against the humiliation snaking around inside her, threatening to destroy what was left of her self-esteem.

She opened her eyes.

There were more important things to worry about. Biting her lip, she focused instead on the intruder. The image of his body sprawled across the stairs flashed through her mind and she shuddered with revulsion. She'd never seen the man before, but she wasn't so certain he was a run-of-the-mill burglar.

It seemed far more likely that one of the men from Alex's past had caught up with her. There had been so many debts. Could the dead man have been sent by Alex's creditors? She flinched, thinking of the car in the lane.

Why would someone come after her now? It had been two years. Alex was dead and gone. She was boxing with shadows. Mac jumped up on the bed, nestling beside her. She stroked the soft white fur on his neck. "What are we going to do?"

The dog cocked his head as if he were contemplating the question.

"I know, I know. You want to stay here," she sighed. "Me, too, but I'm not sure it's possible anymore."

She shivered, feeling helpless and alone, despite the fact that Braedon was sleeping just across the hall. The wind rattled against the windowpane and she jumped.

Swallowing her fear, she walked to the window and checked the latch, relieved to find that it was firmly locked. She turned back to face Mac. "All we have to do is disappear. It's not like I haven't done it before."

Mac lifted his head, his gaze looking reproachful.

"Maybe we could go to Spain. You'd love it there. It's warm all the time." She heard the indecision in her voice. The truth was, she didn't want to leave. For the first time in her life, she'd made a real home. She had friends in Lindoon. And something more.

She dropped down onto the bed next to Mac.

There was Braedon.

But there was also the threat from Alex's enemies. And there was her father's legacy.

Millicent.

Her father's wife hated her. Hated her with a vehemence that was almost deadly. Kacy was an undeniable reminder of her husband's infidelity. And if anything happened to put Kacy in the limelight, her father's reputation would suffer.

Millicent had made that perfectly clear. Kacy had to protect him. Save him from Millicent even in death.

She ran a hand through her hair, conflicted. Loyalty to her father was as natural as breathing. All her life she'd done as he'd directed. Changed her name, her residence, anything it took to stay in his life—to remain his daughter.

All she'd wanted was for him to acknowledge her. To let the world know he had a daughter. He'd promised that some-day she could come out of the shadows, step into the light—with him. But someday had never come, and now it was too late. She was left protecting a memory.

There could be no normalcy for her. There would always be someone digging into her past, asking questions that couldn't be answered. If it wasn't Alex's creditors, it would be someone else. And then Millicent would make good on her threat. No, she had to run.

She stared at the door to the hallway, wondering if Braedon was asleep, wondering what it would be like to wake up in his arms, to feel cherished and safe, even if just for a moment. She was halfway across the room before she even realized her intent. She stopped, knowing she was being foolhardy. Going to him would be a mistake, an entanglement she didn't need. Like Alex.

Alex.

What a mistake that had been. Once in her life she'd let her passions reign and look where it had left her.

Alone.

And hunted. Her trust betrayed.

Even before he died, he'd thrown it all back in her face. The charm had faded and the man had grown menacingly cold. What a fool she'd been. What a stupid, bloody fool.

Squaring her shoulders, she turned back toward the bed. Sleep. She needed sleep. Things would look clearer in the morning.

Like hell they would, the little voice in her head whispered.

*   *   *

Braedon sat on the sofa, looking at the envelope in his hand, wondering what it was about the name that seemed familiar. He turned it over and read the embossed return address. Some realty company in New York.

What had Kacy said? Misdelivered mail. He frowned at the envelope. She'd believed what she'd told him. He was learning to read her eyes, and her reaction had been instant and honest. There was nothing to this.

Still, something nagged at his brain.

He slit the envelope open, feeling only a slight trace of guilt. It wasn't like he was reading Kacy's mail. He pulled out some papers and unfolded them, frowning as he studied what looked to be a legal document.

A contract of some kind. Real estate from the looks of it. He flipped to the back. There was a deed attached. Turning the pages, he noted the signatures at the end. Giles had signed, his handwriting slanted and curling, almost unreadable. There was another signature, too. The seller. But it was impossible to make out the illegible scrawl.

He flipped back to the first page and the clause identifying the seller. Miguel Ruiz. The name was unfamiliar, not that he'd have expected to recognize it. He shrugged. The paperwork looked routine. Evidently Giles had bought some property in South America, an island from the looks of it.

Braedon folded the papers and stuck them back into the envelope. M. Giles was probably sitting on his island right now, drinking piña coladas and enjoying the sunset. Hell, he almost envied the man.

He tossed the envelope into the fire, absurdly grateful that the papers had nothing to do with Kacy.

Max stood at the window of his hotel room, willing Anson to drive into the parking lot. A single light cast a harsh yellow glare across the rows of cars. Where the hell was he? Max slammed his fist down on the windowsill. Pain shot up his arm. God, he hated feeling powerless.

He turned to look at the clock, surprised to see how late it was. Surely the man should have been back by now. There must have been trouble.

Max grimaced and peered out the window again. Anson was more than an employee. He was a friend. The only thing he had left now that Alex was . . .

After all this time he still couldn't bring himself to say the word. Alex had been his world. His whole world. He'd have done anything, *had done everything,* for his brother. Five minutes older, he'd always taken care of Alex. He'd felt an intense responsibility for his twin right from the beginning.

When their mother had failed them, he'd personally seen to it that Alex had everything he'd wanted. He'd schemed and struggled, always one step ahead of the law, trying to make life easy for his brother. He'd protected Alex. And ultimately he'd sacrificed his freedom for his brother.

But it had been worth it. Every minute of it.

Until that bitch came along. Something changed between them when Alex married Kirstin. He'd stopped coming to Rikers to visit. Stopped calling, writing. Max hadn't seen his brother at all the last few months of his life.

Because of her.

She'd bewitched him. Pulled him away from his own blood. Opened her legs and sucked Alex inside.

Max closed his eyes, remembering the way the little slut had rubbed her body against Braedon Roche's. Hardly the grieving widow. He ground his teeth together, clenching his fist.

She'd killed Alex. He was certain of it. Somehow she'd gotten wind of the forgery scheme and killed his brother for the money, taking away the only person Max had ever loved. Alex had been his twin. His soul. His heart.

Hatred seared through him, hot and bitter. He'd make her

pay. If it was the last thing he did, he'd make the bitch pay. But first, he had to find Anson.

Braedon couldn't sleep. His mind was too full of questions, too full of thoughts of Kacy. Crossing the room, he picked up the poker and stirred the dying embers of the fire. Flames flickered to life, and he caught a glimpse of something white caught between the peat bucket and the stones of the hearth.

He reached down and snagged the piece of paper, a photograph. Curious, he took it back to the sofa and held it in the light of the table lamp. Kacy smiled up at him, her green eyes full of laughter. His throat tightened and he felt his heart flutter. Hell, even her picture made his senses leap.

She was standing with a man, in front of a limousine. The man embraced her, his arm wrapped tightly around her. Braedon stared at the photo, his mind imagining the worst. Kacy with her lover.

He frowned, studying her paramour, realizing he recognized the face.

Caldwell Bremmerton.

What in the world was Kacy doing with a bastard like him? The man was a piranha, smelling fear and feeding on insecurity. He ate corporations for breakfast. People were just appetizers.

Braedon had only run up against him once, early in his career. But it had been enough to teach him a few things about manipulation and sheer ruthlessness. Caldwell Bremmerton had drummed Braedon into the ground and left him for so much garbage.

Braedon tensed, remembering. God, how he hated to lose. Hated it more than anything. But this had been more than just defeat. Bremmerton had enjoyed humiliating him, taken pleasure in setting him up and zeroing in for the kill.

Braedon had sworn revenge, sharpening his skills, waiting

patiently for the right opportunity. But the son of a bitch had died before he could exact vengeance. He looked back at the picture, old anger surging through him. He hated the thought of Caldwell's hands on Kacy.

His Kacy.

He blew out a breath, laughing at himself. He was actually jealous of a photograph of a dead man. Dropping the picture on the bookshelf, he turned back to the sofa, his thoughts centering on Kacy.

There were so many questions and so few answers. He no longer believed that she was in any way tied up in Alex's schemes, but something here was obviously very wrong. The events of the last few days couldn't be merely coincidence. There had to be a connection.

All he had to do was find it.

Kacy opened her eyes and looked at the display on her clock for the hundredth time. Fifteen minutes. Fifteen lousy minutes. It felt like hours. She sat up, pushing the hair out of her face, her mind working overtime. At this rate, she'd never get any sleep. The lamp cast a pale glow across the bed, shadows dancing at the edge of the light.

She was tired of being alone. She wanted Braedon, wanted him with a strength of desire she hadn't known she possessed. And he was here, a room away. All that separated them was a hallway. And a magnitude of secrets.

Her secrets.

She lay back against the pillows, careful not to disturb the sleeping dog. Maybe it was time to trust someone. Trust Braedon. Her heart cheered. Her brain revolted. There was too much at stake to make a mistake. She stared at the ceiling, watching the shadows dance across the plaster, shifting shapes fading into the night.

Maybe she could tell him some of it. The part about Alex. About the men from New York. Braedon might have contacts.

Maybe he could actually help. Do more than the police had been able to. And she didn't have to betray her father. She could trust Braedon with a little and let him help her.

She rolled over, staring at the clock again, indecision warring inside her. She'd made so many mistakes. What proof did she have that this wouldn't just be another?

None.

Trust your heart, Kacy. Her mother. The voice echoed through her head and was gone.

"Oh, Mama," she whispered. "I've tried to protect you. All these years, I've guarded your secret. And Father's. But I'm so tired of running. Tired of being alone. Tell me what to do, Mama. Tell me what to do."

Kacy waited, waited for answers that wouldn't, couldn't come. Her mother had sacrificed everything for love. Everything. And now her daughter was left to live with the consequences of that sacrifice.

Trust your heart.

She drew a deep breath and walked toward the door.

Chapter 14

SHE LOOKED LIKE an angel, standing in the doorway, the moonlight washing over her, silvering her hair. Braedon felt desire flash through him, his breath catching in his throat. She was so beautiful. And not just a surface beauty, but something deeper, something intrinsic.

She shifted from one foot to the other, looking young and uncomfortable. Braedon found himself wanting to soothe her, to erase whatever it was that haunted her.

"We need to talk." Her voice was low, trembling.

She stepped into the room, the light turning her nightgown translucent, the shadowy outline of her body sending his senses reeling. A dull but demanding ache spread through his groin and he fought the urge to pull her into his arms and show her just how much he wanted her.

Instead, he pulled air into his lungs, his brain clamping down on his need. "I'm here." The words came out a whisper, but under the circumstances he was grateful they'd come out at all.

She stopped a few feet in front of him, the coffee table between them, her fingers fumbling with the lacy edge of her gown. "There's something I think you should know." Her eyes were huge, heavy with anxiety and indecision.

He smiled, hoping to allay her fears. "Come on, sit over here." He patted the seat next to him, his hand smoothing the sheet-covered cushion.

She edged around the table, looking a lot like a guilt-ridden schoolgirl. She stopped just short of sitting, twisting her hands together, her teeth worrying her bottom lip. He reached for her hand, tugging gently until she sat down beside him. He took her other hand. "Whatever it is, we'll deal with it together."

"I think I know who's been doing this."

"This?" Her fingers trembled and he tightened his grip.

"The dog, the car, the d-dead man." Her voice shook, emotion laid raw.

He lifted a hand, smoothing back her hair, his touch seeming to calm her. "Take a deep breath."

She obeyed, sucking in a ragged breath. "Alex. It was Alex."

"Alex is dead, Kacy. We've been through this." The strain of the past few days had obviously taken a bigger toll on her than he'd realized.

"No." He opened his mouth to argue, but she held up a hand. "I know he's dead. That's not what I mean." She blew out a breath, closing her eyes. When she opened them, they were steady, clear. "When Alex and I married, I didn't know anything about him. I don't have any excuse for that. I was rebelling, trying to prove I could make my own decisions."

Braedon frowned, trying to follow the thread of her conversation. "Rebelling against what?"

Her jaw tensed. "It doesn't matter. The point is, I didn't know my husband. Looking back on it, I realize there were signs, things I should have seen." She was twisting her hands again. "But I didn't."

"I don't see—"

"I'm getting there, but I need to tell you all of it."

"All right." He sat back, watching the emotions chasing across her face.

"Most of my life I've followed the rules. I was always the kid least likely to make waves. The one who faded into the background." She stopped, lost in her past. He could almost see her remembering. "A couple years ago, I decided I'd had enough, that Kacy Macgrath was long due a little excitement. And so *Kirstin* Macgrath booked a vacation."

She stood up, crossing to stand by the window, her back to him. "I chose the Cayman Islands. An exotic place for the phoenix to rise from the ashes. It was beautiful there. Blue waves, white sand. Everything I wanted it to be." She paused, her hands gripping the windowsill. "But I was alone. And somehow it seemed tragic to start a whole new life all by myself."

The pain in her voice hung in the air, surrounding him, but he knew instinctively that if he interrupted, she'd never be able to finish.

"And then there was Alex. I met him at one of the bars on the beach. You know the kind with straw canopies and umbrellas in the drinks. He was dashing. And I never really thought I'd use that word in a sentence, much less meet someone like that." She turned around again, the ghost of a smile on her face. With a sigh, she leaned back against the window frame. "And he was charming. No one like him had ever paid attention to me before. I know it sounds foolish when I say it, but it felt so good. For the first time in my life, I felt desirable."

Her fingers stroked the front of her gown as she remembered, and Braedon wanted nothing more than to kill a man already dead.

"After that, things moved at hurricane speed. We had a lot in common. He loved art. And he was alone in the world— like me."

"He didn't have *any* family?"

She shot him a quizzical look. "No. They were all gone. He mentioned a brother once in passing. But he died, too."

Or was serving twenty to life in Rikers. He opened his mouth to tell her the truth, but stopped, realizing it would only raise questions he didn't want to answer. "So you were traveling at hurricane speed."

"Right. One minute we were dancing, the next we were in bed, and the next we were married. I felt like Cinderella at the ball." She wrapped her arms around herself. "And almost as quickly it was over. I knew I'd made a horrible mistake, trusted someone I never should have, but I thought . . . I thought he loved me."

Her gaze met his and he choked at the anguish he saw reflected there.

"But he didn't, at least not in the way a husband should love a wife." A shudder rippled through her, and her hands clutched mindlessly at her gown. "He wanted to own me. Like a possession or a prize. And he wanted to use me. To hurt me. I . . . I never knew it could be like that. . . ." She broke off, obviously unable to finish.

But Braedon could imagine. "Kacy . . ." He moved toward her, wanting to hold her, to ease her pain.

"Don't." She held up a hand to stop him. "I need to finish."

He nodded, calling on more willpower than he'd known he possessed, and sat back on the sofa, waiting.

"I kept thinking that I'd done something wrong. That the changes in Alex were my fault. I thought I could fix it. Bring back the man I'd married. Make him love me again. But before I had time to sort through it, to understand what was happening, he died."

She sat down, her back sliding along the wall until she reached the floor. "And I was left holding the bag. A very mortgaged bag. It seems my husband had a problem with money. He spent it as fast as he got it. And worse, he gambled. A lot.

"So when word got out that Alex was dead, his creditors came to me. And we're not talking bankers here." She shivered. "These men were vile, threatening me when I refused to pay them. They even broke into the house once, ransacking it." She closed her eyes, wrapping her arms around her knees. "I told the police. They looked into it but said without proof there was nothing they could do. And of course I had nothing concrete."

Her eyes flickered open and she tilted her head, staring at the ceiling. "So I tried to give them something. I sold everything I could get my hands on. The house, the furniture, even my wedding ring. But it wasn't enough."

"What about the antiques?" The question was thoughtless, but the words were out before he could take them back.

She didn't seem to notice. She was too caught up in the past. "I sold almost everything, but I couldn't part with it all."

"And the trust fund?"

"It's all tied up in investments and things. I get a monthly allowance, but the terms of the trust keep me from liquidating any of the assets. I gave them what I got, but they knew there was more, and the fact that I couldn't get it didn't seem to matter a bit." She laid her head on her knees. "Anyway, naively, I thought they'd get tired and go away, but instead, it was like sharks smelling blood. They circled closer and closer, taking the little I had to offer and then demanding more, threatening to kill me—or do worse."

Another shudder racked her body, and Braedon waited, holding his breath.

"Until I couldn't take it anymore. So I ran away. Ditched Kirstin once and for all. Became Kacy again. I just wanted to pretend like it had never happened." She lifted her head, her eyes pleading with his for understanding.

He ran his hand through his hair, trying to let go of the image of Alex with Kacy. Alex seducing her. Alex hurting her. Alex destroying her. He clenched a fist.

The bloody bastard.

"So you think these loan sharks are the ones that are after you now?"

"I don't know. In some ways it makes absolutely no sense, but it's the only answer I can come up with."

"Kacy, it doesn't make sense that they'd wait two years, and then start to hunt you down again. There has to be something else."

She looked away, staring at the floor. "If . . . if there is, I don't know what it is."

His heart cried out for him to tell her the truth. To tell her that he suspected Alex was involved in far more than living the high life. But he had no proof. Everything was a blasted dead end. And there was nothing to connect the incidents over the last few days with the forgeries. Nothing except instinct.

And the truth was, if he told her about his suspicions, he'd have to tell her who he was. And he wasn't ready for that. She'd see it as a betrayal. And just at the moment she didn't need more treachery. He'd tell her. But first he needed time to think. To figure out what to do next.

Kacy's face was pressed against her knees, her muffled sobs filling the room. And his heart threatened to break in two.

She still had secrets. But, hell, so did he. And somewhere inside him, he knew that whatever it was she was still hiding, it had nothing to do with Alex and everything to do with Kacy. The part of her Fin said she kept locked away.

He knew, too, that he could wait, *would wait,* until she was ready to tell him. Tomorrow he'd talk to Matt. His friend would help him figure out what to do. But right now, he needed to hold her, to feel her heart beating next to his. To let her know that she was desirable just as she was. As Kacy.

He walked over to her and held out his hand. "Come here."

She looked up at him for a long moment, tears still glistening in her eyes, and then, with a breath of a sigh, she took his hand and let him pull her into his arms.

All thoughts of mobsters, danger, and threats flew out of her head as his arms closed around her. For the moment, it was enough that he was holding her. She tipped back her head, her lips parted, waiting for his kiss. And when his lips met hers, she opened her mouth, drinking him in like a sun-parched sojourner lost in the Sahara. She wanted more—so much more. And she was positive that without it, she would perish.

Her body burned for him, the fire licking at her, building deep inside until she thought it might incinerate her. His tongue traced the line of her teeth, sending tiny shivers of desire coursing through her. God, how she wanted this man.

She twined her fingers into his hair, drawing him closer, meeting his tongue, swirling around it, tasting the essence of him. The kiss deepened and she felt as if he were touching her deep inside. Sensations exploded inside her, his mouth branding her, making her his with nothing more than a kiss.

But she knew there was more, and she wanted it with every fiber of her being. She shifted, meeting his gaze. His eyes were dark, the blue almost black. The flecks of gold had enlarged, becoming swirls, twirling in the murky depths of his pupils.

"You're sure?" His voice was hoarse, raspy. It slid across her skin as if it were a tangible thing.

She slid her nightgown off her shoulders and let it drop to the floor, her eyes never leaving his.

His intake of breath was audible and he reached out, skimming a palm along the contours of her shoulder and breast, his touch so light, she almost couldn't feel it. With a sigh, she closed her eyes and leaned forward, forcing the pressure, the touch, to deepen. His fingers fluttered slightly and then began to massage, tracing a languorous path back to her shoulder, stopping to caress each of her breasts.

She reached for the buttons on his shirt, fumbling to undo them, finally tugging until they popped away. He shrugged out of the shirt, standing before her, awaiting her pleasure. With a trembling finger, she traced the rugged planes of his chest, reveling in the contrast between the hard muscle and the soft curls of chocolate colored hair.

Bending her head, she substituted tongue for finger, tasting him. His flat nipple hardened under the heat of her tongue and she felt a surge of pleasure, and something else—power.

He groaned, the sound rippling through her, adding to her desire. He pulled her head back, his lips finding hers, his kiss full of promise. She pressed against him, the warmth of his chest searing through her.

His hand found her nipple, and she bit back a moan when he rubbed it between his thumb and forefinger.

"No, don't hold back. Let me hear you, Kacy. I want to know that I'm pleasing you." His whisper tickled her neck, his warm breath teasing her with its touch.

He lowered his head and took her breast into his mouth. Her nipple hardened to a throbbing bud and she sighed, her voice trembling with passion. He suckled harder, rolling the nipple between his teeth, his other hand massaging its partner, the flame inside her building in intensity until she wasn't certain she could survive it, wasn't sure anything could be as wonderful as the feel of his mouth on her breasts.

His hand slid downward, stroking and teasing her as it dipped lower and lower, his mouth still caressing her nipple. Something deep within her tightened, an ache spreading through her, demanding release.

His fingers circled the secret place at the junction of her thighs, and then moved lower to the smooth skin of her legs. She groaned and pushed against him, wanting him inside her.

He lifted his head, a hint of laughter in his eyes. "Patience, my love, patience." His words soothed her, and she drank them in much as she had his touch. His lips found hers and his tongue plunged deep into her mouth, just as his finger finally found its way to her center. She cried out in ecstasy, and he swallowed the sound, the action somehow more intimate than anything they had done.

His finger and tongue began to move in tandem. In and out, in and out, caressing, withdrawing, caressing, withdrawing, until she was balanced on a precipice of light and energy, waiting to explode.

She flung back her head, eyes open wide, waiting for the moment she knew would take her to heaven. But he stopped, withdrawing his hand and his mouth, leaving her stranded, alone.

"Wait. Not yet. I want to see you. Feel you. I want to watch you."

She shivered at the passion in his voice as he lifted her into his arms, laying her on the rug by the fire. With a minimum of effort, he shed the rest of his clothes and she gasped at the sheer size of him, again feeling the fleeting moment of power, knowing that she was the reason for his arousal.

He knelt at her feet and, with gentle hands, spread her legs, shifting so that he knelt between them. His eyes met hers, his lids low, heavy with passion, and with a crooked smile he bent his head and blew softly on the tender nub that marked the center of her passion. She squirmed, sensations rocking through her, and he placed his hands, hot and heavy, on her thighs, holding her still.

A thousand thoughts swirled through her head, the intimacy making her embarrassed. She shifted again, nervously.

His hold tightened. "Let me love you, Kacy. Let me show you how beautiful you are."

Biting her bottom lip, wanting him to touch her *there* more than she could possibly admit, she nodded. Again he smiled, and this time it reached to her soul. He dipped his head again, his breath caressing her an instant before his tongue found her. She bucked against him, unable to control her body's reaction to his touch. His dark hair fanned out against her skin, caressing her thighs as his mouth caressed her very essence.

His tongue flicked lightly across her, and she shivered with the deliciousness of his touch. Then his tongue tightened and drove into her, a prelude of things she knew would follow.

Again and again he stroked her, driving her higher and higher. Her hands tangled into his hair, pushing him deeper and deeper, until the world spun out of control, light splintering into shattered fragments, and she hit the sun, only to fall, swirling into the light.

Closer and closer she came to the heat, certain it would consume her, destroy her, but then, suddenly, through the blinding light, she felt his heat surround her, his arms holding her, and she knew she was safe.

It was almost enough to taste her, to know she'd been fulfilled.

Almost.

Who was he kidding? He ached with need for her. He had wanted to show her how beautiful he thought she was, to see the expression on her face when he brought her to the edge and sent her flying. But he knew that it wasn't enough.

He needed more.

He needed to possess her, needed it with every fiber of his being.

A part of him—the only part still thinking rationally—cautioned again that he should confess everything to her, build this newfound trust on reality. But her body burned against him and he rationalized that there would be time to talk later. Now was a time for passion.

He felt her stir against him and tilted his head so that he could see her eyes. They were a dark, storm-tossed green. He felt his body tighten with anticipation.

She grinned slowly and reached for him, closing her tiny hand around his heat. He bit back a groan, and her smile widened. "I want to hear you, Braedon. See your passion." Her words echoed his, but there was no mockery, only desire—blazing hot desire.

She was magnificent. "I want *you*," she whispered against his lips.

"I want you, too." And he did. More than he'd ever wanted anything in his life.

He pulled away, his eyes surveying the room, settling on a mahogany lyre-back chair. An antique. A moment waiting to happen. He smiled and rose, offering a hand to pull her to her feet. They stood for a moment, eyes devouring the other. And then, with a tug, he pulled her toward the chair.

Her eyes widened as he sat and patted his lap, his manhood turgid against his stomach. Then understanding dawned, and she licked her lips, the motion threatening to undo him. She started to straddle him, but he smiled, turning her so that she faced away from him. She looked over her shoulder, a question in her eyes, but his smile widened into a grin.

"Trust me." The irony of his words mocked him, his heart calling for a reality check, but he pushed the thought aside. Tomorrow. Time enough for truth tomorrow.

Her lips quirked into an answering smile and she turned away from him, her beautiful buttocks nestled against his hardness. She squirmed into place and he almost lost it. She was so hot, so sweet.

Placing his hands on her hips, he raised her, and, with a little moan, she impaled herself on him, encasing him in moist, silky heat. He groaned, trying to hold onto his control. She leaned against him, her back to his chest, and his hands drifted upward, circling her breasts, his nostrils full of the sweet floral scent of her silky hair.

God, he loved this woman.

The thought slammed into him, leaving absolutely no room for discussion. With a sigh of pure need, she shifted, rising and then slowly, slowly, sliding down.

Leaning forward, kissing her neck, he reveled in the feel of her, surrounding him, stroking him. And then, suddenly, she was moving, with a steady motion that set his soul on fire. He released her breasts, his hands settling on her hips, guiding her, urging her.

The pace grew frenzied and he gripped her, feeling her body sliding against his. Deeper, deeper, faster, faster, until he exploded in a fury of light and color. From far away he heard his name and answered.

Kacy.

Kacy.

She filled him, surrounded him, until there was no beginning, no end. They were one, spinning toward the stars. And he danced with her, holding tight as the intensity grew, threatening to burn him alive, and knew that at last, he'd found love.

Chapter 15

THE SOFT PATTER of rain against the window pulled Kacy from sleep. She stretched contentedly, feeling like a cat. Braedon shifted in his sleep, one leg thrown across her possessively. She smiled, luxuriating under the heavy warmth, the attachment running deeper than skin.

She turned her head to look at him. His face was softer in sleep, the harsh lines of life washed away. Still, it was a strong face. His chin was shadowed with the bristle of the beginnings of a beard, the same sooty brown as his hair. She reached out and trailed a finger along the line of his jaw.

Blue eyes flickered open, and his mouth curved into a slow smile. "I was dreaming about you." His words whispered across her ear.

"You were?"

He nodded, his gaze locking with hers. "Shall I tell you what happened?" There was laughter in his voice, and a raspy thread of passion.

"No," she sighed, answering his smile with hers. "I think I'd just like to imagine it." There was something wonderfully intimate about lying here, just being together.

He rolled onto his side, propping his head on his hand, his look turning serious. "Kacy, we really need to talk about all that's happened."

She laid a finger against his lips, shaking her head. "Not

157

now. There'll be time enough for that tomorrow. Right now, I just want to be here—with you. I want to feel like this forever."

"Like what?"

She tried to find words for her feelings. "Like we're safe within a magic circle. Like as long as we're together, nothing bad can ever happen."

He tucked a strand of hair behind her ear, the touch of his fingers sending an arc of fire shooting through her. "What if there is no such thing as a magic circle, Kacy?"

"There has to be. Otherwise there's really no sense in living, is there? I mean, that's got to be what it's all about. Finding that secret place. A safe harbor. Somewhere where you can always know you'll be loved and accepted."

He reached over to trace the curve of her lip, his touch gentle, almost reverent. She searched his eyes, waiting for his response. "I've been so busy building an empire, I think that I've forgotten some of the things that are most important in life. The magic circle you were talking about."

"It's easy to do. We get lost in our ambitions and forget the things that matter most."

"Well, I, for one, am definitely guilty of that. But somehow, here with you, I almost feel like it isn't too late."

"It's never too late for anything, Braedon. You just have to want it badly enough."

"And if I want you?"

She sucked in a breath, her heart beating a staccato rhythm against her side. "Then I suppose you need to step into the circle." She held out her hand, waiting, terrified of the step she was taking, yet certain it was where she wanted to be— needed to be. Certain, too, that he belonged here, with her. That somehow she had something he needed, too. And that, together, they would be two halves making a whole.

His fingers closed tightly around hers as he pulled her gently into his arms. "Let me be your safe harbor, Kacy."

She sighed and moved against him. "I think that you already are."

Their lips touched and the familiar sensation began to build, their bodies fitting together like pieces of an intricate jigsaw puzzle. Her breath caught in her throat at the fire in his eyes. There was desire there, and something more.

She swallowed, touched by the raw emotion reflected in his gaze. She was hesitant to put a name to it, but hope flashed inside her and, for a moment, she dared to believe that this meant as much to him as it did to her.

Sparks flew between them and she pushed against him, wanting the contact, amazed at the intensity of her need. He smiled and rolled on top of her, bracing his arms on either side of her. She met his gaze, a tiny smile curling the corners of her lips, her eyes locking with his, her heart laid bare.

She reached over, fumbling for the switch on the lamp, not wanting to break the contact.

His hand covered hers. "I thought you were afraid of the dark."

She smiled, flipping the switch and settling back into the warmth of his arms. "Not when I'm with you."

Enrico Gienelli couldn't sleep. He paced the worn carpet in front of the fireplace, wondering if he'd ever feel warm again. Mrs. Macnamara's house was like ice. Despite constant prodding, his fire merely smoked, the glowing coals mocking him, refusing to put off any real warmth.

He'd tried the bed, buried in blankets, but his mind was whirling and his thoughts only added to his discomfort. So now he was reduced to pacing, wrapped like a mummy in a shroud of worn blankets.

Ireland was a godforsaken wilderness. Give him Italy any day. Specifically Milan, with its elegance and culture. His mind turned to azure skies, crimson wines, succulent pasta, and beautiful women. For a dago from the Bronx, he'd certainly come a long way.

He shivered. Reality returning.

At least there was one bright spot in this ever darkening nightmare.

Kacy Macgrath. A beckoning pool of innocence on a canvas of rotting black. There had to be a way to save her—protect her from barracudas like Max Madison and Braedon Roche.

He sat down in a chair, suddenly feeling dizzy. He pulled the blankets closer, wondering if he had the courage to be a hero. Probably not. He was too old. To much a product of Madison's world.

His thoughts turned to Max. The man was a loose cannon. He'd always been a bit of a wild card, but his need to protect his brother had kept him grounded. Now, without Alex as an anchor, Max was adrift in anger and nothing would stop him from exacting revenge. Rico sighed. No matter who got hurt in the process.

Rico thought about the brothers, wondering for the millionth time why he'd gotten involved with them. There had been something unnatural about their relationship. Something almost parasitic.

Max had protected Alex to the point of controlling the man. Alex had been little more than an amiable puppet. A mouthpiece for his brother. If Max said jump, then Alex would ask how high. Rico stroked his moustache. And yet that didn't quite characterize it either.

There had been something more to Alex, a stillness, a deadness. As though he'd always worn a mask. At least with Max, what one saw, one got. But with Alex, there had always been a feeling of uncertainty. As if the charming shell hid something deeper, more dangerous.

Rico shook his head at his wild imaginings. Alex Madison

was dead. He posed no threat to Rico now. It was Max he had to worry about. Max and that goon of his. Anson.

Rico considered calling in long-owed favors to dispose of his problems, but dismissed the idea. Killing was messy, and no matter the wise guy, there was always the chance the hit would be traced. Besides, a favor called in would put him back in the middle of a world he'd sooner forget.

One thing people could say about Enrico Gienelli, or at least about Eduardo Baucomo, he learned from his mistakes. No, the best thing to do with Max was to watch him and wait for the opportunity to stop him. Something short of violence, hopefully.

Rico shrugged philosophically. In the past he'd always managed to land on his feet, and, one way or the other, he'd find a way to handle his old cellmate.

In the meantime, he had to deal with Roche. In some ways Roche made men like Max and Alex seem like cartoon characters. Roche was a predator. Pure and simple. Oh, he hid it behind the legitimacy of business, but he was still ruthless. What he wanted he simply took and used it until he had drained everything of value from it.

Rico hadn't ever dealt personally with the man, but he knew the type. Knew it intimately. A man like Roche had taken his life away. Leaving him to rot in jail for something he hadn't done.

Bitterness flooded his mouth, the taste sharp and vile. He swallowed, pushing the memories down. The past was over.

Dead, and buried deep.

But he couldn't, wouldn't let Kacy Macgrath become Roche's latest victim. *He* would protect her. *He* would save her.

And with what he knew—*il pezzo di tórta*. He smiled, translating the thought into English. It would be a piece of cake.

"Oh, my God, the professor." Kacy sat up straight, the sheet clutched in her hand.

Cold air wafted across his body, and Braedon shivered, reaching to pull her back to him, delighting in her warmth. "You're not going anywhere." He pulled her head down, brushing his lips across hers.

"Wait." She pushed back, laughing, straddling him, her hair cascading around her shoulders. "I'm serious. The professor will be here in less than an hour. I can hardly meet him at the door like this." She gestured, the movement emphasizing her lack of clothing.

He ran his hands across the smooth skin of her belly. "See that you don't. I'm not a sharing kind of man."

She bent to kiss him, her hair curtaining their heads in a fragrant cloud of silk. Twining his fingers in the soft strands, he pulled her closer, wanting somehow to lock her inside him until he was certain she was safe.

She met his passion with her own, kissing him until he felt dizzy with need. Then with a laugh she was up and gone, the physical separation almost painful for him.

He reached for her, and she gave him her hand. He caressed it with his thumb, trying not to pull her to him again. "Don't you want me?" He kept his voice playful, but the question was serious.

Her gaze stroked him, tracing the lines of his body, touching him as surely as if she had used her hands. "Make no mistake, Braedon Roche." Her voice was hoarse with unspent passion. "I want you." She blew out a breath, breaking the intensity of the moment. "But right now, I need a shower."

"With me?"

"I suppose that could be arranged." She smiled impishly and dashed toward the bathroom.

He was on his feet and had her in his arms in an instant, carrying her toward the bathroom.

God, he loved this woman.

* * *

Braedon sat on the bed, watching as she brushed her hair, the movements smooth and serene. It felt simultaneously soothing and sensuous. She touched him on so many different levels. "Kacy. We need to talk."

She frowned at the tone of his voice, coming to sit by him, her eyes questioning.

"I . . ." He faltered. Unsure of where to begin, only knowing that he needed to tell her the truth. The whole truth. This thing between them was too important to be based on lies. Well, not lies exactly, omissions of truth. He ran a hand through his hair, for the first time in a long time at a complete loss for words.

"Braedon?" She took his hand, the concern in her voice almost undoing him.

"There are just some things I need to tell you. About Alex and—"

"The things I told you about last night," she cut him off, her grip tightening on his hand. "I probably shouldn't have said anything. I had no right to dump my problems on you. In fact, I shouldn't have involved you at all. It's just that I wanted to be completely honest." She met his gaze, her green eyes searching his. He prayed she couldn't see his guilt.

"Kacy, no, that's not it. I want you to share things with me. I can help."

Hope blossomed in her eyes as she smiled.

He held up a hand. "But there are some things you need to know. Things I should have told you from the beginning."

"Braedon, whatever it is, I'm sure we can deal with it together."

He hoped so, oh, dear God, he hoped so.

She laid a hand on his face, her eyes filled with compassion and something else. Something he was afraid to put a name to for fear he was wrong.

"So what is it you need to tell me?" She sat back, waiting, with no idea at all the bombshell he was about to drop.

He blew out a breath. But it had to be done. If they were to have any chance at all, it had to be done. "I'm—"

The doorbell rang, its incessant buzzing cutting into his words.

Kacy jumped and then smiled. "The professor." She glanced over at the clock. "Right on time." She grinned and leaned over to kiss him, her touch sending shivers of delight coursing through him, a delicate contrast to the dread filling his heart.

The doorbell rang again.

"Looks like it's your turn to be saved by the bell." She rose and headed for the hallway.

"Kacy?"

She turned, her hand on the doorframe.

"We'll finish this later. Okay?"

She smiled, the action seeming to light the whole room. Hell, his whole life.

"Fine. But right now, I have to work. Which means you need to go."

He walked with her to the door, watching as she pulled it open, greeting the little Italian as if they were old friends.

"Professor." He forced a note of cordiality into his voice. It wasn't that he really had anything against the man. It was just hard to be certain who to trust.

"Signore Roche." The man gave a dapper bow.

Braedon almost expected him to click his heels together and pull out a monocle. The man seemed to be harmless enough and it was obvious he was crazy about Kacy. "I was just going."

The professor nodded politely, turning his attention back to Kacy, taking her hand and lifting it to his lips. "It seems I am always interrupting the two of you, no?"

Braedon's blood pressure increased as he watched the man's lips linger on her skin. He forced himself to remain calm. He couldn't judge a man's character based on his own jealous reactions. Maybe Matt would have something. Or not—which, frankly, would be even better. In the meantime, he needed to withhold judgment. Kacy liked the old geezer.

Like Bremmerton, the voice in his head whispered.

Braedon clamped down on his rising emotions. He prided himself on being clearheaded and in control, no matter how desperate things got. This situation was no different, and imagining rivals where there were none was ridiculous.

Baucomo was watching him with amusement, as if he could read his thoughts. Braedon shrugged and the little man turned back to Kacy. "I'll wait in your studio, my dear. Good day, Signore Roche." He inclined his head politely and withdrew.

Braedon placed both hands on Kacy's shoulders. "Look, I know you need to work and I have some things I need to tend to, but I'll be back as soon as I can. I want you to wait here with the professor until then. It's not safe for you to be wandering around on your own."

"I'm a big girl, Braedon. I can take care of myself."

He looked into her eyes, willing her to listen to him. "Then do it for me."

"Fine."

"Promise me, Kacy."

"All right, I promise. I'll stay right here."

"With the professor."

She sighed. "With the professor. Now go."

He bent to kiss her, his mouth lingering over her sweetness. Finally, breathless, he pulled away, satisfied to see that her breathing was equally ragged. They stood for a moment lost in each other's gaze, and then she pushed him away.

"*Go.* I'll be here when you get back."

"And we'll talk."

"And we'll talk," she repeated with a thread of exasperation in her voice.

He stepped onto the stoop, the door clicking shut behind him. Alone, he looked into the gray Irish mist, praying that when he told her who he really was, she'd understand what he'd done and forgive him.

Chapter 16

"I LIKE WHAT you've been doing." Rico examined the miniature with the magnifier, admiring her work. The scope of her talent was amazing. The hat had been restored to its full glory, the colors vivid and crisp, but still a perfect part of the old keepsake.

Kacy leaned back so that he could see better. "I'm not completely happy with the left-hand corner." She shifted in her chair and they looked at the little painting together. "I'm tempted to start over."

Rico frowned, concentrating on the blue velvet drape in the background. "Well, I see what you mean, but I think that you've done the best you can. The canvas is warped slightly and it's not like we're dealing with a true masterpiece." He stepped back to take in the painting as a whole. "I think you've accomplished what the owner requested."

Kacy bit her upper lip, still studying the miniature. "Maybe, but I'm still not totally happy with it. I'll wait until it dries before making the final decision, and then I'll start on the dress."

Bits of paint had flaked away from the bodice the woman wore, the pale green fading into the pigment of her skin. He looked back at the work she'd already completed. It was meticulously restored. Yet she wanted more.

She wanted it to be perfect. Even better than the original.

Her instincts were solid and, in art, that was everything. He smiled at her. She was an amazing woman.

Stroking his moustache, he pulled his thoughts back to the painting. "I'm sure it will look marvelous when you finish. Have you had time to look at the other one?"

"No." Kacy ran a hand through her hair and Rico noticed for the first time how tired she looked. "I'm afraid there was a little excitement here last night."

Rico clenched his teeth. *Max.* He forced himself to relax and smile. "Tell me what happened."

"Sure. How about a cup of tea? I could use a break." She stretched and stood up, turning off the lamp over the drafting table.

"That would be lovely." He followed her into the kitchen, watching as she plugged in the kettle, wanting to shake her into telling him what happened, knowing that he couldn't. She reached to a shelf above the sink, brought down the tea tin, and began to struggle to open it, a perfect reflection of his growing impatience. "Here, let me." He took the tin from her and, using a spoon, popped the top off. "Why don't you let me get the tea? You sit and tell me what happened last night."

She smiled gratefully and sank into a chair. "I'm not quite sure where to start."

He placed two mugs on the table, along with the cream and sugar. "Well, the beginning is always a good place." The kettle began to wail and he turned it off, pouring the boiling water into the pot to steep.

"True enough." She watched as he set the teapot on the table. "There are cookies in the breadbox." She nodded toward the red and white metal box.

An antiquity these days. His mother had owned one. Hers had been tin. He smiled at the memory, opening the packet and spreading the shortbread on a plate. "Here we are. All settled." He poured the tea and handed her a steaming mug. "So tell the professor everything." He leaned back into his chair, biting into one of the buttery cookies, trying to hang on to his composure.

"Well, the long and short of it is that there was a dead man on my stairs last night."

He almost spit out the cookie. "I beg your pardon?"

She smiled, but he noticed it didn't quite reach her eyes. "I'm sorry, that was a rather brutal way to put it. I guess I've had time to get used to the idea." She shivered delicately. "Or as used to it as one can get." She took a sip of tea. "It was an accident. He fell."

"Fell?" Rico's mind was reeling, wondering who exactly had fallen. Anson probably. Although it would certainly be handy if it were Max.

"Yes. The police think he was searching for something, and when he was coming down the stairs, he tripped and fell. Sort of an open and shut case."

"Any idea who he was?"

"No, that's the awful part, aside from the fact that he managed to kill himself in my home."

He stared at her, amazed at her strength. He'd underestimated her. She looked so fragile, but evidently there was steel underneath. All the better, though. It would make what he had to tell her easier, but first, he needed to know more about the dead man. "Did he take anything?"

"No. He tore the place up pretty badly. He . . . he ruined the Monet." Her carefully schooled features slipped a little and Rico had a glimpse of real pain. Interesting. So the steel was an act, albeit a very convincing one. His admiration for her rose a notch.

He reached across the table, covering her hand with his. "I know how much you loved it."

She nodded, her mouth thinning to a narrow line. "I think part of me died with that painting."

"I understand." The words were inadequate, but true.

"I know you do. Only another artist could really comprehend what it's like to lose something you've put heart and soul into. Even if it was only a copy."

Rico squeezed her hand and then released it. "Especially if it was a copy."

She smiled weakly. "I'm sorry. It's just been a bit much to take in."

"Of course it has. Despite all the talk about violence on TV anesthetizing us to this sort of thing, at the end of the day, there is really no comparison to the real thing. Violent death, even an accident, is horrifying, and especially in the sanctity of one's own home."

She nodded, holding her mug with both hands. "You sound like you're speaking from personal experience."

"I suppose in a way, I am. When I was a young boy, I saw someone gunned down."

She looked up, startled. "In Italy?"

"No, in New York."

"That must have been terrible for you."

"At the time it was overwhelming. But now, it seems like something that happened in someone else's life." He took another bite of shortbread. "So, tell me, are the police looking for your intruder's identity?"

"They said they would, but I didn't get the feeling it was going to be a priority. The man managed to kill himself, after all. And from what I can tell, although loads of things were destroyed, nothing was taken." She shrugged almost casually, and he'd have bought it, except that her knuckles whitened as she tightened her death grip on the mug. She cared a great deal more than she was letting on. "I guess they figure he's paid his debt, so to speak."

"What did he look like?" The second the words were out of his mouth, he regretted them. He hadn't meant to sound so callous.

She set down the cup, studying her hands as if she didn't know what to do with them. "I can't say really. There was . . . um . . , a lot of blood. The only thing that sticks out in my mind is all the blood drying on his balding head."

Anson. The man sounded like Anson. "*Dolce Maria.* What was I thinking? Kacy, I'm sorry. It was an insensitive question. I am a stupid old man."

"No. You're not. It's just that I can still see him there." Her eyes widened, all semblance of her mask gone. "If Braedon hadn't been here, I don't know what I would have done."

Roche. She was giving him an opening, but now that the time had come, Rico was having regrets. She'd already been hurt so much. And she obviously trusted Roche. Still, in the end, this was best for her. He squared his shoulders. "I'm glad he was here for you. Although I have to admit I was a little surprised to find him in Lindoon."

"You know Braedon?" She looked confused now and somehow even more vulnerable.

Santa Maria. What was he doing?

Braedon stood in the phone box, watching the rain run down the glass window, listening to the clicking as the long-distance line connected. Whatever answers Matt had, he needed them right now. He needed the reassurance that Kacy was safe with the professor, and even more, he needed to figure out if the events of the last few days were in any way tied into the forgeries.

"Hello." The voice on the other end was groggy.

"Matt? It's Braedon."

"Braedon?" There was a pause. Braedon could hear Matt fumbling with the phone. "I'm here." This was followed by a loud yawn. "Do you have any idea what time it is here?"

Braedon glanced at his watch. "I figure it's around five o'clock."

"In the morning," came the grumbling reply.

"I'm sorry. But I need some information."

"Well, I got what you wanted on the Italian guy."

"Anything interesting?"

"For the most part he seems to be exactly what you thought he was. A low-level art professor from Milan. He's developing a reputation in art history, but nothing high profile." There was a pause and some knocking noises as Matt fumbled with the phone. "Sorry, just trying to get comfortable."

"Baucomo?" Braedon tried to keep his impatience out of his voice.

"Right. He's been at the university in Milan for a couple of years."

"And before that?"

"Well, that's where it gets interesting. There isn't anything on him before his appearance in Milan. There's paperwork, but nothing to support it."

"So you think Baucomo is a phony?"

"Well, the man appears to know art. That's not something you can fake. But the name is certainly suspect."

"Any leads on who he was?"

"Yeah, maybe. There was a punk named Enrico Gienelli. Got sent to Rikers on some bogus racketeering charges. Looks like the Feds were hoping the kid would roll."

"And he didn't?"

"Nope. Served his full time."

"So what's the connection?"

"Well, like I said, nothing concrete—yet. But the physical descriptions match. And it seems Enrico disappeared right after he got out of Rikers. Not that I blame him. His New York connections would send anyone running for the home country."

"You're talking the Mafia."

"Yeah. The man was well connected, but they didn't exactly treat him as family, if you know what I mean."

Braedon frowned, trying to make the information fit somehow with what he knew about the forgeries. It seemed totally unrelated. Hell, it probably was. "Any connection to Solais?"

"None that I can find, but I'm not through looking."

"Good. I want the information, if there is any, as soon as you find it. Call the pub, and if I'm not there, tell Fin to find me."

Matt stifled another yawn. "You got it. Anything else?"

"Yes. It's probably nothing. Just a long shot. But I need to know if Max Madison is still in prison."

"The brother?"

"Yeah."

"You think there's a connection?" He could hear the frown in his friend's voice.

"I honestly don't know. But Kacy Macgrath wasn't involved, and I'm still convinced that Alex couldn't handle it by himself."

"But Madison's incarceration doesn't exactly make him a likely suspect."

"I know. I said it was a long shot. But just at the moment, that's about all I've got."

Matt whistled into the receiver, long and low. "So what makes you think the girl's in the clear?"

Braedon paused, trying to decide how much to say.

"Like that, is it?" Matt had always been too damn good at reading his mind.

"It isn't like anything, Matt. She just wasn't involved."

"And you're not going to tell me anything else, are you?"

"Nope." He smiled, picturing the frustration on Matt's face. "Just get me the information."

"Right. Can I go back to sleep now?" he grumbled, his voice full of laughter.

"Only after you find out about Max."

"That serious." Matt sobered.

"Could be a matter of life and death."

"Jesus, Braedon, what have you gotten into?"

"Nothing I can't handle."

"All right, but watch your back, my friend."

"I will." Braedon replaced the receiver and hoped to hell he *could* handle it. He had the feeling things were going to get a lot worse before they got better.

"Forgive me, Professor, but I'm not following what you're saying." Kacy felt her pulse rate accelerating. The professor looked so kind and concerned.

"I recognized Signore Roche the first day I saw him."

"That's not surprising. He's a well-known businessman." She hated to sound like she was defending him, but she couldn't help herself.

"Well, yes. But then of course you would know that. I'm sure you are old acquaintances."

Now she was really confused. "I'm afraid I don't understand. I just met him. In Fin's pub. He's here to see the sights."

"Yes. You mentioned that. The forts, wasn't it? But now I am confused." He frowned at her, his eyebrows drawing together to form a straight line. "Surely you are pulling my leg about not knowing him."

"No."

The professor shot her a bewildered look, his face awash in confusion. "But with your connection—"

"My connection?" she interrupted impatiently.

The little man sighed and reached for her hand. "I have obviously misspoken. Please accept my apologies. I just assumed that you knew him."

She shook her head, feeling more frustrated by the second. "Why would I know him?"

The professor squeezed her hand. "Because of your husband."

She jerked her hand away, stiffening. "You know my husband?"

"But of course. I am only a small fish, but the pond is not so big." He shrugged. "And Solais is an important gallery."

She ran both hands through her hair. "I don't understand what any of this has to do with Braedon."

"I'm getting to that." His eyes were sympathetic and she shivered, wondering what it was he had to tell her. "Braedon Roche dabbles in many businesses."

She sucked in a breath, waiting, her brain whirling. She'd recognized his name. Recognized it when she'd first heard it. But she'd dismissed it, assuming she'd seen it in a magazine or something. It tantalized her now, the exact nature of the connection remaining stubbornly out of reach.

"One of those is a string of art galleries," the professor continued, his face still reflecting confusion mixed with concern. "High profile galleries." The little man sat back, waiting.

She choked on a breath, trying to inhale before exhaling, the memory coming suddenly clear. "Solais?" She heard Alex's voice tossing off some comment about his boss. *His boss.* Braedon Roche.

Oh, God.

A picture of Braedon holding her husband's photograph flashed through her mind, pretending he didn't know who Alex was.

He'd lied.

Her stomach sank to somewhere around her knees and she stared at the professor, willing him to take the words back, knowing that he couldn't, that he was speaking the truth. "Do you know why he's here?"

"Because he believes your husband stole something from him."

Pain ripped through her, tearing her in two, threatening to shatter her. "What?" The words came out a tortured whisper.

"I thought you knew. And now I have, how do you say, muddied the waters? *Dolce Marie,* I wish I had never spoken." He looked so stricken she almost wanted to comfort him. *Almost.*

Braedon had lied to her. Used her. The words kept spinning around in her head. Taunting her. Threatening to tear her apart.

Drawing a deep breath, she reached inside herself and pushed the pain away. Squaring her shoulders, she met the professor's concerned gaze. "Tell me all of it."

"Well." His hand fluttered through the air. "I do not know that much. Only the rumors."

She waited, her gaze unflinching.

He sighed. "Very well. A month or so ago, a forgery surfaced, a very good forgery. The painting had been bought several years before—at Solais in New York. The authorities seemed to think the switch had occurred there. Once word got out, other forgeries began to surface. And each of them had been sold from the gallery in New York." He paused.

She bit her bottom lip. "Do they know who was responsible?"

"There was an audit of course, but the records were clean. For a time the police suspected Roche."

"But they cleared him." She was surprised how relieved she felt.

"Yes. The files are still open, but—" He gave a Teutonic shrug. "—it is only art, not rape or murder, so for all practical purposes, the case is considered closed."

"But not for Braedon." She knew it as surely as she knew her name. He'd never let it rest until he had uncovered the traitor. Her eyes widened as realization struck her. "He thinks Alex did it."

Again the professor shrugged. "It would seem possible."

Pain tore through her, its sting razor sharp. "And he thinks I was part of it. That's why he didn't tell me who he was."

"Kacy, I'm sorry."

She squared her shoulders, shaking her head slowly. "No. No, you were right to tell me." She stopped, her mind spinning with the implications of what she'd just learned. "You don't believe . . ."

"That you were involved? No, my dear, I do not."

"A-and Alex?"

"I cannot say. I did not know your husband. But if he were involved, it would seem the secret died with him."

"How did you know all of this?" She shot him a suspicious look.

"I'm afraid it's common knowledge in art circles. I assumed you knew it, too."

Kacy shook her head. "No. But I live a rather isolated life." She should have known there was something more to Braedon. Something beyond Irish forts and deep blue eyes. He knew Alex. Suspected him of stealing artwork. And he suspected her.

"I cannot tell you how sorry I am. I feel responsible." The little man looked ready to cry.

She laid a hand on his arm. "You couldn't have known. Of course you would have assumed that I knew him."

"What will you do?"

"I don't know. But I intend to get to the bottom of this. And until I do, I won't let him near me. The bastard. I trusted him. I lo—" She bit off the word. There was no need to tell the professor exactly how foolish she'd been.

"Let me make you some more tea." The professor picked up the pot.

"No. I think I need some time alone." She met his sympathetic gaze. "Would you mind?"

The little Italian frowned, putting the teapot back on the table. "I don't like leaving you here on your own."

"I'll be fine. I have Mac. And besides, I'm well aware now who my enemy is."

"All right then, if you're sure?" He still looked hesitant.

Kacy fought the sudden need to scream at him to leave. No sense murdering the messenger. "Please, just go."

"I'll call and check on you. And we'll meet again to-morrow at our usual time?"

"That'll be fine." The words sounded so normal. She al-most laughed. Everything had fallen apart and still the world went right on.

The professor stopped at the kitchen door for a last look. "Kacy, I'm so sorry."

"I know. But it's not your fault. You're not the one who lied to me."

He flinched. Or maybe she imagined it. "Take care of your-self, child. Until tomorrow."

She nodded, watching as he left the room. A minute later she heard the front door shut. With concerted willpower, she stood up, forcing her legs to move one in front of the other. Her hand was trembling and her stomach churning. She knew from past experience that the rest of her body would soon follow suit. She needed to lock the front door first.

Mac rubbed against her side, comforting her, sensing her turmoil. Together they walked into the hallway and she threw the bolt in the door, using the last of her strength.

Sobs smashed through her, collapsing lungs against heart, making it impossible to breathe. She wrapped her arms around herself, leaning forward as if to ward off blows. With her back to the wall, she slid to the floor and curled over her-self, knees to chest. It was worse than the night Alex had drowned.

Much worse.

Braedon had hurt her far more than her husband had. She'd never loved Alex. Not truly loved him. Any more than he'd loved her. And it hadn't been Alex's fault he deserted her. He'd died.

Braedon, on the other hand, was still very much alive. And he'd knowingly betrayed her. Seduced her. Lied to her.

And she loved him.

Dear God, she loved him.

Chapter 17

"KACY, OPEN THE door."

Kacy raised her head at the sound of a voice. Braedon's voice. The hall was dark, the patter of rain against the walls of the cottage a soft counterpoint to the pounding on the door.

"Kacy." There was an edge of panic to his voice.

Good. Let him panic. After what he'd put her through, he deserved more than a little worrying.

The doorknob rattled ominously. Mac circled in front of the door, whining, looking back at her.

"Kacy." This time he was yelling. There was a thud and the door shook in its frame.

"Go away." Her voice was hoarse, hardly recognizable as her own, but it carried. She leaned her head against the wall and waited.

"Kacy? Are you all right?" His voice was calmer now, but the fear was still there, fear mixed with confusion.

"I'm fine. Now go away."

Silence filled the hall, broken only by the ticking of the parlor clock. Kacy waited, holding her breath until she was certain that he was gone. She sighed, disappointment mixing with relief.

She didn't want to see him. Not even a little bit. He was the enemy. He'd tricked her. Used her. She clenched her fists, staring at the locked door, tears welling again. She hadn't thought there were any left.

With a metallic click, the lock rotated and the door creaked as it swung open. Mac barked joyfully.

Traitor.

"What in hell is going on here, Kacy?" Braedon looked furious, his hair slicked back with rain, his coat and pants soaked through.

"How did you get in?" she asked wearily.

He held up her key. "The planter."

"I see. Well, kindly put it back on your way out." She fought to keep her voice mild. Uninterested. She couldn't— wouldn't—let him see how much he'd hurt her.

He crossed the hall in two steps, pulling her to her feet, his eyes searching hers for answers. "What's going on? You're scaring me."

"I'm scaring *you*?" She struggled to escape his hold, but his hands tightened on her shoulders. "I think you've got it backward. It's you who's been scaring me. And lying to me and . . . and . . ." She trailed off, unable to put words to her feelings without losing control.

"What are you talking about?"

She looked into the dark blue of his eyes, seeing nothing but confusion and concern. Oh, he was good. "I'm talking about Solais."

He lowered his hands. "How did you find out?"

"It doesn't matter. It's enough that I know."

"The professor."

"I should have seen it myself. I recognized your name. I just didn't put it together." But she should have, the voice in her head taunted. She should have.

His eyes pleaded with hers. "I can explain."

"I'm sure you can. You've got an explanation for everything, don't you?" She stepped away from him, the physical distance strengthening her resolve. "How stupid do you think I am?"

"Kacy, I—" He reached out to her, eyes imploring.

"Save it for someone else. I don't want to hear about it. What I do want is for you to get the hell out of my house." She stepped past him, her stomach tightening as her hand brushed his. She yanked open the door and stood beside it, waiting.

"Kacy, after everything that's happened, you need someone to watch over you."

"Someone to watch over me? That's a laugh. I can take care of myself."

"Have you forgotten about the dead man?"

"No. He'll haunt my dreams for the rest of my life. He can join his place in my nightmares right next to Alex. And you. At this rate, I'll probably never be able to sleep with the light off again." She swung the door wider. "Now get out."

"For now." She could see a muscle moving along the line of his jaw. "But I'll be back."

"Don't bother." She was barely hanging on to her emotions. She wanted him gone. She refused to fall apart in front of him. That would be the final humiliation.

"This is far from over, Kacy. I'm not going to let my omissions come between us."

"Omissions?" Rage surged through her. "I think you're understating things just a little, *Mr. Roche.*" She ground out his name. "*Lies* would seem a more appropriate word. Lies, and deceit. And, for the record, I did not kill my husband."

"I know that."

"Oh, really? And are you also satisfied that I didn't forge any of your precious paintings?" She paused a heartbeat and he nodded, the gesture only fueling the fire. "Really? And when, may I ask, did you come to that conclusion? When I was spilling my guts about my dead husband? Or wait, let me guess, it must have been the moment on the chair, when I—"

"Stop it." His hands closed on her shoulders again, shaking

her, his angry gaze meeting hers. "You know that isn't true. Last night was—"

"A lie." She wrenched free, her breathing coming in painful gasps. "Now go."

"Fine. But this is the truth, Kacy. Remember it." He tilted his head, and before she realized what he was doing, his lips crushed into hers, the jolt of the kiss coursing through her, lighting a blaze that had nothing to do with her anger. As quickly as it started it was over. He released her, stepping out into the rain. "I won't let you go without a fight, Kacy. I was going to tell—"

She slammed the door in his face, the reverberation lingering in the hall. It was over.

She'd won.

Shouldn't she feel elated or something? She waited for the feelings to hit her, but nothing came. She was empty.

Empty and alone.

She sank back to the hallway floor, suddenly exhausted. Tracing the curve of her lip with a finger, she remembered his kiss, wondering how she could possibly still love him.

But she did.

Braedon took the curve at Mrs. Macnamara's without benefit of braking. The car swerved as it skidded in the rain, but managed to hold its traction, remaining safely on the road. Braedon truly couldn't say whether he was grateful or sorry.

How could he have been so stupid? Anger warred with concern. If she was in danger, she needed protection. But then she'd made it perfectly clear that she didn't want that someone to be him. Anger won. He accelerated around another curve, the wheels whining in protest.

For the first time since his mother died, he actually cared about another person. All right, not just cared, *loved*. He loved another person. And how had he demonstrated these new feelings? By deceiving her. And now she believed it had all been a lie, that he'd been using her.

He slammed on the brakes, determined to go back to have it out with her. And even if she refused to listen, he'd stay there. In the car if necessary. Anything to keep her safe. The car's tires locked, sending it into a skid ending with one wheel stuck in a ditch. Accelerating, he tried to spin out of the hole, but the tire just dug itself in deeper. He slammed a hand against the steering wheel.

Bloody hell. Wasn't this just par for the course?

He wrenched open the door and stepped out into the steady downpour, his already wet clothes instantly wetter, the cold rain dripping down his neck and into his eyes. The perfect complement to what was turning into a disastrous day.

He started up the lane. Hopefully there'd be help at Mrs. Macnamara's. He kicked a rock and stepped into a puddle, the frigid water instantly soaking through his sock.

Damn and blast.

He wasn't going to lose her. She was the best thing that had ever happened to him, and he sure as hell wasn't going to stand by and watch her walk away.

Granted, it was his fault they were in this mess, but he could get her to forgive him—if he could just get her to listen. He gritted his teeth and turned up his collar, remembering at least one reason why he'd been happy to leave Ireland. The bloody rain.

He tried to concentrate on something else, but the only image his mind seemed capable of projecting was Kacy, the anguish of his betrayal etched in tight lines across her stark face.

Hell, he was a bastard, there was no getting around the fact. But he loved Kacy, and he was certain, with time, he could make her understand why he hadn't told her who he was. Well, he was almost certain.

Who was he kidding? He didn't have an icicle's chance in hell.

A gust of wind buffeted him, and the rain began to fall in solid sheets. He sneezed and slogged forward. He'd built an empire from nothing. The beggar from Dublin was now one of the most feared men on Wall Street. Surely he could manage one slip of a woman.

Again he saw her face, but this time, he could see the determination in her eyes. Kacy Macgrath had been hurt a lot in her lifetime. Her defenses were tough, and thanks to him, they were up in full force and probably stronger than ever.

Well—he squared his shoulders with resolution—he'd just have to breach the walls. Hell, the prize was greater than anything he'd ever fought for before.

And there was no way he was spending the rest of his life without her.

"You're telling me that Anson is dead?" Max scowled at Rico.

Rico settled more deeply into the comfortable armchair in Mrs. Macnamara's study. Taking a slow sip of coffee, he studied Max over the rim of his cup. The man sat rigidly on the edge of a wingback chair, the companion to Rico's. His face was mottled with color, a curious combination of burnt sienna and umber, anger radiating from his gaze.

Rico took another sip of coffee. "Yes, I'm afraid so."

"And you want me to believe he tripped and fell."

Rico sighed. Everything always had to be so complicated. "It isn't a matter of what I want you to believe, Max. It's a matter of public record. The police were there. And according to Kacy, they believe it was an accident."

"Kirstin." The word exploded from Max's mouth, more a curse than a name. "If you weren't such a feeble old man, I'd say you had feelings for the bitch."

Rico felt a stab of anger at the condescension in Max's

voice. "It has nothing to do with emotion, Max. She's quite talented artistically, and, given the opportunity, I intend to capitalize on that talent."

Max drained the liquid in his cup and slammed the delicate porcelain into the saucer on the table. "I wouldn't bank on that, Rico, my friend. I'm afraid I have other plans for our little Miss Macgrath." His eyes lit up with an unholy glee.

Rico squelched a tremor of apprehension. This was certainly not the time to lose his nerve. He glanced at the study door, relieved to see that it was firmly closed. He set his cup on the table and leaned forward, his nose inches from Max's. "I don't think that would be wise, *my friend.*"

Rico stared at the other man, his gaze unflinching. "It's only a matter of time before the Garda discover who exactly it was that died in Kacy's cottage. And when they do, it won't take them long to trace Anson back to you. And with Braedon Roche around, it's only a tiny leap from there to the fact that you were behind the forgeries."

"Along with you."

"Along with me." Rico sat back. "So my suggestion would be that you go home, establish one hell of an alibi, and try to forget all about Miss Macgrath."

"And let her get away with murder?" A vein pulsed against Max's temple.

Rico sighed. "Max, she didn't murder Alex."

"So you say."

"So I know. And even if she did, is revenge really worth going back to prison for?"

Max stroked his chin, his eyes narrowed in thought. "Maybe."

"Max," Rico coaxed, picking up his cup again.

The man blew out a breath. "I suppose not."

"I thought you'd see it my way when you thought about it. Now, I want you to go back to your hotel, pack your things, and head for the States. You'll be safe in your bed before any one even knows who Anson was."

Max's face darkened with anger again. "What if she killed him, too?"

Rico wanted to scream with frustration. "Max, she hasn't killed anyone. The fool fell. He tripped and broke his neck. I'm sorry. I know you had feelings for the man, but that doesn't change what happened, does it?"

"No." The word was spoken grudgingly. "I suppose it doesn't."

"All right then. Go home. I'll tie things up here and we'll let the whole thing die with Alex."

"With Alex," Max echoed, rising from the chair and striding from the study without another word.

Rico sat in silence, staring into his coffee cup, wondering why he felt like he'd only managed to make things worse.

Max shifted his car into gear, cursing the fact that Anson was gone. He reversed down the drive, wipers slapping time against the windshield.

What a godforsaken place. He'd be well out of it.

Unfortunately, it wasn't quite time for him to leave. Rico had been easy enough to pacify. There'd been no reason to argue with the little man. Max shifted into drive and turned onto the lane. The Macgrath woman might have bewitched Rico, but Max wasn't as easy to fool, and he knew she was responsible for his brother's death. Anson's, too, most likely.

His hands clenched on the steering wheel as he thought about his friend plummeting to his death.

Women were never to be trusted. He thought about his own mother—the bitch. She'd called them her little gentlemen. Alex and Maxie. She'd sworn she loved them, but in the end, she'd loved her two-bit hustler boyfriend more, deserting them without ever looking back.

He frowned. God, he hated women.

All women.

Kirstin Macgrath most of all.

The car swung around a corner, its wheels spraying water onto a man walking beside the road. Served the asshole right, walking along the edge of the road like that.

He gunned the engine, wishing for a moment that instead of drenching the stranger, he'd run him down. There was a certain satisfaction in the thought. Too bad he hadn't acted on it; perhaps then he'd have released some of the rage that threatened to undo him, but he placated himself with the knowledge that soon enough he'd have the pleasure of killing Kirstin Macgrath. And that would make him very happy indeed.

Braedon stood on the side of the road, dripping water. It was everywhere. In his eyes, in his nose, running in rivulets down his neck. It was even in his briefs. He stared at the taillights of the retreating car.

The bloody bastard hadn't even seen him.

Considering how well the day had started, it was going downhill fast. He grimaced and slogged forward, his feet squishing in his shoes with each step. He walked up Mrs. Macnamara's drive, trying to avoid both the puddles and the mud, only managing to truly evade the former. Hadn't anyone in Lindoon ever considered paving their driveways?

Reaching the steps to the front door, he ducked under the overhang, grateful to escape the downpour, although he was long past the point where that truly brought comfort. What he really needed was a hot shower.

And Kacy.

He shivered, and for the first time since he left the shelter of his car, it wasn't caused by the cold.

Pounding on the door, he hoped the proprietress could hear him over the storm. Fin had told him all about the widow Macnamara, including the fact that she was nearly deaf. If she didn't answer, he'd be forced to hike back to the pub. And the idea of another jaunt in the rain wasn't at all appealing. He pounded harder.

"Hang on to your hat, I'll be there in a minute."

Braedon scowled at the irritation in the voice on the other side of the door. The man, whoever he was, was warm and dry, and in Braedon's book, that gave him little room for complaint. The door cracked open and a weather-worn face peered out at him.

"Is Mrs. Macnamara at home?"

"That she is." The man waited, eyeing Braedon as if he were a mangy dog rather than a man. Not that he could blame the fellow, he probably did resemble something the cat had dragged home.

"Could I speak with her?"

The man frowned. "Well, now, who would I say was asking?"

"Braedon Roche." He bit out the words, his temper rising.

"The Yank?" The man's eyebrows lifted.

"The very wet Yank."

The man grinned then, and opened the door wider. "Well, why didn't you say so? Come in and set yourself by the fire."

Braedon stepped into the entry hall. "What I really need is the phone. My car is stuck in a ditch just up the road."

The man smiled again. "What you're needin', I'm thinking, is a spot of whiskey."

"Well, there's truth in that, but my car—"

"Never you mind. I'll see to that, or my name's not Tolly Macnamara." The ruddy-faced man gestured toward a closed door. "Study's in there. Mam is taking a nap, but there's whiskey on the dresser. You get your wet things off and I'll see to your car."

Braedon hesitated. He doubted the man could move the car on his own.

" 'Tis not a problem. I'm the local mechanic." Tolly'd read his mind. "I've got a tow truck."

"Then I'll accept the offer."

Tolly grinned and pulled on a weathered mackintosh and a tattered cap. "Be back in a jiff."

Braedon shrugged out of his coat and slipped off his shoes. He was still soaked, but he figured decency won out over comfort in a situation like this. He opened the door to the study, the heat in the little room reaching out like a warm friend.

The feeling was short lived. The professor was sitting across the room, dwarfed by an overstuffed wingback. *"You."* It wasn't an eloquent greeting, but at the moment it summed up Braedon's feelings nicely.

The little man shrugged, looking absurdly at ease in Mrs. Macnamara's parlor. "Forgive me, but you are not, how shall I say it, looking your best?"

Braedon laughed mirthlessly at the understatement. "It hasn't been the best of days. No thanks to you." Kacy's anguished face popped into his mind. He ruthlessly pushed it aside. "And to top it off, I've had car trouble."

The Italian cum Bronx resident shifted in his chair, lifting a glass half full of amber colored liquid. "Come, join me. Tolly will no doubt put things right."

"I'd rather join you in hell." He grated out the words, feeling like an adolescent posturing for superiority.

"I'm sure that can be arranged, but in the meantime, have a drink." The professor waved a hand in the direction of the drinks table.

Braedon frowned at the little man, but crossed to the table and poured a stout measure from an open Bushmill's bottle. Perhaps there was something to be gained here, and, truth be told, he needed the fortification.

But he also needed to know that Kacy was all right. He crossed to the bureau and picked up the phone.

"She won't answer." The man's audacity was getting under Braedon's skin.

"Just who the hell do you think you are?"

"Kacy's friend."

He tried not to let the little man get to him, but the hollow ringing of the phone seemed to underscore his words. He replaced the phone in the cradle. "She could be in trouble."

"But she isn't. She's only avoiding you."

There were subtexts here he wasn't following. He took a swig of whiskey, the liquid burning a path down his throat. "How would you know?"

The man took a sip of his drink, considering the question. "Because I am her friend."

Braedon ground his teeth together, trying not to hit him. "You said that."

"I know, but I wasn't certain you were listening."

If the professor was goading him, he'd get what he deserved. "And what makes you think that she'd want to be friends with a con artist, *Rico*?"

The little man eyed him with something close to amusement. Certainly not the reaction he'd expected.

"Everyone has a right to reinvent themselves, Signore Roche. You of all people should know that."

Braedon narrowed his eyes and drained the rest of his whiskey, pouring some more. "So what's that supposed to mean?"

"Does Fermoy ring a bell?"

Braedon drained the glass again and eyed his adversary. "So you've done your research. Why?"

"Same reason as you. I want to protect Kacy. And frankly, from where I'm sitting, you have a lot more potential to hurt her than I do."

"I'm not going to hurt her."

"I think you already have."

"I was going to tell her the truth."

"But you didn't. Instead, you stole her heart under false pretenses. I had no way of knowing what you were thinking, but Kacy is easy to read. In many ways, she is like an open book, no?"

"So *you* hurt her."

"No, my friend, you hurt her. I only pointed out the truth, thereby allowing her to salvage some modicum of dignity."

Braedon met the little man's gaze, studying it, and finding nothing but a hint of sadness and something that bordered on earnestness.

"I did what I thought was best for Kacy, Signore Roche. If I have offended you, then I am truly sorry. But you should have recognized what it was you had, and taken greater care with it."

"I can't argue with that." Braedon tipped his glass, draining the contents, the alcohol doing little to numb the ache in his heart. He wanted to blame the professor, but the truth was, he'd done this to himself. Taking his anger out on the little man wasn't going to help anything.

"You're good to go, man." Tolly Macnamara sauntered into the room, his ruddy face even redder due to the wind and cold. "Fortunately for you, there was no damage to the car. I left it in the drive."

Braedon stood, reaching for his sodden wallet. "What do I owe you?"

The man waved his hand in the air. "Not a thing. 'Twas my pleasure to be helping. Now, if you'll excuse me, I'll just be off to check on me mam."

Braedon opened his mouth to say thanks, only to be faced with an empty doorway.

"Signore Roche?"

He turned back to Baucomo.

"Don't hurt her anymore. She deserves something better."

"And I suppose you think you can give her that?" Braedon clenched his teeth, squeezing out the words.

"Not in the sense that you mean it, no, but I *can* offer her something she's always wanted."

"Oh?" He lifted an eyebrow. "And what's that?"

"Confidence."

"I beg your pardon?"

"Kacy doesn't believe in herself. People like you have managed to beat her down to the point that she has no faith in herself. I have the power to help restore that."

Braedon was going to hate himself for asking, but he couldn't stop himself. "And just how do you propose to do that?"

"By making her a world renowned artist."

Braedon opened his mouth to reply, his mind conjuring a picture of Kacy, flushed with excitement, telling him the professor wanted to show her work. "I can do that, too." And he could. Probably better than a two-bit hustler masquerading as a success. Like you, the little voice in his head whispered.

"At least for the moment, Signore Roche, I think there is a difference. I am still her friend. She trusts me. You, on the other hand . . ." The little man shrugged, raising his glass in a mocking salute.

The bastard. Braedon fought for control of his temper. How dare he?

Because, his mind taunted, he's right.

Chapter 18

KACY LIFTED HER head. The gloom had deepened and the rain still smattered against the door. Her legs were cramped and she moved one slowly, straightening it with a wince. Mac lifted his head, tail thumping hesitantly.

"It's all right, fella." She reached over to scratch between his ears. "It's going to be all right." She had no idea whom she was really talking to. Herself probably. Suddenly the shadowed hallway seemed claustrophobic. She pushed to her feet, toes tingling as circulation returned. She'd definitely been sitting too long.

She grabbed an anorak from the hall tree and slipped into it. "What do you say we get out of here for a while? It'll do us good."

Again, she knew she was really talking for her own benefit. She pushed the hair out of her face, considered washing up, and then rejected the idea as ridiculous. No one cleaned up before going out into a rainstorm. She sat on the bench and pulled on a pair of rubber boots.

Yanking open the door, she stepped out into the dreary afternoon. It was hard to tell the time, the heavy clouds obliterated any normal light, but at least the downpour had slowed to a steady drizzle.

She pulled up her hood and set out for the stone fort. There was something compelling about Dunbeg any time, but in the rain it was particularly inspiring, the mists making the walls seem whole, the barrier of time somehow thinner.

She smiled at her own whimsy and whistled to Mac, who had dashed up the road after a bird. The rocky ground was wet, almost marshy, and she was grateful for her boots. The air was fresh and crisp, laden with a hint of the sea nearby. Almost imperceptibly, her spirits began to rise. This was Ireland at its most beautiful. The wild colors accentuated by the refraction of light, water, and mist.

Dunbeg shone white against the expanse of green meadow and gray sky, its concentric circles looking more fearsome in the gathering dusk. Kacy stopped on the rise, looking down at the remains of the fortress. The inner wall was still almost completely intact with an arched lintel that probably had served as the entrance.

In places, the wall towered up to nine feet or so, but at other points, time and man had reduced that, leaving only parts of the original wall. Stone steps built into the inside of the rampart formed a great X. From this distance, Kacy could see the remains of a walkway high atop the inner wall.

The outer wall was less well preserved, only built up on three sides, the cliff and the sea below it providing natural protection to the west. Scattered sections remained, with gaping holes where marauders had plundered the stone for other purposes.

There were three entrances to the souterrain. At least, three that she knew of. The one that had collapsed was in the outer wall, situated at the bottom of the southeast corner, a stony slope leading down into the passageway.

A second entrance was hidden in the inner rampart, enclosed behind a low semicircular stone wall, with remains of steps leading into its depth.

The third entrance was far below the fort itself, cut into the stone of the cliff, faced by a tiny stretch of rocky beach. She'd actually seen it only once, when a local fisherman had taken her out in his boat.

The passageways themselves were all interconnected, some parts opening up to large rooms or caverns. A fortress within a fortress. Suddenly she felt an intense kinship with the people who'd built Dunbeg. She had need of protection, too.

Mac barked and she jumped, pulled out of her thoughts. Best not to dwell on it all anyway. She whistled for the dog and together they made their way down the hill to the fort and the cliff edge. It was her favorite spot, the sea stretching out for miles below her, the stony promontory of Dunbeg behind her.

Here, she felt at peace. Almost as if the little fortress were protecting her, watching over her. She shook her head at the thought. She was obviously living in fantasyland. There was no room in her life for peace. Not with betrayals and dead bodies littered everywhere.

She sat on a tumbled pile of rock, arms circling her knees, letting the wind and rain swirl around her, the last vestiges of the gray day beginning to fade into the deeper shadows of night.

The bewitching hour.

As if on cue, stones clattered behind her. She whipped around, heart pounding.

Mac's canine grin appeared through a gap in the wall. "You scared me," she admonished, her voice sounding harsher than normal.

Breathing deeply to calm her racing heart, she turned back to the ocean, the illusion of peace evaporating into the wind. There was no safe harbor. No bolt-hole waiting to shelter her from her enemies.

Rocks rattled again. This time Mac growled. Kacy stood up and turned to survey the fort.

Nothing moved.

She waited, holding her breath.

"Kirstin."

Her name whispered across the ruins, carried on the wind. She bit back a scream. Obviously her imagination was working overtime. After everything that had happened, surely that was understandable.

Her eyes darted around the clearing, looking for something that explained the noise. Mac whined and moved closer to her. "Some watchdog you turned out to be." She rested her hand on his head, grateful for the contact.

This had been a really stupid idea. She was isolated out here. Vulnerable.

The wind shifted suddenly, whipping her hair into her eyes. She reached to push it back, freezing with it gathered into a ponytail behind her.

There, in the archway. A figure.

A man.

Mac growled, low and threatening, the hairs on the back of his neck rising. She tried to summon the strength to run, but only managed to take one step backward.

The figure moved, stepping from the shadow into the half-light of the evening. Kacy released her hair, clutching at her throat, trying to make herself breathe.

Alex.

He took a step toward her, the sardonic twist of a smile tilting his lips.

Mac barked and Alex moved forward again, sending Kacy scrambling backward, one hand held up to ward him off. The feeble movement had no effect, and he came another step closer.

"Alex?" The word came out in a pitiful hiss, her mind whirling with the enormity of the fact that Alex was standing in front of her. Alex. *Alive.* The turf ended with sudden finality and her foot dangled over the precipice. Jerking back, she teetered there, eyes locked on her dead husband, the mist twining around him like a phantom lover.

"Kirstin." Again he whispered her name, the sound whipping away in the wind.

Mac stood between them, teeth bared. At least she had someone on her side. Swallowing nervously, she shifted her weight from foot to foot, trying to make sense of the nonsensical.

One minute she was standing on firm ground, and the next, it felt more like shifting sand. She lost her balance and careened backward, hands rotating helplessly through the air.

There wasn't even time to scream.

Plummeting downward, her arms and legs banging against outcroppings of rocks, Kacy tried frantically to find a handhold, something to break her fall.

She smashed into a small ledge and managed to grab onto a root of some kind, the action bringing her to a jarring stop. Half on and half off of the ledge, she shot a fervent prayer heavenward and managed to climb up onto the protruding rock.

It was narrow, barely wide enough for her body, and every time she moved, dirt rained down to the rocky beach below, but just at the moment it felt a little bit like heaven.

Mac barked from the top of the cliff, and if she hung her head out over the edge, she could make out his nose as he looked down at her. She was well and truly stuck. Physics was certainly not her forte, but from the looks of it, she'd fallen about seven or eight feet. Which meant there was still a hell of a drop below her, ending in bone shattering rocks.

A shudder of panic mixed with relief rippled through her. She tried to sit up, but when a chunk of earth broke away and fell to the beach below, she gave up the effort. The rain had begun in earnest again, its icy droplets stabbing into her face and hands. The anorak was ripped at the shoulder on one side, and water seeped in through the opening, soaking her shirt.

Her breathing ragged, fear lacing through her, she leaned out and looked up at the cliff again. Mac was still there. No sign of Alex. If it had been Alex, her mind taunted. A trick of the light. Or a trick of the mind.

Alex was dead.

"Mac," she yelled, her voice cracked and hoarse. "Go get help. Please, Mac. Get help."

The dog cocked his head, listening, and then disappeared. Great, she was in the Irish version of *Rin Tin Tin*. She just prayed Mac had enough sense to find help. *Braedon*. Somehow, despite everything, in her mind, the words were synonymous.

He'd find her. And rescue her. And after that she'd go back to being angry with him. Or maybe she'd wait to be angry until after a nice, hot shower . . .

Her mind drifted, and she tried to focus, to stay conscious. The cold was seeping into her, stealing her strength.

She leaned out again, hoping to see some positive sign that help was on the way. It's too soon, her mind warned. But she looked up anyway, hope springing eternal and all that. Black edged her vision as the blood rushed to her head, and she rolled back onto the safety of the ledge, her breath coming in gasps.

Maniacal laughter filled the air and she closed her eyes, trying to shut out the vision of her not-so-dead husband leering down at her over the edge.

Braedon stared at the phone, willing it to ring. He needed to talk to Matt. He sat on the bench by the phone, and then stood up again, pacing nervously.

Kacy might be convinced that she hated him, but he knew that somewhere, deep inside, she cared about him. Last night's passion hadn't been a fluke, and he was determined to get past her barriers and convince her that his feelings for her were real. No matter how long it took.

But first, he had to get to the bottom of what was happening. The phone rang and he grabbed it before the sound had a chance to repeat itself. "Roche."

"You know," Matt drawled, "I kinda like this side of you."

"What side is that?"

"The side that's totally dependent on me."

"Well, don't get used to it."

Matt laughed. "Believe me, I'd never make that mistake, and if I were tempted to, that grizzly bear attitude of yours would scare me off once and for all."

"What'd you find out?"

"Not too much. But you were right about Max."

Braedon tightened his grip on the phone. "He's out of prison."

"Yup, for about a week."

"Any idea where he is now?"

"Not definitively, but I got a feeling you're going to tell me."

"He's here. At least I think so." Kacy had seen Alex. Or at least who she thought was Alex.

"It's certainly possible. He was seen in and around Greenwich right after his release, but then he just disappeared. No sign of him, and his brownstone is closed down tighter than a drum."

Braedon sat down on the bench. "Airline records?"

"Not a thing. If Madison did fly to Ireland, he used a charter."

"How soon will you know for sure?"

"By tomorrow."

"Any chance he had a companion with him?" Braedon saw again the twisted body on Kacy's stairs.

"Funny you should mention that. Seems Madison has a chauffeur. More of a man Friday I'd say, name of Anson Forbes. The last time Madison was seen, they were together. I don't want to jump to conclusions, but it's possible Forbes is with his boss. Why?"

"Because we've got an unidentified dead body. You still have contacts with the Irish police?"

"Nothing direct. Friends of friends, that sort of thing. Let me see what I can find out."

"Or better yet, steer them in the right direction."

"I take it you prefer to maintain a low profile."

"For the moment."

"Fair enough. By the way, I'm still working on the Gienelli/Baucomo connection. Nothing to report yet. If the professor is Gienelli, then he's turned straight arrow. There's not even a whisper of scandal surrounding the old geezer."

"Oh, he's Gienelli, all right."

"How do you know?"

"I confronted him with it."

"And he admitted it?" Matt sounded skeptical.

"Well, not in so many words. But he didn't deny it either." The son of a bitch had actually used it to turn the tables on him.

"So, do you think there's a connection?"

"I don't know. It seems so damn coincidental. But I think he genuinely cares about Kacy." Despite his dislike for the man, there was no denying the emotion he'd seen in the professor's eyes. He cared all right. And right now Kacy could use all the allies she could get. No matter what he thought of them.

"So you want me to drop it?"

"No. Keep digging." It wouldn't hurt to stick it to the bugger a little. He owed him one.

"No problem. I kinda hated the idea of letting it go anyway. You know me." There was a hint of laughter in his friend's voice.

"Yeah, I do."

"Anything else you want to tell me? You don't sound so good." Laughter changed to concern.

"Nothing I can explain on the phone. Suffice to say that I've screwed up royally, and only divine intervention with a lot of groveling is going to get me off the hook."

"Now that's something I'd like front row seats for." The laughter was back. "Braedon Roche groveling."

"Thanks for the support."

"Anytime. I'll call you tomorrow."

"I'll be here." Braedon placed the receiver back in the cradle.

He ran a hand through his hair in frustration. Things were certainly heating up, pieces beginning to fall into place. He needed to find Kacy, to tell her the truth, and to tell her what he'd found. But to do that, he'd have to gain at least a tentative truce. And that wasn't going to be easy.

With a shudder, he recalled the icy fury on her face the last time he'd seen her. He blew out a breath. It was going to take a lot of groveling. But then, he'd always been a man willing to do whatever it took to get what he wanted.

And he wanted Kacy Macgrath—now and forever.

He glanced at his watch with a sigh.

No time like the present.

Braedon got out of the car, wondering what kind of reception he'd get. Not a good one, he'd wager. Even with time to calm down, Kacy would still be angry. And rightly so. He had behaved abominably, but to his credit, he'd wanted to tell her everything this morning. Probably too little, too late, but surely it should count for something.

The rain was still falling. A continuous sheet of water, drenching everything in sight. He pulled his raincoat closer, grateful for the warm sweater underneath. He knocked, and when there was no answer, felt in the potted plant for the key, both relieved and annoyed to find that it wasn't there.

At least she was safely locked inside.

Another thought occurred to him, and he reached out to grasp the door handle, turning it slowly. He felt it click into the open position, and bit back a curse. She was so damn trusting.

Exactly what got her in trouble with you, me boy.

The voice was his mother's, and he bit back a grin. It had been a long time since his mind had allowed him to remember that voice. It brought comfort, even in scolding.

He started to open the door, and then paused at the sound of barking coming from the side of the house. Turning, he stepped off the porch just as Mac came tearing around the corner, barking like the hounds of hell were after him. When he saw Braedon, the bark changed to a whine and the dog circled in front of him, clearly agitated about something.

"Hang on there, boy. What's wrong?"

The dog stopped and then barked again, backing up and looking toward the meadow beyond the house. All in all, it was a damn good imitation of a *Lassie* episode, only he didn't feel much like Timmy.

The implication of the thought hit home, the hairs on the back of his neck rising. Kacy was in trouble.

"Okay, Mac, take me to Kacy." He stopped at the car and grabbed a flashlight.

The dog set out at a run, stopping from time to time to see that Braedon was still with him. As they came over the rise, Braedon caught his breath, looking down at the fort. It was wreathed in mist and the eerie cast gave him a sick feeling in the pit of his stomach. He could still hear the collapsing stones of the souterrain. What if another wall had fallen?

Mac barked again, obviously impatient, and offering a silent prayer heavenward, Braedon followed him.

Chapter 19

IT WAS COLD, not pleasantly chilly or refreshingly bracing, but bone deep frigid. The kind of cold that sets in, digging inside until there's no escaping it. Shivers racked Kacy's body, the movement causing a shower of dirt and rocks to fall to the beach below. She tried to still the tremors with no success.

The rain fell incessantly. The deluge had lessened, but the lack of visibility made it seem worse. She stared up, no longer able to discern between the shadow that marked the cliff and the gray-black of the sky.

Tears or raindrops ran down her face. She couldn't tell the difference anymore. In fact, she wasn't sure it mattered. Time had no meaning either. Her watch had broken in the fall and between the rain and the creeping darkness, there was no way to mark the minutes, the hours.

Another piece of the ledge, this time inches from her shoulder, crumbled and fell. She sucked in a breath and willed the trembling to stop. So much for mind over matter.

At least she seemed to be in one piece. Nothing seemed to be broken. Physically, she was okay. Mentally, she wasn't so sure. Fear circled through her, matching the cold step for step, the two dancing together, threatening to destroy her.

She was tired and growing more and more disoriented. Sleep was her enemy, but a seductive one. It would be so simple to slip away. She closed her eyes and relaxed, just for a moment letting a sense of warmth ease through her.

No.

The word echoed through her brain and she fought against the lethargy, forcing her eyes open. *Braedon.* She focused on Braedon. He would come. No matter what lay between them, he would come.

All she had to do was wait.

Braedon followed the dog through the fort to the cliff, his heart in his throat. Mac stopped and laid on the ground, his nose over the edge, whining softly.

"Here?"

He looked over the edge, the sound of the ocean the only indication of what lay below. The dusk and the mist hid the rocky shore. Fear ate at him. If she was down there, if she'd fallen . . .

He inched toward the edge, his foot hitting loose rock. The stones disappeared into the gloom, the echoing clatter as they hit bottom taking forever to reach his ears. No one could survive that fall. No one.

He knelt beside Mac, peering down into the darkness.

"Kacy?"

A small whimper floated back to him.

"Honey, are you down there?"

"Braedon?"

The voice was weak, but clear. A shadow shifted below him. He could just make out the ledge. Relief surged through him. He flipped on the flashlight, and almost wished he hadn't. She was wedged on a narrow outcropping just below him. Lying on her back, she looked so tiny and fragile, her face white and drawn. "Sweetheart, are you all right?"

"I've been better." The ghost of a smile lit her face.

He released a breath he hadn't realized he'd been holding. "Can you stand up?"

"I've been afraid to try. I think the ledge is unstable." As if to emphasize the point, rock from the outcropping clattered down into the darkness below.

"Look, it's holding your weight now. I think, as long as you move slowly, it should be all right for you to try to stand."

There was silence for a minute, then she struggled to a sitting position. More rock fell, but the ledge held steady. "All right. Here I come." She looked up and their eyes met.

Braedon's stomach tightened. In such a short time, she'd become so important to him. He laid across the cliff top, hanging down over the edge, arms extended. "Reach for my hands, Kacy."

She pressed herself against the rock and reached upward. His fingertips dangled uselessly above hers. She maneuvered herself onto tiptoe, and still she remained out of reach. Her wide-eyed gaze met his, her face completely devoid of color. "Now what?"

"We need something to bridge the gap."

"Got any rope on you?" Beneath the false bravado, he heard a trace of fear.

"No, but I have the next best thing. Hang on." With a contortion worthy of a gymnast, he pulled his belt out of his pants, looping one end around his wrist, using the buckle. Grasping the length of leather with both hands, he dropped it over the cliff. "Okay, grab hold."

"I've got it."

"All right, I want you to use it like a rope. Brace your feet against the cliff and climb. When you get to my hands, I'll grab you and pull you up."

"Can you do that?" She sounded hesitant.

"Kacy, we don't have a choice. Now come on."

With a nod, she began the ascent. Her weight pulled at his arms, but the pain was preferable to the alternative. Losing Kacy. "Come on, just a little farther. You can do it."

Her hands inched up the leather. He watched, waiting, and

when her fingers brushed against his, he released the makeshift rope with one hand and grabbed her wrist. "I've got you. Now on three I want you to let go of the belt and grab my other hand."

"All right."

"One. Two." He sucked in a breath, bracing himself. "Three." He released the belt and circled her arm as soon as her hand touched his. She swung outward with the motion, her weight pulling his muscles taut.

Like a pendulum, she swung inward again, her feet planted firmly against the side of the cliff, relieving some of the pressure.

"Perfect. The Flying Wallendas couldn't have done it better." He concentrated on supporting her weight. "You ready?"

"Oh, yeah."

"All right then, this elevator is ready to go up."

A crack echoed through the gloom and the ledge beneath her splintered into fragments of rock, spiraling down through the mist.

"Good. I don't think down is an option." She managed a smile, but it was so slight it would have been easy to believe he'd imagined it.

"Okay, I'm going to pull." He shimmied backward on the ground, pulling with every ounce of strength in his body.

One minute she was dead weight, and the next, she was collapsed on the ground beside him, their labored breathing a symphony to his ears. He rolled over, pulling her into his arms, holding her tight against his pounding heart.

She tipped back her head, her eyes searching his. "I knew you'd come."

With a groan, he covered her lips with his, drinking in the taste of her, grateful for the feel of her in his arms, the smell of her skin against his. She sighed. And with a strength of will that surprised him, he pulled away. She was vulnerable now.

And cold. He could feel her trembling through her anorak. He stood up, pulling her to her feet, both hands on her shoulders. "Tell me what happened."

"It was Alex. Alex was here." She was shivering uncontrollably now, an edge of hysteria coloring her voice.

"It wasn't Alex, Kacy."

"But I saw him." The rain began to fall again in earnest, the water striking like icy needles.

He took off his raincoat and wrapped it around her. "Come on, we need to get you home. We'll talk there. After you're warm and dry."

She stared at him for a minute and then nodded, leaning into him when he put his arm around her. Mac ran joyous circles around them, delighted that his mistress was on her feet again, as the three of them set off across the meadow for Sidhean. And, just for a moment, Braedon felt that all was right with his world.

"I did see Alex. I'm sure of it." Kacy snuggled under the afghan, her feet curled underneath her. The sofa cushions were covered with sheets and turned facedown, but she could still imagine the ripped cushions, the image reminding her of the insanity of the last few days.

Braedon moved to sit beside her on the sofa. "Why don't we start at the beginning?"

"All right." She shivered, remembering. "I was at the ruins, with Mac, and *he* was watching me from the shadows of the wall. I was sitting by the cliff, thinking about . . ." She stopped, embarrassed.

His voice softened. "It's okay, sweetheart, just tell me exactly what happened out there."

She nodded. "I heard a noise. Rocks rattling. When I turned around, he stepped out of the shadows. He wanted me to see him, Braedon. It was different from the restaurant. I think I surprised him there. But this time, he definitely wanted to be seen."

"Did he say anything?"

"Only my name." She pulled the afghan closer. "And then he started to walk toward me, this really sick little smile on his face. I panicked and tried to walk away, but I was too close to the edge. The ground gave way, and the next thing I knew I was on the ledge." She stopped and looked up, meeting his gaze. "You believe me, don't you? I mean, that I saw Alex."

He leaned forward, his hand on her arm. "I believe that you think you saw Alex."

Indignation flared. "It wasn't my imagination, Braedon. I swear it."

"I didn't say that it was."

She frowned, confusion warring with resentment. "So, what are you saying?"

He blew out a breath. "Alex has a brother."

"I know that. He's dead."

He reached for her hand. "I'm afraid Alex lied to you, Kacy."

She searched his eyes, trying to make sense of what he was saying. "So you're telling me that Alex's brother is alive?"

He nodded. "Max is Alex's twin." He paused, letting the impact of his words sink in.

Her heart twisted as her brain processed the information. "An identical twin?" The words came out a low whisper.

"Yeah."

"Why didn't you tell me before? At the restaurant? You let me believe . . ." She snuggled closer into the afghan, holding the edges, a tightly woven shield of sorts.

"Because I thought that Max was in prison. And because I didn't want you to realize who I was—what I knew."

She held up a hand to stop him. This wasn't the time. She needed to understand about Alex—and Max. "He was in prison?" She raised her eyebrows, waiting for him to explain.

"I don't know all the details, but evidently Max and Alex were grifters."

"Con men?" Well, that certainly fit. She must have seemed like an easy mark.

Braedon squeezed her hand reassuringly. It was uncanny how easily he read her mind. "Anyway, they got caught embezzling money. Or Max did. And he was incarcerated for it."

"But Alex got off?"

"I think Max covered for him, but of course there's no proof. Anyway, the point is, I was wrong. He's not in prison. He was released a week ago."

Kacy chewed on the side of her lip, her mind racing a mile a minute. "So it was him I saw at the hotel and at the fort. Alex is really dead."

"Yes, Kacy. Alex is dead. But Max doesn't want you to think so."

"But why? Why would he want to torment me like this?"

"I think it has something to do with the forgeries."

"The ones from Solais."

He released her hand and stood up, walking over to stand in front of the fireplace. "I gather the professor filled you in."

She pulled the afghan closer, reminding herself that he had betrayed her. "Some. You thought I was involved."

He nodded, his eyes boring into hers, the intensity there almost frightening.

She shook her head, clearing her thoughts of Braedon. Right now she wanted to think about Max. "And if you thought I was involved somehow—"

"Then it wouldn't be too big a leap for Max."

"So he thinks what? That I helped Alex?"

"Maybe, or that you hurt him."

"You think Max believes I killed his brother?" Her voice rose almost to a shriek.

"Look, sweetheart, the truth is, I don't know what Max is thinking. This whole thing is just conjecture." He ran a hand through his hair, his frustration reflected in the action. "We don't know what this man is capable of. Hell, we don't even know why he's here."

"Well, at least he's not a ghost." She pushed her hair back and tried for a smile, but failed miserably. "Anything is better than what I've been imagining. But there's still a problem with your little scenario."

"And that is?"

"Max was in prison. I'm not sure how that sort of thing works, but I do think it precludes any direct involvement in the forgeries."

"True, but he could have been the brains behind the scheme. All he'd have had to do was direct his brother."

"Yes, but Alex didn't paint those copies, Braedon. There had to be a third person involved." A thought forced its way front and center. "Do you think it could have been the man on the stairs?"

"Maybe. But I think he was Max's lackey. A guy called Anson Forbes."

"I see." The information was coming too fast. There was more here than her brain was capable of dealing with. She stifled a yawn.

"You're tired."

"It's been a long day." She twisted a strand of hair around her finger. "I just want this all to go away."

He took both of her hands in his, his steady gaze meeting hers. "We'll get to the bottom of this." He pulled her to her feet. "I'll take care of you, Kacy. I promise." He leaned closer, his eyes searching hers.

She pulled away from him, wrapping her arms around herself, suddenly feeling frightened and alone. There was a madman tormenting her and a liar standing in front of her. The world, it seemed, was full of people waiting to take advantage.

"But I can't trust your promises, Braedon."

Something flickered across his face and then was gone.

Pain. Remorse. And something else that Kacy couldn't put a name to. Wasn't certain she wanted to. "Kacy, we need to talk."

Hurt battled with need. He'd saved her. He'd betrayed her trust. One feeling clashed against the other and she sighed, realizing she simply didn't have the energy to fight with him.

"We do." She sat back down on the sofa, drawing the afghan tightly around her.

"I don't know where to start."

"Someone told me today that the best place to start was the beginning."

Braedon nodded and sat in the chair facing her, studying his hands. "I've worked really hard for what I have. For my reputation as well as my money." He rubbed his chin, still not looking at her. "Until recently, my reputation was the most important thing in the world to me."

She wanted to ask him what he meant by that. There was so much between them. But now wasn't the right time. She needed to concentrate on the subject at hand. "And the discovery of the forgeries threatened that reputation."

He looked up, the vulnerability in his eyes making her want to cry. "The police thought I did it. That I sabotaged my own business."

"But you didn't." She said it softly.

"No, I didn't."

"Well, neither did I."

He sighed, rubbing his eyes, elbows propped on the arms of the chair. "I know that."

"Now."

"Now." He looked up at her, his eyes tortured.

"You didn't tell me who you were." The sentence hung in the air, embodying everything that stood between them.

"No. I didn't. And believe me, if I could take it back, I would. But I can't."

"That's true, but you can try to explain to me why you felt

the need to lie to me." She watched him, trying to control her battling emotions.

He blew out a breath. "I thought Alex was involved. He was the only one besides me who could have pulled it off. He had access to everything in the gallery. He knew when paintings were due in and when they were being delivered after they sold. With the right connections, he could have made it work."

"And I was his wife." She squared her shoulders, meeting his gaze, her own steady.

He nodded. "An obvious connection. You were conceivably the closest person to him. And when you couple that with the fact that you disappeared without a trace . . ."

"I'd say that's a little bit of an exaggeration, Braedon. I mean, you are sitting here."

A ghost of a smile traced its way across his face. "Well, it wasn't easy to find you, believe me." He shifted uncomfortably in the chair. "And there was the money."

"Money?"

"Alex's share of the forgeries." Braedon looked miserable, but held her gaze, his eyes steady, his meaning crystal clear.

"You thought I had Alex's money?"

"It seemed logical. I mean, you had the wherewithal to disappear. And then there's all this." He gestured to the antiques filling the room.

"But I explained—"

"I know. And I wanted to believe you. In fact, on some level I did believe you." He looked down at his hands, studying them as if they held the answers to all the secrets of the world.

She shivered with the memory of those hands on her body. Maybe they did hold all the answers. His words wounded her, but not as much as she'd thought they would. Her icy façade slipped a little, emotion rushing through the chink. Maybe it would be all right. Lord knew, she wanted it to be all right.

There was logic in his train of thought and she had a feeling she knew where he was going next. "Then you saw the Monet."

He shrugged. "What was I supposed to think? I mean, I came here expecting to prove you guilty, and there was the proof right in front of me."

"But you said you believe I'm innocent."

"I do. You were so honest about everything, even admitting that the painting was your copy. It didn't make sense. But you have to understand, Kacy, part of me desperately needed you to be guilty."

She frowned, confused by his words.

He stood up and began pacing in front of the fire. "You were a paradox. On the one hand you were the last link with Alex. My last hope for finding out what really happened."

"And the other side of the paradox?"

He stopped, turning to face her, his heart in his eyes. "You were the most wonderful woman I'd ever met. Honest, endearing, beautiful . . ." He stopped, their gazes colliding, and Kacy suddenly found it hard to breathe.

"And a forger." She sank back against the sofa, trying to put physical distance between them.

"No. I didn't believe that. I knew you were innocent, but things had gotten complicated and I just never found the right time. Hell, this sounds lame even to me." His eyes pleaded with hers. "I tried to tell you this morning, remember, but Baucomo interrupted. And then when I got back—"

"I wouldn't listen."

"Well, you had good reason." He knelt beside her, taking her hand in both of his. She shivered at the contact, his warmth shooting up her arm, kindling a fire deep inside her. "Kacy, I don't want to lose you."

"I'm not sure that you ever had me, Braedon." She spoke instinctively, regretting it before the sentence was completed.

She wasn't sure she could survive losing *him* and so she'd opted for self-preservation.

The pain reflected on his face hurt her. "I see."

"Braedon, I just need a little time." She squeezed his hand. "I haven't had much luck with men and I don't trust my own decisions. I want things to be good between us. But I need to know that I can trust you."

He released her and moved to stand. She reached out and stopped him, laying a hand on his cheek, reaching inside herself for courage. "I think I'm falling in love with you, Braedon, and it scares the hell out of me. I don't know what to believe. So much is happening. You—us." She stroked his cheek, feeling his body tremble at her touch, her words. She lost herself in the strength of his gaze. "I'm afraid. There's a dead ringer of my husband out there somewhere trying to drive me around the bend. Or worse. And I don't even know why. My dog was p-poisoned, there was a dead man in my house, and last n-night . . ."

He covered her hand with his. "We found something very special, Kacy."

"I believed that. But then today you took it away from me with your lies."

"I'm just asking you to give me a chance."

She met his gaze, searching for any hint of insincerity, but there was only regret. With a sigh, she made up her mind. There were shadows to fight and she didn't want to be alone. She wanted to trust him. She wanted to take the chance— needed to take the chance. "No more lies?"

He smiled, recognizing the answer in her eyes. "No more lies."

She tipped back her head, waiting for his kiss.

Chapter 20

"So WHAT DID you find out?" Kacy asked, looking up as he walked into the kitchen. She was holding a teacup so tightly that her knuckles were white.

"Not a damn thing." He sat down next to her at the table.

"Nothing?"

He blew out a breath, shaking his head. "Matt hasn't turned up anything new. He's going to turn up the heat, but until he can find something more, we're on our own."

She carefully put the cup back into the saucer, concentrating on the action as though the world depended on it. It broke his heart to see her like this. He damned Max Madison to hell and back again. Not that it did any good.

"What about the Garda?" She lifted her head, her troubled gaze meeting his.

"There's nothing they can do. We haven't got anything to pin on him."

"But I saw him at the fort. He left me there."

"There weren't any witnesses, Kacy. Even if it is illegal, it would be your word against his. Not to mention the fact that at the moment we don't even have a *him*."

"But we know he's here. Somewhere. I can feel it." She rubbed her arms with her hands, shivering.

"I called the hotel, too."

Hope flashed in her eyes. "And?"

He hated to douse the light in her eyes, but he had no choice. "Nothing. There's no Max Madison registered at the hotel. And, at least according to the front desk, no one answering to his description."

She shook her head. "But they have to protect their guests, don't they? They have no reason to tell us the truth."

"Well, I'm not a man without influence. Although I don't think the guy on the phone knew me from Adam's off ox."

The ghost of a smile chased across her face. "Adam's off ox?"

"Something my mother used to say." He shrugged, answering her smile with a grin. If nothing else, at least they were working together again. "Look, let's go over what we know. Maybe between the two of us we can come up with something."

"Seems worth a try." She stood up and crossed to the sink. "I'm going to make a sandwich. Do you want one?"

"Sure." He watched her movements as she pulled out bread and sliced some cheese. Even in the simple act of cutting cheddar, she managed to look irresistible. "Okay, so what have we got?"

"Well, from my end, there's the car, and Mac's poisoning, and the dead man. Plus the two sightings of Max." She laid a plate on the table in front of him.

"And the little fact that he left you out on that ledge to die."

She sucked in a deep breath, her eyes meeting his. "Well, I didn't die. And if I have my way about it, I'm not going to. Max or no Max."

"I certainly second that."

She picked her plate up off the counter and turned to face him, her eyes narrowed in thought. "You know, now that I think about it, there have been other times when I thought someone was watching me."

"You mean the way he was today?"

She nodded, sitting at the table, her plate in front of her. "Yeah. At the fort, actually. A couple of times when I was there with Mac, I thought I heard something. At the time I wrote it off as my imagination. But now . . ." She stopped, her mind obviously puzzling over something. "What about the wall at the fort? The footprint. Could that have been Max, too?"

Braedon swallowed a bite of sandwich, his brain churning. "It could be. Or it could all be totally unrelated. We don't have a shred of evidence that Max is even here."

She fixed him with an indignant stare. "Are you saying I didn't see him?"

He raised a hand in peace. "No. Not at all. I'm just saying we don't have anything to prove he's really here. Nothing to tie him to anything that's happened."

"There's the body. Did you tell the Garda about this Anson person?"

"Yeah, I did. And they're going to look into it. But things move slowly in the country. And it could be a while before they know anything."

"Can your friend Matt help to speed things up?"

"I think so. Hell, I hope so."

"Maybe we're going about this the wrong way. Maybe instead of concentrating on where Max is, we should be concentrating on why he's here."

"What do you mean?" He finished off the last of his sandwich, surprised at how hungry he'd been.

"I mean that Max is obviously here for a reason. If we can figure out what that reason is, then maybe we can figure out what's going on." She paused, chewing on her bottom lip. "And how to stop it."

"All right. So we're assuming that this has something to do with the forgeries, right?"

"Yes. It seems to make sense. And, despite your comments earlier, I think we can assume that Max isn't trying to kill me."

"Kacy," he said, shaking his head. "I don't know if I'd go that far."

She held up a hand to stop him. "Hang on a minute. If you think about it, he hasn't really done anything to hurt me."

"What the hell are you talking about? He left you stranded on a ledge in the middle of a rainstorm. That's not exactly a gesture of goodwill." He stopped, realizing that he was yelling at her.

She smiled slowly. "I know. But he didn't push me, did he? And if you separate that instance from the others, then what you have is a search. Even the police thought it was a robbery."

"All right, I'll accept that. Although I still think there's more to it. Hell, Kacy, he destroyed the Monet. If that wasn't a malicious act, I don't know what is."

"Look, I'm not trying to make excuses for the man. I just want to get to the bottom of this. Besides, it wasn't Max who tore the house apart. It was Anson."

"Or we think it was Anson." Frustration reared its ugly head again. All they had were dead ends.

"The bottom line here is that Max seems to think that I have something he wants."

"But what?"

"I don't know. Nothing of Alex's. I sold everything of value and threw the rest out. I didn't want any memories."

"You kept his picture."

"I know. I tried to explain it before. I feel responsible for his death."

"Even after everything he did to you?"

"No one deserves to die like that, Braedon."

He thought about Anson's death. Her words then had been almost the same. Kacy was a compassionate woman.

More so than he was. He wanted nothing more than to bring Alex back to life simply to have the privilege of killing him again.

"Besides, at the time, I wanted him back. I still believed that I could make it work."

"And now?"

She smiled slowly, sending shivers of need down his spine. "Now I know better."

He shook his head, focusing on the issue at hand. "Didn't Alex ever share anything with you? Anything that would give us a clue about what Max might be looking for?"

She shook her head, pain flickering across her face. "No. There's nothing. Alex never told me anything."

"And you didn't ask."

"If I asked a question, he lied to me or found a way to throw it back into my face. I know I should have done something more. But I didn't."

"I didn't mean to bring it up again." He lifted his hands in testament and then dropped them again uselessly. "I just hoped there was something . . . anything."

"There's nothing. Honestly. I barely saw Alex after we were married. And when I did, talking was the last thing on his mind." She shivered at the memory.

"He hurt you."

Her eyes met his, telegraphing an answer he didn't want to hear. "I still have nightmares about it."

"That's why you're afraid of the dark."

She nodded.

"Oh, God, Kacy." He half rose from his chair, wanting to pull her into his arms, to make it all right, but she shook her head, holding him off with just a look.

"We covered this ground before, Braedon, and I don't want to relive it. There are things we can see with hindsight that we can't see when we're in the middle of the storm. The important point here is that I survived."

There was something in her voice. A new note. Somehow in everything that had happened, Kacy had grown stronger. "And now you have to let it go."

"I don't know about that. Things have a way of resurfacing when you least expect them to." She pushed her uneaten sandwich away, suddenly deflating.

Damn Alex Madison and his brother.

"We're going in circles here. We need more information. And until we get it I doubt we'll uncover anything."

"Is your friend going to call back?"

He nodded, reaching across the table to take her hands. "As soon as he finds something. Listen, why don't you get some sleep? I'll stay here and keep watch."

"You think he's coming back." Panic flashed across her face, but as quickly as it appeared it was gone. She was obviously determined to put on a brave front.

"I think it's possible. But I'll be here, Kacy. I'll watch over you."

And by God, he was going to do whatever he could to keep Max Madison from hurting her. She'd been through enough. And he'd be damned before he'd let anyone else hurt her.

"But, Braedon—" She looked up at him, her green eyes flashing with emotion. "—who'll take care of you?"

Braedon leaned back in his chair, watching her sleep. Her hair was splayed across the pillow, a silky curtain slipping across her cheek. One strand had separated from the others and lay across her mouth, lifting and falling with each breath she took.

He resisted the urge to crawl into bed next to her, to wake her with kisses. It was too soon. Besides, after everything he'd done, the invitation had to come from her.

The house was quiet. Mac slept at the foot of the chair, his nose resting by Braedon's toe. It was a domestic scene.

Tranquil.

Deceiving.

He sighed and rubbed his eyes. Sleep threatened to over-take him, but he fought against it, knowing he needed to stay alert.

He'd gone over it a million times in his mind and still nothing made sense. What could Kacy have that Max wanted? The only answer he could come up with was money. But Kacy didn't have any. And even if she did, how did Max plan on get-ting it? And for that matter, if Max had truly been the brains behind the forgeries, wouldn't he have already known where any money was hidden?

Unless Alex had died before he could tell Max where the money was.

Braedon frowned, trying to piece it together. Kacy had said she met Alex in the Cayman Islands. A damn good place to stash ill-gotten gains. But still, there'd been time to tell his brother. Unless it had been a double cross. Had Kacy and Alex been working together? But that threw suspicion back on Kacy. And damn it, he'd been down that road before. He trusted her, and by God, he was going to prove it to her.

Hell, this was all so complicated. He stood up and walked to the window, still thinking about Max. If Braedon had jumped to the conclusion there'd been a double cross, then Max would, too. And Max would no doubt believe his brother was innocent.

Could the whole thing be that simple?

The storm had blown itself out, leaving behind a beautiful night. The moon shone brightly against the rocky ground, sil-vering the stones that dotted the meadow. If Alex had died without telling his brother where the money was, then it was logical that Max would believe Kacy might know where it was.

Was it possible that Max had been jealous of Kacy's involvement with his brother? Or worse still, did Max believe Kacy had something to do with his twin's death?

It was all so bloody confusing and, without confronting Max, impossible to straighten out. Braedon watched a cloud drift lazily across the moon. No. He would find a way to get to the bottom of this. For his own peace of mind and for Kacy.

If Max Madison had anything to do with the forgeries, Braedon intended to see him put away for a long time. And if he was indeed behind all that had happened to Kacy, well, then he'd be lucky if he lived long enough to see prison again.

There was still an overriding problem, though. Before he could do anything else, he had to find Max Madison.

Max stood at the hotel window, watching a cloud briefly obliterate the moon. It was almost full. A hunter's paradise. He smiled. He was soon to be the hunter. He'd made up his mind. Tomorrow was the day.

He'd take out the bitch and nail that greasy little wop, too. Nice and tidy. And if he was lucky, he'd convince Kirstin to tell him where the money was hidden. If not . . .

He shrugged. It wasn't as if he was hurting for cash.

Revenge was far more important than money. He owed it to Anson. And, more important, to Alex.

Max watched as the moon bathed the Irish countryside in shimmering light. This time tomorrow, Kirstin Macgrath would be dead and his brother could finally rest in peace.

"For you, Alex. Always for you."

Kacy stirred, opening sleepy eyes. Braedon slept sprawled out across the chair. It didn't look particularly comfortable, but he seemed to be past caring. His face in slumber lost the hard edge it often had when he was awake. As though the man he'd become was discarded for the time being, and the boy he'd been was allowed to come out to play. It was a whimsical thought and she smiled at her flight of fantasy.

Braedon was who he was. And she loved all of him. So she'd try to forgive the part that had lied to her. The hurt wasn't gone entirely, but the anger was. She honestly couldn't say she'd have done anything differently if the situations had been reversed.

In fact, truth be told, she had kept things from him. Maybe not as ruthlessly as he'd done, but certainly with the intent to conceal. Braedon had no idea who she really was. Again, she smiled. In some ways, he knew her more intimately than anyone ever had, but the fact remained that she had lied to him, too. At least by omission.

"You're awake."

She started out of her reverie, meeting his sleepy gaze. "Just barely." The moon was still out, its light coming in through the window, mixing with the glow of the table lamp.

He came to sit on the bed, reaching for her hand, his eyes concerned. "How are you feeling?"

"Sore." She stretched, her muscles groaning with the movement. "And sleepy." And content. The thought echoed around in her brain, but she dared not repeat it out loud. With Braedon here, somehow everything seemed right with the world. All the rest of it held at bay. Suspended, at least for the moment. She was in the magic circle. And part of her was loath to say anything that would break the enchantment of the moment.

"Kacy, I've been thinking about what happened this morning. What I didn't say. What I should have said. I was wrong. And I really am sorry."

She stared up into the deep blue of his eyes. "I think I understand why you did it."

"I don't want secrets between us."

"Neither do I." And she meant it. For the first time in all her life, her father's voice was silent, and she knew what she had to do. "I haven't told you everything either." His brows drew together and a shadow crossed his face. She shivered, but forced herself to continue before she lost her nerve.

"I haven't told you about my father." She drew in a breath for fortification.

Chapter 21

"YOUR FATHER? I don't understand." Braedon's voice reflected his confusion.

Kacy stared at the ceiling. Remembering. Trying to make it sound like something romantic and not something sordid. "My mother was a beautiful, talented woman, but she was from the proverbial wrong side of the tracks."

"Fin said she was from Lindoon."

"Then you probably know some of it already. She left home when she was young. I think she thought she'd find riches at the end of the rainbow. And the end for her was in New York. She found modest success as a model, but it was long before the supermodels ruled, and so she only got by, really."

She stopped, not certain she could continue. He squeezed her hand encouragingly. "She met a man. The love of her life, actually. He was young and handsome—and he was married. But that didn't stop them. They began to see more and more of each other. Always in private, away from prying eyes. My mother quit modeling. It was too public and he thought it was dangerous."

"Dangerous how?"

"It was a different time, Braedon. People didn't get divorced as much. And even when they did, it wasn't acceptable, especially in society circles."

"There had to be more to it than that."

"There was." She sighed, knowing that somehow it was time to lay all her ghosts to rest. "My father married into a very powerful family. He spent the better part of his life working his way to the top of his father-in-law's company. I'm not sure that anything mattered to him as much as his quest for power."

"But that alone wouldn't prevent him from having a mistress. It wasn't exactly the dark ages."

"There was his wife. Millicent. She was very possessive. And my father believed that if she found out about my mother, she'd divorce him."

"And there goes his meal ticket." Braedon's voice sounded harsh, judgmental.

"It wasn't as bad as all that. Really. My father just didn't want to lose what he'd worked so hard to build. Anyway, my mother and father were happy in their own way, I think. And before too long, there was tangible evidence of their affair."

"You." His voice was gentle now, and he stroked her arm lightly with one hand.

"Me. I was born in upstate New York. Father bought a house for us. He visited as often as he could, but of course it wasn't nearly enough. And the rest of the time we were completely isolated."

"Why?"

"Because of Millicent. She couldn't have children. And that only made her more possessive of my father. She threatened him."

"With divorce," Braedon offered dryly.

"With more than that, I think. My existence was a reminder of Millicent's failings." She shivered. "My father never talked about it all that much, but I think he believed that if she ever discovered I existed, she might actually harm me. So we stayed on the estate. Always."

"But what about shopping and school?"

"We had staff to handle the shopping and I had tutors. All generously paid to keep our secret."

"What about friends?"

"There weren't any. We couldn't take the risk."

"It must have been a lonely childhood."

"In some ways it was. But when my father was with us it was wonderful. We were a family." She nervously ran a hand through her hair. "It was a lot harder on my mother than it was on me."

"What do you mean?"

"She withered and died a little each day he was away. He was her whole world."

"But she had you."

Kacy smiled wistfully. "She loved me. But not like she loved him. And when he was with us—she was magnificent. Charming, beautiful, funny. But when he was gone, she went inside herself somewhere, to a place I couldn't reach."

"As time passed, he came less and less. Not because he didn't love us, you understand. But because he had another life, a life we couldn't be a part of. And the more he was gone, the more she withdrew, until one day, when I was eight, she swallowed a bottle of pills and never woke up."

"Oh, Kacy." He pulled her into his arms and she nestled into his warmth, letting it comfort her, give her strength.

"I thought it was my fault." She spoke into his chest, the sound muffled. She felt his hand as it stroked her hair. "I thought I did something to make her go away. To die."

"You didn't do anything, Kacy."

She pulled back, leaning against the pillows. He stretched out beside her, keeping an arm around her shoulders. "I know that now, but not then."

"What happened?"

"I was sent away. To boarding school in Switzerland. I thought I was being punished. It was all very hush-hush. I wasn't even allowed to use my real name."

"Sister Margaretta."

"Exactly. Kirstin died and Kacy was born."

"Did your father visit?"

"Sometimes. But mainly I had holidays alone. I wasn't allowed to go with any of the other girls. They might accidentally figure out who I was. The threat of Millicent was always there, lurking in the shadows. Kacy Macgrath—persona non grata. For all practical purposes, I didn't exist."

He tightened his hold on her. "It must have been horrible for you."

"Not really. I'd never lived any other way. Sometimes I'd see other families and wish that was me. But most of the time I accepted it. The only time it was ever different at all was when I was really little. I used to come here with my mother, to my Granny Macgrath's. Lindoon was magical. I felt normal here. I never was allowed to stay long, but while I was here, I could pretend I was like other kids. I could pretend the secrets didn't exist."

"That's why you came here after Alex drowned."

She nodded. "I thought it would provide sanctuary."

"But it hasn't."

"No. I should have known better."

"But surely when you grew up you escaped from your father's prison?" He sounded angry again.

"No. For a little while I had something approaching normalcy. My father had attained great power by that point. He ran his father-in-law's company, making millions. But then the old man died."

"Your father?"

She shook her head. "No. His father-in-law. And the noose my father had been wearing all his life tightened again. Millicent's father had left everything to her. All of it. Everything my father had worked for all those years. Millicent had him in a stranglehold."

"One of his own making, Kacy."

"Don't judge him so harshly, Braedon. He had to keep me in the shadows. Not just to protect himself, but to protect me."

"From Millicent." He frowned, stroking her hair with one hand. "That's not love, Kacy."

She tensed, pain shooting through her. "I think he thought it was. I've always been taken care of. The best of everything."

"Except a life."

"No, I even had a life. An odd one, to be sure, but it had its moments." She smiled up at him, willing him to understand. "Even after he died, he took care of me financially."

"The trust fund."

"I have enough to keep me comfortably."

"When did he die?"

"Just before I married Alex. That's why I . . ." She trailed off, embarrassed to admit she'd married a stranger out of loss and grief and loneliness.

"That's why you used Kirstin again."

"It was stupid, really. A little rebellion after years of perfect behavior, but I was angry and hurt. I didn't even know he was ill."

"Sometimes there isn't time for good-bye, Kacy."

"No. He was sick a really long time. He knew. He arranged for me to be taken care of, all duly cloaked in secrecy, accounts transferred to other accounts and then on to others, but he never took the time to say good-bye. Not even a letter."

She stopped, trying to pull herself back into control. "I loved him so much. And I don't think I was ever anything to him but a painful reminder of my mother. Every time he looked at me, he saw her. And he wanted her."

Hot tears spilled down her cheeks, and Braedon pulled her close again. She could feel the steady beat of his heart against her skin and she let it soothe her, calm her. "I guess I'd always thought that someday, he'd acknowledge me. He promised he would. Stupid, I know, but I had dreams that he'd whisk me off to his penthouse in New York, introduce me to the world as his daughter.

"I wanted so much to be a normal part of his life. But I couldn't be, and frankly, I don't think he ever wanted me to be. And then when he died, I knew it would never happen. That my legacy was to protect his secret for the rest of my life."

"From Millicent."

She bit her lower lip, nodding. "And for one stupid moment I rebelled."

"Your marriage."

She nodded miserably.

"Did Alex know about all of this? About your father?"

"No. Even in my rebellion I couldn't talk about it. Maybe it was too ingrained in me. Or maybe even in the midst of my foolish attachment to Alex, I realized he couldn't be trusted. I don't know. All I know for certain is that I acted like a fool, and you already know where that left me."

"With Alex's mess."

She rolled away, wiping the tears from her eyes. She needed to finish this. Finally let it go. "His mess, yes, and my own stupidity. When Alex's goons came after me, I foolishly thought Millicent might help me."

He rolled over on his side, facing her. "You told her who you were?"

She met his gaze, the moment at hand. "Yeah. Kirstin Macgrath—Kirstin *Caldwell* Macgrath. My father was—"

"Caldwell Bremmerton. Of course. How could I have been so stupid?" He laughed, his reaction not exactly what she had expected.

"I don't think it's funny." Her heart constricted. She felt deflated, hurt. He thought this was a joke.

"Oh, honey, I'm not laughing at you. Honestly." He reached out and tucked a strand of hair behind her ear. "I'm laughing at me. I found a picture of you with Bremmerton and

I thought . . ." His voice trailed off and he sheepishly met her gaze.

"You thought my father and I were—" She couldn't bring herself to finish the sentence.

"I certainly didn't know he was your father. I saw how you were looking at him. I was jealous, Kacy."

Relief flooded through her. He wasn't laughing at her. And he wasn't repelled either. In fact, he'd actually been jealous— of her father, no less. A bubble of laughter rose in her throat, but died before it could escape. "You were going through my things?"

"No." He held up a hand in defense. "I found it on the floor. By the fireplace. It must have fallen there when the cottage was trashed."

She breathed a sigh of relief. "But you knew my father."

He blew out a breath, looking decidedly uncomfortable. "Yes. I knew him. We had business dealings."

She searched his face. "And you didn't like him."

"No, Kacy, I didn't. And I can't say that your story makes me feel any differently." He pulled her back into his arms, his lips brushing her hair. "But I'm not certain I can be objective. Tell me about Millicent."

"There isn't much to tell."

"I take it she wasn't pleased to discover Caldwell had a daughter."

"She threatened me. Threatened to destroy my father's memory and to make my life a living hell."

"And you believed her?"

"I didn't really analyze it. Between Alex's goons and Millicent's threats I just wanted to escape. So I did what I do best. I disappeared. Again."

"Until I found you."

"Until then." She knew suddenly that what she wanted more than anything was to be with this man, to have him hold her like this every night for the rest of her life. She sighed and nestled closer, feeling his heart beat against hers.

He kissed her gently, holding her safe in the circle of his arms. "Try to get some sleep, princess. Everything will look better in the morning."

The words were nice. Comforting. But she knew they weren't true. Couldn't be true. Not until they'd figured out how to stop Max Madison.

Chapter 22

BRAEDON WOKE TO the soft drumming of rain on the roof. He groaned. Memories of yesterday chilling him right through the bedcovers. Kacy stirred, her head tucked tight against his chest. He groaned again, his body responding just to her nearness. *Torture.* She snuggled closer, one leg thrown across him.

Oh, but what a way to go.

She moaned softly and tilted back her head, green eyes open, sparkling with desire. "Braedon." His name was a whispered entreaty. One he did not have to have offered twice. He rolled over, pinning her beneath him, his hands tangling in her hair.

He searched her eyes, making sure of his welcome, and then when she smiled, he lowered his mouth to hers, teasing her with his tongue, tasting the sweet honey of her lips. He traced a path with his mouth along the soft curve of her chin, down the column of her neck, relishing the tiny shivers his touch sent streaking through her.

He slid the strap of her nightgown off of one shoulder, his fingers curving around her smooth skin, massaging lower and lower until he held her breast in his hand, the nipple tight and hard against his palm. She arched against his hand, driven by her need, and his body reacted immediately, desire surging through him, a tidal wave of emotion threatening to unman him.

234

With fumbling hands, they removed their clothes, touching, exploring—the need to be skin to skin driving them to a frenzy.

Finally, when they were both naked, she kissed him, her tongue leaving trails of hot fire as it traced the contours of his mouth. Their gazes locked, her eyes dark pools, flecks of silvery gold dancing across the cool green. Eyes a man could lose himself in. And Braedon knew he was already lost. With a sigh, he rolled again, this time positioning her on top of him, her body molded to his.

She sat up, legs straddling him, and lifted her hair, back arched, breasts teasing him. Then she released the gleaming strands, and the soft-spun gold drifted down around her shoulders, caressing her breasts.

He groaned and reached for her, his desire to hold her, to possess her, greater than any he had known. A soft smile played about her lips, and as their eyes met, she lifted, impaling herself on him with one fluid motion. He circled her waist with his hands, amazed at how tiny she was. Pulling her forward, he suckled at her breasts as she began to ride him, their moans mixing together as the delicious tension began to build.

Up and down, up and down, like a pony on a carousel. She threw back her head, closing her eyes. He watched as she moved, sliding along the length of him. Taking him deeper with each thrust, lost in the magic of their dance.

Tears filled his eyes as the sweetness that was Kacy surrounded him—loved him. Her hands dug into his shoulders and he closed his eyes, letting her take him higher and higher, the world changing, simplifying until there was only the two of them, dancing together, riding the carousel. Color and light filling the air.

Around and around, up and down, faster and faster until the world flew apart and shattered into fractured colors. Reds and yellows and greens.

It was magic.

It was love.

Kacy rested her head on Braedon's chest, the cadence of his heart a counterpoint to the patter of the rain against the window. Outside the wind howled, but here, bodies intertwined, the world seemed safe and warm. She snuggled closer, enjoying the pressure of his arm as it tightened around her, the feeling of belonging.

Tracing lazy circles across his chest with her fingertip, she sighed, emotions spent, contentment curling inside her like a purring kitten.

"I lived most of my life in this country." His voice rumbled up through his chest. Stereophonics in bed. She bit back a smile. He stroked her hair absently with one hand. "You'd think in all that time I would have grown accustomed to the rain."

"I think it's wonderful. There aren't gardens anywhere in the world as marvelous as here. And they couldn't look like they do without all the rain."

"I've never thought of it like that." There was a smile in his voice. "You always see the bright side of things."

She laughed, the sound ringing out through the room. "Or maybe I just like the rain." She twirled a finger around the springy hair on his chest. "So what made you leave Ireland?"

He was quiet for so long she didn't think he was going to answer. She wanted to take back the words, but couldn't. Braedon was a private man and their intimacy was newly found. She didn't want to jeopardize it. Still, she had told him her secrets.

"I guess, indirectly, my mother dying."

"Indirectly?" Kacy frowned, confused.

"Yeah, in and of itself, that wasn't the reason I left. It was everything added together, really."

She held her breath, waiting for him to continue.

He shifted slightly, pulling her closer. "My mother and I were on our own right from the beginning. My father left for a pint one night and never came back. We were better off, though. He had a wicked right hook." The words themselves were issued with a bantering tone, but underneath, Kacy could hear the pain of the little boy.

"So your mother took care of you."

"We took care of each other. It wasn't easy. The people in the village where I was born were less than forgiving. They didn't cotton to an unmarried woman on her own with a child. So we moved to Dublin, thinking the big city would have opportunity to spare."

There was bitterness in his voice, and Kacy wanted to comfort him, but knew it was best, for now, just to listen.

"We didn't have any money. And most of the time not even a place to lay our heads, but she always made me see the adventure of it. Magic in the dreariness, hope in the face of despair. She'd say that we were lucky to have each other and that there were lots of folks in this world who had no one."

His accent had thickened and she could hear traces of the Dublin boy in the rhythm of his voice. "She worked in a factory. Godawful hours, with pennies for pay, but it put a roof over our heads and a bit of food in our bellies. When I was a lad, I thought that everyone lived like that. I'd no idea how destitute we really were. She never let on. Never complained. Just worked shift after shift after shift."

"And what did you do?" Kacy wanted to understand this part of Braedon. The part that still hurt after all these years.

"At first I stayed with the woman who lived in the flat above us. Then, when I grew older, I started doing odd jobs. Anything I could find to bring in a few quid. Anything I could do to make her life a little easier. And, for a while, we did all right. Even managed a holiday once, to Whitegate. It was the first time I'd ever seen the ocean."

She ran her hand lightly along his chest, needing to touch him, to let him know that she was there.

"After that, things went to hell in a hurry. She got sick. Really sick. She said it was a virus. The kind of thing that comes on sudden and then refuses to go away, but I knew it was something worse. I was twelve, a man grown in the world we lived in."

Kacy's heart twisted at his words. She understood only too well what it was like to be thrust from childhood too soon. "What happened?"

"She didn't get well. We went to a doctor, and then to another." He sighed, the movement and sound communicating itself through his chest, his pain becoming hers. "They all said the same thing. Almost like a litany. An aggressive form of lymphoma. Too advanced. There wasn't a damn thing anyone could do about it." He paused, his breathing ragged, his heart pounding.

"But surely there was hope?" Kacy reached for his hand, pulling it to her cheek, trying to communicate her sympathy with a touch.

"Hope?" His laugh was harsh and humorless. "Hope was for the wealthy, not the inhabitants of a broken-down flat north of the Liffey. I wanted so much to help her, to make her well. I wanted answers. I wanted miracles. I thought that if I had enough money, enough power, I could save her."

"But you were only a child."

"I was the man of the family. I was all she had. Little by little, it ate away at her, this cancer, until there was nothing of her left but her spirit and her driving need to stay with her son. And I let her down. I let her die."

"No. You did everything you could. I know it. *I know you.*" She tipped back her head, meeting his tortured gaze.

"But it wasn't enough, Kacy." He closed his eyes and she reached up to run a hand along the contour of his cheek, wanting nothing more than to ease his pain. "After she died, I was on my own and I swore I wasn't going to be poor anymore." He paused, opening his eyes, a slight self-mocking smile curling his lips. "Sort of like the woman in *Gone with the Wind.*"

"Scarlett O'Hara?" Kacy didn't know if she wanted to laugh or to cry.

"Right. Only without the hoop skirts."

She smiled up at him, amazed at his ability to challenge his grief. "So you set out for America?"

"Not exactly. I went on the dole. I was just a kid, but Ireland provided for me. A series of foster homes, I think you call them. Hellholes would be a more accurate description. I kept running away, until finally when I was fifteen, they washed their hands of me once and for all."

"But you were still so young."

"Only in age. Truth be told, I was a streetwise punk. A punk asking for trouble. And that's just what happened."

"You were arrested?"

"More than once, princess." A touch of laughter edged his voice. This time without bitterness. "But, no, I got my comeuppance from a world-weary Dubliner with an eye for potential. Patrick Mahoney. Then, he took me in and gave me a job and slowly, oftentimes the hard way, my self-respect. I worked my way up in his company, watching and learning, determined to find a way to make it on my own someday. Paddy taught me everything he knew."

"About business?"

"Business and life. He taught me how to talk without letting the world know where I came from. He taught me to play with the big boys without letting them get the better of me. He taught me how to figure the odds and how to win. He taught me to muzzle my emotions and lead with my head. Paddy Mahoney took a raw, angry boy and polished him into a man. And then he died, too."

Braedon leaned back against the pillows, staring at the

ceiling, lost in the memory. "He left me some money. I think he'd meant for me to stay on, but I knew it was time to try my own wings."

He ran a hand lightly across her shoulders, tracing a path down her back, his touch sending her senses reeling, but he was lost in thought and unaware of the effect he was having on her.

"I wanted to make my mark on the world and I figured the States was the place to do that." His voice was low, noncommittal.

"And did you?" she queried.

"Did I what?"

She shifted slightly, so that she could see his face. "Make your mark?"

He laughed, quietly, to himself. "I'm successful, if that's what you mean."

"I don't know what I mean, really. It's just that it seems to me that people get it all wrong. They think the answer is in the game or the winning. But there isn't really anything to that, is there? I mean, at the end of the day, it's what you come home to that matters."

He pulled her close. "Do you have any idea how wonderful you are?"

She flushed, embarrassed at the naked emotion swimming in his eyes. "I . . . it's just . . ."

His mouth closed over hers, effectively cutting off her sentence, which was just as well, since she had no idea what she'd been about to say.

His kiss was demanding, full of the passion he'd held at bay for all those years. It called to her, pulling her deeper and deeper, until she wondered if she would drown in the pure sensation of him. A prospect that, she had to admit, sounded rather appealing.

His hand found her breast and she bit back a moan, pushing against him, her hands stroking, exploring the hard contours of his back.

"Let me love you, Kacy." The whispered words blew soft against her cheek, sending desire rippling through her, hot and heavy.

She opened her legs, welcoming the feel of his throbbing heat against the apex of her thighs. Her need burned strong, but this time it was laced with something more. An overriding feeling that this was right; that somehow, here, with him, was where she was meant to be.

With a groan, he thrust into her and she welcomed him, cradling him deep within her pulsing heat. They rocked together, the rhythm coming naturally, as if it had been specially choreographed for them long ago. She clung to him, sensation splintering through her, knowing that she had found the other half of her soul. And for the first time in her life, Kacy knew she wasn't alone.

"Let me take you home, Braedon."

"I'm already there, love. I'm already there."

Chapter 23

KACY OPENED HER eyes and looked sleepily toward the window. Rain still ran in rivulets down the window-pane, but the world outside was discernibly lighter. She stretched and yawned, comforted by the heat of Braedon's body next to hers. Morning had come. And despite the uncertainties looming out there, she felt like it was going to be a good day.

Braedon rolled over with a groan, throwing an arm across her waist. "I suppose you're going to tell me that we have to get up?"

"Well, as a matter of fact—"

He cut her off with a kiss, his ministrations making her giddy and hot all at the same time. Then, with a decidedly male grin of satisfaction, he released her and rolled to a sitting position on the side of the bed, rubbing one sun-bronzed hand over the stubble on his face. At the sight of his naked torso, a stampede of stilettos tangoed through her insides like beginners' night at Arthur Murray's ballroom dance studio.

"I need to call Matt."

His words were like a splash of cold water. The dancers quit their fumbling and her desire evaporated. There was so much at stake. Time enough to explore their fragile new relationship when Max Madison was safely behind bars.

"So who exactly is Matt?"

Braedon stood up, pulled on his jeans, and walked to the

window. "Matt is an old friend. A very well-connected old friend."

"You mean in society?" Kacy failed to see how that could be of any value to them.

Braedon smiled, sending her heart singing. "Sort of, but more important, he used to work for the government. And in his line of work he formed a lot of attachments. People who know things."

She smiled, recognition dawning. "You mean like the FBI or something."

"CIA, actually. Hell, probably the 'or something,' too." He turned around to face her, leaning casually against the sill. "He works for me now." He grinned, obviously a private joke of some kind. "At least as much for me as he's ever worked for anyone."

Kacy was losing track of the conversation, in part because she was having trouble concentrating on anything but the man in front of her. "And he's been helping you with all this?"

"He was the one who located you."

She flinched, the memory of yesterday's pain raising its ugly head.

He crossed to the bed in one stride, tipping her head back with one finger. "Kacy, we've been there and back again."

"I know. I just . . ."

He sat beside her, both hands on her shoulders, his blue, blue eyes looking into hers. "Kacy, I love you."

Her heart actually stopped beating. "You do?" Now there was a witty thing to say at maybe the most important moment of her life.

He smiled and slowly covered her mouth with his, speaking against her lips. "I do."

Braedon sat down on the bench in the hallway by the phone. He couldn't remember ever feeling like this. So content, so happy. He smiled at the thought. Such a simple word for such complex emotions. Kacy was humming off key, the sound drifting out of the open door of the kitchen, absurdly comforting.

He picked up the receiver and waited for the buzz of the dial tone. Nothing. Frowning he tapped the switch hook. Still nothing. "Kacy?"

She poked her head around the corner, eyebrows raised in question.

"The phone's dead."

"It's probably the storm." The rain increased from a gentle rhythm to a steady drumming as if to emphasize her words. "It happens all the time."

"Well, hell."

"Sorry."

"Matt could have been trying to reach us all night."

"You'll have to go to the pub. Fin's on a better line than mine. Cable or something. It'll probably still be working."

"Okay, so we'll go to Fin's."

She looked at the clock on the table. "I can't. Professor Baucomo will be here any minute."

Braedon ran a hand through his hair in frustration. "Look, I know reviving your career is important to you, but I think at the moment we have a few more imperative things to consider."

"Braedon, I'm not going to be of any help while you're talking on the phone, and besides, I want to go through some of the papers in the attic again. Maybe there's something there we missed."

"But—"

She cut him off with the wave of a hand. "I'll be perfectly safe here with the professor."

"We don't know that."

She leaned against the doorframe, her arms crossed, her expression mutinous. "I know you probably don't like Professor Baucomo. After everything he did, I even understand why. But I like him, and I trust him. He was only trying to help me, Braedon."

"Maybe. But there's more to the professor than you realize, Kacy."

She sighed. "More secrets?"

"It's probably nothing, but I had Matt look into our little professor's background."

"Was that necessary?" She narrowed her eyes, the green taking on a fiery cast.

"Yes. And what's more, he found something. Seems your professor has a past."

"Everyone has a past, Braedon." She shot him a meaningful look and he had the grace to feel embarrassed.

"I realize that, but until we find Max, I don't want to take chances." And besides, the bastard had practically ruined his relationship with Kacy. *No.* Truth was, he'd done that all by his lonesome. "I don't trust your safety with anyone but me."

She dimpled. "I like the way that sounds. But I'll be safe here. I have Mac." The dog appeared at her side, looking back and forth between them. "And I'll have the professor. And I really want to look at those papers. Besides, you won't be gone that long, right?"

He shrugged, knowing when he was beat. He'd be gone no more than half an hour. Less if he drove really fast. And despite his feelings about Baucomo, Kacy was right. Everyone had a past. And there was nothing to connect Baucomo's to Max or Alex. "When is the professor due here?"

As if in answer to the question, the doorbell rang.

He kissed her hard on the lips, and then released her. "I'll be back as soon as I can. Be careful, Kacy."

She reached for the doorknob. "I will. And maybe I'll have found something by the time you get back, or maybe Matt will have some news for us."

He hoped so. Dear God, he hoped so.

* * *

The church bells wouldn't stop. The steeple rose ominously into the sky, casting a black shadow over the cemetery. The sound built, the ringing echoing, crescendoing across the silent churchyard. He covered his ears, trying to shut out the incessant sound.

A grave rose from broken ground, taller than the others, the stone glaring and white. Its epitaph blurred, unreadable. But he knew who it belonged to. Knew it with a certainty that echoed through his brain, a terrifying counterpoint to the ringing of the bells.

He closed his eyes, trying to erase the vision of the mound of earth, but the image was still there, taunting him. Under the cacophony of the bells, he heard someone call his name. His heart pounded and his breath came in raspy gasps.

Fear coursed through him, holding him captive, frozen in this hellish place. Slowly he opened his eyes, already knowing what he would see. It stood half in, half out of the grave, hands extended, mouth open, calling his name. Its eyes were hollow sockets—or what had been eyes, the opaque balls sightless, staring. Seaweed clothed its bony body like a slimy suit.

It moved, one halting step at a time, like something from a horror movie. Only it was real. Bile rose in his throat and he retched, trying to look away, to shut it out. The bells increased their frenzied ringing. Bringgg, bringgg.

The creature had almost reached him. He opened his mouth to scream. He knew who it was. Knew it in his soul, despite its grotesque appearance.

Alex. His brother. His twin.

Bringgg.

Max sat up in his bed, sweat momentarily blinding him, the phone beside the bed jangling.

A dream. It had been a dream.

He gulped in air, reaching for the receiver. "Yes?"

"There's a message for you, sir."

The front desk. Max forcibly swallowed the remainder of his fear, pushing the dream aside. "What is it?"

"A Mr. Baucomo called. He said to meet him at a Miss Macgrath's. It says here that 'things have changed.' "

Max frowned, wondering what Rico was up to now. "When did he call?"

The clerk fumbled with the phone while she consulted the message. "Looks like late last night, sir. There isn't a time, but the signature is the night clerk's."

"Fine. Thank you."

"You're welcome, sir."

He hung up the phone. If Rico had changed his mind, that could only mean one thing. Kirstin knew something. Something that put them at risk. He smiled. Gienelli had played right into his hands.

Alex's revenge was at hand.

He drew a deep calming breath. Maybe then the nightmares would stop.

Braedon crossed the empty pub, heading for the common room and the phone, hoping desperately that Matt would have some news. It was imperative that they find Max as quickly as possible. He still had no idea what the man thought Kacy knew, but until he was apprehended, she wasn't safe.

"Morning, Braedon. Just getting in, I see." Fin came through the swinging door leading to the kitchen, two cups of steaming coffee in his hands.

Braedon's mouth watered in response to the aromatic brew. "That for me?"

The man smiled. "Well, now, that depends on where you spent the night last night."

Braedon answered with a grin of his own. "Surely you know that a gentleman never tells, Fin."

"Aye, that I do." He shrugged with exaggerated drama.

"But how's a poor barkeep to update the rumor mill when his patrons refuse to spill the beans?" Fin handed him a cup and fixed him with a narrow-eyed stare. "As long as it's more than a dalliance, you have my blessing."

Braedon met the barman's steady gaze. "Oh, it's more than that. I promise you."

"So be it, then." Fin moved around the bar to a stack of papers by the register. "I've a message here for you." He thumbed through the pieces of paper. "Ah, yes, a telephone call, it was. Caitlin took it."

"From the States?"

"I've no way o' knowin'. It doesn't say." He held out the slip of paper.

Braedon took it. The note was handwritten, the writing loopy, feminine. And it didn't say much of anything. *The man you're looking for is at the hotel.* "This is it?"

Fin shrugged. "I guess so. If there was more, I'm sure Caitlin would have written it down."

Braedon read it again. Cryptic. But possibly useful. "Where is Caitlin?"

"Unfortunately, she's up and out this morning. I've no idea when she'll be back. Is it a problem?"

"No." He looked at the message in his hand. Most likely it was from Matt. Just like him to be cryptic. But he ought to check to be sure. This was not the time for making mistakes.

"I'll be right back." He nodded at Fin and headed for the phone. Punching out the numbers, he thought about Kacy— about all that she had been through. Once Max Madison was out of their lives, he intended to spend the bulk of his time showing her just how great life could be.

The phone continued to ring, echoing in his ear. "Damn it." He slammed the headset back into the cradle and strode back into the main room.

"Did you get hold of your friend?" Fin raised a quizzical eyebrow.

"No. But I think I'll head over to the castle and see what this is about." He waved the note in the air for emphasis.

"Good enough." Fin raised his eyebrows, obviously curious, but too polite to ask.

Braedon turned to go, trying to calculate how long it would take him to drive to the hotel and then get back to Kacy. It was an impossible situation, but she was with the professor. And she had Mac.

"Braedon?"

He turned to look at the barman. "You never told me why you left a lady as lovely as Kacy on a morning as fine as this." The man grinned, an almost envious look on his face.

"The phone. Kacy's isn't working. She said it was the storm." He shrugged.

"That's odd." Fin's voice sounded unusually serious.

"What do you mean?"

"Nothing, really, just that I talked to Tolly this morning, no problem, and usually when the line is down, his phone is out, too." Fin scratched his head.

A niggle of worry shot through Braedon. "Look, Fin, would you mind going out there and checking on her? It won't take me long to handle this, but I'd feel better if someone I trusted looked in on her."

"She's alone?" Braedon was relieved that Fin wasn't asking for more explanation.

"No. She's working with Baucomo this morning."

"Fine, then. I'm waiting for a delivery. It should be here any minute. So as soon as it comes, I'll head over to Sidhean. Is that good enough?"

"That'll be grand, Fin. And thanks."

"Not to worry, boyo, I'm not doing it for you. I'm doing it for Kacy." The smile in his voice took any sting out of his words.

"Okay, I'm off to check this out, then I'll call Matt and meet you at Sidhean."

The Irishman nodded and Braedon turned to go, sending a prayer heavenward, hoping that he was doing the right thing.

"So, you've forgiven him."

Kacy looked at the professor over the rim of the box she was sorting through. He was sitting on the sofa in her studio, sipping coffee and looking at her with troubled eyes. "Yes. I have."

"I see."

"You sound like you don't approve."

The little man sighed and set his cup on the side table. "It isn't for me to approve or disapprove, my dear. I just don't want to see you hurt."

"And you think that Braedon will hurt me."

"I cannot say with any certainty, but I know his type, and so, I think, yes, it is a possibility."

"I appreciate that you care about me, but—"

"But you would like for me to quit meddling in your life, no?"

She nodded, glad that he understood. She liked him, and the fact that he seemed to be so concerned for her only deepened her feelings for him. As odd as it sounded, she felt as if the little Italian was a kindred spirit of sorts.

"So be it then." His worried gaze met hers. "I'm truly sorry if I misspoke yesterday."

She took a deep breath, memories of yesterday's pain already dimming in the light of the new day. "You didn't. And I'm glad you told me. But Braedon was going to tell me, too. Would have, in fact, had you not arrived when you did."

"And I suppose he had reasons for lying?"

"Good reasons."

The professor looked at her, his brows drawn together, waiting for further explanation. Kacy realized there wasn't much she actually could tell him. At least not until things had been cleared up. Besides, the truth was she really didn't know all that much.

The doorbell rang, interrupting her thoughts. "That'll be Braedon."

The professor started to rise. "Shall I leave you?"

"No, absolutely not. Sit down. I'll be right back."

She walked through the hall, her step light. It was amazing how much the prospect of just seeing Braedon lifted her spirits. "Well, that took you entirely too—" She stopped, the words dying in her throat.

Alex.

"Good morning, Kirstin." He leveled his gun. "I thought it high time we had a little talk."

Chapter 24

BRAEDON SLAMMED THE door of the rented sedan. A wild goose chase. Matt had sent him on a bloody wild-goose chase. God, where was his head?

With Kacy.

Well, at least Fin was with her, and the professor. He'd check in with Matt and then head for Sidhean.

The pub was almost empty. The old man was in his place, newspaper in hand. Braedon wondered if he even had a home. A leggy looking redhead was behind the bar. The elusive Caitlin O'Brien no doubt. Up until now, he'd never actually seen her.

"If you're looking for Fin, he's left."

"Actually, I was just going to use the phone. I'm staying here."

She smiled at him, her face alight with laughter. "I know who you are. Fin talks about you night and day. You and Kacy—" She winked. "—if you take my meaning."

He liked her. An imp in an angel's body. He grinned, sharing a moment of camaraderie.

"The phone." She tipped her head toward the common room, her blue eyes dancing with amusement.

"Right." He turned to go and stopped, his eyes drawn to a painting on the wall. He knew it.

Knew it really well.

Hell, he'd owned it.

Sold it.

And been informed that it was a fake.

The Transformation mocked him.

"Like it?" Caitlin had come up to stand behind him.

He scrambled to pull his scattered thoughts together. No sense in discussing his fears with a stranger. Even a friendly one. "It's an interesting piece. I've never seen it before."

"We just got it back today. It's been at the framers."

"Where did Fin get it?" He already knew, but perversely he needed to hear it.

"It's one of Kacy's. A copy. The original was by some guy named Marty, Marvin, something."

"Martin." He said the name quietly, the painting holding his full attention.

"Righto, that's it. Anyway, Fin loves it. And Kacy's never liked it. Reminds her of her dead husband. I think she painted the copy for him." A patron sauntered up to the bar. "Uh-oh, duty calls." She smiled and left him alone with the Martin.

That it was the real Giles Martin, Braedon hadn't a doubt. If necessary, he could prove it. There would be a gallery mark on the back of the canvas. He blew out a breath, trying to figure out what the hell it meant. Had Kacy lied to him? Did she know she had the original?

He felt sick. The room blurred.

No, he told himself firmly. She couldn't know. If she had, she'd have never dared give it to Fin. He pictured the Irishman in the kitchen at Sidhean, painting thrust under his arm. Kacy hadn't batted an eye.

He turned from the painting and headed for the phone, angry at himself for having doubted her.

Kacy took an involuntary step backward, her hand fluttering at her throat, her thoughts coming in scattered bursts.

Alex.

No. Not Alex.

Something in the way he stood, the way he looked at her. *Not Alex.*

"Max." The word escaped from her throat, more a mangled whisper than something spoken.

"You recognized me." He sounded disappointed. "Aren't you going to ask me in?" He stepped across the threshold, reaching back to close the door, the little gun still aimed at her heart.

"Kacy? Who is it?" Professor Baucomo stepped into the hallway and froze. His eyes on the man with the gun.

"Hello, Rico, or should I call you Eduardo?"

Kacy shot a look at the professor. "Rico?" He shrugged apologetically. *"You know him?"*

"You could say we have a relationship."

Max laughed, a low throaty sound that sent shivers of dread up Kacy's spine. He motioned them into the parlor with the gun. The professor took her elbow, his hand trembling a little.

"Have a seat," Max said. It was not a conversational request.

She sat, her back ramrod straight. The professor moved to the sofa, balancing himself on the edge. She had the insane desire to flick him like a marble, certain that he would roll off and bounce across the floor. She bit back a swell of hysteria, trying to assure herself that this would somehow have a happy ending.

Mac growled from the kitchen door, teeth bared. "Call him off, or he's dead." Max scowled at the dog.

Kacy whistled softly and Mac came to her, settling by her feet, his hair raised in protest.

"I was relieved to get your message, Rico. I'm glad you came to your senses concerning our little problem." He gestured at Kacy with the gun, a thin smile twisting his lips.

It was almost like looking at a caricature of Alex. The facial structure was the same. The line of the nose, the hair, the eyes, even the curve of his ear was identical. But it was as if the picture had been subtly altered somehow. A mirror image gone awry. Lewis Carroll would have had a field day. Kacy just felt sick.

The professor—Rico—frowned. "What message?"

"Now, don't play coy with me. I know you have feelings for our Kirstin. It was evident from our conversation the other night. I'm just glad you've come to your senses. All that rubbish about her being innocent."

"She didn't do it." The professor's voice was so low Kacy had to strain to hear it.

"Didn't do what?" Kacy was beyond confused and she wasn't sure she wanted to hear the answer, but at the same time, it was kind of like the guy in *Dirty Harry*—she just had to know.

Max focused on her, his eyes narrowing to slits. Pure hatred blazed there. Kacy shivered. "Kill my brother," he hissed.

Kacy opened her mouth to protest, but all that came out was a small squeak.

"You found out about the money, didn't you? That's why you killed him."

"What money?" she asked, trying to make sense of the nonsensical.

"That's right, play innocent with me." He sneered at her. "Alex may have been a sucker for a pretty face, but make no mistake, I know exactly who you are."

Kacy knew she was on the edge of sheer panic. She gripped her hands together tightly, the painful sensation helping to keep her grounded. "Alex didn't have any money. And I didn't kill him. He drowned." Hearing the fear in her voice, Mac growled. She laid a hand on his head. "Hush," she whispered, certain that if he didn't, Max would kill him.

"There is no way my brother could have drowned. He was an excellent swimmer."

Memories of that night filled her head. "It was a horrible storm. No one could have survived a wave of that size."

"Look at her, Rico. The picture of virtue. What garbage."

Anger surpassed fear. "I'm telling the truth."

"She is, Max," the professor added quietly.

Max ignored them both, waving the gun. "Where's the money?"

"There isn't any," Kacy ground out.

"There has to be. Alex banked all of his and all of mine."

"Well, if there was, the secret died with him. All he left me was a pile of debts and creditors named Guido who carry guns."

He hesitated for a moment, glancing at the professor. "Did you know this?"

"No, it's the first I've heard of it. But it makes sense. If she didn't know about the forgeries, then she probably didn't know about the money. So it would follow that when Alex died, the whereabouts of the accounts went with him."

"Professor, I—"

"Shut up." Max trained the gun on her again. Mac growled and leapt to his feet.

"No," Kacy screamed, moving toward her dog.

Too late.

Max fired and Mac keeled over, yelping in pain, blood darkening his fur. Kacy flung herself at the dog, crying his name.

"Get her away from him," Max snapped at the professor.

Gently he pulled her back. Mac whined and tried to raise his head, but couldn't. Kacy was choking on her tears.

"You bastard." She stared at Max, knowing that her hatred matched his, feeling for feeling. If she could, she'd claw him to death with her bare hands.

"Sit down, Kirstin, or I'll shoot him again, and this time he'll die. Just like my brother." His eyes were a little wild. She realized, with a shudder, that he *was* going to kill her. Oh, he might toy with her first, but ultimately, he was going to kill her.

Amazingly, the knowledge calmed her more than it frightened her. Suddenly she had nothing to lose and everything to gain. And by God, she wasn't going down without a fight. "Professor? Tell me what the hell is going on here." She snuck a look at Mac; his eyes were closed, but she could see that he was breathing. Relief swelled through her.

"Yes, Rico, do tell our little black widow what it is exactly she's stumbled onto."

The professor loosened his shirt collar, beads of perspiration dotting his forehead, looking first at Kacy and then at Max. "Well, you know about the forgeries."

Kacy nodded, grateful for the time to try to figure out what to do.

"I was the forger."

Her attention jerked to the professor. "You?"

"Yes, my dear, I'm afraid so. I told you I hadn't any imagination and so was not particularly successful with my own work, but I'm afraid I neglected to mention that I seem to have quite a talent for copying someone else's work." He shrugged, looking more like an embarrassed grandfather than a criminal.

"So you and Alex were—"

Max shook the gun at her. "I was the mastermind behind the forgeries. Me. Not Alex. He was only useful as our front man. Alex was always the charming one, even when we were little, but it takes more than charm to get through life. You need intelligence. And fortunately, I have that area well covered."

"You organized the forgeries." She eyed the door to the hallway. If she could distract him and make a run for it . . .

"I wouldn't try it, Kirstin." He raised an eyebrow, looking eerily like Alex. "You'd be dead before you made it out of the chair."

She sighed and leaned back. Surely if she could keep him

talking, there'd be another opportunity. "What gave you the idea?"

"Rico's talent."

"But I thought you were—"

"Incarcerated? I was. But so was Rico." He smiled at the professor, but there was no mirth reflected there.

"Rico?" Kacy turned to the professor. The little man looked miserable.

"Enrico Gienelli—" He inclined his head. "—at your service."

"But what about the university, Milan?"

He shrugged. "A useful alias."

"You mean you're not an art historian?" Kacy felt like her world was tumbling into a great chasm, taking her spinning along with it.

"No, no, I am. It's just that I find it useful to keep my other life separate."

"And Eduardo Baucomo?"

He shrugged again, looking very Italian. "My better half."

"So Braedon was looking for you?"

"In a way, yes. Of course, he thought it was you and I'm afraid it was useful for me to let him."

"And to try to break us up." She glared at him, satisfied to see him flinch.

"I'm sorry, Kacy. I didn't mean for you to get hurt, but it was a matter of self-preservation."

"Enough with the pity party. I've got other things to do with my day. In fact, the truth is, I think we've come to the end of the line." Max studied her over the barrel of the gun. "How my brother thought someone like you could ever replace me is totally beyond my comprehension, but I guess he's paid the price for his misplaced trust."

A flicker of guilt fluttered through her mind. It had been her fault Alex had gone out in the storm.

Max smiled, his lips thinning to a fine line. "You did kill

him, didn't you?" It was almost as if he sensed her agony, pouncing on it like a cat toying with a mouse. "Maybe not with your bare hands, but with your wiles and your words. How does it feel to know you've killed a man, Kirstin? Or was Alex not the first?"

"I've never—"

"You're just like the rest of them," he cut her off. "Prancing about, seducing and beguiling. Lying, saying you loved us when you didn't. You knew you were leaving, and still you called us your little men. Telling us we were the center of your world, all the while knowing we were nothing to you. Nothing." His voice rose in pitch, sounding almost child-like, his eyes clouded, and Kacy realized he was lost in memory, talking to someone else, someone from long ago.

She inched off the chair, poised for flight, waiting for her moment. She glanced at Mac. He was breathing. She could see his side moving up and down. She bit her lip, indecision tugging at her. Out of the corner of her eye, she saw the professor nod, his eyes signaling her.

Go.

She shot upright. Max's eyes cleared and he leveled the gun, clicking back the hammer.

Kacy tried to get out of the way, but something hit her hard, driving her to the floor as the gun's report echoed through the parlor.

Chapter 25

"I DON'T KNOW what the hell is going on, Matt, but I sure as hell intend to find out." Braedon paced in front of the phone, turning each time he reached the end of the cord.

"That's two hells in one sentence. I'd say something has you pretty upset."

"Save the analysis and tell me what you know." He hadn't meant to snap at Matt, but damn it, he needed answers.

"All right, but at some point in the near future I would like to know exactly what's going on." Matt's voice held a ring of exasperation.

"As soon as I know something, you'll know something, okay?" He had a hell of a lot to discuss with Matt, but right now Braedon didn't have time to talk about it.

"Fine. In the meantime, I've got some information about your pseudo Italian."

"What?" Braedon tightened his grip on the phone.

"Seems the good professor né Enrico Gienelli was in Rikers the same time Max Madison was."

"I think I was really hoping there wouldn't be a connection." His mind started whirling, pieces falling into place.

"Yeah, and it gets better. They were roomies."

"Son of a bitch." He stopped pacing, his heart taking up the rhythm.

"Something like that."

Panic knifed through him. Kacy was with Baucomo/ Gienelli—or whoever he was. "Matt, I've got to go." He slammed the phone down, knowing that he had to get to Kacy, and he had to get there now.

He ran into the front room, skidding to a stop beside the bar. Caitlin was talking with a man in coveralls. "When did Fin leave?"

"Excuse me." She smiled at the man and then turned to look at Braedon, her brows knitting together, her irritation obvious.

He didn't give a damn, but he forced himself to keep from grabbing her and shaking the information out of her. It wasn't really her fault. She had no idea what was at stake. "Just tell me when he left."

"I don't know. Not long ago. He was waiting for the painting. The framer was delivering it and the man was late. As soon as he got it on the wall, Fin waylaid me and headed out the door." She met his gaze. "Is something wrong?"

"I hope not. I sure as hell hope not."

Kacy froze, waiting for another shot. Something heavy covered her body. Dead weight. She tried to shift, to see what it was. Cautiously she turned her head.

Eyes. Wide, sightless eyes. Eyes attached to a face.

She screamed, surprised to find that no sound came out. Only a harsh, hissing exhale of breath.

With concerted effort, she shoved the body off of her. It rolled onto its back, one lifeless hand still draped across her chest, palm up, entreating her.

The professor.

Tears welled in her eyes. The little man had saved her.

"What a fool."

Max.

Instinctively Kacy tried to scramble away, but there was nowhere to go. The coffee table blocked her on one side and the professor's body on the other. At least his hand wasn't touching her anymore. The tears slid down her face as she looked at him. He'd never meant her harm, of that she was certain.

Max towered above her, his eyes wild, the gun still pointing at her. "The stupid bastard."

Anger rose past terror and she found her voice. "How dare you speak of him like that."

"I'll speak of him any way I please, Kirstin. I am in control of this situation, not you." For emphasis he clicked the hammer back again.

Terror shoved past anger again, and she felt her hands trembling as she pressed against the table, one sharp corner digging painfully into her shoulder.

"In a way," he continued almost absently, "it simplifies things." He watched her, a look of satisfaction spreading across his face. "Yes. A professional spat, shall we say. Between forgers. It's perfect. Two for the price of one." His smile widened, and he aimed the gun. "Say good-bye, Kirstin."

She closed her eyes, knowing it was too late. There was nowhere to run. If this bullet didn't get her, the next one would. She wondered what it felt like to die. Wondered if she'd see the professor.

Wondered if Braedon would miss her.

Mac whined, and she snapped out of her lethargy just before the gun discharged again. She dove under the coffee table, forcing her body into the small space.

Max laughed. "This is quite entertaining, Kirstin, but I'm afraid I haven't time for games."

She pushed herself farther under the table, knowing it couldn't really protect her, but appreciating its solid comfort nevertheless.

Max squatted, the gun resting casually against his knee. "Shall I say good-bye to Braedon for you?"

"I don't think you should say good-bye to anyone just yet, Max."

That voice. She'd know it anywhere. In fact, she'd heard it recently, whispering her name. Gooseflesh crawled along her arms and the hairs on the back of her neck rose to attention. It was true. She hadn't been mistaken.

"Alex?" Max's voice was choked. He rose slowly, and from her cramped position she saw him thrust out his hand, almost as if to ward off his brother.

"Give me the gun, Max."

He obeyed in a dreamlike fashion, his movements jerky, his hands shaking.

Alex took the gun and smiled at his brother, the charm of the gesture failing to reach his eyes. Why hadn't she noticed before how cold his eyes were? "Come out from under the table, Kirstin."

She shook her head, her arms and legs refusing to budge an inch. He reached down and closed a warm, strong, living hand around her arm and yanked her to her feet. She slammed her head on the table, the pain biting into her, momentarily making her dizzy.

"What, no welcoming kiss for your long dead husband?" He jerked her forward, his lips pressing against hers. She shuddered with revulsion, wondering what she'd ever seen in this man.

He stepped back, a tiny smile twisting his lips, and turned toward his brother, the gun dangling from his hand. "Hello, Max. Long time no see."

"I thought you were—" Max stood staring at his twin, his eyes wide, his mouth still moving, trying to form the rest of the sentence.

"Dead?" Alex slowly rubbed a lazy finger down the barrel

of the gun. "The reports were greatly exaggerated, I'm afraid."

"Where the hell have you been?"

"Paradise." His lips curled into what should have been a grin, but somehow it came off more like a caricature of one. His eyes remained empty, icy.

Kacy took a step backward, toward the door.

Alex spun around, his hand closing on her arm. "Not thinking of leaving, I hope. Why, we haven't had a chance to get reacquainted yet." He ran the barrel of the gun across her cheek, the cold metal making her shiver. "Sit over there, where I can see you." He motioned toward the sofa.

"Let me check on my dog first."

"He's fine. And if he isn't, well, there isn't a damn thing you can do about it. Now sit." He pointed the gun at her.

Reluctantly she walked toward the sofa, stopping quickly to check on Mac. He was breathing easily and the bleeding seemed to have stopped. He whimpered a little when she rubbed his head.

"Now, Kirstin."

She made her way to the sofa, stepping around the professor, trying not to look at him.

"I don't understand this, Alex. Why didn't you tell me you were alive?" Max had regained his composure and stood facing his brother, his mouth drawn into a tight line.

"Because I didn't want to." Alex tilted his head and watched his twin, a look of contained amusement playing across his face.

"I don't understand." Max was repeating himself and he looked deflated somehow. As if someone had given him his favorite dessert and then taken it away.

"It's simple, Max. I wanted to disappear. I had a few— problems. So I decided to start a new life."

"But the storm—"

"Provided an excellent opportunity," Alex finished for him.

"But, Alex." Two dark heads swung around to look at her. So alike. So different. "I saw you on the pier. The wave smashed into you. You were there and then you were gone. There's no way you could have faked that." Her mind was spinning.

Reality was a lie.

She hadn't watched him die. He was here, in front of her.

With a gun.

"I didn't plan the wave." He shrugged. "But when I came ashore a few minutes later and heard you screaming my name, I recognized a golden moment and seized it."

"So you left me there, thinking you were dead?" Kacy tightened her hands into fists, trying to contain her emotions.

"Regrettably, I had to. As you are no doubt aware, I had some very outstanding debts and some rather unpleasant creditors. But more important—" He shot a look of loathing at his brother. "—I had a millstone around my neck." He focused his attention back on Kacy. "I'd already set the plans to disappear in motion. I was merely waiting for the right time. The storm provided the perfect alibi. Dead is dead, after all."

"Apparently not." Kacy almost let her anger get the better of her, forgetting for a moment who held the gun.

"I knew he never loved you." Max sounded childlike, as if he were gloating. He'd obviously missed the significance of his brother's words.

Alex smiled at Kacy, his eyes exploring her body, mentally undressing her. She pushed back into the sofa, trying to put more distance between them. "I don't think love was ever a part of it. But there was a certain chemistry. Wasn't there, Kirstin?"

Tears welled again. She scrubbed them away, angry that

she'd let him get to her. But then that's what Alex was good at. Manipulating people.

He smiled at her, a crooked smile that had once seemed so enchanting. Now she saw it for what it really was. An artifice. An actor, wooing an audience. The look carefully contrived to gain maximum effect. She shuddered.

"I can see why you wouldn't have contacted her. But why would you want *me* to think you were dead? We're brothers. We're twins. You're a part of me. My other half." Max's gaze was tortured, filled with hurt and confusion. "I've lived my life for you." He took a step toward his brother and Alex moved back, keeping the distance the same.

"Well, you see, that was the problem." Alex sighed. "The fact is, you made my life a living hell. I couldn't breathe. I had no life of my own. I didn't even have an identity apart from you." He narrowed his eyes, his loathing written across his face. Kacy almost felt sorry for Max.

"But I . . ."

"What? You *loved* me." The word was spoken as if it were a curse. "Max, you smothered me. Always telling me what to do, how to dress, what to think, how to live. I'm surprised you didn't give me a daily pissing schedule." He waved the gun in the air, his composure slipping. "I hated your meddling."

"Meddling?" Max gasped. "I was taking care of you. Without me, you wouldn't have been anything but a charming loser. You needed me. And I was there for you. I even went to prison for you." He was almost screaming.

"Well, now, there was a really stupid thing to do. I'd have beaten the rap. But no, instead, my idiot brother comes charging to the rescue and takes the fall for me," Alex said, his voice filled with derision.

"You ungrateful son of a bitch." Max's face was ashen and he spoke in a low voice, barely above a whisper.

"This is exactly why I had to disappear." Alex was in control again, his voice light and conversational. "You can understand that, can't you, Kirstin?" He turned to look at her and Max followed suit. They stared at her, identical looks on their faces, waiting for an answer.

Suddenly she felt like she was facing Tweedledee and Tweedledum. A totally insane moment. Reality caving in on itself, leaving a nightmare from which she wasn't likely to awaken.

She nodded.

There was no right answer, and thankfully the twins didn't seem to care. They turned to face each other again, Max red-faced and angry, Alex looking amused.

"I can't believe you've been alive all this time and haven't tried to contact me."

They were back at their dance again, one moving forward, the other moving away.

"Believe it." Alex smirked.

"What about the money? My money?" Max screeched.

"I used it to buy an island. My island."

They continued to circle each other, sounding more like little boys than grown men.

"I want my money."

"I'm afraid you can't have it."

They stopped moving, Max standing across from his brother, the anger fading from his face. He laughed. "This is crazy. I can't believe I'm really seeing you. That you're alive."

Kacy watched the brothers with horrified fascination. Alex smiled slowly, the expression still not reflected in his eyes. "Now you see me."

His hand twitched and the gun exploded.

A crimson flower burst into bloom on Max's forehead. He opened his mouth, astonished, and then dropped to the floor with a sickening thud. With a whoosh, he exhaled once and stopped breathing.

Alex looked at his brother dispassionately. "Now you don't."

Chapter 26

 KACY SCREAMED, THE sound resounding off the walls of the little room.

"Shut up," Alex snapped. "Or you'll be next."

She clamped down on her fear, trying desperately to rein it in, staring at the body. *Bodies.* Her eyes darted between the two fallen men. The professor and Max. Blood was spattered everywhere, on the wall, across her carpet. She tightened her hold on sanity and forced herself to look at Alex. "What happens next?"

He was calm almost to the point of being comatose. It was eerie. His face was devoid of all emotion. He'd just killed his brother, and he was standing there as though he were waiting for tea.

"It's interesting that you should mention that, Kirstin." He pointed the gun at her and she sucked in a breath.

Sanity and insanity struggled for control, sanity winning by a nose. "If you're going to kill me, too, just go ahead and get it over with." She glared at him. Anything was better than waiting and watching him stare at her.

"Darling, you wound me. I have no intention of killing you." He waved the gun at her. "Yet." He smiled, the gesture devoid of humor. "We've only just found each other again. And I do so want to rediscover the carnal side of our union."

Kacy felt bile rising in her throat, burning her esophagus.

269

He took a step closer, looking at her like she was the main course at a banquet, and she shrank back, wishing she could disappear.

"But first, I need you to write a little note."

"What?" The change of subject left her feeling disoriented, confused.

"A note. I want you to confess your guilt to Roche."

"My guilt?" She managed to choke out the words, but knew she sounded like an idiot.

"Yes. Such a shame, really." He handed her a piece of paper and a pen. "A quarrel with your compatriots." He gestured toward the bodies. "And such a terrible ending. But then, you always were a passionate woman." He licked his lips and let his eyes travel slowly up and down her body.

She swallowed hard, fighting to keep from throwing up. "You want Braedon to think I did this?"

"Exactly. And that you've run away."

"But surely you know they'll find me." As soon as she said it a tremor of pure terror ran down her spine. Of course they wouldn't find her. Not alive, anyway. And Alex would be in the clear. Case closed.

"It won't matter then, will it, Kirstin?" His voice was smooth and oily. It suffocated her with its silky cadence. "Write the note."

She reached inside her, summoning every ounce of courage she had. "No. I repeat. If you're going to kill me, do it now." She spoke slowly, enunciating each word as if he were hard of hearing.

Alex smiled and she felt her brave front slipping away. "I can do that. But first, I'll have to kill your dog." He pivoted the gun slightly, taking aim at Mac.

The dog whimpered and lifted his head, his trusting gaze meeting hers. Her heart shriveled.

The hammer clicked into place.

"Stop. I'll write the note."

Alex swung the gun back to her. "You always were a smart girl."

She wanted to laugh at the irony of that statement. She'd married a psycho. Hardly something one would consider an intelligent move. She blew out a breath. "What do you want me to write?"

Braedon pulled up to the cottage in a spray of gravel. There were cars parked everywhere. Fin's Mini, the professor's rental car, and a black Mercedes he didn't recognize. A shiver of alarm washed through him and he leapt from the car at a run.

Bounding up the steps, he flung open the front door and skidded to a stop in the foyer. The house was quiet, too quiet. He walked across the hallway and stopped in the doorway to the parlor, fear changing to horror.

The room was littered with bodies. He took a hesitant step forward, stepping gingerly around blood pooled on the floor. The professor lay on his back, sightless eyes staring up at the ceiling.

Across from him, another body lay curled on its side. He poked it with his foot and Alex's face looked up at him, the handsome features frozen in lifeless surprise.

Max.

His heart began to pound as his eyes searched the room for Kacy, uncertain whether he was praying to find her or not.

"She's not here."

Braedon whirled around, tensed, ready for battle.

Fin.

He relaxed, meeting the Irishman's green-eyed gaze. Fin's normally genial face was creased with a frown.

"How long have you been here?" Braedon demanded.

Fin winced, shifting from one foot to another. "Only a few

minutes. Tolly Macnamara needed my help with an engine. It took a bit longer than I'd thought it would. I'm sorry, Braedon."

"Don't be. If you'd been here, you'd most likely be dead, too." He ran a weary hand through his hair. "I take it there's no sign of her?"

The big man pulled something from his pocket, looking decidedly uncomfortable. "I found this." He held out a folded piece of paper. " 'Tis addressed to you. I . . . uh . . . under the circumstances, I'm afraid I read it."

Braedon took the note, not certain he wanted to read it. The handwriting sloped and looped across the page. He looked up at Fin. Stalling for time. "You recognize the writing?"

Fin dipped his head. "I do."

"I see." He forced himself to look at the page, to read the words.

> *Braedon,*
>
> *I figured at the very least I owed you an explanation. I'm afraid that I haven't been completely honest with you. In fact, the truth is, I've told you nothing but lies. You were right about me all along. I was a part of it. Alex was more than my husband, Braedon, he was my partner. And when he died, I realized I had an opportunity to be rich beyond my wildest dreams.*
>
> *So I took the money we were holding for Max and disappeared. I kept in touch with the professor and from time to time we did a little business. You even said yourself, I'm one hell of a forger. And it keeps me in pretty things. Max knew I'd double-crossed him, and so when he got out of prison, he showed up here.*
>
> *I really wasn't planning to eliminate him. But it was him or me and I think, even under the circumstances, you'll have to admit you're at least a little glad it was him and not me. The professor wasn't my doing. Max did it. I'd never*

*have hurt him. I'm truly sorry the old man is dead. But we
mustn't cry over spilled milk.*

 *I'm disappearing for good this time, so don't bother
trying to find me. I enjoyed the ride, while it lasted. You
were amazing in bed. But there was never really anything
to it. I'm afraid my heart will always be with Alex.*

 Kirstin

Braedon crumpled the paper in his hand, blood pounding
in his ears, feeling like an absolute fool. *Kirstin.* She was
everything he'd thought she was and more. He looked at the
carnage before him. Much more.

He stopped himself. Angry at the train of his thoughts.
There was no Kirstin. Never had been. There was only Kacy.
And she needed his help. There was an explanation here. He
just had to find it.

"You don't believe it, do you?" Fin's worried voice broke
through his angry internal diatribe.

He focused on the man, shutting out the note and the dead
bodies. "No. Kacy isn't capable of doing this."

Fin nodded his agreement. "Besides, she'd never willingly
leave Mac."

Braedon frowned. "Mac is here?"

"In the kitchen. I was working on him when you came in.
He's been shot, too."

"Is he dead?"

"No, he's going to be fine. Paddy Fitzgerald's on the way."

The information was coming too fast. Braedon's head was
still reeling as he tried to understand what was happening.
"The phone's working?"

Fin shook his head. "I used my cell phone. Called the
Garda, too."

"So now we have to figure this out." He looked at the note
again, this time with the eyes of a man trying to solve a riddle.

"Figure it out?"

"Yeah. We'll take it bit by bit. The truth is here; we just have to find it." He studied the note and then handed it to Fin. "First off, Kacy didn't need money. She has a trust fund, but I don't think anyone knows about it."

"Well, that would rule out stealing money then. And there's the part about loving Alex. We know that's a load of rot. Whatever there was between the two of them, it was never love."

Braedon closed his eyes, seeing the pain in Kacy's eyes, remembering her confession. No, she'd never loved Alex. Ever. He crumpled the paper in anger.

A thought pushed its way front and center in his brain. *Alex.* He frowned, the whole picture remaining stubbornly just out of his grasp.

"What're you thinking?" Fin asked anxiously.

"I'm not entirely sure. Just bits and pieces that are suddenly making some sense." He shook his head, trying to force clarity. But whatever it was, it remained stubbornly on the edge of his conscious mind.

Fin massaged his temples. "This is all my fault."

"You don't know that, Fin." Braedon stood up, responding automatically, his brain still trying to figure out what was bothering him. He was missing something. But what?

"If I hadn't waited for the framer to bring the bloody painting back, none of this would have happened."

"That's it." It was as if his brain adjusted the focus; what had been blurry suddenly became crystal clear.

"What's it? I'm not following you."

"The painting."

"What has Kacy's painting got to do with any of this?" Fin frowned, confusion drawing his brows together to form a rusty *V*.

"It's not Kacy's painting."

"Well, it most certainly is. I got it right out of the studio there. You saw me."

"I saw you take a painting. But unless I'm mistaken, you don't have Kacy's copy of the painting. You have the original."

"The original Martin? But how in the hell did—"

Braedon held up his hand, interrupting. "It's not really important now. What matters is that I think Alex took it."

"But Kacy—" His face looked mutinous.

"Didn't know, Fin. She thought it was her copy, just like you and I did. He fooled us all."

"He who?"

"Alex."

"All right, I'm trying to stay with you here, but you keep losing me. How does the painting in the pub tie in with all that—" He gestured toward the front room. "—in there?"

"It ties in because I think Alex Madison is still alive."

Kacy tried to sit up, but before she had risen a couple of inches, bindings of some kind pulled her taut and held her firmly in place. She dropped back against something lumpy and soft. A mattress maybe.

She strained to see where she was, but there were too many shadows. She couldn't see. Something dug into her wrists and ankles.

Rope.

She was tied into place with rope, the rough hemp holding her spread-eagled in what appeared to be a dark, damp cavelike room. Occasional drops of water fell onto her body, adding their icy touch to her already chilled skin.

Skin.

She struggled to look at herself, already knowing what she'd see. She was naked.

Fear ran through her with the power of a freight train, her

memory replaying the last few hours with startling clarity. Mac, the professor, Max—*Alex*. She struggled to escape her bonds, only succeeding in abrading her wrists, leaving blood dripping down her arm.

He'd done this. Alex.

She'd written what he'd told her, trying to word it so that Braedon would know it was a lie. But would he? Their relationship was so fragile, so new. Did he trust her enough to believe in her?

She lifted up, straining against her bonds, bucking against the rope, trying to break free. Finally, exhausted and hurting, she dropped back onto the mattress. Another drop of water hit her, this one right between her breasts, the moisture sliding down her body, pooling at her abdomen. She sucked in her stomach, trying to get the icy water to roll off her, succeeding only in making it worse.

Where the hell was she? What had he done to her?

She'd finished the note and handed it to Alex. Then she'd gone to Mac to make sure he was all right. The next thing she remembered was being here. Something had to have happened in between. But what?

She struggled to remember, sorting through the fractured memories in her head.

Pain.

She remembered pain. Alex must have hit her. Knocked her out. That would explain why she didn't remember coming here. Wherever here was.

She tried to see something in the gloom, but it was too dark. More droplets of water splashed down, running in tiny rivulets over her body. As accommodations went, these weren't exactly the best.

There was a leak. A serious leak. And unless she figured a way out of here, it was going to drive her crazy.

Tears filled her eyes, the salty liquid running down her

nose, into the corners of her mouth. Great. All she needed was more water.

She closed her eyes, trying to picture Braedon, feel his warmth surrounding her. He'd said he loved her. He wouldn't believe that she'd murdered Max. Somehow he'd figure it out.

He'd find her. He had to.

Chapter 27

ALEX PACED THE confines of the chamber, and Kacy strained to keep him in her vision.

"This fortress—" He gestured to the rough-hewn room, deep under the hillside surrounding the fort. "—is an ancient testament to mankind's continuing need for a way out, a back door. I can't help but feel a kinship."

Kacy struggled against her bonds, certain that Alex was insane.

He stopped and rubbed his temples. "I ought to feel relieved, exuberant—energized. But I don't. It was there for a moment. One tiny moment. But now it's gone." He came to stand over her, his eyes boring into hers. "What I need is release, Kirstin." His smile was nefarious. "There is a certain rush of adrenaline that comes in the instant one's quarry realizes the game is over." He trailed a finger down the soft underside of her arm. "It's an addiction. One I relish."

He squinted his eyes, massaging his head. "One would almost think I was actually feeling remorse about Max's unfortunate demise." He snorted with derision and began pacing again, moving in and out of Kacy's line of vision. "But I'm not. I'm glad that my brother is dead."

Kacy opened her mouth to say something, but then shut it again. Surely there was wisdom in not drawing the attention of a madman.

"There is something liberating in all this, Kirstin. You

278

should try it. But then you don't have it in you, do you, my dear?"

He prodded her, evidently wanting a response, so she shook her head, finding that words had deserted her.

"Everything I do is magic. It's all falling into place. All the loose ends. Max always told me to tie up the loose ends. There is a certain irony, isn't there?

"Shall I tell you about it?" He tipped his head to one side, studying her, his eyes dilated, wild. And then without waiting for an answer, he continued. "First there was the banker in the Caymans. I did that in spades. An unfortunate boating accident, helped along by a clogged fuel line."

He smiled, turning her blood to ice. There was evil here—real evil. He'd stepped over some invisible line, all things redeemable lost in the action. There was nothing left of the charming grifter. Nothing at all.

"There was such a thrill, Kirstin. Watching the boat explode, fiery refuse drifting through cloud studded skies, splashing into the water. It was my first. A virginal experience. I didn't come down from the high for days."

He seemed to be on a roll, forgetting she was even there. "Next came the passport counterfeiter. A fussy little cockney man with an attitude. Now, that took some planning. But I was up to the task. The man lived in London. It was so damn easy. A mugging gone bad. That's what the newspapers had said."

Alex closed his fist. "I can remember the feel of the knife in my hand, the resistance as blade met flesh, the satisfaction as it finally slid home, twisting deeper and deeper." He grinned at the memory. "I almost climaxed there in the park."

Kacy tried to fixate on Braedon. On hope. But Alex's evil surrounded her, leaching everything good in its wake.

"It started with necessity, a way to assure that my new identity was safe, but somewhere along the way it became fun, a game of sorts, one that I always managed to win. There was a realtor and a cleaning lady who was simply in the wrong place at the wrong time."

He stopped pacing and stared down at her. "In some ways she was the best of all." He stroked his crotch, lost in the moment. "After that it was Anson. The stupid oaf. He was fondling your things, Kirstin. He had to be stopped. Before he found something that tipped off my stupid brother. I twisted his neck until it snapped, like a Tinkertoy."

Kacy fought the urge to be sick.

"And then, there was Max. *My* nemesis. My twin. He couldn't believe I'd do it. His eyes were full of questions, confusion, joy mixed with fear. And I put it there. *Me.* In the end I controlled my brother. In an irrevocable, wonderful way, I won. And now there's nothing to stop me. They'll blame you. And I'll disappear again. Dead forever. Once I have the painting."

"Painting?" The question came out more a squeak than a word.

Alex caressed her cheek with the back of his hand. "*The Transformation,* Kirstin." He turned his hand, trapping her skin between thumb and forefinger, twisting viciously. "You didn't think I'd forget my painting, darling. If it weren't for that damned mongrel, I'd have it now."

She bit her lip to keep from crying out. She would not let him have the pleasure of enjoying her pain. "You hurt Mac?"

"I should never have left it behind," he continued as though she hadn't spoken. "I even broke into the beach house to get it. Quite a risk, actually."

"It was you?" Her brain was spinning, the information coming too fast to process.

"Yes. Don't you remember me coming to you? You smiled in your sleep that night."

Visions of her nightmares filled her brain. Alex touching her, stroking her, surrounding her with maleficence. It hadn't been a dream at all. She shuddered. It had a been a memory.

He released her, moving away, resuming his pacing; she could hear his footsteps against the stone floor. "But it wasn't there."

"I sent all my paintings ahead of me, to Ireland. For safekeeping."

"I should have known. But you paid for that, didn't you, darling? I destroyed the Monet. A painting for a painting. Tit for tat."

"You destroyed the Monet?"

He bent low to her, his breath washing across her face. "Don't you know by now that you can't keep anything from me, Kirstin?"

"So you came here for *The Transformation*?" The words came out in a tumble. Her gaze locked with his, and she recognized insanity swirling in the depths of his eyes.

"I came for loose ends. I thought I'd made that clear, Kirstin." His tongue flicked out, serpentlike, tracing the contours of her upper lip.

She tried to twist away, her stomach roiling with revulsion.

"But then I saw you. And I realized that I still want you, Kirstin. I want to feel you writhe beneath me. I want to plunge into you until you cry out in pain. And then, my love, I'll do it all again and again. I'll use you, ride you, until there is nothing left.

"And then, Kirstin, I'll squeeze the very essence from you. Watch your life drain from your naked body." Alex's mouth slowly twisted into a smile.

Kacy fought back a scream, wanting more than anything to tell him that she wasn't Kirstin. Never had been.

"Alex is alive? We are talking about the same Alex that Kacy watched drown, are we not?" Fin's look of astonishment was almost laughable.

"Yes, we are. Bear with me. I'm not sure I'm completely clear myself." The thoughts were coming faster and faster and Braedon was trying to straighten them out and put some order to them.

He sucked in a breath, forcing himself to remain calm, in control. "All right. I didn't have time to verify it, but I'd wager a lot on the fact that the Martin in your pub is the real thing." He sat on a kitchen chair, eyes narrowed, trying to piece it all together. "The one that was supposed to be the original turned up a month or so ago. During an appraisal it was discovered to be a forgery." Along with a hell of a lot of other paintings sold by Solais.

Fin sat down opposite him, his elbows propped on the table. "Kacy told me once that Alex really loved *The Transformation*, that's why she painted the copy." He shot a look at Braedon. "And that's why she gave it to me."

"Right, so if Alex loved that painting as much as she says he did, it seems to me that it would be next to impossible for him to resist the temptation to own the real thing."

"So you think that Alex sold Kacy's copy and kept the original?"

"I do. It would have been easy enough. The forgery ring was most likely already in place."

"Sweet Jesus." Fin whistled through his teeth. "But I still don't see how any of that proves Alex is alive."

"It doesn't, at least not by itself. But I found a contract with a deed in Kacy's attic. It was addressed to an M. Giles. She said it was a mistaken delivery. To their New York apartment. I thought she was right. Now I'm not so sure."

"Wait, I think I see where you're going with this." Fin rubbed a hand across his chin. "You're thinking the initial M stands for Martin?"

"Exactly. Giles Martin—Martin Giles. It's just a hunch, really. But think about it. Alex loved *The Transformation*. Man going from misery to joy, morphing from a black-and-white existence to Technicolor."

"So you think that's what he was planning to do? Make

himself over and live a new life?" Fin narrowed his eyes, his expression shrewd. "But how in the world would we prove such a thing? Short of the man signing his name to a confession, there's no bloody way to be certain."

Braedon felt like banging his hand against his forehead. The answer was suddenly so obvious. A true V8 moment. "I'll be damned. It was right there in my hand. I knew something was off. I just couldn't place it."

"Well, don't go all blabbery on me, man, tell it." Fin leaned forward, his eyes fierce.

"It's the signatures."

Fin frowned again in confusion. "You've lost me again."

Hell, the whole thing was so crazy he wasn't certain he hadn't lost it himself, but he could see the slanted handwriting clearly in his mind. In fact, he'd seen it twice. "On the contract and on Kacy's marriage certificate. The signatures. The names were different, Fin. But I'd swear that the handwriting was the same."

"When did you see the marriage certificate?"

"In the attic, the same time I saw the deed." Braedon closed his eyes, remembering the handwriting. It was distinctive, and though the letters were different, the style was identical. He opened his eyes, meeting Fin's anxious gaze. "I can't be sure, but I think both signatures were written by the same hand."

"Where are the documents now?" Fin asked impatiently.

Braedon tightened a fist. "I burned them."

"What in hell for?"

"I didn't think they were important." He'd been thinking about making love to Kacy. Nothing had seemed important. "Look, there's probably something else in the attic that can tie Martin to Alex. Kacy said there was more mail. The police can look when they get here."

Fin glanced at his watch. "*If* they get here. One of the downsides to living in the country."

"Well, we can't just sit here and do nothing. That maniac was here. He did this. I'd stake my life on it."

"If you're right, then he has Kacy. And that can't be a good thing."

Brandon's stomach tightened into a tangled knot, fear surging through him. Fear mixed with rage. His gaze met Fin's, seeing his own helplessness mirrored there. "How in the hell are we going to find her?"

"Hello, darling. Comfortable?" Alex's voice filled the room, setting Kacy's teeth on edge, sending a tremor of fear down her spine. The mattress dipped as he sat down beside her, running one finger along the swell of her breast. "You are so lovely. It's too bad you couldn't have been loyal as well."

Anger surged through her. "Loyal? You're the one who faked your death and left me behind to clean up the mess." She croaked the words, her throat dry, her voice barely audible.

"But you're the one who kept my letters and my painting."

"What are you talking about?"

His face twisted with rage. "The deed, Kirstin. The only thing linking my old life with my new one."

"I have no idea what you're talking about."

He continued as though she hadn't spoken. "And then there's *The Transformation*. What the hell did you do with it, darling?"

"I gave it away, Alex." She spat the words out, anger swelling through her. "So that I could forget about you."

"Impossible thought, Kirstin. How could you forget this?" His finger circled her nipple, the touch light, almost casual, an afterthought. She tried to twist away, but the ropes kept her firmly within reach. "You know what they say about wives, don't you? It's best to keep them locked up safely. Away from strangers."

He closed his hand, his forefinger and thumb digging into the tender skin. "I saw you with him, you know. Through the window. I saw what he did to you. What you let him do. You've been a very naughty wife, Kirstin." His knowing gaze met hers, his eyes flashing.

Her blood ran cold. He'd seen her with Braedon. Her face flamed with anger. "You bastard."

"Yes, Kirstin, I probably am. But from now on I'm the bastard who butters your bread. And if you value that pretty neck of yours at all, you'll do what I tell you." He leaned down, his breath fanning her face. "Starting now."

He framed her head with his hands, holding her still, and then slowly lowered his head, until his lips brushed against hers. His tongue traced the curve of her mouth and she closed her eyes, trying hopelessly to twist away.

"Hold still." His grip tightened and sharp pain pierced her lower lip, and she realized with horror that he was biting her. She cried out, the sound lost against his mouth, and shrank back into the mattress, willing him to stop, to go away.

He sat back, an insolent smirk on his face. "Don't ever forget that you belong to me, Kirstin. I decide what you do and what you don't do. And only I have the right to touch you. Here." He ran his fingertip across her neck and breasts. "And here." The finger dropped lower and she bit back a scream, glaring at him.

Hating him.

He pulled his hand away, the sardonic smile still firmly in place. "That's enough for now. I like the anticipation. It makes me hard, Kirstin. Hard for you." He touched himself and she wanted to throw up. "I've brought you something to drink." She retched as he moved toward her again, laughing. "Ah, dreaming of drinking me? Maybe later. Right now, I've brought water."

He lifted a glass and Kacy had to fight to keep from begging. Despite her best intentions, her mouth opened of its own volition.

"Now, now, let's don't be greedy." He dipped a finger in the water and trailed it along her lips.

She sucked at the drops, the moisture easing her dry mouth. He lifted the glass for her, holding her head with one hand. She tried to drink, but the angle was off and the water trailed down her chin and onto her chest.

Alex pulled the glass away. "There now, that's enough."

She whimpered with need. She was so thirsty.

"I'll bring you more later. But now, a little prelude, I think." He held the glass over her, tipping it slightly so that the water ran in a thin trickle, splashing across her breasts. Like the water droplets, it pooled below, on her belly.

Before she realized what he was going to do, Alex dipped his head, his tongue lapping at the water on her skin. Tears of humiliation and anger squeezed from behind her tightly closed eyes. She tried to separate herself from the body on the mattress, to find some safe place to go.

She thought about Braedon. And prayed that he would come. Prayed that he would kill Alex.

Braedon sat on the front steps of the cottage, watching as Fin helped Paddy Fitzgerald settle Mac into his car. He was going to be all right, but Paddy needed to get the bullet out and patch him up and they'd decided—against Mac's wishes, based on the way he was howling—it was something best taken care of at the surgery.

Fin thought Mac was in pain. Braedon knew he was frantic over leaving his mistress. Wherever she was. He buried his face in his hands, the feeling of helplessness robbing him of his strength. God, how had he let this happen?

The Garda had come and gone, taking the bodies with them. They were doing all that they could. They'd searched the house inside and out for clues but there was nothing definitive. They had agreed to watch the airports and ferries, but until he could prove that Alex Madison was alive, they would no doubt remain cordial but skeptical. He hadn't told them about the note. Fin had agreed with him that, under the circumstances, it was too damning.

Between he and Fin, they'd canvassed everyone in the village. No one had seen a damn thing. It was as if the man was a bloody ghost. He ran his hands through his hair, trying to stay focused. It was up to him to find her. But how? He tried to think, but his brain was running in slow motion, a creeping sort of lethargy snaking through his body.

Fin dropped onto the step beside him. "Well, that's that. Now what?"

"I honestly don't know. She could be anywhere by now." He lifted his head, hating the vulnerability in his voice. He was supposed to have taken care of her. He never should have left her alone. And now, because of his stupidity, she was God knows where, possibly hurt or worse. He clamped down on the idea, unwilling even to consider it.

"This isn't your fault, you know." Fin placed a hand on his shoulder, reading his mind.

"Isn't it? I keep thinking about her telling me she'd seen him at the hotel. I didn't believe her. I should have at least suspected that it was Max. But I thought the bastard was still in prison."

"You couldn't have known, man."

"But I should have taken it more seriously when she said she saw Alex at the fort." He closed his eyes, a picture of Kacy floating through his mind. Not out on the ledge, but that first morning at the ruins.

He smiled, remembering the way she'd looked, the mist curling around her. If it hadn't been for the falling stones, he would have kissed her. With a start, he realized that he'd loved her even then. His heart sank. If he lost her now . . .

His brain overrode his emotions, a single thought telegraphing its message insistently. He opened his eyes, his senses trained on trying to decode what his subconscious had dredged up.

The fort. The rock slide.

Kacy had said the stones had collapsed. He frowned, forcing himself to concentrate. "The footprint." He grinned suddenly, his lethargy gone.

"What footprint?" Fin raised his brows quizzically.

He hadn't realized he'd spoken out loud. "The one at Dunbeg. It's the key, Fin. There was only one." He stood up, his mind already trying to figure out what to do.

"What in the world are you blethering about now?"

He looked at his friend, too impatient to try to explain, and then relented when he saw the distress reflected on the big Irishman's face. "Come on. I'll explain on the way."

"Way where?" Fin questioned, but rose to follow him as he set off across the drive.

"Dunbeg," Braedon said, stopping at his car to grab his flashlight. Fin caught up with him and together they headed for the fort. "When Kacy and I were exploring the ruins, a section of wall broke off and collapsed. Kacy explained that the wind and rain and years of pilfered stones make that sort of thing a common occurrence."

"So?" Fin held his hands wide, palms up.

"So, we went to check it out. And found that part of an entrance to the souterrain had caved in. There was a footprint in the mud by what was left of the opening. Kacy was worried that someone was trapped inside."

"What does this have to do with Alex?" Fin interrupted impatiently.

"I told Kacy that the footprint was pointed away from the door."

Fin frowned, his brows knitting together. "Meaning someone was walking away, not into the falling rock."

"Right. And that's all I thought about it." He felt himself

grow hot and shrugged. "There were other things on my mind."

The ghost of a grin swept across Fin's face.

"Anyway, the point is I missed the fact that there was only one print. It was raining cats and dogs. Mud everywhere."

Fin quickened his step, hope lighting his ruddy face. "And if someone had walked away, there would have been more than one print."

"Exactly. It was more like someone had stepped out and then back again."

"Someone who saw his wife with another man?"

Braedon grimaced. "Someone who saw his wife in the *arms* of another man."

Fin blew out a breath. "And in anger, created a distraction."

"Seems plausible."

Fin nodded, caught up with the idea. "Those tunnels riddle the hillside. They even lead down to the sea. A man could hide in there for years."

"And he could hide someone else." Braedon shuddered, rage twisting through him at the thought of his Kacy trapped somewhere underground with a madman.

Fin grabbed his arm, hurrying him along. "Come on, then. Let's go find the bloody bastard."

Drip.
Drip.
Drip.

Chinese water torture would have been more humane. Kacy wanted to scream. She was cold and her muscles protested in agony. And on top of everything else, something was in here with her. She was certain of it, could hear it creeping around, skittering about. Her mind was inventing all sorts of creatures and she shivered as much from apprehension as from cold.

She strained against her bonds. Nothing. She'd managed to loosen the rope around her left wrist, but not enough to allow her to escape. She bit back an oath and slammed her head back down against the mattress.

She had no concept of time, but she was tired and hungry and she had to . . . well, she just wasn't going to think about that.

More than anything, she had to get out of here. It was all well and good to think about Braedon riding to her rescue, but it was probably good to develop a plan B, just in case. Tears threatened again and she dug her nails into her palm, driving them away. She jerked her left arm, twisting her wrist at the same time. The rope dug into her flesh and she bit her lip to keep from crying out in pain.

Alex was not going to get the best of her. She wouldn't let him. She twisted her wrist again, and this time felt the rope slide a little. The skin was raw and it burned from where the restraint had cut her, but considering some of the alternatives, whatever she did to herself, right up to cutting her hand off, would be more than worth it.

She squeezed her eyes shut, folded her hand until it was as narrow as she could make it, and yanked. Searing pain shot up her arm, but she forced herself to ignore it and wrenched her hand free.

She lay for a moment, waves of agony washing through her, and then with steely fortitude, she pushed away the pain. No way was Alex going to get her without a fight. She reached for her other hand, looking down her arm as she fumbled with the knot, gritting her teeth with determination.

One down, three to go.

Chapter 28

KACY SAT UP, her left wrist throbbing. It was hard to see in the dim light, but from an upright vantage point she could make out rock and dirt walls. She was sitting on a makeshift bed and dilapidated mattress. She flexed her feet, inspecting her ankles, relieved to find that other than a few abrasions and some serious bruising, they were fine.

She could walk. Granted, she wasn't up to a marathon, but under the circumstances she'd take what she could get, as long as it meant getting the hell out of Dodge.

Her wrist hadn't fared so well. It didn't look good. It was purple and scraped raw in places, the bone dipping inward, forming an odd crater in the center of her wrist, and her hand was swelling, her fingers ungainly and stiff. She swallowed back nausea as a wave of pain washed through her.

There wasn't time for this. She'd feel sorry for herself later. Right now, she had to move. She eased off the bed, finding her balance, waiting until her head stopped whirling. Finally steady on her feet, she held her injured wrist with her good hand and surveyed the room, trying to figure out exactly where she was.

Faint light filtered through chinks in the rock wall directly behind the bed. Crossing over to it, she braced herself with her good hand and tried to peer through a small gap, hoping to see what was on the other side. The stones under her hand shifted, scraping against each other, plummeting outward, leaving a larger hole.

She stumbled, lurching backward, grateful when she regained her balance without falling. Sucking in a deep breath, she froze, staring at the patch of sky through the gap, her mind reproducing instant replay of the rocks tumbling end over end to the beach below.

The souterrain.

She must be in one of the little chambers along the passageway. One that fronted the cliff. She shivered, remembering for the first time that she was not exactly dressed for the occasion.

A ratty looking sheet covered the mattress and she grabbed it with her good hand, twisting it around her torso in a makeshift toga. Surely what all the well-dressed madmen's concubines were wearing these days.

She swallowed her panic. It wouldn't do to lose it now. Alex would be back.

She shuddered, remembering his touch.

Oh, yes, he'd be back.

Her mind flashed images of his leaning over her, touching her, licking her . . . Her stomach churned at the thought of what had almost happened. She drew in a shaky breath. But it hadn't. For whatever twisted reason, he'd stopped and the fact remained, he hadn't.

But she also knew he'd be back to finish the game. She ground her teeth together, fortifying herself for battle. If she had any say in the matter, he'd never finish any game ever again.

She took a step toward the far side of the chamber. The feeble light played out, the shadows taking over. She couldn't really see the wall, just a slight change in the darkness, the sense of something solid. But there had to be a way out. And her money was on the wall.

Arms stretched in front of her, she moved cautiously forward, trying to ignore the white hot pain shooting down her left arm. Step after step, one foot in front of the other until her hands hit rock. Then, inching first one way, and then the other, she felt for the door.

Finally, in the farthest, darkest corner, she felt wood.

Strong, solid, impenetrable wood.

The door.

Not a centuries-old rotting door. A new and completely unopenable door.

She fumbled for the handle and tried to pull it open, knowing already what she would find. If Alex had gone to the trouble to install a new door, he wouldn't leave it unlocked.

She sank to the floor, cradling her mangled wrist.

She was trapped.

"Where the hell does this thing go?" Braedon shone the light down a dark, curving corridor of the souterrain.

"I haven't been here in years, but if memory serves, the main passage runs in sort of a *Y*." Fin's whispered words sounded hollow, bouncing off the shadowed walls.

"So what? That's the tail?" Braedon motioned to another opening with the flashlight.

"I think so. It's hard to keep a sense of direction in this hellhole."

"I thought you said you played here when you were a kid." Braedon stooped to pick up an iron rod lying in the passageway. The thing resembled a poker—a rusty poker. But it was still a weapon—of sorts.

The flashlight illuminated Fin's rueful grin. "I'm afraid age has made me a bit more cautious. Not to mention the small fact that there's a madman loose in here."

Braedon shuddered with the thought, his overactive imagination picturing Kacy. "Which way?"

Fin eyed the two passages, shining his pocket torch at first one and then the other. "I've no idea. Maybe we should split up."

"All right. I'll take this one." He took a step down the straighter part of the tunnel. "We'll meet back here, unless we find something."

"Fine." The Irishman took a step down the other corridor. "Good hunting."

"Aye." Braedon smiled at the Irish lilt, realizing somehow that it felt good—right. "You, too."

He moved into the passageway, shining the thin beam of the flashlight into the gloom. The pathway angled sharply downward, then curved, disappearing around a turn in the wall. He tightened his grip on the poker, staring into the dark shadows of the opening.

If the situation wasn't so dire, he'd laugh. He could wither a boardroom full of men with a single well-placed look, but when Kacy needed him, all he could manage was to arm himself with a rusty fire tool.

Great.

He was no better than a weekend warrior. And he seriously doubted a thin piece of iron was going to make much of a statement against a loaded gun. Hopefully backup was on the way. Fin had called the Garda. But no matter his choice of weaponry, he couldn't afford to wait for them.

He started down the pathway, the little light cutting a swath through the dark. The tunnel was quiet. Oppressively quiet. The only noise the hollow dripping of water and the occasional rattle when he hit a loose rock.

He tried to clear his mind, to form a plan, but all he could think about was Kacy—Kacy with Alex. Blistering rage flowed through him, leaving burning resolution in its wake. If that bastard had hurt her . . .

He clenched his fist around the poker. Gun or no, he'd

enjoy taking on the son of a bitch. He'd be damned if he was going to stand by helplessly and wait until it was too late.

A rock rattled in the passage outside the door. Kacy raised her head, fear surging through her. She scrambled to her feet, fighting to maintain balance, muscles protesting the movement.

She looked around frantically for a weapon. There were some small rocks on the floor, but nothing big enough to do serious damage and she was fresh out of slingshots.

The door shook against the wall, the sound rattling through the room.

Alex was here.

She grabbed a piece of rope from the bed, not certain what she was going to do with it, but needing to have something in her hand. Visions of strangling Alex ran through her head, but she quickly discarded the notion. He towered over her. She'd be lucky if she managed to cut off the blood supply to his stomach.

She backed against the wall, trying to press herself into it, to disappear. Hiding in the deepest shadows, she listened intently, shivering when she heard something slide against the outside of the wall.

She tried to hold the rope in both hands, but her left was swollen and starting to go numb. No amount of willpower was going to make it serviceable. Maybe she'd lasso him. Now there was a brilliant thought. Fear was making her slap-happy. She clamped down on her panic and tried to focus on the situation. She needed her wits about her.

One way or another, she wasn't going down without a fight.

"Kacy?" The whispered word sounded louder than a scream—a beautiful, wonderful, scream.

"I'm here." Her voice was hoarse, but she knew he could hear her and that was all that mattered.

The door squeaked as it opened, and she sucked in a breath, waiting.

With a muffled wail, she launched herself at the shadowy figure. *Braedon*. Strong arms closed around her and she greedily consumed the comfort of his touch.

"What has he done to you?" Braedon's voice was tight, filled with emotion. He released her, pulling her gently into the pale wash of light, his eyes moving from her head to her toes, taking in her injured wrist, her bruises, and the bed sheet.

Wordlessly he spun around, taking in the ropes and the bed. His fists clenched and he uttered a string of curses. He turned back to her, his face twisted with rage. "Did he—"

She held out her hand, wanting to soothe him, reassure him. "No. He . . . he touched me, but he didn't . . ." She shuddered, unable to finish the sentence.

His face softened, concern replacing anger. Yanking off his sweater, he carefully eased it over her body, loosening the makeshift toga, allowing the tattered sheet to fall to the floor. The sweater hung to her knees, surrounding her in his warmth, his scent, somehow soothing her, forming an invincible shield. In the middle of what could only be described as madness, Kacy suddenly felt safe. As long as he was beside her, she could face anything.

Gently he pulled her to him, enclosing her in the warmth of his embrace. Their lips met and Kacy's breath escaped on a sigh as she drank in his taste, his essence—trading her soul for his.

With a groan, he stepped back, a faint grin chasing across his face. "Hold that thought."

She tilted her head back, smiling up at him. "I will."

He lifted her injured hand, bringing it gently to his lips, his reverence bringing tears to her eyes. Their gazes met and held. His full of promise. Hers full of love.

He pulled away. "Sweetheart, we've got to get out of here."

The magic in the moment evaporated in an instant. Alex was still here, somewhere. And if he found them . . .

"Can you walk?" Braedon looked down at her bare feet.

She nodded, the ever present fear rising again. "I'll be fine, let's just get out of here."

He reached down and picked something up. She squinted at it, recognizing its shape. Not exactly the Uzi she'd been hoping for, but it was a definite improvement over the rope.

He wrapped an arm around her, drawing her back into the shadows surrounding the doorway. With a faltering step, she let him propel her forward, toward the door.

"Leaving so soon? And here I was thinking we were going to have a party." Alex's voice floated out of the dark chasm marking the opening to the passageway, the disembodied sound sending shivers of fear racing down Kacy's spine.

Braedon pushed her behind him and raised the poker menacingly.

Alex laughed, stepping into the room. "I win." He tilted his head, a sinister smile lighting his face. "I think a revolver trumps a poker every time." He waved the gun for effect. "Drop it."

Braedon's hand tightened on the iron rod and then with an exhale of breath, he let it go. It clattered against the rock floor.

"Now, kick it over here." Braedon complied and the poker rolled into the darkness.

"Well, now, isn't this cozy. The wife, the lover, and the husband." Alex raised his brows, watching them, an almost bored look on his face. Kacy knew better. She knew what a mask he wore, how easily he hid his feelings. A master con artist. But underneath it all lurked a madman.

"You won't get away with this, Madison." Braedon's voice was barely more than a growl.

"Oh, but I already have. All I need to do now is tie up the last few loose ends. And you, with your attempt at heroics, have just made that easier for me." He leveled the gun, pointing it at Braedon's chest.

With a stifled cry, Kacy dove in front of him. Braedon's hands circled her shoulders, pushing her to the floor, his big body covering hers.

Alex's laughter echoed off the walls. "Splendid display of loyalty. Wasted, of course. I do have more than one bullet. Stand up, both of you."

Braedon moved off of her, carefully keeping himself between her body and the gun.

Kacy moved to his side, equally determined to protect him. "Let him go, Alex. You know it's me you want."

Alex shifted slightly, the gun leveled again on Braedon. "Oh, yes, darling, I want you, but I also want this bastard to pay for taking what belongs to me."

Braedon took an angry step forward.

"Call him off, Kirstin, or I'll shoot him right now."

"Braedon." Her whispered plea held her heart in it. He stopped.

"Now, where were we?" Alex stroked his chin. "Ah, yes, we were discussing Kirstin's infidelity."

"You son of a bitch." Braedon's eyes narrowed and his whole body tensed.

"Actually, you're not far from the truth. But that's neither here nor there. What does matter is that you've not only caused me a great deal of trouble, you screwed my wife. And where I come from—" He smiled as if they were discussing a day at the fair. "—that's a punishable offense." He aimed the gun.

A shadow detached itself from the wall, leaping at Alex. Kacy screamed and threw herself toward Braedon, the report of the gun ringing in her ears, a vision of Max dying filling her brain.

Not Braedon, her heart pleaded, never Braedon.

He moved under her, throwing her off, rising to his feet, crouched low. Kacy sat back against the bed, dazed, watching as two figures struggled in the half-light. A glint of red hair caught her eye.

Fin.

Braedon moved forward, obviously wanting to join the fight, but hesitant to endanger Fin. With a sickening thud of bone against rock, the two figures separated, one dropping to the floor in a shadowy heap.

Alex turned to survey them, a twisted smile on his face, blood dripping into his eye from a cut on his forehead. He looked like something dragged from the depths of hell, and the hatred in his eyes made Kacy gasp.

Braedon launched himself at Alex, his bulk hitting the other man with an audible crunch. Something clattered across the floor. The two men struggled, locked together in combat. Kacy's beleaguered brain suddenly ran up a red flag.

The noise.

Metal on stone.

The gun.

Scrambling around the edge of the room, away from the fighting men, she fumbled in the dark, trying to find the weapon. It had to be there. It had to.

Nothing.

Braedon groaned and she turned in time to see Alex slam a fist into the side of his head. She waited until she saw that he was still upright and then turned back to her search. The only way she could help him was to find the damn gun.

Her fingers hit something cold and pliable. She jerked back. A hand. A human hand.

She bit back her fear, her brain back in charge. Fin. She'd found Fin. With a trembling hand, she felt for a pulse.

It was there, faint but steady. She sucked in a breath and

sent a prayer heavenward. For now, she'd have to let someone else worry about Fin. Right now, she had to concentrate on helping Braedon.

Moving past him, she resumed her search, trying to shut out the sounds of the battle behind her. Her hand hit the wall and something shifted. Reaching out into the darkness, her fingers closed around cylindrical metal.

The gun. She had the gun.

Pulling herself to her feet, she held up the gun, bracing her right hand with her maimed left, determination filling her mind. "Braedon, move." The words were amazingly steady and some other part of herself watched with amazement as she waited for the moment.

The two men froze for an instant, and then each reacted to her command. Braedon dropped to the floor, and Alex turned to meet her gaze, his eyes narrowed, his face bloody.

Ice-cold fury washed through her, flushing away all other emotion. This man had used her, abused her, and tried to take away the things that meant the most to her.

He took a step backward, his look changing, fear rising in his eyes.

She hesitated, unsure for an instant. And then she saw Alex smile slowly, his fear dissipating, replaced by the certain knowledge that he had won.

Her finger tightened on the trigger.

One minute he was smiling, and the next, his eyes widened in surprise. He clutched at his chest, careening backward against the outer wall. With a deafening thunder, the stones collapsed under his weight, dropping away, falling to the rocks below.

Alex teetered for a moment, his eyes locked with hers, and then, arms pinwheeling, he fought for balance and lost, falling back into the blue of the sky, his scream echoing through the suddenly still air.

* * *

Braedon staggered to his feet, his eyes locked on Kacy. She closed her eyes, the gun slipping out of her hand. In one stride, he was across the space that separated them, pulling her close, holding her warm and alive against his chest, her heart beating in tandem with his.

"It's over, sweetheart," he whispered in her ear, his hands stroking her hair, her back, reveling in the feel of her safe against him. Her body shook as great choking sobs racked her, all the torment of the last few days—hell, the last two years—finally finding release.

He rocked her in his arms, whispering words of comfort, words of love. If necessary, he vowed, he'd stay with her here, like this, until hell froze over. Whatever she needed, he'd find a way to give it to her. She held his heart. She was his life.

"Is he dead?" The words were soft, hesitant, murmured against his chest.

"No one could survive that fall, Kacy."

"I need to know for sure." She pulled back, meeting his gaze.

"I'll look." He started to move away.

"No. I have to do it." The resolve in her voice made him proud. His Kacy was a survivor.

He gently reached for her hand. "Okay. But you don't have to do it alone."

They walked to the edge of the crumbled wall, and with a little hiss of breath she looked down. Braedon tightened his grip on her hand, his eyes searching for and finding the battered remains of Alex Madison on the rocks below.

"He's dead," she whispered, the words holding the trace of a question.

Braedon winced. The bastard still had a hold on her even in death. He pulled her away from the grotesque display, wrapping his arms around her. "He's gone, Kacy. Forever. He can never torment you again."

She nodded against his shirt and nestled closer. He felt tears sting his eyes. It was finally over.

"So what in sweet hell happened here?" Fin was sitting up in the corner, rubbing his head, a confused look on his face.

Kacy tipped back her head, a smile lighting her eyes, laughter filling her voice. "You saved me."

She was answering Fin, but her words were meant for Braedon alone.

Epilogue

KACY STOOD IN the front room of the cottage, looking down at the huge diamond sparkling on her finger, the light catching its facets, turning it into a rainbow of color. As of this morning, she was officially Mrs. Braedon Roche.

And this evening their friends were here to honor them, to share in their joy. It was an eclectic mix. Saville Row suits blended with coveralls and corduroys. Fisherman's sweaters stood arm in arm with Armani. New York chic and Irish charm.

Kacy had never been so happy.

All traces of the nightmare were gone. Her little cottage was painted and polished, cleaned and renewed. Just like her life.

She sipped from her champagne flute, her eyes automatically searching for Braedon. He was in a corner, deep in conversation with Paddy Fitzgerald. She drank in the sight of him, wondering if she would ever grow tired of simply staring at him.

As if sensing her gaze, he looked up, his blue eyes crinkling into a smile. He mouthed the words *I love you* and blew her a kiss. She smiled back, a shiver of desire rippling through her.

"Ah, what a lucky man he is."

Kacy flushed with embarrassment, pulling her gaze away from her husband and turning to face Fin. "I bet it'll be your turn before you know it."

"Well, now," he said, stroking his chin in exaggerated thoughtfulness, "I don't think that's a wager you should be making. What with the only eligible women around here being my sister, who by the way is sorry she couldn't be here, and old Irene Macnamara, I'd say I haven't the pope's chance in hell." Fin lifted his beer glass in salute to the elderly woman, who was looking every bit the village matriarch, dressed in black chiffon edged with white lace.

"Seriously, though—" He reached for Kacy's hand, the one still encased in a cast. "—I can't think of two people I'm happier to see together. The only shame in it is that you'll be living so far away."

"Oh, but we won't. At least not all the time. I'm surprised Braedon didn't tell you. He's decided he wants to come home. So he's moving things over here. We'll be in Dublin some, but we're keeping the cottage. And we're opening a gallery here, in County Clare."

"Well, I'll be damned. The boyo has come to his senses. I always said he was one of us."

Kacy laughed and held up her glass. "That you did, Fin."

They clinked glasses. Beer against champagne. "To you and Braedon."

"Thank you, Fin." Braedon joined the toast, his cobalt gaze meeting Kacy's, his glass joining theirs. "If you'll excuse us for a minute, I'd like some time alone with my wife."

Wife. What a lovely title. Kacy linked her arm through his and together they wandered toward the kitchen, trailed by Mac, who seldom let Kacy out of his sight these days. "So what's this all about?"

He pulled her into the quiet of her studio, his arms trapping her against one wall, his lips doing wonderful things to the soft skin of her neck. "Can't I enjoy a private moment with my wife?" His whispered words sent pinpricks of red hot need racing through her.

"Not unless you're prepared to throw every one of our guests out on their well-dressed behinds." She shivered as his teeth pulled at her ear, his breath stirring her hair. "Oh, Lord, Braedon. I can't take this."

"Fair enough. *We'll leave.*" He stepped back, his eyes teasing her. She almost melted onto the floor, a puddle of raging hormones. God, she loved this man.

"We can't just leave our guests," she protested half-heartedly as he helped her into her coat.

"Fin will make sure they're well cared for. He's good at that sort of thing."

"True enough." Kacy smiled up at him as he escorted her into the kitchen to the back door. "So where are you taking me?"

"Patience, my love."

Mac followed them to the door, tail wagging, begging to be included in the party. But at Braedon's firm "no," he dropped resentfully to the floor of the kitchen.

"He's never going to forgive me." Braedon pulled her out the door, ignoring the baleful whine from the dog.

"He'll get over it," she said, laughing. "Now tell me what you're up to."

His blue eyes twinkled and he leaned in and kissed her on the nose. "Nothing much. Just a little fairy magic."

"Can I open my eyes now?" Kacy asked, wondering if Braedon had taken leave of his senses. It was cold out, and the mist was penetrating. She could think of a lot of things she'd rather be doing with her new husband than traipsing over the Irish countryside.

"Not yet. Just a few more steps." There was laughter in his voice, and something else. Worry? She smiled. Braedon was actually nervous.

He led her forward two more steps and then stopped. "Okay, now."

The meadow was awash in swirling half-light—the last of the afternoon sun shining through the mist. Dunbeg was off to her left, its stones shining white against the meadow. In front of her, perched on a rocky promontory, was a small stone building ornamented with a garish red bow.

"What's this?" Kacy looked up at her husband.

His arms around her tightened. "A wedding present."

"A house? Braedon, we already have a house. Three, in fact."

He propelled her forward. "This isn't a house, Kacy. And it isn't mine. It's yours." He opened the door.

Kacy walked inside, her heart beating joyously. *A studio.* Braedon had built her a studio. Even in the gray of the day she could see the potential for light. One entire wall was glass, the view of the sea breathtaking. She turned in a circle, drinking it all in, then froze as her eyes fell on the back wall.

"My God, Braedon how did you . . ." She broke off, tears welling in her eyes. The Monet—her Monet—filled the wall, its canvas unmarred by Alex's evil.

Braedon's hand closed around hers and she leaned into his warmth. "It was just a matter of finding the right person." His hand stroked the curve of her head and she sighed with contentment. "It's from Professor Baucomo as much as me, really. I took a chance and contacted one of his colleagues—a student of his. Anyway, the man was delighted to help and I thought it fitting that a protégé of the professor's be the one to restore it for you."

Kacy moved toward the painting, her eyes locked on its lush colors. She thought of the professor and his last act of kindness, and she hoped that somewhere—somehow—he knew, despite everything, how much he meant to her.

She turned to face Braedon, banishing the professor from her mind. Today was a day for celebrating. "*You* gave it back to me."

"It's not perfect, but the lighting helps. And I knew how much it meant to you."

She ran to him then, throwing herself into his arms. "I love you, Braedon Roche. And I love the studio and the painting. I can't think of a better wedding gift."

He pulled her closer, his eyes speaking volumes. "Well, I think the fact that we're standing here, free of shadows, is something."

She nibbled on her lower lip, thinking of the one thing that she still had to fear.

Millicent.

Braedon held out a folded blue document.

"What is it?"

"Another wedding present. Millicent has agreed to a settlement. You're free to announce your parentage as long as you make no claim to her estate."

"But I don't want any of her money."

"I know." He smiled, and she thought her heart might actually take flight.

"You're a miracle worker."

He shrugged. "What good's a mogul if he can't work a few miracles? Besides—" His expression grew serious. "—I'm your safe harbor. Remember?"

"I remember." Her gaze met his, her heart swelling with joy, and she reached for his hand. "Braedon? I can think of another wedding gift we ought to consider." Her eyes strayed to a pile of blankets spread cozily by the fire.

"Oh, really?" His blue eyes turned black with desire. "And what might that be?"

Braedon looked down at his wife. She looked beautiful in the last light of the Irish afternoon. Her hair spread across his chest, her skin alabaster silk. He had never felt so at peace. At last all was right with his world.

He nestled back against a pillow and pulled the blankets

closer around them, one finger lazily trailing along the smooth curve of her shoulder. "I think I'm in heaven."

"Me, too." Kacy snuggled against him, tipping back her head to meet his gaze. Braedon was satisfied to see the spark of passion flaring in the swirling green depths of her eyes.

With a slow smile, she threaded her good hand through his hair and pulled his lips to hers. The kiss started as a fairy touch, all magic and light, but then she opened her mouth and he was lost. This was the woman he had dreamed of all his life. And she was his. A fierce swell of possessiveness washed through him. Possessiveness and pride.

"Shall we adjourn to the cottage?" His voice was hoarse with passion.

Her dimple appeared, creasing her cheek. "Why? I think we have everything we need right here."

A last ray of sunshine broke through the clouds, reaching in through the window to lightly kiss the intertwined couple, and then dance on to illuminate the painting on the wall. The Monet's colors glowed in the basking light, its magnificence reflecting the love that filled the room.

Read on for a sneak peek
at the next thrilling romance
from Dee Davis . . .

JUST BREATHE

Coming in Summer 2001.

Prologue

 Volksgarten, Vienna, Austria—1985

THE WIND WHISTLED through the trees, whipping the rose bushes into a frenzied dance, their canes thrashing in the wind like bony arms reaching for something. *Reaching for me.* Lisa pulled her sweater around her, shivering.

The night air was chilly and laden with the heavy scent of roses in bloom. Masses of them. She hurried along the narrow pathway, trying to stay focused on the task at hand. Leaves rustled. She glanced from the path to the roses. In the dark of the night, they were no more than black on black, ghostly shadows weaving in the wind.

Stop it.

She shook her head and clutched her sweater even tighter. She really wasn't cut out for this cloak-and-dagger stuff, but a good reporter always went to the source and, unfortunately, the voice on the phone had been insistent that this was the source—or rather that the statue of Elisabeth was.

There was something ironic about it all. A Cold War dead drop and the statue of a Hapsburg Empress murdered by an anarchist. Perhaps the caller had a sense of humor. Or perhaps this was simply a wild-goose chase. Perhaps there was nothing to find. She left the main trail, stepping into the deeper gloom of the trees.

The pressing question was one of credibility. Could she

trust the caller? She squared her shoulders. She'd damn well better be able to. She'd gone out on a proverbial limb for this one. Despite the fact that certain people—very *credible* people—thought the promised information was at best a hoax, and at worst, the ramblings of an addled brain.

The path split, one branch snaking off to the right and the other curving left. She stopped, trying to remember the way. Everything looked different at night. *Sinister.* She sucked in a breath, and chose the left-hand fork. This was not the time for the willies.

If her source was telling the truth, this could be the beginning of a very promising career. The kind of thing that wins journalism prizes. All she had to do was find the bloody statue and retrieve its hidden treasure. Proof positive. She shivered again, this time with anticipation. The trees began to thin a little, the path twisting out of sight behind a closely clipped hedge.

Almost there.

Something hissed past her cheek. She slapped at it, thinking that it was too early for midges. Another hiss, this one followed by a burning sensation in her chest. Her hand automatically covered the site, and she recoiled at the feel of something sticky.

Blood. *Her blood.*

Ducking instinctively, she forced herself to run, her mind still scrambling for an explanation. The crunch of shoe leather on gravel broke the silence of the night. Someone was on the path. Veering right, she scrambled into the trees, hot pain searing through her body. She stumbled and fell, the soft spring grass cushioning the fall.

She tried to roll over, to get up, but the world went all wobbly, her strength draining away, pooling beneath her with her blood. She gasped, trying to force air into her lungs, but the effort was almost more than she could stand. The wind whispered through the trees, pulling the branches back like hands on a curtain. Stars twinkled in the night sky.

Benign magnificence illuminating evil.

A branch snapped, and Lisa turned her head. Moonlight flickered against pale skin and dark eyes. Knowing eyes. Satisfied eyes.

The eyes of an executioner.

The eyes of a friend.

Chapter 1

 Sudbahnhof, Vienna—Present Day

"SO TELL ME, dear, have you ever actually had a multiple orgasm?"

Chloe Nichols's eyes widened as she pulled her Sony Walkman's earphones from her head. "I beg your pardon?"

"I asked if you've ever had a multiple orgasm." Charlotte Northrup tilted her head to one side, one perfectly penciled eyebrow raised in question.

Chloe's face heated to lobster red. Great, she resembled a crustacean. Not exactly glamour girl material. The train rumbled along, its clickity-clacking rhythm seeming to underscore the question. She struggled to find words, trying not to stare at her seatmate. Charlotte pursed her lips, obviously waiting for an answer. She looked so earnest—so interested.

"I mean these books," the blue-haired dowager tapped her well-manicured finger against the cover of her romance novel knowingly, "make it sound so wonderful." The last was more of an exhale than a word. "My ex-husband barely gave me enough time for one orgasm, let alone a whole slew of them." She leaned forward, eyeing Chloe as though she were the shaman of sex. "So have you? Had one, I mean."

If possible, Chloe's face burned even hotter. She hadn't had a single orgasm in, well, forever. And frankly, romance novels depressed her. All those happy endings. Chloe sighed, wishing their other companions would return. She needed reinforcements.

On the other hand, maybe that wasn't such a great idea. Wilhelmina Delacroix and Irma Peabody were cut from the same cloth as Charlotte Northrup. Willie and Charlotte had been friends forever. Lord, they probably talked about these sorts of things all the time. And Irma? Well, her Midwestern practicality would certainly shed new light on the subject. The thought of the three of them, together, discussing multiple orgasms was simply beyond comprehension.

For better or worse, the compartment door stayed stubbornly closed, and Charlotte raised an eyebrow again, obviously waiting for some snippet of coital wisdom. Chloe struggled to think of something to say. Charlotte looked so hopeful. There was nothing to do but lie. It was the only way. She opened her mouth to answer, just as the train lurched to a stop.

Static crackled over the loudspeaker, a message blaring in three equally unintelligible languages. Thank goodness, a reprieve. "I think we've arrived." Chloe glanced out the window at the train platform. It was an underground station, and the dim lighting made it hard to see anything clearly.

"We'd best hurry." Charlotte closed her book with a snap and stuffed it into her bag. "You know what Thomas said about getting off the train quickly."

Chloe nodded and gathered her luggage, tucking the Walkman under her arm. Thomas Hardy—obviously a man with a literary mother—was their tour director. She smiled thinking of his dour face and neatly trimmed beard.

He reminded her of someone's butler, or what she imagined a butler to be like. She'd never had any firsthand experience with that sort of thing, but if there was a butler type, Thomas definitely fit the mold. And right now, the memory of his clipped accent was ringing in her ears, warning them that European trains didn't stop for long. "Look sharp, ladies, and move quickly."

Chloe followed Charlotte, stopping at the compartment door to adjust the strap of her bag, balancing it against the weight of her overstuffed backpack, and wondered what in the world had made her decide to carry all this stuff when there was a perfectly good porter assigned just to them.

Chloe sighed. She'd blame it on all those years as a Girl Scout. *Be prepared.* Or was that the Boy Scouts? Well, either way, a girl never knew what she might get into. Chloe winced. She was certainly walking proof of that statement.

She stepped into the crowded aisle of the train, squeezing between other departing passengers. Charlotte had already disappeared from sight and the rest of the group was nowhere to be seen either. They'd probably already disembarked. She'd best get a move on. Thomas was a stickler for punctuality. And given the circumstances, she didn't want to do anything else to annoy him.

The woman directly in front of her was obviously a devotee to the Chloe Nichols plan for lugging luggage. She was loaded down with three suitcases, and trying to juggle them as she struggled along seemed to be more than she could handle.

With a muffled and rather unladylike curse, the woman fumbled her burden, two of her suitcases tumbling to the floor. Chloe skidded to a stop and something hard and solid slammed into her back. She looked over her shoulder directly into a pair of amused gray-green eyes set into a wonderfully masculine face. *Chiseled* was the word that came to mind. Chiseled and gorgeous. Her heart actually did a half-gainer into the general region of her stomach.

His hand steadied her elbow as the overloaded woman struggled for balance, her suitcases swinging precariously with each motion. "I don't think she understands the meaning of 'pack light.' "

His whispered words sent tremors of heat chasing through her, adding to the electricity of his touch. At this rate, she would be answering Charlotte's provocative question affirmatively without ever removing her clothing—or even knowing the man's name. She smiled at the ridiculous turn of her thoughts.

Another passenger stepped out of his compartment, pushing between them before she could respond. A surge of disappointment rocked through her, surprising her with its intensity. Luggage lady finally moved forward, and Chloe followed, pushing all thoughts of the handsome stranger firmly out of her mind.

The steps down from the train were daunting, and she paused, trying to figure out the best way to approach them. The last thing she needed was to wind up sprawled on her butt in a pile of her unmentionables, especially with Mr. Make-Her-Heart-Sizzle somewhere back there.

A ferret-faced little man, cursing all women and their suitcases, shoved past her, pushing her off balance as he descended the steps. She teetered, then fumbled for footing, hanging onto her luggage like a lifeline. Not that it was doing a bit of good.

She felt her stomach drop three stories, and then she careened downward, something stinging her arm as she collided with the pushy man. He broke her fall, but did nothing to preserve her dignity. She ended up straddling him, blood staining the sleeve of her blouse, her skirt hiked up to her thighs, her self-respect taking the next train out of the station.

Amazingly, the platform had cleared and there were only a few people milling about. She grabbed an errant lipstick and comb, stuffed them into her purse, then fumbled for a CD that had managed to escape its case, sighing when she saw the condition of her Walkman. It was doubtful it would ever play again. Except for the throbbing in her arm, she seemed to be unhurt, and she was thankful no one was staring. At least there were no witnesses to her latest debacle. It seemed even Mr. Wonderful had disappeared. She breathed a sigh of relief.

As if on cue, he materialized, kneeling beside her, his face a scant two inches from hers. She could smell his aftershave. Feel his heat. Charlotte's words slid down her spine again. *Multiple orgasms.*

"Move."

Her addlebrained daydreaming vanished in an instant. She slithered off the ferret-faced man, noticing for the first time how still he was. "Are you all right?" The little guy didn't move. In fact, he hadn't moved since she fell. Concern spiked through her, and she reached out to touch him.

"Come with me. *Now.*" Mr. Wonderful, who was rapidly turning into Mr. Bossy, yanked her to her feet.

She turned to face him, meeting his steady, green-eyed gaze. "He needs help. We have to do something." She shivered, a trace of fear running through her.

Mr. Bossy started to move, pulling her with him, his eyes sweeping across the platform, looking for something. "I'm afraid there's nothing you can do for him now."

"Of course there is. It's my fault that he fell. The least I can do is call for some help."

He urged her forward as he increased the pace. She struggled to hold onto her luggage, grateful when he took it from her. "Right now, the most important thing we can do is get you out of here."

"But the man—" She looked back over her shoulder.

"Is dead."

Sabra Hitchcock unscrewed the silencer from her gun and slid them both back into the inner pocket of her black leather coat. She didn't particularly enjoy killing, although she couldn't say that it really bothered her either. As far as she was concerned, there were really only two reasons to kill someone: to end a threat or to acquire money. And this job had been about threat.

Charles Messer was dead. And for the moment that was enough. She eyed the body dispassionately from across the platform. The walkway was almost clear. Just a few stragglers, and the bimbo who'd literally fallen over the body.

Why was it that klutzy women always managed to get themselves rescued? It was as if they had neon emblazoned on their foreheads, flashing out the message, *Save me. Save me.*

Sabra blew out a breath in disgust as she watched a magnificently formed male rush to help the bimbo to her feet. He was tall, his shoulders wide, his ass tight. She was all legs and hair. Probably boobs, too. Sabra felt a rush of adrenaline and wondered if it was because of the man or the woman.

Barbie or Ken. Equally appealing.

She started to smile, but the movement quickly twisted into a grimace as the dark-haired man turned toward her. His features were unmistakable, even from this distance. Pain laced through her, sharp and hot. He wasn't supposed to be here. Her heart rate accelerated, sweat popping out on her brow.

Damn him.

Time had done nothing to lessen his hold over her, his mere presence enough to send her into panicked flight. He mustn't see her. Mustn't know. Her eyes locked on his powerful body, and she stepped deeper into the shadows of the station.

Matthew Broussard.

Her nemesis. Her obsession. She closed her hand around the cold comfort of her Sig Sauer. *Matthew Broussard.* She watched as he hurried the brunette away, one arm locked protectively around her shoulders. Some things never changed. Matthew the protector. A policeman appeared at the far end of the platform. She pulled herself together, wrenching her gaze away from him.

Time to make an exit.

With a last glance at the body, Sabra moved in the opposite direction, years of training helping her to blend into the background.

A nonentity. A nobody.

She forced herself to look straight ahead, fighting the desire to turn for a last look at Matthew. Even now, like this, she wanted him. She licked her lips nervously, still fingering her gun.

Ben was going to shit a brick.

"Dead as in . . ." The woman jerked to a stop, turning to look up at him.

"Dead." Matthew tried to move her forward, but she was rooted to the spot.

"Are you saying I killed him?" She blinked once, her eyes wide, her look confused and a little frightened.

She had the bluest eyes he'd ever seen. Clear like a mountain lake. Innocent eyes. He'd never met anyone with such an open trusting look. People like that didn't turn up much in his line of work. "No. He was dead before you hit him."

He felt her relax slightly. A little breath escaped through her lips with a whoosh. Soft brown hair curled around her face, just brushing the tops of her shoulders. "But he's still dead." She looked back over her shoulder as he propelled her forward. "Shouldn't we—"

"No. Best we get you out of here. Whoever did this doesn't need to get a good look at you." He felt her shudder, a delicate ripple that started at her shoulders and moved downward.

"But surely the police need to know?" She looked up at him, her bottom lip caught between her teeth, her eyebrows arched in question.

"They already know. And besides, there's nothing you could tell them that's worth endangering your life."

"And how exactly would I endanger myself by talking to the police?" Little sparks danced in her eyes.

Backbone. An innocent with backbone.

He was beginning to like this woman. Hell, if the circumstances were different, he might—but they weren't. He tightened his grip on her arm, propelling her forward again. "I'll explain later. Right now we've got to keep moving."

She shot him a look but kept pace, matching her stride to his. It was almost two-to-one, his long legs easily outdistancing her, but he had to give her credit, she was hanging in there. Most women would be yelling by now, and a scene was the last thing they needed.

He scanned the platform, but there was still no sign of the killer. It had been the work of a pro from the looks of it, and although he was probably long gone, Matt wasn't about to take a chance. Unless he was way off his game, the bloodstain on her shirt had come from a bullet. A bullet intended for Messer. And whoever was responsible wouldn't like loose ends, especially a wounded one. He wasn't about to let the bastard get to her. And right now, he was her best chance.

Matt sighed. From the frying pan into the fire. Charles Messer was dead. Whatever secrets he'd been carrying had died with him. And now this woman, whoever she was, had landed, literally, in the middle of it all.

What the hell had Messer been doing on the train? Their meeting wasn't scheduled until tomorrow, and there was no way the little man could have known he was coming in today. He'd been too careful—not certain what it was exactly he was walking into.

A maelstrom from the looks of things. Matt frowned, his instincts sounding a warning. At the end of the platform, he saw the familiar green uniform of the Austrian *Polizei*. Showtime. He looked down at the woman walking beside him. Her face was composed, but he could feel the tension in her body, and there were little lines of stress radiating across her forehead. Her breathing was coming in small gasps.

Certainly nothing that would alarm the officer in and of itself, but later, when he'd discovered the body, he might remember her and wonder. Matt's trained mind went into high gear. What he needed was something to make them blend into the background. A blinding glimpse of the obvious. The officer drew closer, a semiautomatic machine gun thrown carelessly over one shoulder.

Matt blew out a breath. Ah, hell, in for a penny and all that. With a quick maneuver, he pulled the startled woman into his arms, his mouth close to her ear, his breath lifting the curls of her hair. "Follow my lead."

Her gaze was wide-eyed and laced with questions, but she nodded. Quickly he bent his head, covering her mouth with his, pulling her body tightly against him. It was a kiss for show, an effort to conceal her from the policeman, but when her lips trembled under his, he forgot all about reason and logic. Hot fire swept through him, electricity threatening to stand his hair on end.

Her lips parted and he didn't have to be asked a second time. His tongue swept in, tracing the contours of her teeth, reveling in the hot, sweet feel of her mouth. Her tongue met his, shyly at first, and then with something approaching abandonment. He stroked the line of her back, one hand coming to rest on her waist, the other moving lower to cup the curve of her bottom.

This was heaven.

A titter of laughter accompanied by the sound of applause broke through his libido-driven ecstasy. Heaven with an audience. Matthew hated audiences. He pulled back. His liplock partner was staring panic-stricken at the area just beyond his shoulder. He turned, having the sinking feeling he was going to regret it.

Three pairs of perfectly made-up eyes were staring at

them, running the gamut from mildly amused to openly envious. One of the ladies, a purple-headed dowager in a Chanel suit, poked her companion in the ribs. "Now that, Charlotte, is a romance hero."

Matthew started to smile, but sobered immediately. A fourth pair of eyes—male—blinked at him over the rims of an oversized pair of tortoiseshell glasses, the glitter of annoyance hard to miss. He wasn't sure what the connection to his brunette was, but he had a feeling he was about to find out.

Without thinking, he slid an arm around her, his palm gently covering the bloodstain. No sense tipping their hand, until he knew how the cards lay. She trembled at his touch, and he wondered vaguely what emotion caused the reaction.

Tortoiseshell cleared his throat in the contemptuous way only certain members of English society can pull off. His eyebrows danced above his glasses, and Matthew's companion stepped closer, two bright spots of color staining her cheeks.

"Miss Nichols, we've been looking for you everywhere. And then I find you . . ." he trailed off, his hands flapping uselessly in the air. Sucking in a breath, he drew himself to his full height, which probably wasn't more than five and a half feet, narrowed his eyes, and glared at her. "I think you owe us an explanation." Icicles could have formed on every perfectly enunciated word.

The little prick. Matthew felt his temper rising, but clamped down on it. Three uniformed men were huddled around the body down the platform. Now was not the time for a scene.

"Now, Thomas." One of the women, a white-haired grandmotherly type with what looked to be a sympathetic face, placed her blue-veined hand on Tortoiseshell. "I'm sure Chloe has an explanation."

Chloe. He liked it. Soft, yet strong. He pulled her closer, wanting for some absurd reason to protect her. Three pairs of geriatric eyes fixed on them again. Chloe was definitely out of her age bracket with these gals.

Chloe opened her mouth and then closed it with a little snap, obviously at a loss for words. She bit the side of her lip, her face turning even redder.

"Well, Miss Nichols, I'm waiting." Tortoiseshell did everything but tap his foot. This guy had to have been a schoolmaster in another life. More green uniforms appeared in the platform doorway. "First the cow, then the altercation in the hotel room, and now this. We are not amused." Matthew eyed the police and then the Englishman. He'd actually use the royal *we*. Who the hell did he think he was?

"Surely you aren't going to object to—" another septuagenarian—this one with blue hair—eyed him from head to toe "—him." Her tone was just short of x-rated. Matt felt himself flush under her scrutiny.

"He's certainly better than the cow." The first woman, purple-hair, sighed wistfully.

"And a lot more pleasant to look at than that Alfredo person was." This came from blue-hair.

"I think his name was Alberto, Charlotte. But you're right, this one is definitely an improvement. Even you have to admit that, Thomas." The dowager eyed Matt with something bordering on open lust.

"It's not him." The little man deflated, his tone becoming almost woeful. In an instant, he changed from belligerent to beaten, all his bluster dissipating. "It's all of it." He waved his hand through the air. "We're frightfully late now. And worse still, I actually lost one of my charges. Granted," he eyed Matthew wearily, "it seems that she was in perfectly good hands." A titter from the ladies. "But the point is," he pulled out a pocket watch and consulted it with a sigh, "I'm going to have to call the home office again."

"Well, at least they're getting used to it." Blue-hair—Charlotte—offered helpfully.

"I suppose so." He released another tortured sounding breath. Matthew almost felt sorry for him. Whatever was going on, his bark was evidently much worse than his bite. "I shouldn't have snapped at you, Miss Nichols. It's just that this is my first tour and I do so want to impress the home office. And even you have to admit that most of my problems can be linked directly to your little *escapades*."

Matthew glanced at Chloe. Her color was still high, and she fidgeted against his side, obviously embarrassed. Even when flustered, she was charming, and he fought the desire to kiss her again.

"I'm sorry, Thomas, really I am. There is an explanation." Everyone turned their attention back to Chloe. She shot a look down the platform. Matthew followed her gaze. The officers were dispersing. A good sign. But telling this crowd about the body was not going to help anything.

He sighed. There really was no help for it. Thomas needed an explanation. And the truth was simply not an option. He had to get involved. After all, he needed to make certain there were no repercussions for what she had, or hadn't, seen today. It was in his own best interests after all. Besides, until he sorted things out, he could use a cover, and Miss Nichols might be just the ticket. He assured himself there was no other motive. None at all. His lips tingled in silent dispute.

With firm resolve, he pushed all thoughts of the kiss aside and looked down at Chloe. "Let me tell them, darling."

Chloe shot him a confused look, then glanced back down the platform. "All right."

He looked up to meet Tortoiseshell's gaze. "I'm afraid it's my fault you're running late." For an American, Matthew managed to add a nice little bit of ice to his voice, but then he'd had a hell of a lot of practice.

Thomas raised an eyebrow in question, some of his bluster returning. "And you would be?"

"Matthew Broussard." He held out his hand and the English-man took it limply, his bluster evaporating as quickly as it had come.

"Oh dear, not of *the* Broussards?" His face drained of color.

"One and the same." Matthew smiled.

"Oh my," said Charlotte, fanning herself with one plump hand. "I knew your mother and father."

Poor woman.

It never failed. One mention of his surname and the world seemed to collectively hold its breath. No need to point out that he wasn't exactly the Broussard poster child.

Two of the policeman passed by. They glanced at the group but dismissed them immediately, mumbling the word *aus-landers*. They'd pegged them as tourists. Perfect. Matt looked back to the group. Time to get out of here.

Thomas was still staring at him, doing one hell of a Lady Macbeth impersonation with his hands, mumbling some-thing about the home office.

"I'm sure, under the circumstances, the home office will understand, Thomas."

"I don't see how."

"Well, you see, Miss Nichols—Chloe," Matt pulled her closer and smiled down at her, "is my fiancée."

Chloe almost choked, the three ladies sighed simultane-ously, and Thomas grew even paler. Served him right. Blam-ing his own ineptitude on her. Not that she hadn't caused quite a stir, especially with the cow. But it had been an honest misunderstanding.

Anyway, the point was, it was nothing compared to the things she'd undergone in the last twenty minutes or so. In short, she'd fallen from a train, straddled a dead man, shared the most mar-velous kiss with the most marvelous man, and wound up en-gaged to him. At least technically that's what Matthew was saying. Although for the life of her she couldn't understand why. Her brothers would be having a heyday with this one. Even for Chloe this was turning into quite an adventure.

She forced herself to focus on the conversation. If she didn't, the way things were going, she'd wind up married with children. Matthew was speaking to Willie, the others listening with rapt attention. "So, I was hoping to join her here, but wasn't sure that my business would allow it. Thankfully, there's been a change in plans. Hence, the reunion. And now, ladies, I think we've kept Thomas waiting long enough, don't you?"

Everybody smiled and nodded. Somehow, in only a few moments, he'd managed to disarm them all, even crotchety old Thomas. But then he was quite a disarming man.

And even if it was all make-believe, it was a marked improvement to the state her love life had been in an hour or so ago. She had a fiancé—at least for the moment. And as far as fiancés went, this one was a winner, even if it was a charade. She ran a finger across her lips remembering his kiss. Maybe there was such a thing as a romance hero after all.

And she could always face reality later. In private. After all, she'd practically done a lap dance with a dead man, and frankly, if she was going to have an ally in all this, she'd choose Matthew Broussard in a minute. Although she had absolutely nothing concrete to base that on. But she trusted her instincts and even though she knew there was more here than she was seeing, she believed that when push came to shove, this was a man a woman could trust. Absolutely, irrevocably.

Her father would be rolling his eyes, her mother applauding her faith. Time would tell who was right. She glanced up, and was embarrassed to find gray-green eyes regarding her steadily, a hint of amusement lurking in their misty depths. She was definitely out of her league with this one. But somehow, she had the feeling it was going to be worth the ride.

"Shall we go, darling?" Even though she knew his words

were spoken for their audience, they teased her with their intimacy and she shivered in response. If he could do that with words spoken without meaning, imagine what he could do with true emotion backing his verbiage. Multiple orgasms were probably an understatement.

Chloe met Charlotte's amused gaze and blushed, certain that she'd been reading her mind. She opened her mouth to respond, but was cut off when Matthew bent his head to kiss her, his lips warm against hers.

"Just keep smiling," he whispered against her mouth. *Like that was going to be difficult.* "I'll come along with you to your hotel. We still have to talk about what happened."

Chloe breathed in the smell of aftershave and Matthew, and wondered if it was a sin to thank a corpse.